Saving Elijah

Saving Elijah

Fran Dorf

G. P. PUTNAM'S SONS
New York

G. P. Putnam's Sons
Publishers Since 1838
a member of
Penguin Putnam Inc.
375 Hudson Street
New York, NY 10014

Published simultaneously in Canada

Library of Congress Cataloging-in-Publication Data

Dorf, Fran.
Saving Elijah / Fran Dorf.
p. cm.
ISBN 0-399-14630-X
1. Mothers and sons—Connecticut—Fiction. 2. Sick children—Fiction. 3. Spirits—Fiction. 4. Connecticut—Fiction. I. Title.

PS3554.O6715 S28 2000 99-088125
813'.54—dc21

Printed in the United States of America

1 3 5 7 9 10 8 6 4 2

This book is printed on acid-free paper. ♾

BOOK DESIGN BY AMANDA DEWEY

For

Michael

Heal me, O Lord, for my bones shake with terror.
My whole being is stricken with terror.

PSALM 6

All right, who are you then?
A humble part of that great power
Which always means evil, always does good.

GOETHE

One should not grieve too much for the dead, and whoever grieves excessively is really grieving for someone else.

SHULKHAN ARUKH

Saving Elijah

prologue

When the woman phoned, I couldn't place her name until she said she was Maggie's mother. Then I knew.

They'd made quite a pair at the hospital, my son and her daughter. Eight-year-old Maggie was stricken and hairless and exhausted, her ashen face steroid-bloated beyond all reason. Five-year-old Elijah, with his thick glasses and crossed eyes, looked like a weird little Martian, his red-blond curls pasted to his skull with goop, an electrode and wire bonnet attaching him to a rolling EEG machine. He giggled when he saw himself in the mirror.

"Yes, I remember now."

I stood in my darkened bedroom, the phone hot against my ear. I could hear my children's laughter like the pealing of chimes through the house. Kate, fifteen, and Alex, fourteen, were amusing Elijah with a game of tag.

"Maggie's well again," the woman whispered.

Why was she calling *me?* She wasn't my friend; I'd only met her that once.

"Did you hear me, Mrs. Galligan?" she said. "Maggie's leukemia has gone into remission. The doctors said she only had a few months to live, and now her white count is normal."

Suddenly. Unexpectedly.

"Miraculously," Maggie's mother told me. And then, softly: "Elijah has the gift."

Faint as a cat's whisker grazing my cheek, I could sense the corrupt metallic odor that was already beginning to infiltrate everything.

I had visions of long, desperate queues on the street in front of our house, of frantic faces at our door, a procession of the hopeless and the crippled and the diseased. Night and day, hobbling, limping, dragging, wheeling up my lawn, sunlight and moonlight glinting off the bright metal surfaces of their wheelchairs and gurneys and battery packs. They would come to this house seeking miracles of their own. Save me, God.

What happened between the two children had certainly been extraordinary, no question about that. Miraculous, even, although I interpreted that particular event of that momentous time in my life quite differently than she had. I told her how glad I was that Maggie was well again. If she believed Elijah had somehow healed her daughter, who was I to dissuade her of the notion?

What I did not say is this: While God's purpose is ultimately mysterious, God's gifts come in an infinite variety of packages. Sometimes God bestows gifts in glossy silver paper wrapped up with iridescent bows. A crazed gunman comes into McDonald's and riddles the place with bullets, but you hide under a table and are somehow spared. A shiny, easy miracle, no? Well. Certainly not for those who did not hide under the table, and those whose cancer hasn't gone into remission. If their loved ones are looking for miracles, they will have to struggle and grieve and search. The miracles they find then will be of the deepest, truest kind, because those miracles have to do with the giving and the cherishing of our blessings rather than the getting of them, or the asking for them. Miracles of friendship and forgiveness, hope and peace and faith, can always be found by those who are willing to search, even in the darkest of packages.

My name is Dinah Rosenberg Galligan. I'm an ordinary woman, in my mid-forties as I tell this. I have auburn hair and freckles across my nose. I was a chubby kid who became a slender woman—bony, even. Some have called my face pretty; I've always thought my neck too long. "I love your neck, Dinah," Sam said, all those years ago. "It's beautiful. Like a swan's." Personally, I think ostrich is more like it. But I was stirred by his love talk. It was part of the reason I married him.

I am perhaps more educated than most, but I would still call myself ordinary. I am Jewish, my husband Catholic. I realize now that when I was in the thick of all this I was mired in self-loathing and blame. Was I too vain, full of hubris, lacking somehow? Perhaps I had been trying to be superwoman, what with the children, the husband, the house in Westport, the psychology practice, the twice-monthly column in the Connecticut *Star*, and the volunteer writing class for the elderly every Thursday afternoon. I cannot change the past, nor would I want to, certainly not by unlearning life. I was, I suppose, where I needed to be then. The future is another matter.

Once upon a time, I didn't believe we could ever know the future, let alone change it. I didn't believe in demons, or ghosts, or prophecy, or miracles, or anything of the sort. Psychologists as a general rule don't believe in free-floating evil. The only demons exist within, and only in the metaphorical sense, though we admit evil can be caused by circumstances without. You can't sit all day and listen to other people's stories and not admit that. But psychologists believe in ids, psychoses, obsessions. Human beings are damaged, traumatized, deviant, or lacking in impulse control: Their fathers abused them, their mothers neglected them, their egos are fragile, they were poor and deprived. Not to mention they have too many Y's in their X's and Y's, too little serotonin in their synapses, and dopamine out the wazoo. If they hear voices and see visions or demons or ghosts, they have a chemical malfunction of the brain that must be treated and cured.

I no longer believe rational answers explain everything, partly because of what I've seen and felt and know, and partly because if there are no demons, there are no angels. Yet an angel lives in my house. At least one. His name is Elijah.

Our stories make us who we are. Most of us believe we must hold them inside if they are very painful and raw, because no one will want to listen. Here is where psychology and theology surely agree: Suffering buried inside is a bitter poison indeed. And chief among God's miracles is human compassion, which is often thought of as mere altruism, but which actually offers very sweet fruit in return. Every new day is a miracle, is it not?

I did not tell this story to Maggie's mother, but I want to tell you.

An Angel in Intensive Care

one

He was a clever demon. His song seemed like comfort, when I could find none.

I was praying. There in the Pediatric Intensive Care Unit where the death of children was everywhere, and my own child's death a distinct possibility, I heard a disembodied voice, a melodious tenor, and acoustic guitar accompaniment. A virtuoso performance this was, syncopated rhythms and slides and chord progressions that seemed beyond the instrument's capabilities. Yet the song I heard in the air was a simple lullaby, the same one I sang to my boy each night.

Wynken, Blynken, and Nod one night
Sailed off in a wooden shoe,
Sailed on a river of crystal light,
Into a sea of dew.

Who would have such nerve, to play music where children were dying?

Dr. Jonas was examining Elijah, and the song sluiced through my ocean of pain as I watched the young doctor manipulating the flesh of my flesh, slack limbs of my limbs. I watched and I prayed. Oh, where are you, baby? What distant land have you sailed to? The song offered a kind of warmth in that season of absolute zero. I took it for an angel's song, or even a lullaby from the throat of God.

I had been awaiting God's appearance, one way or another, so this was not a surprising conclusion. I don't know whether it's true that there are no atheists in foxholes, but if there are any mothers in the PICU thinking life is just a meaningless, random game of craps and I've lost, too bad, I wasn't one of them. At least I didn't think I was. For a week (or was it two?), whenever I could gather a coherent thought, I'd been believing in God with all my might. And praying, arguing, pleading, crying, screaming, damning, denying, apologizing, waiting.

Waiting, mostly, for God's answer.

What would the sound of God be like when it came? A sonic BOOM, a booming God-like voice, like the Voice that spoke to Charlton Heston when he played Moses? Would God speak in exalted language, using words no one but God would ever have the chutzpah to utter, words like "Behold!" and "Thy son is saved!"? Would there be saving angels with halos and wings? Maybe the hospital rabbi would come and say a simple *Mi Shebeirakh,* a prayer for healing, and my son would awaken, just like that, and say, "Mommy."

But Elijah had that tube in his throat. He couldn't say "Mommy."

I heard singing. This is a sign, I thought. What else would I think in the silence of waiting that felt to me like God's rebuke, like a parent's betraying slap on the bare buttocks of a child: But why, Mommy? You gave me these crayons.

Don't punish Elijah. Don't punish me.

Wait. Stop. I heard singing, even over the screaming inside my head.

The PICU never stops. You'd figure a PICU would have a lot of small private rooms, like on TV. This was a huge space, all open except you could barely see the patients for all the technological marvels hovering over the beds like whispering, gossiping women, the huddles of suck-*hissing,* click-clicking, beep-beeping, *whoosh*-pumping machines, and the labyrinth of tubes connecting innards to equipment like spacemen to the mother ship.

But you could see the buzzing doctors and nurses, the parents having the worst moments of their lives in front of everyone else, and the big desk in the center where computers monitor every sigh.

All in all, it reminded me of ground control at Cape Canaveral. My parents took me and my brother there as children in 1962, after John Glenn circled the earth. I was six, and my movie-star-beautiful mother held my hand tightly. I felt so special to have her as my mother. At that age I wanted to be just like her, to wear white pointy sunglasses with little rhinestones and a sheer pink scarf tied just so over my hair, which was almost the same glorious auburn color as hers. I tried to imitate the way she glided along in her white pedal pushers and high-heeled mules as if she were on a moving promenade. Our family stood at the launch pad. "Dinah, Dan," my father said to my brother and me, "you're witnessing history." Sergeant Marty Rosenberg, PFC, served in the South Pacific during World War II. Men were bayoneted right in front of him. He's very serious about history. As my own personal history goes, the PICU was right up there. Ground control to Major Tom, beam me up, Scotty.

At each end of the PICU, there were two private rooms with glass walls and doors, called Negative Air Rooms—NARs in acronym-happy hospital-speak. Negative air seemed appropriate; I had been turned inside out, after all.

The place was full of technomiracles like NARs, which somehow managed to suck in, keep in, and reuse air. Even when you opened the door, NAR air didn't leak into the general PICU air supply. The last thing children sick enough to be in the PICU needed was a blast of bad, contagious air on top of everything else. One of these rooms was where they had put Elijah. They weren't sure what was the matter with him, but they put him in the NAR, just in case. He had just turned five. We'd had a birthday party, with paper hats and chocolate cake that ended up smeared all over his face. A messy eater, my Elijah.

Dr. Jonas was listening to his lungs. I started praying again:

"Please, God. I know Elijah's in bad shape, he's in a coma, but he can't be as bad off as some of these kids here. Like Kenny, the teenager with cancer eating his liver. And the toddler named José, whose mother keeps screaming in Spanish. He must be really sick because he's always wrapped in a silver blanket, and he's hooked up to more machines than anyone else. And what about the boy with Down syndrome, something wrong with his heart, and a cleft palate, too, often how it works, as I well know from Elijah, problem on top of problem? As in when it rains it pours, it would be so much fairer if it drizzled on everybody just a little, instead of soaking the same kids over and over and—

"No. Wait. Sorry, I didn't mean that, I don't care that Elijah has some problems, neurological glitches, learning disabilities, PDD, obsessive-compulsive disorder, crossed eyes, a heart defect, sensory issues, yada yada. Just give him back to me, just the way he was, I'm not asking You for *corrections.*

"It's just that I have to warn you, God, we're into some really horrible stuff here, so if you can't take it You'd better stop listening right now.

"Wait. What in the world is the matter with me? Of course You can take it. You've seen far worse than this, the Black Death, racks and tortures, even murders in Your good name. What about millions marched into ovens? What do You do, hide Your face, like my friend Julie and I used to do when we went to a scary movie and knew from the music that a bad part was coming? You can close Your eyes if You want, but please don't leave now, when I need You most. We're talking about my Elijah here, Elijah Galligan. My boy who loves Elvis Presley.

"When he was three, Elijah saw Elvis on television, and he's loved to get naked and dance to Elvis ever since. The kid's a born nudist. I bought a tape for him. 'Hound Dog.' You should see that kid wiggle. I mean, of course You've seen it, but if You've seen it how can You just let him lie here like this? Is it me, is it *me?* Do I not love him enough?

"A coma. Please. Help."

I stopped my prayer and listened. I still heard a lullaby, definitely. I'd forgotten there was such a thing as music. The praying of mothers had been the only music before, a moving bass figure or drumbeat, contrapuntal to the main PICU melody, but constant. You could hear the mother-prayers under the din of the machines, rising *crescendo sempre agitato* toward the fluorescent lights.

"Do you hear that, Sam?"

My husband, sitting at the other side of Elijah's bed, had been crying before Dr. Jonas came in. Wailing, really. The man I loved, with whom I had three children, the man I'd seen cry maybe once in twenty-four years of knowing him, was making a sound in his throat like lowing into a megaphone. I wanted to go to him, but my body felt so heavy, bloated and stinking with fear and despair. I couldn't move, not a muscle, not a finger, not a toe.

That is what happens. You want to comfort each other, but grief is everywhere, even inside your mouth. You are flailing about, swallowing water, it's filling every organ and cell, and you are going down for the last time, glub glub. How do you offer a husband—anyone—a lifeline when you're drowning yourself?

The voice, the song. My lifeline. I grabbed hold with everything I had. I wanted Sam to come with me.

"The singing," I whispered. I had not spoken in perhaps an hour.

"What are you talking about, Dinah?"

"Shhh. *Listen.*"

He listened. "I don't hear anything."

No matter. *I* heard it. I closed my eyes and let the song carry me. Just a lullaby I sang to Elijah every night before he went to bed. I'd help him get into his Big Bird footed pajamas, then I'd sit on the bed and sing to him and Tuddy, the Day-Glo green puff-a-lump with a huge funny turtle face and orange bow tie he carried everywhere. My singing voice isn't great, but Elijah wouldn't even try to sleep unless I sang. Loud. If I didn't sing loud, he nudged me.

When I opened my eyes, I was no longer in the PICU. Blue sky and ocean and sea air had somehow materialized around me, replacing the sight and smell of that hospital room. I was with Elijah in a glorious place. I even knew where I was, though I'd never been there. There is a spot on the eastern coast of Australia, where swimming fish and sea creatures flash by in a kaleidoscope of color and design, where endlessly varied coral formations rise high from the ocean bottom, where anemones and sponges undulate to the music of the gently swaying sea. Behold: the future in a waking dream. When Elijah turned seven or eight, we were going to travel thousands of miles together on an airplane to see the city of coral. A vacation, perhaps. Or maybe Sam, a copywriter for an ad agency, would have a client there, and the whole family would go with him. And my pain? Gone—the PICU but a dim memory of a nightmare I had once, a long time ago.

We are on a small boat in a great azure sea, bobbing above the Great Barrier Reef. The expanse of water spreads for miles in every direction. We're still wearing our swimsuits after swimming with the fish. So. Elijah will learn to swim after all, he has always been so afraid of the water. Our skin has dried now, drenched in the warmth of the noon sun. His skin has darkened, his hair lightened from its normal reddish color to a lustrous golden-blond. Our snorkel masks and fins lie on the boat deck, and Elijah is sitting on my lap while we examine a piece of coral together. I am so proud of him, he has learned so much. He still can't read very well, but he talks in sentences and he makes up stories, and I love him more and more. God granted him great progress after his recovery from the coma, an additional gift.

I kiss Elijah's fingers—he has scraped the skin on his fingertip against the rough, pocked surface of the coral.

"Look, honey, do you see all these little holes? In each of these tiny holes there used to be an animal."

He pushes his glasses up on his nose. "An elephant?"

I'm about to tell him about tiny sea creatures, but he looks so hopeful that I say, "Well, if you want elephants to live in each of these holes, then that's what lives there. Tiny little elephants with funny little trunks smaller than toothpicks."

He laughs and peers at me from behind his glasses. "You're silly, Mommy."

"You're silly, too." Beneath the surface of the rippling water, I can see brain corals, stag corals, honeycombs. Tall and fat, tiny and towering, reds, whites, greens. And crevasses between the coral for brilliant fish, electric blue multitudes, yellow schools, resting places. We all need resting places, do we not?

A giant turtle swims right by. "Look, Elijah!"

With a smile, Elijah puts his hands up at his shoulders and flaps them, imitating the turtle. I laugh. He shoves his glasses up on his nose again and rests his elbows on the side of the boat, his chin on his hands.

The little stars were the herring fish
That lived in the beautiful sea.

The song, now coming from nowhere and everywhere.

Elijah sits up again and looks around. "Who's singing?"

This music has become all things to me now, a hymn, a dirge, a concerto, a symphony. Solemn and joyful, a reverie and a mazurka, both a major and a minor key. Liquid silk and rock and roll and razzmatazz, too. Debussy, the Fifth Brandenburg, the Rolling Stones, Art Garfunkel singing "Bridge Over Troubled Water," and Jobim on guitar. All of it, all at once. And the voice? A virtual choir that seems to contain every emotion, every sensation, lifting me up like a strong wind, soothing me like a tenor sax, rousing me like a bass, loving me like a violin, rocking me like a drum.

"It must be God singing from the heavens." The secrets of the universe contained in every measure and chord.

"Heaven is where dead people go?" My son lazily dips a finger in the water.

I nod. "That's what they say, Elijah."

"Is that where I almost went?" Back down to resting his chin on his hands, elbows on the side of the boat.

"Yes, I suppose so."

"It must be a very big place, to hold all the dead people."

I laugh. My Elijah will become a child who speculates about such things, who imagines.

"Yes," I tell him. "God's arms are very big. And isn't God's song wonderful?"

He turns his head toward me without lifting his chin from his hands. "I don't know, Mommy. I kind of like Elvis."

I laugh and laugh and laugh.

"Mrs. Galligan? Are you all *right?*" Dr. Jonas, bending over me. "Can I get you something?"

Where was the azure sea?

The world collapsed inward, and I heard a sucking sound as I crashed back into the place where I could not be, where I could not live, where Elijah, lying mute on a bed, entangled in tubes, might never reach the age of seven or eight.

"Are you all right?" Young Dr. Jonas always had a bland expression, probably a good thing for a guy who watches children die. Of course Jonas also helped children live, I knew that. Some kind of genius, I guessed—I hoped—to be in charge, at so young an age in this New York City medical center where people came from all over the world, where they transferred you when your local hospital didn't know what to do. Or some kind of a lunatic. Or maybe he just had a God complex. Who else would seek this out day after day? I knew about lunatics and God complexes, being a psychologist.

On the other hand, I liked Jonas a lot more than I liked Dr. Moore, the attending doctor, a tall, bulky, fiftyish neurologist who never looked you in the eye. When I mentioned Moore's eye-wandering propensity to Sam, he said he hadn't noticed. How was that possible? This guy's eyes darted everywhere but never landed on you. Or maybe it was only me.

Now from the other side of the bed Sam was staring at me oddly, the dark circles under his eyes like bruises, punctuating despair. No wonder he was looking at me that way. I had been laughing maniacally in the PICU.

It was a sign. God would never let me imagine my child as an eight-year-old if he would never get there.

"I'm. All. Right," I said. There was that weird voice again. Ever since my son fell into this coma, the voice that came out of my mouth didn't sound like mine. There were out-of-place breaths between the words, no tonal inflections, no cadence or phrasing or beats. It didn't sound like a human voice at all. More like a machine.

"Is there any change?" Sam asked Jonas, who had finished his examination.

"We're scheduling him for an MRI tomorrow," Jonas said, as if that answered the question.

"Why an MRI?" I asked. "Dr. Moore says he's going to wake up any day." Elijah was still conked out, Moore kept saying, because of all the medications they gave him at the other hospital to stop the seizure, before they transferred him here. A drug cocktail, Moore called it, disparaging what they'd done there, I thought. I was reminded of the time we remodeled the upstairs bathroom and the shower floor ended up looking like a sliding board. The tiler blamed the Sheetrocker, the Sheetrocker blamed the carpenter, the carpenter blamed the electrician, who blamed the plumber.

"Sounds like he thinks they did the wrong thing," I said when Moore left the room after expounding his drug cocktail theory for the third time.

Sam said I was being ridiculous. From the moment we got here, Sam hadn't understood anything I said, or he understood and disagreed. Could I have been sadly mistaken all these years, believing Sam and I were complementary halves of a whole, that together we were more than what we were individually? Perhaps my robotic speech was an unknown language.

Dr. Jonas unhooked Elijah's chart, made a note or two. I had read the chart myself, some of it: *Elijah Galligan, 5 years old . . . history of present illness . . . admitted 9:02 AM Jan. 4, status epilepticus . . . non-responsive . . . bluish extremities . . . patient intubated. Loading dose administered, 9:14 AM, Ativan, 5 mg . . . 9:25 AM Dilantin administered, 250 mg . . . 9:48 AM . . . phenobarbital administered, 300 mg. Mother states . . . transferred . . .*

I hadn't yet been able to read any further, because the letters always started to swell and melt into meaningless black marks.

Jonas hooked the chart back to the bed, pressed his hand into my shoulder in a gesture he meant to be comforting, I'm sure.

"We'll do an MRI because we just want to be certain of everything," he said, then he left.

Left us, without telling us anything. Again.

I looked at my son lying there, his little glasses useless on the night table, his Tuddy beside him. No. There was something wrong with that. The doctor had moved Tuddy to examine him. I placed Tuddy back under his arm, and arranged his hand the way it was supposed to be.

I squeezed my eyes shut and tried to conjure up the vision again, the sea and salt air, my son in his future, but I saw nothing. I heard nothing. There was nothing to smell in the air except my own sweat and parfum de hospital.

"I need to draw some blood."

I opened my eyes. A technician was standing in the doorway, holding a white plastic tray packed with tall skinny vials.

"Again?"

"I'm sorry."

I took my son's hand. Maybe this time he'd feel them sticking him, and it would wake him up.

The technician had so many vials to fill, had to be thirty, at least.

I couldn't watch him take still more blood. I closed my eyes, and that was when I heard the guitar song again. "Wynken, Blynken, and Nod." Was it possible there was a singing vampire in the hematology department?

No. It had to be a sign from God, a little number God dreamed up, exactly like the Great Barrier Reef. Who else could possess an instrument that yielded the sound of a symphony; a melody so simple and yet so complex; a lullaby, hymn, spiritual rock me baby? Who could make those frets shout "Hallelujah" like a whole gospel choir? Who could hold a note for so long without taking a breath, or would even know the lullaby I sang to my son?

Who, indeed?

two

After the technician left, Sam closed his eyes and rested his forehead on the bed. He really didn't hear the music. Incredible. Now it seemed to be coming from a source just outside the room. I looked through the glass wall to see if there was a troubadour playing a guitar in the PICU. There didn't seem to be one as far as I could tell.

The nurse was taking Elijah's temperature again. She was a kind woman with a large bosom, plump cheeks, and quiet eyes. I'd had the thought of wanting to rest my head against her chest.

"He has such long eyelashes," she said, placing the electronic thermometer in his ear but laying her palm on his forehead, too, as if she were taking his temperature that way, as a loving mother would. Wait till she saw his blue eyes when he opened them.

I searched my son's face one last time for any twitch, then walked out. My husband didn't even look up, though I hadn't left the room in hours, maybe a day or two, even for a meal. What was the point of eating when my son had to be fed through a tube in his nose with a watery whitish liquid that looked like infant formula, only thinner?

I wandered into the PICU, where pandemonium had erupted as it did here at intervals, clattering metal wheels across the floor, nurses and doctors descending. I shrank up against the wall to let them race in with a child on a gurney, terrible purplish lesions all over her body, terror-struck parents following close behind. Right. A bed had been vacated that morning. Someone's child had died right there in front of me, or been moved down to the regular pediatric floor for further treatment. That was about it for the choices. No one got tossed right from the PICU into the street.

Still hearing the music, I started across the PICU again, passing by the other NAR. That was where Jimmy was. Eleven years old, he'd been hit by a bus. Oh, Lord, that poor boy looked bad, though I couldn't see him right now, because the curtain was drawn. I could only see his parents' feet shuffling about underneath it.

The music seemed to be emanating from the corridor outside the PICU. Into the corridor I went, and when I came out I saw a man—not a man, exactly, since the color of his skin wasn't right, it was much too pink, like a television picture that needs a color adjustment. But he was sitting on the plastic sofa near the elevator, strumming a guitar and singing.

"Where are you going, and what do you wish?"
The old moon asked the three.
"We have come to fish for the herring fish
That live in this beautiful sea."

He was very gaunt and tall, though I couldn't be sure because he wasn't standing. He had a broad forehead, a wide mouth, fleshy, coal-black lips that were definitely not made of flesh. Dark stuff that looked like twine hung down in front of his shoulders, partly obscuring his face. He was wearing clothing of a style popular two decades ago, when I was in college: bell-bottom blue jeans, a studded black leather jacket, a belt with a heavy silver buckle. The strap on his acoustic guitar was embroidered with peace signs, though at its edges the strap seemed to be covered with mold. And his clothes were tinged with mold, too. His shirt seemed fitted closely to his angular body, a button-down monstrosity, purple and green flower splashes, with a large open collar. He wore heavy black boots caked with mud, and leaves were clinging to his clothes.

There was no one else in the corridor, and I walked right up to him.

"So it's been you playing the music?" My voice sounded normal, not robotic, but I wasn't a hundred percent sure I'd actually spoken with my mouth.

The guitar player just kept playing and singing.

The old moon laughed and sang a song
As they rocked in the wooden shoe,
And the wind that sped them all night long
Ruffled the waves of dew.

I was reminded of the folk music of my generation, an acoustic guitar and a simple melody, Cat Stevens, Simon and Garfunkel, James Taylor. Music I loved when I was a hopeful young woman, incapable of imagining something like this could happen to *my* child.

"How do you know the lullaby I sing to my son?"

He played. He sang. He occupied space but seemed to have no weight or mass, and the outer edges of him were fuzzy, like the blurred outlines of a watercolor painting.

I pointed to his boots. "This is a hospital. The children are sick. You shouldn't bring dirt in here."

In fact, he seemed to be covered with a faint coating of dirt and green slime, as if he'd recently had a close encounter with a mud puddle. *This* was my son-saving angel?

He stopped playing and looked up at me. That was when I noticed his eyes, flat and all dark, not a speck of reflected light, or of white. Perhaps this should have frightened me, but it didn't. Nothing could have been as frightening as Elijah in the PICU.

Is there some archetypal belief mechanism that comes into play when we find ourselves in the presence of a phenomenon beyond ordinary reality? Perhaps I was able to interpret what I was seeing because I was already way beyond ordinary reality, I was anesthetized with shock.

"Had an accident," he said. "Ended up in the dirt. Can't help it." His voice was a whisper of wind, with an undertone like the cooing of pigeons. He articulated each word distinctly, as if he believed everything he uttered was significant, and spoke languidly, as if he had all the time in the world. Yet as he talked, he kept those dark lips pursed together as if he had to hold something in his mouth at the same time. An affectation, to be sure.

"Accident?"

"Motorcycle. Damned things are deadly, you know. Only loons drive them." He cupped his hand to his mouth and whispered, "And people who think they can cheat the Angel of Death. That one hangs around here a lot. Always nearby."

I looked around, but the corridor was empty.

He started to laugh, a twittering sound, like the rustle of tree birds and leaves. "You'd notice him. He's full of eyes. Pretty hard to miss."

"Eyes?"

He leaned toward me. "As in when Master Angel Death comes looking for you, there's no place to hide." More twittering. "Should be here any time now, for Jimmy. Could be tomorrow. Next day at the outside." He raised one long pink finger to his lips. "Listen. The Angel is already approaching. You can just hear it, if you listen really hard. Jimmy. Jimmy."

I listened but heard nothing and didn't want to hear. "Please don't tell me this."

He made a shrugging motion. "Why not? Jimmy's not *your* son. What do you care?"

"You think I shouldn't care just because he isn't my son? Don't you care?"

"Not a bit. Why should I?" He strummed a few chords on his guitar, then stopped, sat back and regarded me. "Want to tell me you aren't glad the Angel is coming for Jimmy instead of your son? Just go ahead and try, and I'll call you a liar." He grinned and went back to his strumming. "You can't cheat that Master Angel, you know. When it's your time, it's your time."

There was something disturbingly intimate about his warbled mur-

murings that reminded me of the way Sam and I had always talked to each other late at night, after we'd made love.

"Unless you're very smart, very quick. You have to know certain secrets, too." I noticed that when he spoke or moved any part of him, his mouth, his arm, his head, the outline of him mingled with the air, as if it were dissolving, then rippled outward in concentric circles, like the surface of water when you skip a flat stone.

"What secrets?"

"Why should I tell you?"

"You don't have to bother, because no Angel of Death is coming for my son. Dr. Moore told us it was just a little drug cocktail."

"Ah, Moore. The big cheese at the big hospital." He drew his finger to his lips. I noticed then that his finger, his whole hand—both hands, in fact—were covered with dark gashes, like desiccated blood. Maybe this accounted for the pinkness of skin, or whatever he was made of. Like a watercolor wash, he was white mixed with red makes pink.

"Sometimes doctors lie," he said. "And sometimes we are in denial, are we not?"

Denial? "I'm not in denial. And Moore isn't lying. Anyway, I've had a vision of my son in his future."

He stared at me with his lifeless eyes. "Oh, have you now?"

"Yes. That proves my son will have a future."

"Of course," said the guitar player, and strummed a few more chords.

The elevator opened and two nurses came out. They walked right by us, chatting without so much as a glance.

"Why don't they see you?"

His laughter echoed from one end of the corridor to the other, bouncing off the ceiling, the soda machine, the linoleum floor, the walls. "Well, now. You are certainly not the brightest of bulbs, are you? For all your fancy degrees. They can't see me because I'm dead. I'm a ghost."

One of the nurses was putting coins in the Coke machine.

"Why do I see you and they don't?" I asked him.

"Oh that. Molecular incompatibility."

"What?"

"They aren't configured to see me, my Dinah. I'm for you. I'm all for you."

The two nurses took a left into another corridor. "Did they think I was talking to myself?"

"Well, now, ho, hum, you're not actually talking. It's a trick, sort of like mental telepathy." He shrugged, a favorite gesture of his, and this time I noticed that whenever he did it the air around him seemed to blister. And sometimes, if I blinked, certain features and details of his seemed to fade out of focus, or disappear, a part of a shoulder, an ear, a finger. "Of course, there is also the possibility that I'm not really here and you're talking to yourself."

Was he trying to confuse me?

"On the other hand," the ghost said, "if they *did* see you talking to yourself, I doubt it would surprise them. Parents in the PICU can get pretty weird." He leaned forward, sotto voce. "One time, there was this father. Now this guy was loaded. Head of some big real estate company. Told Dr. Kay that if he would only save his son, Mr. Big Shot would build a wing on this hospital and name it after him."

"Did his son live?"

The ghost moved his mouth into a smirk. "Lived to disappoint his father, too bad. The kid's all grown up, in a detox unit at the moment. Fathers bribe and yell and demand and make phone calls. Not Sam, of course."

I stared. How did he know about Sam?

"And another time," the ghost said, "this Japanese lady got down on her knees and put her face at the feet of young Dr. Jonas, her face right to the floor. She actually licked his Reeboks and begged him to save her daughter."

"That must have been awful for Dr. Jonas."

The ghost cooed, "Oh no. Jonas loves the power of it all. It's a real rush for him."

I hadn't heard the word "rush," used that way, in years. "Did her child make it?"

The ghost sighed melodramatically, with a jerk of his shoulders. "Afraid not. Sometimes—a lot of the time if you want to know the truth—it doesn't matter what the doctors do. No matter how like little gods they think they are."

I bowed my head. No, please, God. That couldn't be true.

"So," the ghost said, "I see you've been praying."

"Of course I have."

"That's probably a good thing, that you're not the proverbial atheist in the foxhole."

Was he reading my mind? I'd spent some of the day making mental lists of all the things I wanted to apologize to God for, and that was one of them: for never *really* having thought about whether I believed or not. For not praying enough, never truthfully. For not having devoted my life to God, or to selfless works or something. For not being Christian or Buddhist, or Muslim, if any of these are God's religion of choice. For marrying out of my faith. For not loving Elijah enough. For having ever questioned His sending me a child with some physical and mental disabilities. Even for having a sense of humor some might call irreverent. (Fine. I'll never crack another joke, never write another column, hang up my computer.)

And I'd been humbling myself. (The nerve of me, to ask for God's help after questioning His existence.) And demanding. (How dare God do this to my innocent boy?) And promising, and bargaining, I admit it. (Anything, I'll do anything. My leg, my arm, my life! Take me, me, me.) Over and over, these lamentations, an obsessive on overload. Mania, hysteria, a psychosis composed of grief and terror.

"Whoa," the ghost said now. "You really are off the wall, aren't you?"

"What would you expect, with my son lying there?"

He crossed his arms over his chest. "I didn't say *all* parents got weird. Some manage to keep it together."

I decided not to even try to defend myself. "Why were you on a motorcycle if you think only loons ride them?"

"I think that now. I didn't think it then. Being dead tends to alter one's ideas about things. In life, we really are 'foolish prating knaves,' you know." He made a gesture like a sneer. "You don't recognize the quotation?"

Hamlet, who had his own ghost to contend with.

"You don't look like any kind of ghost I've ever heard of," I said.

"Hey. I've gone to a lot of trouble with this." He stood up and stretched out his arms, as if to demonstrate how handsome he was. "I made it out of bits of memory, and it was the best I could do." He turned around and showed me the back of his head, and I gasped. There wasn't much there; his skull was a smashed pumpkin. I could see gray matter and pink bone, the sheen of bone and blood, sticky clumps of hair clinging to it.

He sat down again and reached for my hand. He was not made of solid matter, and I felt my hand pass through a speeding, stinging windstorm cold enough to instantly strip my skin off my bones. I yanked my hand back. My skin was still there.

He sighed, positioned his hands on his guitar. "Do you want me to play for you again?"

"I can't stay here. My baby, Elijah. He's in the PICU."

"I like that name, Elijah," he said. "Do you know that Elijah is the name of the last prophet?"

I knew very little about the etymology of the name. I knew I left a cup for the Prophet Elijah at our family's little Passover Seder every year, and I had named my son in the Jewish fashion, after my mother's father, Elijah Blake. I never got to know Grandpa Eli very well, since my mother was estranged from her family, but I knew he was an immigrant who'd managed to build a huge carpet business in Georgia. One of those restless, high-strung men, huge in size and spirit, possessing energy of awesome proportions, dominating the lives of everyone close to him.

"Bet you didn't know that the Prophet Elijah will perform the last miracle before the coming of the Messiah," the ghost said. "Did you know? Pretty funny, don't you think? God has to enlist the services of a Messiah to fix things, like a common employer? The Almighty Master of the Universe needs *help?* Pay no attention to the man behind the curtain."

"What in the world does the Messiah have to do with anything?"

"I should think, given the situation, you'd make an effort to understand this God you're praying to. Take that little dream you had."

"It was a vision of the future."

"Ah, the future. One of my favorite subjects. So there you are in the future, on the Reef with your boy . . ."

I closed my eyes and tried to recall the great beauty of that place, and the peace I had felt. I suddenly remembered having read somewhere that the Great Barrier Reef was the only living thing on earth you could see from the moon, as if there on that spot, God placed a fingertip on the surface of the ocean, fifteen hundred miles long, and said, "Here! Here is where I will build *My* city!"

My eyes flew open.

The ghost was sneering. "I'd say your God is reminding you how great and powerful He is. He's telling you He holds the power of life and death over your son."

"How?"

He sighed. "Why go to the trouble to show you His own coral city, which is so much more beautiful than any city created by mankind? Why show you this if not to remind you of your insignificance? That's benevolence? From the One who's trying to comfort you? In my humble opinion, it's downright petty."

I felt a current inside me, like a volt of electricity.

"Anyway, I was just giving you a little insider information before. I'm well aware you named your son after Grandpa Eli. A man of great, shall we say, appetites." He spoke the word "appetites" with a rumble from the back of his throat. "Business, and food. Am I right?"

It was true. The first time I met Grandpa Eli I was seven, and he was already very fat.

"And women, too," the ghost said. "The women just loved him. Am I right?"

"I don't really know." How did *he* know?

"Well, sure you do. Some guys got it, and some guys don't." He jumped out of his seat again, parting the air in his wake. He began to gyrate his pelvis.

"Stop that," I said.

He sat down, moved his mouth and black lips into an expression that seemed like a pout. Then he looked around himself and began swatting at the air, as if he were surrounded by a swarm of insects that I could not see. He kept on whacking at the air for a while, even smacked himself once or twice, then just ceased, and looked back at me, as if nothing had happened.

"Well, I know Grandpa Eli was a great phil-an-thro-pist!" He pronounced the word with great drama. "He gave large sums of his money away. Thirty-thousand, thirty-one thousand, thirty-two thousand, thirty-four, thirty-six, thirty-eight, forty, one, two three four five six seven eight nine ten—"

"Hel-*lo.*" It seemed he would have gone on with that infernal counting forever if I hadn't interrupted him.

"Well, Grandpa Eli did give his money to Jewish causes. Right?"

"What's wrong with that?"

"Ho, hum. If he thought of himself as such a great Jew, and loved his people so much, how come he changed his name to Blake from Aaronov?"

"It was the South, in the thirties. What do you expect?"

"Well, well, how tolerant of you. Not so your mother, though. Right? Didn't she always say that her father thought women were only good for two things? Well, three, if you counted taking care of the house?"

I'd heard her say that once or twice. My mother left Atlanta when she was nineteen because Eli had promised handsome positions for his sons in his carpet mills, but excluded her. Still, after he died, Charlotte seemed to have no recollection that she used to call her father "the Bull." Suddenly, she claimed undying love for him. Even asked me to honor him by naming my second son after him.

"How do you know so much about me and my family?" I asked.

With an air of indignation, he said, "Do you think I just showed up here without some sort of preparation?"

"Preparation for what?"

"It takes some doing for a ghost and a mortal human to have a conversation, you know. This doesn't happen every day." He patted the place next to him, and his hand seemed to mix into the plastic fabric. "Sit, babe."

I sat down. *Babe?* Who had called me that?

Oh, the stench of him, of moist earth and rot, of dankness and loam.

"You stink," I said.

He bent toward me. "I knooooow. It's *just* terrible, isn't it? But this was the best I could do. The best, the top, the max! I already told you that."

"So what if you told me already?"

"Well," he said with a shrug, "we're never going to get anywhere if I have to keep repeating myself."

"Where do you think we're going?"

He raised an eyebrow. "Where would you like to go?"

"Your singing soothed me," I said, ignoring his insinuating tone. "You have a beautiful voice."

He swelled and puffed out as big as a bloated pink moon. "People have told me that." His smile turned sly. "*You've* told me that."

What was he talking about? I certainly would have remembered it if I'd ever met a ghost.

I stared at what purported to be his face. The air shimmered all around him, then he disappeared and materialized on the other side of me.

"What kind of a trick is that?"

His nod moved the air like a breeze. "Simple trick. Nothing to it."

"How do you play the guitar with your hands all gashed?"

"Doesn't hurt. Been dead a long time."

"Where have you been since then? What does a ghost do?"

He moved his mouth into a frown. "Help people, if he feels like it. I'm here to help you."

I started to cry.

He lay his guitar against the bench and held out his arms. He embraced me, then he rocked me, enfolded me within that swift current of air, and I barely noticed the odor and cold. Now he began to sing, softly, the lullaby that I sang to my son. He rocked me and sang it to me, and it eased me some. I was willing to take comfort from wherever it came.

He was starting to dematerialize, and I felt myself falling, falling. I pulled away and sat up. "You *are* a ghost."

"Well, duh!" he said. By then I had to squint to see him. He was now little more than a bright white haze, edged in pink and black.

I stood up. "I'm going back to be with my son."

He was filling in again with detail and color, fingers, blue jeans, boots. He positioned his guitar on his lap. "Good. Fine. Go back and be with him. While you can."

I stared at him.

The ghost laid his guitar down on the white linoleum tiles and smiled. "Hope is a snake that keeps slithering out of your hands. Is it not? And when you finally manage to catch it again, you just can't seem to hold on. No?"

My blood seemed to stop moving through my veins. I was as still as inert gas. And it's really true that when you see a ghost, the hair at the back of your neck stands on end.

"Tell me if you know something."

"Why should I?"

"Do you know if God plans to let my son live? Tell me!"

He crossed his arms over his chest and made a *psshing* noise. "Do you think there is any creature on earth who knows the plans of God? Even a ghost?"

I started to flee.

"On the other hand, a ghost can see the future."

I turned back. "You know the future? Then you do know if my son will wake up?"

"Ha, ha, ha. Two roads in a wood . . ."

"Why are you deliberately trying to be cruel?"

He made a sound in his mouth, between his teeth. "Me? *Moi? Mi? Mich?* Well. If you ask me, there's only one cruel One here. God is the cruel one. Innocent babies die, are even tortured and murdered, and this is supposed to be the will of a benevolent God! *Free* will?" He laughed that twittering sound again. "What a master gamester. I really don't understand why you humans don't realize it's a scam. God pulls this kind of stuff, and you *still* worship Him, you think He's going to help you. What a joke."

I ran as fast as I could, and didn't look back.

three

I suspect the demon had been stalking me for a long time, just waiting until I was weakened and confused and vulnerable before it moved in for the kill in that hospital corridor. Perhaps it was lurking nearby for the happy times, too: the morning Sam and I first made love; the birth of our children; the day I walked up to a rostrum to accept my doctoral degree after five long years of study. Was it perched beside my parents in the stadium that June day, playing riffs on the guitar, invisibly mocking them, mocking me?

Charlotte was beaming. How could I ever forget that? We're talking about my mother here: tough, determined, rigid, narcissistic as a love-starved adolescent. Part Scarlet O'Hara, part Medea, all barracuda. She'd met my father at nineteen, when he came to do legal work for Allport Designs, where she was then working as a floor assistant, having quit her Atlanta family in a rage, resolved to make her own way in New York's garment industry.

Charlotte purrs, flirts, sweet-talks, scrutinizes; she does not generally beam. But she'd beamed the previous January when my brother, Dan, graduated from medical school, and she was beaming that fine spring day.

I guess it's in the rulebook, even hers. When not one but both of your children become doctors, beaming is required, even if you'd wanted your daughter to follow you into your business, a business having to do with women's clothing whose very content makes your daughter's eyes glaze over. Even if your daughter only became a psychologist, not an M.D., even if you are Charlotte.

Had the demon always been hovering like a hawk, waiting until the season of absolute zero to pounce? How did it know such a season would come? Everyone has troubles, as Sam's mother always says. She says it even now, after everything. Plucky, she is, my Irish mother-in-law. She means it, too, it's not an act. But even Mary Galligan admits not everyone has had troubles like Sam and I have had and certainly not everyone reaches absolute zero.

It had been an ordinary Tuesday, like any other, just a few days after the new year. I had no idea the season was upon me. Who ever knows?

In the morning I saw patients in my office in the Westport Professional, the two-story stucco building on the Post Road with arched windows and Spanish aspirations where I did my thing. My last patient before lunch was a new referral, Danielle O'Connor. She came into my office, a big attractive blonde in her thirties, wearing sunglasses in the middle of winter. I asked her why she'd come, and she took off the glasses. The bruise, compliments of her husband, was raw and dark.

She told me the story the way abuse victims often talk—slow, matter-of-fact, almost dazed, like a prisoner of war. Details change but the plot is always basically the same. In this case, her husband had accused her of flirting with one of his business colleagues at a party. He twisted her arm, he backhanded her across the face, he demanded to know how she could humiliate him in front of everyone he worked with.

"The nurse wanted me to call the police," Danielle said. "She said I should go to the shelter . . . I told them I fell, I always make up something . . . they knew . . . the nurse gave me your card . . . he says he'll kill me if I tell the police." She hesitated, and tears began to slip silently down her cheeks. "If I don't go to these parties, he says I'm a bitch, and I'd better watch it because a man like him shouldn't be with someone like me anyway. So I go." She took a tissue from the box I keep on the table in front of the sofa. "But then he always accuses me of something . . ." She broke off. She was a very long way from realizing that it didn't matter what she did, or didn't do. He was the one with the problem; if he needed to hit her he'd find a reason. The next time it might be for going to the party and *not* talking to anyone, or for making beef stew for dinner when he wanted pork chops. Wham.

"Danielle, what did you do when your husband hit you?" I asked her.

She wiped her nose. "What I always do. Tell him I'm sorry I upset him."

"So you don't argue with him?"

"Arguing just makes it worse." Her look was something on the order of trapped, wounded animal. "It gets worse if I cry, too. He hates it when I cry."

"So what you do is to try to protect yourself from his violence, in a way?" I always try to validate the woman's choices. They have to begin to see themselves as someone who has choices again. "So it doesn't escalate?"

"I never thought of it that way."

"Does it work?"

"Depends on how much he's had to drink. That night was the worst. My daughter heard us, she came downstairs, and he started in with, 'Get over here, Sarah, I want you to see what a whore your mother is.' He calls me these terrible names—my own husband." She put her head in her hands and wept in earnest now.

Whore. In my experience abuser epithet choice number one.

Danielle looked up, bewilderment on her face. "There was this man at our club, it was five years ago . . . I just needed someone to talk to . . ."

So then. She believed she deserved whatever he dished out. And the poor woman was too terrified, too conditioned by years of abuse, too humiliated to even call the police. No one could know what was going on in her life.

Shortly into the session, she began to defend him, of course. He'd apologized, sent her flowers, he was just having a hard time at work, things were going to be better now. Classic cycle: tension building, violent incident, honeymoon. In college, I'd slid briefly into a spectacularly abusive relationship myself, complete with all the rationalizations, the "yes, but all he needs is my love to straighten him out's." Almost died because of it.

I thought I could help Danielle, and wanted to work with her. But first things first. We reviewed her options if and when it happened again, which it would, and worked out a plan for her safety. I spent the rest of the hour getting her family history, which not surprisingly included a verbally abusive father, made an appointment for the following week, an appointment I didn't keep as it turned out, and told her to call if she needed me.

She thanked me and left. I returned a few calls, did some paperwork at my desk, then left to meet my friend Becky for lunch. It was very cold outside, with a bright, blue sky and a strong winter sun that glistened on the sidewalks and streets. I drove over to Main Street, the *très chic* Westport drag where you could pick at a four-course lunch at Café Christina, pick out a $600 decorative pillow at Lillian August, pick up a $28 Gap T-shirt better left to your daughter, an $800 little black skirt from Henry Lehr.

I found a parking space just as I turned the corner off the Post Road, and spotted Becky right away, gazing at a black silk sheath in the Henry Lehr window. She's hard to miss, this tall, exotic-looking mother of three. She's always reminded me of a movie star from the 1920s named Louise Brooks, partly because Becky also wears her ink-black hair in a short swingy bob with cropped bangs. She was skeptical until I dug out a film book and showed her Louise Brooks in *Love 'Em and Leave 'Em.* We had a good laugh over the film's title, and Becky agreed there was a certain resemblance.

"I'm buying," she said as we walked to Café Christina. "I actually made a sale today. Just a condo, but the commission is thirty-five hundred."

I congratulated her, then teased her about the bite that little black number at Henry Lehr would take out of the $3,500. While we munched on our grilled veggie salads, Becky complained about her daughter's new boyfriend.

"He comes to pick her up last Friday," Becky said, "and he's got an earring in his eyebrow and a skull tattoo on his arm. Jennie swears he's a good student, but I thought Mark was going to lose it." She grinned. "Hey, maybe you could make a column out of it."

I laughed. "I could call it 'What to do when Satan shows up at your door for a date with your daughter.'"

I'd begun the column on a lark, really, to amuse myself during my difficult pregnancy with Elijah, which had me spotting until the sixth month, fighting world-class nausea all the way through, and feeling utterly bovine. I'd been a chunky kid with a mother obsessed with thinness. Bovine was not a good way for me to feel. In my seventh month I wrote two hundred words about various little pregnancy humiliations, hormonal imbalances, my appalling increase in sentimentality, a sudden fondness for Hallmark cards and cows. I sent it to the Connecticut *Star.* The features editor liked it and invited me to write another. The "Agitated Observer" was born.

"I'm going to start charging you if you don't watch it," Becky said.

She had, in fact, been the inspiration for the piece coming out in the paper that afternoon.

"So," she said, "how's Elijah?"

"Doctor says he has to have heart surgery." In addition to his many other physical and developmental problems, Elijah had a small hole in his heart. We'd known surgery was coming, but just last week we'd gotten the news that the doctor wanted to do it soon.

"God, I'm sorry," Becky said.

"He says it's not that big a deal. They make this kind of repair all the time."

"It'd be a big deal if it were *his* child."

She had a point. "I feel like the little Dutch boy with his finger in the dike. Every time we plug one leak, another spurts. That poor kid has more specialists than a barrel of eighty-year-olds."

"Maybe so, but you're amazing about it, Dinah. Really."

"You just do what you have to do, right? He is frustrated, though. Me too. I just wish I knew how to help him. At least the tantrums have eased up, and he's been doing a little better in school lately, but when they do circle time, he still wanders over to the window. They paste pictures, he's at the sandbox. He needs so much one-on-one help. I suppose all the kids in the class do. I guess I should be grateful he can walk in the first place. Three of the kids in that class are in wheelchairs."

Her son Brian and Elijah were the same age, but Elijah was in special ed, and his class was full of children with handicaps, most far more devastating than his collection of relatively minor physical ailments and developmental disorders.

She nodded, touched my hand. "As I said, you're amazing."

"Thanks," I said. "Now, of course, my mother doesn't think so. Good old Charlotte. She's been campaigning for some special school she knows about out on Long Island. They're the *only ones* who know how to work with kids like him."

Becky laughed. "I doubt there are many kids like him. Elijah is unique."

"That he is," I said. "Even if he won't be a rocket scientist."

I would never have made such a comment to anyone other than Sam except Becky. I was much too defensive. But she'd been incredibly supportive, right from the beginning, and it had been pretty obvious almost immediately that Elijah had a lot of problems. He didn't roll over until he was almost seven months old, didn't sit up until he was ten months old, then sat there unmoving like a little frustrated Buddha for months, screaming. He never crawled, didn't walk until two and a half. Now he was five, and although he could walk and run, if a little awkwardly, his vocabulary was limited, and it was unclear just how much he could learn, how far he would go, and whether he'd need supervision and support the rest of his life. The future was a great big question mark.

"What the world needs is more cuties like Elijah," Becky said. "And fewer rocket scientists."

I smiled. "Thanks, Beck. Would you please inform my mother?"

After lunch we walked back over to Henry Lehr. The dress was a slip of a thing, with spaghetti straps.

"You could carry it off with those long legs," I said.

"How much could it be?" she said. "Three hundred?"

"You wish."

"Dinah?"

I turned. Ellen Shoenfeld was standing there, wearing her tweed coat. Underneath she probably had on one of her tweed suits, too; she always dressed formally, with stockings and heels.

"How are you, Mrs. Shoenfeld?"

"Very fine." She snapped the words; her accent is heavy, German.

"This is my friend Becky Sullivan. Ellen Shoenfeld. Mrs. Shoenfeld is in my writing class at the Jewish Community Center." She was the only person in the class I didn't call by a first name. I'd just gotten the feeling when I met her that she wasn't comfortable with American familiarity. She didn't correct me, even though I introduced myself as Dinah.

They both nodded and said hello. Becky asked if she liked the class.

"WHAT?" Ellen was always asking you to repeat things. She had two daughters who lived nearby. Why one of them didn't get her a hearing aid, I had no idea.

"Do you like the class?" Becky said, speaking slowly now, loudly.

"Oh, yes, yes. Very much. Thank you."

"Your hair is so beautiful," Becky said.

It was hard not to notice Ellen's hair, which was pure, perfect white, the color of snow. You could see the pink scalp beneath it. She wore it in a loosely braided chignon. It must have been very long, as if she hadn't cut it for many years. Maybe never.

Ellen nodded her head at Becky. "Thank you, and so is yours, my dear."

Becky thanked her. I looked at their two heads, enjoying the dramatic contrast.

Ellen turned to me. "So then. I must go. My daughter is picking me up in a little while. I will see you Thursday, Dinah. Yes?" Ellen's face is deeply lined, her nose beaked, but despite her age and the bow of her back, she still manages to carry herself with a stately dignity, even elegance.

"Wouldn't miss it." I loved that class. Partly because I've always liked hearing people's stories, that's what psychologists do, partly because I loved them.

And what stories I heard from those septuagenarians and octogenerians! Frieda Brodsky had been a mail-order bride. Abe Modell was a retired dentist who called his autobiography-always-in-progress *From the Ukraine to*

Novocaine. When he was nine and his brother Max eleven, Cossacks rampaged through their town near Minsk, killing their mother. The boys were put in steerage on a boat bound for America and a distant relative, who was to collect them at Ellis Island but never showed up.

Some of them were excellent writers, too. Especially Carl Moskovitz, part of a core group who'd been coming since I first started teaching the class seven years ago. Ellen had only the past September joined the class for the first time. At the beginning of every new session, I always had everyone introduce themselves again, for the benefit of the new people. This they all did at length, telling birthplace, age, number of children and grandchildren, and singing the praises of a spouse, dead and alive. Ellen said, "I'm Mrs. Max Shoenfeld. Ellen is my forename. I'm eighty years old and I come from Munich, in Germany. My husband of thirty-six years died ten years ago. He was a fine man, and I miss him every day. I have six grandbabies. Esther, Rebecca, David, Nathan, Allisa. And Jennifer."

Carl always introduced himself by saying, "Carl Moskovitz. Accountant. Retired." A man of few words. He wrote just like he talked. Deadpan, and mordantly funny, whether depicting his brother-in-law's boorish behavior at Carl's wife's funeral, or the time in 1947 when he lost his pants in a bet and had to walk the Coney Island boardwalk in his underwear. They weren't all as good as Carl, but they all tried the assignments. Except Ellen, who just kept saying, "No, no, I just like to sit and listen." Except that she could hardly hear.

"Well, goodbye then." She waved. Her fingers were as bent as winter twigs, the skin on her fingertips puckered, like dried parchment.

"See you Thursday, Mrs. Shoenfeld." I watched her walk away, then glanced at my watch. It was after two. "I have to go pick up Elijah," I said to Becky. "I promised I'd help set up for the Winter Fair tomorrow."

"What'd they rope you into this year?"

"Elijah and I are in charge of the clown toss." When Brian and Elijah were two, Becky and I took them to a local fair. Brian thought the clown wandering around was funny, but Elijah started screaming at the top of his lungs. I had to take him home.

"He's come a long way," Becky said. She planted a kiss on my cheek, then we said goodbye and I headed over to the school.

Most of the children in the class had already been picked up, and Miss Stanakowski was sitting on a floor mat, reading a story to little Isabelle, who had Down syndrome and wore a perpetual smile. Elijah was sitting in the corner next to the piano, by himself. He was tapping a plastic truck on the floor, over and over and over again. His play sometimes mimicked autistic behavior, but he wasn't autistic. There didn't seem to be a formal name for his odd collection of problems, except that he had a non-specific, pervasive developmental disorder.

"Hi, sweetie!"

His face lit. He vaulted to his feet, glasses flashing in the sunlight streaming the large windows. He ran right to me and gave me one of his hugs. Since he didn't have much language at his command, he put his all into a hug, or a dance, or a jump, or any kind of physical movement. His arms were incredibly muscular for a five-year-old, his body was more Schwarzenegger brawny than Galligan lean. When he hugged you, you knew you'd been hugged.

"You know what Elijah did today?" Miss Stanakowski was pregnant. She clapped her hands together. "Go on, Elijah. Show Mom your picture." She always seemed as happy at her students' accomplishments as I'm sure she would have been at her own child's.

Smiling big, Elijah went over to the table where Tuddy and his coat were, and held up his picture. It was actually a cutout of a magazine photo of a horse that he'd pasted on, around which he'd made a few squiggly lines, under which he'd scrawled out the letter E.

"That's beautiful, Elijah," I said, and kissed him.

"He sat through all of circle time," Miss Stanakowski said. "And he counted to twenty. Well, almost. All in all, we had a very good day."

Kate was already home when we got there. Right before my eyes, right under my nose, my daughter is turning into a beauty. Pale, glowing skin, shining auburn hair, luminous dark eyes, the lush fifteen-year-old figure with which each of us is gifted only once in our lives, even those of us who were chubby.

Of late she'd taken to reading books by the feminists of my own era, and confessional women poets such as Sexton, Plath, and Sharon Olds; loudly declaring her independence from men; and wearing ragged jeans and baggy shirts, as protest against the ridiculous lengths women go to for their looks. Her sabotage was unsuccessful at hiding her beauty. Still, Charlotte, wearing Calvin Klein, sniffed, "Kate, honey, I know a nice hobo I could introduce you to." My throat tightened and I started to tell her to leave my daughter alone. But Kate had her own comeback: "Actually, Grandma Charlotte, I'm holding out for a Calvin Klein bum. Heroin chic, you know?" Charlotte actually giggled. Would wonders never cease?

Now Kate was in the kitchen, peering into the refrigerator. Poppy was sitting on his haunches beside her, hoping she was in a sharing mood. Any little morsel would do.

The Galligan family dog is species canine, mix unknown. Body as big as a shepherd, legs as short as a basset hound, brain the size of a pea. We named him Poppy when we first brought him home from the shelter. Elijah, who had a vocabulary of about six words, kept pointing to him and saying "puppy." I suggested we call him Puppy, but his older brother thought that was a dumb name for a dog. "How about Poppy?" Alex said. Even dumber, but it stuck.

Kate glanced over her shoulder at me. "Mom, why don't we ever have anything to eat in this house?" I'd just shopped the day before, in the hour between my morning of seeing patients and the time I picked up Elijah. Sam, who commuted to his job in Manhattan, had been begging me to get a live-in au pair to help out, but I wanted to raise my children and tend my home mostly myself. Not that Nelda, my mother's longtime housekeeper, hadn't done a good job with me.

"Last time I looked there were some apples." I bent down to pet Poppy, who was panting, barking, and wagging his tail at my side, having briefly broken off his stakeout at the fridge to trot over and say hello.

"Apples are boring."

"Turkey sandwich?"

"Mo-om. A turkey sandwich would be dinner." She raised her upper lip in that gesture of disgust all teenagers have mastered that says, What planet did you just drop in from?

"Kaaaaaaate!" Elijah sprinted into the kitchen then, holding Tuddy in one hand, both arms outstretched.

"Hey, little guy!" Kate was half-mother, half-sister to Elijah. She closed the fridge, picked him up. He linked his arms around her neck while she swung him around and tickled him. Still clinging onto Tuddy, he giggled like mad.

"So, how are you doing, baby? Did you have a good day?"

He nodded his head vigorously. "I made horse."

"You did?"

He nodded and wiggled to get down. "Horse. Picture." He ran into the front hall to retrieve it.

"I saw these really cool croakies at the Gap, Mom," Kate said. "We should get him one. His is boring."

Boring seemed to be the word of the day. "What's a croakie?"

"The thing attached to his glasses that holds them around his neck if they fall off."

"Oh." I didn't even know it had a name. Elijah's was just plain old blue. I got it at the place we got him his glasses. He was two when the ophthalmologist prescribed them. For four months, I'd put them on him and he'd fling them across the room. I came up with the idea of putting the glasses on Tuddy. He thought that was hilarious and eventually consented to put them on his own face.

Elijah came back then, holding up the picture.

"Well, that is beautiful," Kate said, touching his head of glossy red-blond curls. "Such talent our little guy has."

He pointed to the collection of pictures I'd tacked on the door into the laundry room. "Put up." I took the new addition from him and got out the tape.

"So, what do you think, Elijah?" Kate bent down so that she could be eye level with him. "Want a really cool yellow croakie with green stripes?"

"Green." He held up Tuddy.

"That's right, Elijah, Tuddy is green, too. Look, Mom, he knows green."

"Of course he does," I said. "He knows all his colors. Don't you, Elijah?"

"Green yellow purple blue red orange," Elijah said. He often strung words together like that.

"Well, I'm getting you a croakie," Kate said. "Then you'll know green and yellow stripes. Right, Elijah?"

Elijah nodded. "Right." He gave her a wide, satisfied smile.

What was he going to do, say no to his big sister, even if he didn't know what a croakie was? Not a chance.

Sam's agency had just gotten a huge new account, one of the major computer companies out in Silicon Valley, and Sam wanted to celebrate. I made a family favorite, chicken Marsala.

"This is delicious, Dinah." Sam never failed to compliment whatever I cooked, even when I tried something new and it flopped.

"Tastes kind of boring to me," Kate said.

"You want something else?"

"Dinah," Sam said, "it's outstanding. Don't make her something else."

I sighed. Of course he was right.

"Is it okay if I stay over at Eddie's on Friday?" Alex was shoveling potatoes in his mouth. "His dad is taking us to a basketball game." My fourteen-year-old had shot up suddenly last year and looked more like his lanky, handsome father than ever.

"I don't see why not," I said. "But Saturday Dad and I want to go out. Which one of you is sitting?"

"He is," Kate said.

"She is," Alex said.

"No way," Kate said. "I'm going out on Saturday night."

"Oh yeah, who with? I thought you said males are the enemy." Alex and Kate's bickering reminded me of my own relationship with my brother, Dan, but they cared about each other much more than Dan and I ever had. And they were certainly united in their love for, and protection of, Elijah, although Alex occasionally blurted out a frustrated remark revealing a wish that his little brother could just be normal.

"None of your business, Alex," Kate said. "And I never said they were the enemy."

Sam winked at me. "Come on, Katie, tell us who the lucky man is."

She shrugged and put her napkin to her lips. "Stop it, Dad-dy."

Sam gave her his big, dimpled smile. "Oh, come on, Kate, I'm having fun."

"Bet it's Greg Laurence," Alex said.

"You don't know what you're talking about, Alex," Kate said, with a haughty shrug of her beautiful shoulders. "We're just going to the movies, a bunch of us. Mom, would you tell him to chill?" A hint of amusement turned up at the corner of her mouth.

I was glad my two older children had a natural, easy relationship, right down to their usually good-natured ribbing. My daughter had a large group of nice friends. In high school I had no gang to hang out with, and only one real friend, whom I hadn't spoken to for . . . well, too long. Tall, gangly Julie Bronstein, with the incredible head of frizzy orange hair. She was forever wrapping, ironing, and processing that hair so she could wear it long, straight, and parted down the middle in the style of the day, an impossible effort. We became known in high school as the Red Twins, even though our two shades of red hair were as different as they could be, mine auburn, and hers, well, it looked like her head was on fire. We were so close we even went to the same university, but by the end of sophomore year, she stopped speaking to me. Julie was not a subject I liked thinking about.

"Or maybe it's Ben Papp," Alex was saying.

"Mom, are you going to tell him to shut up?"

"Give it a rest, Alex," I said.

"Are you coming to my concert?" Kate asked then. She'd taken up the flute when she was ten, and now played the instrument beautifully, with grace and delicacy. Her teacher said she might have a chance for a career in music if she really set her mind to it. So far, it didn't seem to be where she was going, but you never knew. For Sunday's concert, she was planning to play a Bach piece she'd been practicing diligently for weeks. She'd done many a concert before but for some reason this one had her jittery.

"Of course," I said. "We'll all be there. All grandmas and grandpas. And Elijah, of course." Music was one of the few things that consistently held Elijah's attention, whether it was Elvis, Kate playing the flute, or my own off-key lullaby singing. I love listening to everything from folk, to jazz, to doo-wop, to acid rock, but I can't produce anything, instrumentally or vocally, that could remotely be called music. For two years I took lessons from a dictator named Anna Drum, who was unsuccessful in her attempt to hide her disappointment at my lack of talent, the lessons having begun the way everything did, by the command of my mother's fierce will.

I was nine. Charlotte had screamed at me about something or other earlier in the week, and the gleaming white Steinway grand she had delivered to the house we lived in then was her way of making up. She was at work, of course, but Nelda seemed not only to be expecting it but also to know exactly how to rearrange the furniture in our living room to accommodate it. From the sidelines, Julie and I watched her direct its placement, no easy task, as it took up most of the room.

"Who is going to play that thing?" I said finally.

Julie looked at me and grinned. "I have a feeling *you* are."

And that was how I learned that I was to study the piano.

"Kate changed the subject because she doesn't want to talk about Greg," Alex was saying now. "You're not going to buy that load of crap about the movies, are you? What about you, Elijah?"

Elijah didn't seem to be paying attention. He wasn't eating either.

"Give your sister a break," Sam said.

Alex snorted. "Why should I?"

"Because she's the most wonderful sister *you'll* ever have," Kate said.

Just then Poppy yelped. Poppy operates under the assumption that any food stared at long enough will eventually find its way to his mouth. He'd been sitting quietly at Elijah's feet, waiting. I realized that Elijah had been unusually quiet all the way through dinner. Come to think of it, he hadn't even wanted his usual horsy ride on his father's shoulders when Sam came in the door. Before Sam even put down his briefcase, it was always, "Horsy, horsy!"

Not tonight.

Elijah laid his head down on the table then, and he closed his eyes. And that was how it began.

four

"Can I come in?" Becky was standing in the doorway of the NAR. She'd come nearly every day since it began, and she didn't avert her eyes from Elijah when she walked in, the way everyone else seemed to do. She looked this disaster straight on.

I watched her press her lips to Elijah's forehead, careful not to disturb the tube in his nose or the one in his throat. She stayed that way for a moment, lips pressed to his skin, eyes closed. I saw her whisper his name, an act of simple kindness that moved me from numbness to tears. When she stood up she had tears in her eyes, too.

"I need some air," Sam said then. "I'm going for a walk." He glanced at me as he stood up, perhaps expecting a reaction.

That morning I think I must have given him a horrified look when he said he was going for a run. "I've got to get my blood pumping," he said. "Be back soon." And he was gone. Sam has always been a jock, but I had slipped into some other universe where normal routines didn't exist. Why hadn't he? Now I watched him leaving the room again and wondered how he could move so quickly when I seemed to be doing everything in slow motion, like an old LP record grinding down. Had he even noticed that Becky's husband, Mark, the other half of our so-called best friends, had yet to make the one-hour trip?

The ghost was out there singing again, I could hear it above the din of the PICU. I tried not to listen but there was no way to shut my ears.

All night long their nets they threw
To the stars in the twinkling foam.
Then down from the skies came the wooden shoe,
Bringing the fishermen home.

Sam would be walking through the corridor, right now.

"Do you hear that, Becky?" Do (*breath*) you (*breath*) hear (*breath*) that?

"Hear what?"

"I sing that lullaby to Elijah. Every night. Listen."

She peered through the glass wall of the NAR, as if to search for a musician playing a song she clearly didn't hear. "What lullaby?"

"'Wynken, Blynken, and Nod.'" How could I not have told her how Elijah had to have that lullaby and no other before he would go to sleep? It was so very important. All the time we'd wasted on memories, gossip, complaints about our parents and our husbands, exchanges of information about our children and the difficulties of raising them, reports of minor flirtations (one major, in Becky's case), and I'd left the lullaby out.

"I don't hear anything, Dinah."

Obviously no one could see the ghost except me. Nor could they hear his song. Maybe I was imagining the whole thing.

Becky sat down in the empty chair next to me, leaned forward, and stretched out her arms. I couldn't bear it. I was having so much trouble breathing. Just the thought of someone hugging me, touching me, putting pressure on my body—even my friend, even my husband—made me gag. It would cut off my already diminished air supply.

I knew I was shocky. The panic and breathlessness and sleeplessness were unmistakable symptoms. I'd certainly treated enough bereaved parents in my fifteen years of practice to know at least some of the details of Big Time Grief. My own grandmother had lost a child, one of my mother's brothers. He was only four at the time; my grandmother never got over it. It's interesting there's no name for it, for a sonless or daughterless mother, like widow, or orphan.

But was it a blessing or a curse to know I was in shock and even to know some of what I would face if Elijah didn't survive? Did it help or hurt me to know that if my son died I would never get over it, that it would sit like a monster on my head for the rest of my life? That there would be some people I had thought friends who would abandon me?

"I can't." I pulled away from her.

"It's okay, Dinah." She folded her perfectly manicured hands on her lap. "I spoke to Addie this morning. She said she came yesterday."

Addie, another friend, an artist who designs book jackets for a publishing company in New York. When Elijah was born she gave him a small chest she'd hand-painted with white and blue polka-dot dinosaurs.

I nodded, looked down at my trembling hands. I couldn't bring myself to care if my friends came, or if they didn't come. Their coming didn't change anything. Either way I hurt more than I had ever believed possible. If Elijah didn't survive, I would never be able to forgive them for not coming, would never again consider them my friends no matter what their reasons: didn't know what to say, too busy, too far away, too uncomfortable, too scary, too whatever.

"Mark sends his love and prayers," Becky said.

I nodded as enthusiastically as I could. A barely perceptible nod. Where was Mark, anyway? Was he going to be one of the abandoners?

"Is there anything I can do for you, Dinah?" Becky said finally. "Do you want something to eat? It's just about dinnertime."

"I'm not hungry."

"How about at the house? Bring dinner for the kids tomorrow?"

"Sam's parents are staying with them," I said. "Bringing them down in the evenings."

Becky nodded. "Is there *anything* I can do for you, Di?"

I was listening to the ghost's music. But I'm smart. I wasn't going to ask for corroboration again.

"Could you call the Jewish Community Center, tell them I won't be teaching the class for a while?"

"They know, Dinah. Sam must have called. And I saw Mrs. Shoenfeld there the other day, when I took Brian to his swimming class."

Was it only a few days ago that Becky and I saw her on the street? No. It was a week. More than a week.

"I was amazed she recognized me," Becky said.

I wasn't.

"She asked me how you were doing, seemed very concerned about Elijah." Becky glanced at him. "Has she met him?"

"Once." Last summer I'd registered Elijah for Krafty Kids, an art class given at the same time I give my writing class. I'd talked to the teacher about his learning disabilities, and told her the day I brought him in that I'd be right down the hall if there was a problem. There was. Elijah tried to finger-paint one of the other kids, and the teacher brought him to me long before the hour was up. "I told him he couldn't do that," she said, "and he's been sitting in a corner and crying ever since. I'm sorry. It's too much of a disruption." She nudged him toward me, then left.

I introduced him to my class. Even though he went off into a corner and banged a pair of little plastic cars on the floor instead of standing there with me and letting them engage him the way most children would have, they fussed and fawned over him. That made me feel good, of course, and Ellen Shoenfeld was one of the fussers and fawners. But only she acknowledged the obvious, that Elijah was not a normal child. "It must be hard for you, Dinah."

"She asked me if it'd be all right if she wrote you a note," Becky said. "I told her I thought it would."

I felt oddly moved by this. Ellen is a Holocaust survivor. Nobody had told me, but she's eighty and Jewish and speaks with a fairly heavy German accent, which means she probably immigrated later in life, which means circumstances probably found her in Germany when Hitler came to power. Clearly she doesn't talk about it openly, as some survivors do, and when I asked the question all she said was, "Yes, I was there when it happened." Then she walked away.

"She said you're a wonderful woman," Becky said.

"Don't know why she thinks so. She's shown up at every class this session, but so far hasn't written a thing."

"Why would she come but not write?"

"I don't know."

Becky smiled. "You love that class, don't you?"

My eyes were filling with tears, my breath quickening with another wave of panic. Ordinary conversation felt like a runaway train. "I can't talk about the class now, Beck."

"I'm sorry. Look, I'm going to get a sandwich for you—you don't have to eat it, you can just put it on the table and then you'll have it if you want it."

She left. I couldn't possibly eat anything, but I'm sure she was relieved to have a mission. Perhaps she'd come back telling tales of ghosts sitting in corridors, playing guitars.

I rested my head again on the bed next to Elijah's belly and closed my eyes. Even so, I could see six parallel lines on the monitors beneath my eyelids, inching their way across the two screens over and over. Pulse rate, blood pressure, pulse oxygen, expiratory pressure, respiratory pressure, and ventilator rate burnished into my brain. When Becky got back I was still watching lines, listening to the *whoosh*-suck click-pump, and hearing a song of beautiful dreams and fishermen three.

"I got you roast beef on rye, is that okay? And a soda. At least take a drink." She put the provisions on the table next to the bed and sat down. "I didn't see Sam downstairs," she said. "He must still be outside walking."

I nodded. "What do you think he'll do if Elijah dies?"

Becky flinched. "Dinah! Elijah is *not* going to die."

"But if he does?"

"I don't think you should talk that way in front of him. Maybe he can hear you."

And maybe he'd hear me talking that way about him and get mad and open his eyes.

"He's *my* son, I'll talk any way I want to."

She sighed, stood up, and walked over to the glass window, looked out into the PICU for a moment, then turned around. "I think you'd both be devastated. I think Sam would turn to you for strength. And you'd turn to him. But Elijah isn't going to die." She came back over to the bed and squeezed his limp hand. "Isn't that right, Elijah?"

Elijah slept on, his breathing machine *whoosh*-pumping away.

Becky was wrong about Sam and me. You'd think couples would cleave to each other, but they don't. Most don't, anyway. My patient Laura Soffel and her husband couldn't talk to each other about their dead son Tom and eventually divorced because they couldn't talk about anything else, either. Sheila Morrison and her husband talked all the time, Sheila to me, her therapist, the two of them to their parish priest, fellow grief support group members, to a psychic, and finally to a divorce lawyer. And Grandma Elizabeth and Grandpa Eli? My mother didn't speak to them for years and I met them only them eight or nine times, but during those few visits I was witness to my grandparents' bitter battleground of mutual blame.

Sam and Dinah would be no different. What always seemed to melt and mix and mesh perfectly with Sam and me, in exactly the right proportions and measures, in a marriage that tasted sweet and happy, would burst and split apart like a piece of fruit dropped from a great height. I didn't know the words we would use to hurt each other, the blame we would hurl at each other. But I knew that our equation, Sam's and mine, our formula, the ratios that defined our marriage, would no longer apply, do not apply once you lose a child.

I could not imagine Sam without Elijah. And how would I survive if every molecule in my body had been corrupted? I'm not sure when the molecule thing happens, as you carry a child or simply as you mother him, but I was sure that each of my cell nuclei was unalterably made up of four parts, one part me, one part Kate, one part Alex, and one part Elijah. If a crucial Elijah-piece of each cell nucleus were suddenly sliced off at the cellular level, I was certain the missing piece of each cell would defile the whole structure until, eventually, it crumbled to dust. I could feel edges crumbling already.

My patients who'd lost children had certainly been more functional when they left me than when they came to me. Functional? Was that the salient word? Now, in the hospital room, I realized that nobody anywhere, no therapist, certainly, possessed a diagnostic guide for this, no DMRDMC (first edition): *Diagnostic Manual for Rebuilding Destroyed Mother Cells.*

"What does the doctor say?" Becky asked.

"That he's going to wake up soon."

Becky nodded, sat silently for a while again. Then, "Can I get you anything else?"

Could she get me back to before this? Could she trade places with me, could it be Brian lying here like this and not Elijah? No. Wait. I didn't mean that.

I no longer felt like a real human being. I belonged out in the corridor with a ghost.

Sam came back then. He looked so very tired, weary and bleary-eyed. Other than that, he didn't look much different than the first time I met him, while waiting to register for my freshman courses at George Washington University. I was shuffling through my papers to make sure I had everything I needed and dropped my yellow card, the one you had to show to the registrar. It landed right at Sammy's feet.

"That's mine," I said, reaching for it at the same time he did, thinking what a cute guy he was. Gentle brown eyes, tall and lanky, dark tousled hair, wire-rimmed glasses, worn flannel shirt, unbuttoned sleeves. A killer smile, complete with dimples.

"You don't want to forget this." He handed the card back to me. "No money, no tickie."

A boy wearing a Hendrix T-shirt, fatigue pants, and a rawhide headband tapped Sam's shoulder. "Hey, man, it's your turn."

"Hey, man," Sam said with an easy smile at me, "give me a break, I'm talking to a pretty girl here."

Now, in the hospital, Sam sat down, radiating frigid air, smelling of grease, probably stopped in the hospital cafeteria for a bite. "It's cold outside."

"They're saying snow," Becky said.

Right. It was winter. Elijah loved snow. I wanted to tell him it was snowing, whisper it in his ear, shout it in his face, but I didn't want them to see me do this. I would wait until I was alone with him. And then I would tell him and tell him and he'd wake up so that we could go out and play in the snow.

I closed my eyes, again, and, once again the sights and smells of a hospital room vanished and I was transported somewhere else, to another time and place.

My own kitchen. Sam is standing at the sink, loading the dishwasher. The room is as dim as a murky pond, illuminated only by the small lamp on the desk in the corner. How odd it is that he's rinsing and loading in the dark.

"Where were you?" he says, turning around.

"You know I've been at the cemetery. Why ask?"

He dries his hands, flings the dish towel at the counter, takes a sip from an ever-present glass of scotch.

He stacks the last dish in the rack, shuts the dishwasher. "Ann Magill called. She and Jim invited us for dinner Saturday night."

"Oh, please. After all this time she wants to be friends again?"

"Come on, she's tried."

"She called me last week, and she's babbling about Jim's hernia. I *hate* the babblers."

The babblers are worse than the advice-givers, the pain-minimizers, and those who claim access to God's mind: "God must have wanted him." "Bear up for the sake of your other children." "At least he didn't suffer." And that old standard, "Time will heal." The babblers don't say these things. I'll give them that. The babblers want to talk about anything else.

"It's hard for people, Dinah. Are you going to judge everyone we know this way forever?"

"Yes. I am." I fall into a ladder-back chair.

"Won't you please come to the grief support group this week?" Sam says. "Maybe it would help you, Dinah."

"I don't want help." Sour bile rises at the back of my throat. I do not attempt to hide my bitterness. "What's the point of going there, communing like we're some kind of club that no one would ever want to belong to? No one can understand what I've been through, anyway."

He sighs, tinkles the ice in his glass like bells, and downs the last of the scotch, to the very last drop. He's drinking all the time. "We've both been through it, Dinah."

"What do you want from me, Sam? I'm doing the best I can. I'm still living, aren't I?"

He stares at me for a few moments, then starts out of the room with his glass. "I want you to stop being a martyr." I hear him pouring a refill.

"Mr. and Mrs. Galligan?"

I was back in the NAR. A PICU intern was standing in the doorway, holding a clipboard. "I need a history."

"Another history?"

My skin was burning hot, as if I had been scorched by the sun. What had I just experienced? How could another waking dream portend an outcome so opposite the first one?

"I'm sorry," the intern said.

"It's all right, come on in." Sam waved him in.

Becky stood up. "I really have to go anyway."

"Thanks for coming," Sam said.

She kissed us both goodbye, and kissed Elijah again. The intern waited until she left, then pulled over the chair in the corner and sat down, his pencil poised.

"Okay," he said. "Why don't we begin with the pregnancy?"

five

We almost lost Elijah once before, before he was even born. I was two months pregnant, and started to spot during our vacation on Martha's Vineyard. Alex was nine, Kate, ten. The spotting continued through the weekend; I was petrified but didn't tell Sam until we were back in Connecticut. He took me in his arms and rocked me and told me it was going to be all right "no matter what." The same words he used when he asked me to marry him.

We'd be a great team, he said, facing everything together, *no matter what.* We'd work out whatever problems that might arise from our two different religions, face whatever bad stuff came our way, illness, even our parents' deaths, which at the time seemed like the worst thing that could ever happen.

We'd been looking forward to the birth of our third child, even though he wasn't exactly planned. I was already thirty-nine. We'd always alternated using condoms and a diaphragm because birth control pills made me fat and Sam thought the IUD was an unnecessary health risk. The condom broke. We had a laugh about it in bed that night, and when I turned up pregnant again, Sam joked, "When it comes time for your sex talk with the kids, you better warn them that it actually does only take once."

"*My* sex talk?"

He raised an eyebrow. "Well, you're the expert on human affairs here. I'm a mere maker of ads."

I had amniocentesis a couple of days later. The doctor told us there were "no chromosomal abnormalities" when he saw us in his office.

"Does the spotting mean there's something wrong with the baby?" I asked.

He placed his fingertip on the bridge of his nose. "Many, if not most, women who have problems early in a pregnancy like this go on to deliver perfectly healthy children."

"What's the percentage?" Sam wanted to know. I was grateful for his question.

"Well, there could be problems. But the likelihood is that everything will be fine."

"But what if there really *is* something wrong?" I said. "How far along in the pregnancy would I be likely to know? Early enough to have an abortion?" I didn't *want* an abortion, I just wanted to discuss the worst-case scenario, so I could prepare myself. "By the time a few more months roll around and we see if the problems continue, it'll be too late to even consider it. Right?"

"Dinah's a worrier," Sam said, offering me a smile. Now I wanted to slug him, even though he was right. He thought my worrying made me a pessimist. Wrong. I was a realist. He was being Pollyanna.

"I really think you're jumping the gun here," the doctor said. "I'm sure everything is going to be just fine."

The spotting finally stopped in the sixth month, and three weeks early I went into labor. Delivery after forty-two hours was by cesarean section, and Elijah looked like a chicken with very little meat on its bones. His skin was yellow with jaundice, and so thin it seemed transparent, with a mottled, reddish cast. You could see what was underneath, the capillaries and veins. He had an abundance of spiked black hair that made me think of a cartoon character who just stuck his finger in an electrical socket.

Mostly my baby kept his eyes closed in the beginning, but when he did open them he looked right at me and claimed me on the spot. He had Sammy's dimples, you could see that right away, in a face no bigger than a grapefruit.

Elijah wasn't one of the really frightening two-pounders, but he wasn't all pink and plump and squealing with vigor, either. Elijah's cry was more like a kitten's tiny mew. Whenever the other new mothers saw my son's sickly pallor and hanging skin, and the sore raw spot under his nose where the nurses had taped the nasal tube in place, thought bubbles might as well have appeared over their heads: "Thank God that isn't mine." "How terrible for her." But they didn't need to feel sorry for me. My son seemed as utterly wonderful to me as theirs did to them.

Then there was the very young mother, age sixteen at most, with frizzy red hair as bright as Julie's. She lifted her baby girl out of the bassinet, sat down near me in one of the rockers, and began to cry. My hormones in an uproar, I started to cry, too. I was thinking how much I missed Julie in my life. Not for the first time in my marriage, I thought about calling her. She wouldn't hang up on me after all these years. The next day a couple in their thirties came in and held the same baby, who left with them. I never again saw that very brave sixteen-year-old. And I never did call Julie, either.

I spent most of the first three weeks at the hospital, and Charlotte arrived to save the day with my father and Nelda in tow. Kate complained that Nelda kept cooking things she hated, like meat loaf and casseroles involving green beans. I remembered the menu well.

Sam said he'd handle it. And he did.

One night, he sank down in the rocking chair beside me, then bent down to kiss our son, who'd just fallen asleep. Elijah startled. He did that a lot in the beginning, as if something inside had suddenly frightened him. Sam looked tired. No wonder. Commuting to the city every day, dealing with the kids and Charlotte, too. And no doubt my father wanted attention as well, wanted Sam to accompany him on his nightly walks.

For as long as I could remember, my father had taken a walk after dinner, he said to organize his thoughts for the next day. As a kid, I was convinced he did it to get away from Charlotte. They worked together all day running my mother's clothing business; she owns a chain of women's boutiques called Charlotte's Petal, fifteen stores at last count. Too much Charlotte was lethal, as far as I was concerned. I always thought he stayed with her because of Dan and me; now of course I realize it's more complicated than that. I used to go with him, though; walking with Dad was one of my favorite things to do as a kid.

We sat silently for a while. Sammy was intently watching a new Madonna and child: a beautiful black woman with a head of intricate cornrows that cascaded all the way down her back, rocking a magnificent baby, born that morning. Skin the color of deep chocolate, huge black-rimmed eyes, alert and awake.

I reached over to touch him. "You're worried, aren't you?"

He turned to me, then looked down at Elijah. "It'll be all right. He'll be all right."

But we didn't really know that.

"Your mother is a piece of work," he said, changing the subject.

"The meat loaf issue?" I said, letting him.

He nodded.

"Ah. Did you start out with how happy we were that they were helping?"

He laughed. "What do you think, I've got a death wish? I told her how much we appreciated their coming. I said the kids were upset because you aren't there and that maybe it would be better if I cooked dinner, because I can fix things they're used to."

"My husband," I said, "you are a genius." Charlotte would never have let him cook; if you don't want to cook you pay someone to do it, you don't let a *man* do it, for God's sake.

"I know." He gave me a smug, self-satisfied look.

"So Charlotte said . . ." I went into my famous Charlotte-giving-guilt imitation: "'Oh, no, no, don't be silly. Just tell me what Dinah makes and I'll try to follow it.'"

"She tries, you know."

"Hey, whose side are you on? So Nelda's making hot dogs tonight?"

"Not a meat loaf or green bean in sight."

We moved on to talking about more important things, like how many cc's of formula Elijah had taken that day.

Finally, after three weeks, they let us take him home. Kate hovered over him like a little mother, and Alex seemed almost afraid to go near him at first, as if he would break. And Elijah cried. Most nights either Sammy or I had to walk our tiny bawling baby around the house until, gradually, his screams subsided and his red, angry face relaxed.

One night Kate appeared in the doorway of the dining room, where I was circling the table for what seemed the fiftieth time. Standing there in her lavender pajamas, pale, thin arms poking out of short sleeves, auburn hair sleep-matted, she looked younger than ten.

"What are you doing, Mom?" She rubbed her eyes.

I put my finger to my lips and kept walking. Elijah had just closed his eyes. "Sometimes I have to walk Elijah around to help him go to sleep," I whispered.

"You *do?* What time is it?"

"About three."

She stood watching me for a moment, then said, "You said you'd take me to get ballet slippers tomorrow. For the play."

"I will, Kate," I whispered. Then, "I would have walked you around, too, if you'd needed it."

She looked at me. "But I didn't need it. I was a good baby, right?"

"Elijah's a good baby, honey. You and Alex were just calmer babies."

"It's not Elijah's fault he isn't."

Still walking. I could feel his heart beating, smell his baby smell in his hair. "No, of course not."

"I love you, Mom."

"Love you back."

"You should make Daddy walk him around sometimes."

"Daddy does his share," I told my budding feminist. "Let's all go to bed."

Charlotte knew what to do about all of this, of course. Just let him cry. Eventually she realized I was not going to take her advice and insisted I needed a baby nurse. But I wanted Elijah to be my own. I was planning to return to my practice, pared down and part-time, in three months. Until then, no helpers.

"My God, Dinah, that doesn't mean you have to turn yourself into a zombie. What kind of a mother can you be if you're always exhausted?"

I managed to resist telling her that I was a better mother than she had been, whether I had a baby nurse or not.

My mother and I eventually compromised. A nanny came in three nights a week for two months. Charlotte insisted on paying. I ended up grateful for the help, because it became apparent very quickly that Elijah needed an extraordinary amount of care and attention. Wrestling my guilt to the ground, I went back to work when Elijah was four months old. I had to or I'd lose my entire practice and have to start over. I did hire a woman to help, a friend of a friend of Sam's mother. Her name was Bridey and she was lovely and patient. At ten months Elijah was still not crawling, and the testing started in earnest: brain scans and EEGs and blood tests and hearing tests. There was something wrong but they had no idea what.

At twelve months old, he started in a special pre-nursery class designed for kids with issues like his, and I let Bridey go. I could handle it myself from here on out.

When Elijah was seventeen months old I joined a weekly playgroup, just as I'd done with Alex and Kate, even though I was older than the other mothers. Elijah wouldn't even look at the other children, and nestled into my lap with Tuddy, the turtle my father had picked out for him a few months before. It had been love at first sight. Elijah and Tuddy spent the next two hours on my lap munching on our muffins, staring out the window, and occasionally playing with a toy I pulled from my bag. I was disappointed but not surprised. He was always wary of new situations, had to warm up to new things gradually, on his own time.

A few weeks after we started the group, one of the toddlers, Paulie Pearl, brought over a colorful spinning top. Elijah, who was on my lap, watched Paulie place the top on the table and push the shaft to make the toy spin.

Elijah watched him.

Paulie pushed it again, apparently trying to show him how to do it.

Elijah reached out. I held my breath. It looked like he was going to touch it. Elijah froze, then jerked back his hand. I tried to guide his hand again to make the toy spin, but this time, too, he yanked his hand away, clenched his teeth, and began to scream. Was he screaming in frustration because he knew what to do but couldn't yet get his hand to do it? Was it a sensory problem that might improve with occupational or physical therapy? Or was it a mental handicap, which would never really get better? I didn't know. All I knew was that you couldn't force him to do things he didn't want to do, or couldn't do.

Paulie Pearl brought over several offerings that day, but Elijah screamed every time, then finally rewarded Paulie's efforts by hurling a red fire truck across the room, where it collided with a collection of silver-framed photographs arranged on a side table, toppling the lot. One frame crashed to the floor and broke.

"Oh, God, I'm so sorry," I said. "Let me help you clean it up. Say you're sorry, Elijah."

Of course, he hadn't mastered any speech yet.

"No, no, it's fine." Tammy Pearl, Paulie's mother, cleaned up the broken glass, then set the surviving frames up again while I stood, holding Elijah, who clung to my neck for dear life.

"Maybe we should go," I said.

Becky stood up. "Don't, Dinah." She came over and took Elijah's hand. "You just didn't want to play with the truck now. Right, Elijah?"

He hid in my neck.

"Right, Tammy?" Becky said.

Tammy had just gotten the frame arrangement on the table the way she wanted it. "Of course. Anyone want any more coffee?"

The other children went back to playing in the far corner, and the mothers went back to coffee and chatting. Elijah got off my lap and crawled over to the television. I turned it on for him. He was afraid to touch the button, or he hadn't yet figured out things could be turned on by buttons. But he had recently started to point to things he wanted for the first time.

After a few more weeks, some of them were grumbling. "Do we have to have that thing on all the time?"

One day the TV was off and Elijah was grunting and pointing toward it, so I got up to turn it on for him. Tammy Pearl cornered me. "Have you taken him for some kind of evaluation?"

"Of course." No, Tammy. We're trying to figure this out on our own.

"Is he autistic? What's the prognosis?"

I felt myself tearing up. "They aren't sure yet. But, you know, Tammy, when he does manage to learn things, he gives you a smile so big you can live on it all day."

Becky, who seemed to have heard the conversation even though she'd been talking to one of the other women, and the other kids were making a lot of noise, moved toward us. "That's true," she said. "I'm a witness."

The playgroup gradually fell apart, there were more and more absences, until finally all of the women except Becky had dropped out officially. Various reasons.

About six months later I ran into a woman I knew from Alex's middle school PTA, in the supermarket. Elijah was with me, sitting in my shopping cart, eating a donut I'd given him to keep him quiet. Before I had Elijah, it had never occurred to me that I'd feed a child to keep him quiet. Elijah threw a tantrum at the drop of a hat, but I didn't want to confine him to the house because of it.

Amanda and I chatted for a moment, then she said she had to get back with the refreshments for her daughter's playgroup.

Elijah was clapping his hands.

"I joined a few months ago," she said. "Karen really loves the stimulation of the other kids. You probably know some of the women. Leslie Lee? Tammy Pearl?"

One night, Elijah scooted away when I reached for the towel after his bath, and ran downstairs naked. Twelve-year-old Alex was watching television, a history of rock and roll. Elvis Presley was on the screen, doing "Hound Dog."

It was as if Elijah had never heard music before. There was Elijah, age three, dancing naked around the room to Elvis. What a wiggle. You couldn't help but laugh at him, standing there naked and wet, imitating Elvis bumping and grinding, shaking his butt, his little penis wiggling.

Sam came in from a late night at the office while we were all standing around watching this, me holding the towel, all of us just hooting. Then Elijah saw Sam, and he smiled. He closed his eyes and started moving his mouth to the music, too, pursing his lips and then smiling, and pursing and smiling again, over and over. We laughed even harder. I didn't realize at the time that all that pursing and smiling was a compulsive behavior of sorts, one that intensified within the year. At the time it was just funny.

He was adorable, hilarious, irresistible. But no matter how adorable he was, or how much progress he seemed to be making with his language and cognitive development, his physical ailments were perpetual. And on a Tuesday evening, a year after he did his wiggling, wacky Elvis dance for the first time, as we ate a dinner of chicken Marsala to celebrate Sam's success, Elijah quietly laid his head down at the dinner table.

His forehead was cool, but he was obviously coming down with something, again. I put him to bed a little early, hoping to head it off. He slept through the night but in the morning, he did have a little fever. I kept him home from school, canceled a meeting with my editor, got the woman in charge of the Winter Fair on the phone, apologized for leaving her in the lurch for the clown toss, and made an afternoon appointment with the pediatrician.

Elijah sat on my lap all morning with Tuddy. We watched a Willie Wonka tape, his favorite. He loved to say "Wonka." He'd say it three times:

Wonka, Wonka,Wonka—the way he'd said his numbers when he started to speak and count. He had to do everything three times. Three times I had to read his story to him; three times he had to walk through the door; three times I had to kiss his cheek. Sometimes I even had to sing him his lullaby three times.

Everyone seemed to think he wasn't all that smart, but I thought he was very smart, just a different kind of smart. I tried to get him to say "Wonka, Wonka, Wonka" that morning as he sat on my lap, but he wouldn't say it. He wouldn't even wear his glasses. He just sat with his head against my chest and we watched the tapes together, and I read to him.

"He's got another ear infection," the doctor said, after a quick examination.

I'd lost count of the number of ear infections. Well, at least he wasn't screaming. Elijah hated doctors, of course. Hated white coats so much he'd been known to scream at the sight of a butcher in the supermarket.

The doctor shrugged. "And there could be something else going on, too." Casual. Unconcerned.

He prescribed another antibiotic, and by dinner Elijah seemed to be feeling better. He ate some soup. His fever was nearly normal, just over 99.

Sammy helped Alex with his homework while I put Elijah to bed, then I caught up on some of my own paperwork. Looking through a magazine with a spread of the latest creations from Paris, a bizarre collection heavy on feathers and uneven hemlines, I thought I might try a piece on the absurdities of the fashion industry. A "who do they think they're fooling?" kind of thing. But I was simply too tired. Tomorrow. Around 11:30 Sam and I went to bed, turning on the intercom into Elijah's room while we were getting undressed. I'd used it for Alex and Kate when they were babies, was still using it for Elijah at five because of all his problems.

Sam and I made love that night, and right in the middle of it we heard Elijah. *Ah-ba-ba-ah-la* . . . a singsong babbling.

We giggled. With Elijah you never knew what to expect.

"What in the world is he doing?" I glanced at the night-table clock. Almost midnight.

"He's singing, Di."

"Should we go in there and tell him to stop?"

"In your next life."

He was right. Elijah hadn't even slept through the night until he was four. Given his sleeping history, it was best to let him go back to sleep on his own.

Which he seemed to have no inclination of doing anytime soon.

We resumed our lovemaking, but Elijah kept up his odd singsong over the intercom, louder now, as if he were delighting in it: *Ah-ba-ah-ba-LA-LA-La.* We kept dissolving into laughter, so finally we shut the thing off. Afterward, Sammy said, "Wait, I can't fall asleep without my musical accompaniment." So we turned it back on. Elijah had stopped singing.

In the morning, I was cooking pancakes for the kids, trying in my mind to flesh out my send-up of the fashion industry. It was an amusing image—the average woman wearing haute couture to her daily activities, the PTA, the market, the office. What would my patients think if I showed up one morning with a triangular little hat perched smartly on my head, with a feather sticking out of it: "So how are *we* feeling today?"

Alex was erasing and repenciling figures from last night's homework, Kate was grumbling about a history test, Sam was drinking coffee.

Becky called while I was cooking pancakes, and I carried the cordless receiver to the stove. "I just wanted to tell you I loved the 'self-helpaholic' piece," she said.

I'd called it "How to Stop Improving Yourself: The Self-Helpaholic's Survival Guide."

"As the inspiration for the piece," Becky said, "I must protest. You left out my favorite self-help book of all time."

Becky was forever reading the self-help books I wouldn't read and swore I'd never write. "Which one's that?"

"*The Science of Bunnetics.* Now there was a piece of work. Have you seen my *tush* lately?"

Becky and I chatted for a few minutes while I cooked pancakes and stacked them on the plates beside the stove. As I hung up I was wondering whether Elijah would be well enough to go to school. I went into his room to wake him. Maybe he'd be well enough to eat some pancakes, which he loved, though the syrup usually ended up all over his face.

The room was dark and very quiet. He was lying half on his side. I said his name and moved closer. He did not answer or sit up or turn to greet me.

I moved up to his bed. His eyes were open, staring. He was awake, after all. "Elijah?" I reached down to touch his forehead. "Sweetie?"

A steady and rhythmic motion in a bed, delicate, like the wing beats of dying birds.

"Elijah?" I moved in closer.

Why was he staring that way? What was he staring at?

My God. It was a seizure.

Wait. Wait. This wasn't fair. He'd been tested for seizures. He'd never had seizures. And it was quiet, so quiet. Just the tiniest motion of his hand, his shoulder, his head, just like a little bird struggling on the sand.

How long? How long? How long?

Sammy had gone out to get the newspaper from the driveway, and when he came back, everyone in the house was screaming.

This is how it happens. You are just doing normal things, concentrating on the details of your life, counting on the givens, relying on the universe, fixing pancakes. And then the next moment arrives.

Wait a minute. Second-quarter rule violation: Foul.

six

After the intern left with Elijah's history, I realized I wasn't hearing the guitar anymore, hadn't heard it for quite a while. I went out into the PICU and walked past the other NAR. The curtain was open and I could see Jimmy through the glass, swathed in bandages and tubes. His parents were hunched over his bed.

I walked into the corridor. The ghost was gone. Jimmy's sister was there, though. She wandered around the PICU like a second wraith, drifting into the corridor, the waiting room, the room with all the couches where some of the parents slept, the bathroom where you'd go for a sort of break. She was maybe nine years old, pole skinny, and her eyes were wide and strange. She never used her own name, only wanted you to know she was Jimmy's sister. And talked, endlessly.

"What time is it? Aunt Ellen was supposed to be here at six, and if it's six already, I'd better get back in because I don't want to miss her."

"I'm sorry, I don't know." I tried to smile.

"She's going back home to Indiana tomorrow, and this is the last time she'll be coming."

Jimmy's sister followed me right into the bathroom, telling me, again, how if they'd stayed in Indiana this would never have happened because the bus drivers drove a lot slower there.

I looked into the mirror, thinking it was possible I'd become as invisible as dust.

"I'm glad my aunt came." She spoke to my reflection. "But Mommy and Daddy were kind of mad because she only came to see Jimmy *two* times. I want to go back home with her but Mommy and Daddy say I can't. The kids in my new school are nice and all, but I wish I was back home because all my friends are there."

I nodded, splashed some cold water on my face. I wanted to tell her my friends mostly hadn't come either, and they lived only an hour away.

"It's been eleven weeks since our lives changed forever." She always got to that, said it to nearly everybody, as if she were a robot child implanted with an adult computer chip.

"I'm sorry, honey." I wiped my face with a paper towel, then I turned and went out. My own children would be coming soon. In fact, they were there. Sam's parents had brought them. They are a physically mismatched pair, the Galligans. My mother-in-law is so short it's hard to believe she's an adult, and my father-in-law stands over six feet tall.

I took as deep a breath as I could take, and gave each of my children a hug.

Kate was crying. "What should we do about Elijah's hamster, Mom?"

She was looking to me to tell her what to do, and I didn't have a clue. I was trying to remember what day it was. Thursday. Right. I'd missed her flute recital last Sunday. Sam went, though.

"Just keep feeding him," Sam said.

I let my in-laws hug me, then dropped into a chair in a corner.

Shortly, my mother and father came in. But no, this couldn't be Charlotte Rosenberg, of the perfect coif, the flawless makeup, the impeccable taste. Still tall and willowy, even at the age of seventy, Charlotte wouldn't miss the opportunity to wear something dramatic and designer.

She didn't own anything else. And what was the perfect outfit for visiting a comatose grandson? A black cape. On the other hand, for the first time in my life, I could actually see the gray at the roots of my mother's hair.

My father looked pretty bad, too. He had circles under his eyes, and his stocky frame seemed somehow smaller, deflated. He hugged me, then Charlotte hugged me, enveloping me in that black cape. It reminded me of the one she'd worn when we shopped for my wedding gown at the salon of a designer she knew on Seventh Avenue. They kept bringing out heavy brocades, beaded silks, taffetas with skirts wide enough to hide a platoon. "So what is it you *want*, Dinah?" she kept saying, all the while winking at Mr. Jacques, really Jack Mancuso of Brooklyn. Charlotte wanted an elaborate affair at a fancy New York City hotel that would have cost enough to feed the starving children of some small country. I wore an ornate pearl-encrusted gown, in which I felt kind of silly. I did stick to my guns on the place, though, and was married on a beautiful old estate near their home on Long Island where we'd moved when I was fifteen, a move that caused no end of resentment. How could my mother make me move and leave my best friend behind, back in the old neighborhood?

"How is he?" my mother asked now.

"Seems like his color is better," my mother-in-law said.

As I've already said, Mary Galligan is one of those relentlessly upbeat, endlessly energetic women who always has two or three projects going at once. She knits and chats, needlepoints and has a pot of homemade jam on the stove, cleans up while she's cooking. And Lordy, she doesn't just take a walk with you, she swings her arms back and forth for a little exercise and points out interesting things along the way.

I looked at Elijah. Maybe his color *was* a little better. But he was still just lying there.

Mary held her rosary in one hand, leaned over and kissed Elijah. "There, there, wee boy," she said softly. Then she whispered a prayer.

I've always had a lot of respect for Mary, for coming over here from Dublin by herself at so young an age, for the easy way she connected with

Elijah, when everyone else had such a hard time of it. Not that she'd ever admitted Elijah had problems. Yet by instinct Mary somehow knew how to relate to him on his level, which was the only way he could accept. So what if Mary buys kitschy holiday sweaters to wear once a year, a Halloween sweater with orange pumpkins and flying witches, a Christmas sweater with perky trees adorned with little multicolored beads for the lights. All of which goes down really well with my mother in her Armani, of course.

Mary had started to cry, and my mother put her arm around her. Kate started to cry and came over to sit down next to me on the floor. My father teared up and walked out of the room. I could see him through the glass.

After a while, Sam's father said, softly, "Where's the soda machine, Sam?"

"There's one in the corridor," Sam said. "I'll take you, Dad. Did you have dinner?"

"No," Mary said, wiping her eyes, "nor a chance to give the kids dinner, either. I'll take them down to that cafeteria. The sandwiches down there are brilliant."

Come on, Mary. A diamond might be brilliant. An essay, a professor, Einstein. But a sandwich?

"Good idea," my father said. "Dinah?"

I'd seen that cafeteria, hadn't eaten a meal anywhere else since we got here, but I'd stopped going. Everything tasted the same. A donut might as well have been a rancid turkey sandwich.

"You have to eat," Sam said.

I motioned toward the sandwich on the table. "Becky brought me something."

"You haven't touched it," Charlotte said. "Really, Dinah. You must eat."

This really was quite odd coming from the woman who took me to a diet doctor at the age of thirteen, who came into his examination room and told me to get undressed.

"*Completely?*" I was horrified. I'd just gotten my first bra, and had begun my periods only a few months before. But I remembered my mother saying to be a good girl, not to argue, and to do what the doctor said.

There was a little curtained area, and I stood there crying, looking at the sheet folded on the bench, trying to figure out how to disappear into the walls or fit through the tiny barred window that looked out on the brick building next door. When I came out clutching the sheet around my body, he was waiting none too patiently, his arms folded neatly over his chest. I lay down on his exam table, let him put my feet in the stirrups.

I do not remember anything about that man's face but I remember his hands, big and meaty, inside me.

"We'll fix her up in no time," he told my mother when the three of us met afterward in his jumbled office. He prescribed amphetamines.

I dropped almost fifteen pounds that year. By the age of fourteen I could leap tall buildings. At fifteen I was taking five black beauties a day, and Charlotte bullied me into modeling in one or two of her runway shows. At the time, she had ten stores.

By sixteen my periods had stopped and I had almost lost my teeth. Odd for such a young person to get trench mouth, the dentist said when he took a look at my gums. When he told Charlotte they were rotting from all the speed I was taking, she threatened to sue that doctor Glick. I stopped speaking to her until she withdrew the threat. That was when she went to work on my nose—a Rosenberg nose, not a Blake nose, she liked to say. Within a year my nose was fixed but I was fat again. That was the year I started to call my mother Charlotte.

"Are you sure you don't want something to eat, Di?" Sam had an arm around Alex and was heading out the NAR door, his parents in tow.

I shook my head. Was eating suddenly the most important thing in the world?

"What about you, Kate?"

"I want to stay with Mom and Elijah," Kate said.

Charlotte put her hand on my shoulder. "If Dinah is staying, I'll stay, too."

No. I couldn't think about eating, nor about diet doctors who give thirteen-year-olds internal exams. I couldn't even think about ghosts. I had to concentrate on not screaming.

I sleep a little that night, although a dream I have is worse than the reality. In the dream I am walking through a department store so bright it's blinding. Shiny perfume bottles on counters flash around me like strobe lights, well-groomed women in smocks hold out gaudy bottles and tubes. I haven't put on lipstick in a very long time. A chic black suit shoves a bottle in my face. "Giorgio of Beverly Hills?" Her voice lilts up at the end, as if she is asking me a question.

"Coma of Connecticut." My humor has curdled like sour milk.

The well-groomed saleslady rears back like a frightened horse.

I move on. I make my way to the boys' department, collect five pairs of sweatpants, three sweatshirts, five T-shirts, stretchy fabrics, elastic waistbands.

"Easier to pull over steel-hard joints and muscles and limbs."

The saleslady is staring at me.

"When muscles atrophy," I tell her, "limbs wither from lack of use, they become as hard as steel."

The saleslady punches a key on the cash register. *Bbbbrrrrring!*

I woke, back by Elijah's side in the PICU with that word a taint on my lips: Atrophy.

Five A.M. The PICU was quieter at night, the din hushed, the parents settled into reclining chairs next to their children, perhaps sleeping, perhaps not. The nurse who was always in the room gave me a little smile, a nod.

I stumbled out into the PICU for some coffee. Jimmy's father was there at the coffee machine. I made a special effort to say something to him, I guess because of what the ghost had said, or because his son was in the other NAR.

"How is your son?" How (*breath*) Is (*breath*) Your (*breath*) Son (*breath*)?

"Jimmy's in God's hands, Jimmy's in God's hands," he said.

When Dr. Moore came in for his rounds a few hours later, I forced myself to watch him examine Elijah. I hated everything about the man, the way his eyes darted, the rough way he touched my son, the way he shouted in his ear, and adjusted the respirator to see if he would breathe on his own, and thumped on Elijah's thin chest with the side of his hand, as if he were a butcher pounding meat.

When he finished, he stood back. "In a few days he'll wake up and wonder where he is." Dart. Dart.

He'd been saying that for days.

Sam grabbed onto it. "You think so?"

"Oh sure," he said between darts. "When he wakes up he'll probably be as mad as hell and probably wiggle and fall right off the bed."

"You should see him wiggle," Sam said. "If you put on some Elvis music, he'll wiggle like crazy. Right, Elijah?" He squeezed Elijah's hand, then said to Moore, "He loves Elvis."

A half-baked smile appeared and disappeared. "We'd better tie his wrists to the sides."

"*What?*"

"You don't want him to fall off, do you?" Dart-dart.

"I guess not," Sam said. Such passivity. I was seeing certain qualities about my husband that I had never noticed in twenty years of knowing him.

"What's he going to do?" I managed to get my mouth to say. "Fling himself over the bar?"

"Dinah," Sam said, "if the doctor says we should tie his wrists, we'd better tie his wrists."

The nurse was already tying Elijah's wrists to the metal bar. Moore was gazing out into the PICU.

"He'll have his MRI today," the doctor said. "It's a special picture of the brain."

Why was he so damned condescending? Did he think we didn't know what it was? "Why does he need it, if he's going to wake up soon?"

Moore shrugged. "Just to see."

"When?" Sam asked.

He shrugged. "Sometime today."

They never told you when. It was like some sadistic little game, you hanging onto their every word, they being as imprecise as they could.

The MRI department was deep in the bowels of the hospital. It was a good thing they had official transports who knew how to get there; they couldn't very well have distraught parents pushing comatose children on gurneys up and down the corridors, asking directions every other step. When we got halfway down the first hall, I made them wait while I went back for Tuddy. I draped Elijah's arm around the stuffed creature as if he'd decided to hug his Tuddy, and there it stayed all the way into the MRI tunnel chamber. The machine made a lot of loud knocking noises. Sam and I sat there and watched, and I kept thinking that it was yet another bad sign that Elijah was sleeping through all that noise.

I wasn't sure what time it was, but many hours later, we had a white coat convention. Nothing formal, where they invite the social workers, the head nurse, and the chief resident, and everyone sits down in chairs with their hands folded on the conference table. This was impromptu. We were all standing up, right in the middle of the PICU. A pair of nurses, and doctors by the dozen: five neurologists—Moore, the big cheese, and his entourage of four residents; Williston and her two infectious disease residents; a guy from RAD, whatever that meant; a cardiologist; and Jonas, and his three PICU residents. Elijah sure was going to be pissed off when he woke up and found he was in white coat land.

"As of right now," Moore was saying, "his MRI looks completely normal."

My heart felt as if it might drop onto the linoleum floo Moore must know what he was doing, even if he didn't l the eye. He hadn't gotten to be the head of neurology out knowing something. I had no real basis on which to judge the competence of the doctors, since I wasn't an M.D., but a Ph.D. I did know a little something about medicine from my own training, but even if I had at one time learned something useful, my sluggish mind couldn't have retrieved it.

Sam reached for my hand. "The MRI is good, then. Right?"

"It might be good news, he could make a full recovery." Dart-dart.

Three out of four in the neurology camp nodded in agreement. Yes. Yes. Yes.

"Really? It's normal," Sam repeated.

Dr. Jonas exchanged a look with Dr. Moore. Jonas seemed annoyed, and Moore looked around, as if he didn't care what Jonas thought.

"I feel it's better to err on the side of caution when we talk to parents," Jonas said, and the PICU residents nodded.

When we talk to parents?

So. Jonas seemed to think Moore was being overly optimistic about Elijah's prognosis. Sam was just standing there, looking like someone had just punched him. Didn't he catch these nuances? Why was I so sluggish yet so attuned to nuances?

Dr. Jonas said something about different doctors having different approaches. Dr. Moore didn't respond with what he thought about Jonas *or* his approach. He just shrugged his shoulders and avoided looking us in the eyes.

Dr. Jonas said, "Mr. and Mrs. Galligan, it's possible there may be a cellular process going on that won't show up in the tissue for some time."

"Time *always* plays with loaded dice, babe."

I blinked my eyes. The ghost had suddenly materialized next to Moore. Pink skin, black boots, white coat. Neurology resident No. 5.

"*What*?"

"Oh, time. Time, time," the ghost crooned. "Time always plays with loaded dice. That's Yeats, you know. 'The wrinkled squanderer of human wealth.' Old Willie was right."

"What is *wrong* with you?" I asked him. What was wrong with me?

"Tee, hee, hee. Just having a little fun."

"We should have some results back in a few days," said Dr. Williston, a small, round-faced woman with Coke-bottle glasses. I called her the owl. She was the infectious disease specialist brought in because they thought Elijah might have a meningitis infection.

The two nurses didn't get a vote. Of those who voted, the score stood at 4 to 4. My son's recovery was a draw.

Meanwhile, the ghost's eyes were dart-darting—literally—all over the PICU, like a pair of crazed black bullets. Zig and zag. Ceiling. Floor. Desk. Floor. Bed in the corner. Floor. Back in his head.

Had my pain walked me right off the edge? I closed my eyes, and when I opened them again, Sam had his arm around me. The ghost was still there.

"You can't shut me out that way, silly Dinah," the ghost said. "Instead of trying to hide from me, a useless effort, why don't you get a look at your son's MRI? So much more productive. Then at least you'll know what they're talking about when things get hairy."

Oh. They weren't hairy already? "I want to see the MRI," I said.

All eyes turned to stare at me, as if I'd made a request they'd never before heard.

"Well, I suppose you could see it," Dr. Moore said, slowly. "How about tomorrow morning? You come downstairs and we'll show it to you then."

"I don't know how to read an MRI."

Dart-dart. "I'm sure we can give you the short course." He laughed a little, amused for some reason known only to him. That made me hate him more, if possible, than I already hated him. I was beginning to hate everyone—the doctors, the nurses, Becky, Addie, everyone who came and everyone who didn't. I was beginning to hate God.

"Tell him you need the long course." The ghost zipped up to the PICU ceiling, skeletal now and laughing.

I felt cold, as if an icy wind had entered me. "You can't be real," I said.

I saw pink flesh congeal in an instant on those bones, legs, torso, arms, face; then clothes appeared, boots, black leather jacket. "Ah, but what is reality, after all?"

"A riddle?"

He frowned. "Well. Not just any riddle. The ultimate riddle. Is it not?"

I turned away. The doctors had dispersed now, leaving Sam and me standing there alone in the middle of the PICU.

Sam leaned toward me. "Dinah, I don't want to see the MRI," he whispered.

My throat was closing. I couldn't breathe. "Why?"

"I don't know. I just don't want to."

"You're saying because you don't want to, I shouldn't either?"

"No, of course not. You can if you want. I just can't." He stared at me silently for a moment, then walked back into the NAR.

The lights in the PICU flickered. What would happen if the power went out? That had happened on our wedding day. There was a huge storm. Charlotte went nuts, but I reveled in the romance of it, white lilies by candlelight. A guy in the band had an acoustic guitar, and the singer and the drummer just went ahead and sang and played together. Sam and I danced by candlelight, to the acoustic guitar and the sound of rain and thunder. If it rains on the day you marry, his mother told us later, it's a sign you'll have a long and happy life together.

This wasn't part of our bargain, Sam. This wasn't anything close to the deal.

"What a wimp."

I looked up. The ghost was still hovering at the PICU ceiling. He gestured toward the NAR. "Milquetoast. Weakling. Milksop. Chicken shit. Miserable, pathetic excuse for a man. How could you have married him?"

"I loved him."

"Pshh. You just wanted a husband."

"I wanted love, like any girl."

The ghost was beside me again, zip, blink. "So much that you were willing to do what you did to Julie? Dinah isn't much of a friend, now is she? No wonder your friends have all abandoned you now. Evens up the score. No?"

I felt a cool flush at my neck, a buzzing in my head. "How do you *know* about Julie?"

"I've already told you, babe, I'm only for you. I know everything."

He winked. Then he vanished in a theatrical puff of smoke.

seven

I was six when Julie Bronstein showed up on my front lawn on a warm Sunday morning, new to the neighborhood, and bearing gifts, a Barbie doll in one hand, a large speckled frog in the other. We'd moved only a few weeks before to the new development of split levels in Great Neck from a small apartment in Queens, and I didn't yet know a soul on the block except the little boy next door, who only wanted to play with Dan. My mother, who as years went on became only more irritable and short-tempered, even abusive, had screamed at me earlier because I'd left my breakfast dish on the table. Nelda was off that day. Didn't she, Charlotte, have a right to a day off, too?

"All I ask is that you place your dishes in the sink," she'd snapped. "That's all!"

I was outside sulking. We'd gotten back from Cape Canaveral a few days before. It had been so much fun. My mother had been calm and relaxed, I was thrilled by her beauty, the way people would look at her with a kind of longing. We'd played cards in the hotel room, she'd bought me a pair of white pointy sunglasses just like hers, and Dad had taken a picture of us wearing them, our arms around each other. Now she was back to screaming at me.

I'd never seen anyone who looked quite like Julie, that riot of fire-orange frizz, pulled away from her forehead with a blue headband, the freckles covering every inch of her—face, arms, legs. She was wearing thongs. Even her feet had spots.

"Hi, I'm Julie. I found this in my yard. Wanna see?" She presented the frog, its legs dangling out from her grasp.

I reached out to take it, but the creature slipped away from her and dropped to the ground. We spent the next half hour chasing it around the yard, imitating its hops and giggling until we finally cornered and caught it.

"What should we do with it now?" Julie said, panting, laughing, gripping the thing with both hands now.

I motioned toward the Chevy parked in the driveway. "I know. Let's put it in my mother's car." My mother's stores were closed, and she was home.

Julie's eyes widened. "Won't she be mad?"

"Oh no," I said. "She can take a joke."

"Wow!" said Julie. "My mother hates frogs."

We put it in the car, I got my own Barbie doll, and we sat on the front step, playing Barbie and telling each other about our summer vacations. Julie thought Cape Canaveral was much better, but in a way I was jealous because she'd gone to see her grandparents in Maryland, and we never went to see mine. The two of us played and talked and giggled all morning, just waiting until Charlotte came out to go somewhere. Which she did, around noon. When she opened the car door, the frog hopped right out. She jumped backward and let out a short little shriek that sounded like a bark. "What was *that?*"

"We don't know," I said.

Her eyes narrowed, she advanced on me and loomed. (Julie would later name her mad expression the gargoyle face.) "Don't lie, Dinah!"

"We're not lying," Julie said, amazed, she told me later, that someone who was so beautiful could look so ugly. "Frogs can get into really, really small places. It must have climbed in through the engine. I'm Julie, we moved in over there." She pointed at the house across the street. For my part, I was amazed that she could fib with such a straight face.

My mother clucked a bit, and shook her head a few times, then got into the car and drove away. We held our breaths until we could no longer see her, then we let loose and giggled until our stomachs hurt.

I had a co-conspirator and a new best friend.

By the time Julie and I were ten, we had thirty-five Barbie dolls between us, counting Julie's ten. Charlotte just loved to buy me Barbie dolls, I think because she was trying to convince me that Barbie's was the body I should go for, presumably because it was as far from my own body as you could get.

More likely than not that summer we could be found hanging out in my room in the air-conditioning, play-acting our Barbie games, which had become quite elaborate by that time. I'd become a great fan of ghost stories and gruesome tales, and I'd recently read a book about Marie Antoinette. One morning Julie and I made a working guillotine out of two shirt cardboards and a piece of string. We'd line up the dolls as the audience, kneel the accused doll down, shout, "Off with her head," drop our cardboard blade, then pull off the doll's head and laugh hysterically.

When we tired of that one, we played a game we called Humiliation, in which the Kens were modeling in a fashion show, and the Barbies were the audience, only the Kens all came out on our runway without their pants. Julie, who had asthma, was laughing so hard she started to wheeze, and our giggling woke my brother, fourteen and already keeping a teenager's hours. He banged on the wall between our rooms.

"Shut the hell up! Some of us are trying to sleep."

We left the dolls in a jumble in the middle of my bedroom, said goodbye to Nelda, in the kitchen, and rode our bikes over to the original Charlotte's Petal. It was about a three-mile ride, and both of us were huffing and wheezing by the time we got there. We bought a soda at the luncheonette across the street, then headed for trouble.

Charlotte wasn't there that day, she now had eight stores to attend to, and my father had quit his law practice to go in with her. There was only one customer in the store, a really fat lady, fatter even than me. The saleslady's name was Bea Stern and she was trying desperately to find something to fit that customer, who'd told her she was a size twelve. Poor Bea kept pulling dresses off the size-twelve rack and handing them to the lady's arm through a crack in the dressing room door, only to have the customer hand them back and say, "This is too old-looking for me," or "This isn't my color." Finally, Bea pulled a pink mini dress in a crinkled fabric off the size-fourteen rack.

"This is a *fabulous* Pucci," she said through the dressing room door. "They run a little small, so I thought you'd need the next size. If not, I can get you the twelve. It just came in, you *must* try it on." The saleslady was new, but she'd already mastered my mother's style.

"*P-ucci!*" Julie whispered, spitting out the *P.* "P-ucci, P-ucci, P-ucci!" she kept whispering and spitting, and soon we were both giggling.

Finally, the lady came out of the dressing room in the dress and gazed at herself in the mirror. The dress was much too tight on her, she was more of a sixteen than a twelve, and it was very, very short, exposing very fat knees and thighs like tree trunks.

"Oh, it's *you!*" Bea Stern said, standing behind her.

This sent Julie and I into fits of laughter. I cupped my hand over my mouth and said in a stage whisper, "Yeah, it's you if you're Ten Ton Tessie."

The customer heard it, Bea Stern glowered, Julie and I ran.

"Maybe she won't tell your mother." Julie was on her back, staring up at the late afternoon sky through the trees. We'd laid our bikes down on the hill in the park next to the monument to the war dead, and we were horizontal beneath a stand of tall pine trees by the duck pond.

"Right," I said. "And maybe the moon'll forget to show up tonight."

Julie rolled over and propped herself up on an elbow. "Why'd you say it so loud, anyway? Your mom is going to kill you."

"Maybe what I ought to do is just never go home again. Dan would certainly be happy about that."

"You can always come to my house."

"Can I live in your room?"

"Sure. You can sleep in my other bed. Wouldn't that be the greatest, if we could be like sisters?"

I pictured myself living at Julie's house. Sharing her room at night, being able to whisper at three o'clock in the morning if we wanted. Eating dinner with her dad, and her brother, Scott, who loved playing kid tricks like putting fake plastic throw up on Julie's bed, and her mom, who baked cookies and the famous Bronstein strudel, and was so sweet she could make you sick, my mom always said. It wouldn't be so bad at Julie's, but I'd miss my gerbil, and Nelda, who was teaching me to speak Spanish, and my room, and my beloved books, and all my *stuff.* And Dad. Every night after dinner since the summer began, Dad and I had gone for a walk through the neighborhood. He'd even told my mother once when she asked if she could join us that it was a special father-and-daughter walk, and would she mind if we went, just the two of us? She said she didn't and I was glad for that, because I didn't want to hurt her feelings, even though she sometimes hurt mine.

I loved the way the houses in that neighborhood were the same, except they were painted different colors and some had porches and some didn't. It was interesting to me because on the inside everything was so different. Not just the way the people looked, but how they thought, who they were, the rules they lived by. Mrs. Lippincott made her daughter Angela take fifteen vitamins every day. Julie's mom lit candles for being Jewish every Friday night, without fail. My mom believed in charity and justice, and took off from work two times every month to sit with sick people at the hospital, participated in our synagogue's *Tzedakah,* serving dinner at the homeless shelter, collecting soup cans for the poor.

The houses were close to the street so at night you could see right into the rooms, as if the people had turned on the lights to show anyone outside what they were doing. All four McGregors were always watching television, and Mrs. Posner was always cleaning, and Mrs. Samuels sat alone. Julie and I called her the witch because she was mean when you came on her lawn but at night you could see she was just a lonely old lady. That night Mrs. Lapidus was sitting with Mrs. Posner at the Lapiduses' kitchen table.

"Where's Mr. Lapidus?" I said. Mr. Lapidus was always tinkering in his garage with the door up, and you could see the hammers and wrenches hung on the pegboard behind him, the bicycles, spare tires, and Hula Hoops in the corner. He used to smile when you passed and say, "Nice night."

"He and Mrs. Lapidus are getting a divorce," Dad said.

"Why?"

He shrugged. "It's not our business, Dinah."

"I know why," I said. "It's because Mr. Lapidus was supposed to meet his mistress at the airport and they were going to fly off to Tahiti because it's true love. But Mrs. Lapidus found the note Mr. Lapidus wrote and killed his lover and hid her behind the wall in the basement. And so when Mr. Lapidus didn't see her at the airport, he came home but he had to leave again because he kept hearing her heart beating in the basement, louder and louder and it scared him to death." I had just read "The Tell-Tale Heart."

My father smiled happily. He was proud of me. "You certainly have an imagination, Dinah."

I shrugged. "But Dan's smarter. Mom thinks he is."

"No, she doesn't, Dinah. Your mother loves you."

"Sometimes it doesn't seem that way."

"She just gets upset sometimes. Sometimes you deserve it, you know." His face was stern, and I liked it better when he had his arm around me. We walked in silence for a while.

"Maybe you should be a writer," Dad said suddenly. "Since you like to make up stories. And read them, too."

"But I like real stories a lot more."

He laughed. " 'Real' is a funny word. You can take the very same event and two different people might experience it and remember so differently that when you hear them both tell about it, it's hard to say which version is real and which isn't."

My father was a reticent man, almost shy, but he was also quite thoughtful. I wondered what went through his mind when my mother went crazy and screamed at me. It must have been so different from what I was thinking.

"How long do you think I could stay at your house?" I asked Julie now in the park. We were down on our backs again, pine needles digging into our skin through our cotton shirts.

"At least until next year." She propped herself up again. "Hey, who's Ten Ton Tessie, anyway?"

"Well, how the heck should I know?"

Both of us burst into giggles, and pretty soon we were laughing so hard we were rolling around in the pine needles, holding our bellies, begging for mercy.

"Jules?" I sat all the way up, serious now. I loved her so much. "Let's make a pact that we'll always be together. We'll always know everything about each other, and always be friends. No matter what. Even if we get married."

She made a face. "Forget it, I'm not getting married. I already told you."

"All right, even if we don't get married. We can live together in a beautiful house and do anything we want. No husbands to tell us what to do." Except in my house, it was just the opposite.

"You mean like when we're thirty?"

"Yep. Even forty."

She raised an eyebrow. "Well, of course we'll always be there for each other. But not when we're thirty or forty."

"Why not?"

"Because you're not going to make it to eleven." She grinned. "'Cause your mom's going to kill you tonight."

Bea Stern told my mother, of course, and got fired. After all, she'd violated Charlotte's Petal policy: style, fit, quality, and honesty.

And that night I got an all-out dose of Charlotte's Wrath. I was hiding in my room at about six o'clock when I heard the front door slam, then the creak of the steps, then banging on my door. "Dinah! Open the door. This instant!"

I considered jumping out the window, then decided against it and opened the door.

Her eyes were wide, her jaw clenched. "How dare you insult my customer?"

"I didn't insult her, I just—"

She slapped me so hard I staggered back and fell to the floor next to the jumble of Barbie dolls.

"Don't lie, Dinah!" She towered over me, wearing the gargoyle face and her Chanel suit, alligator handbag looped over one arm, keys still in hand. "I hate it when you lie!"

I was crying hard, and holding my hand to the stinging place on my face where she'd slapped me. I heard Nelda banging the pots around downstairs. She knew.

"I want you to apologize. Right now!"

I lifted my face and forced myself to look up at her. Tears were streaming down my cheeks and I clamped my mouth shut. I hated her.

"Apologize. Right now."

I didn't know what good apologizing to her was going to do, but I knew I didn't want another dose of her convincing.

"I'm sorry."

Charlotte sat down on my pink bedspread. "Why would you say such a thing to one of my customers, Dinah?" Suddenly she was a calm, rational person who wanted to discuss something with a daughter she had no memory of slapping less than a minute ago.

I shrugged. I wasn't even sure why I'd said what I'd said.

"It's that Bronstein girl," Charlotte said. "She's a bad influence. You are never to be so disrespectful again. And you will never set foot in any of my stores again."

I said nothing. That was hardly a punishment. What followed was.

"And you are *not* to see Julie Bronstein again, either."

"Mom, you can't—"

"I can do anything I want. Look at this mess. I buy you everything and you never show the least appreciation for any of this." She swept her arms out in a gesture that took in the room, the book-strewn bed, the cardboard guillotine, the leftover scraps of cardboard and scissors, and the pile of Barbies and half-naked Kens.

"You have ABSOLUTELY NO CONCEPT of what my life is like!"

I curled myself into a corner next to my bed. My mother stood up then and said, "You know, Dinah, you're hardly in a position to make fun of someone for being fat!"

She whirled around and stormed off. Of course that wasn't the end of it. She carried on for weeks about her ungrateful daughter who didn't appreciate how difficult it was to be a mother and a successful businesswoman at the same time. Did she think I cared? She was the only mother I knew who worked. She threatened not to send me to camp, in addition to never letting me see Julie again, but in the end, her threats about separating us were mostly bluster.

For the whole first half of my life, in fact, no matter what I was doing, or where I was going, Julie was always there. She was there when I was eleven, and my brother locked me in a closet after we spied on him making out with Liza Tubbman, saw him rubbing her boobs, which were quite impressive, as I remember. Charlotte took Dan's side, as always, believed his story about studying for a test together: "Three hours in that closet!" I argued, in a confrontation that had my brother red-faced, my father's mild protest instantly silenced by my mother, and Liza Tubbman, her shirt hurriedly buttoned wrong, slinking out the door.

As I argued back, my mother's objection, "I'm *sure* it wasn't three hours, Dinah. The way you exaggerate is just tacky!" eventually turned into a full-fledged attack of the gargoyle face, a vicious comparison of the importance of my brother's grades versus my own, and yet another time my mother hit me.

"I just don't know *what* we're going to do, Dinah," my mother said later that night, when I went to apologize to her, at my father's insistence. "I try and try, but nothing I do seems to help. My own daughter! I must be a complete failure, I might just as well kill myself. Then you wouldn't have to look at me anymore."

Of course it would be my fault if she killed herself. Everything was about her.

The next day, when I told Julie what had happened, she listened without saying anything until I was through, then she said, "What in the world does she want from you?"

I shrugged. "She wants me dead. She wants me to just disappear, just kill myself."

Julie shook her head. "I don't think so. I think she wants you to beg *her* not to kill herself." She was eleven years old when she came up with that.

As my difficulties with my mother worsened, Julie expanded her role in my life from mere constant companion, co-conspirator, and bosom buddy, to comforter, confidante, and counselor. She might have been called my savior. When I was working up to kissing a boy for the first time, Julie soothed me when he never called me again. When I was recuperating from my nose job, she arrived at the hospital with a huge stuffed bear on which she'd spent her entire savings. When I came off my amphetamine addiction at sixteen, she helped me, encouraged me, held wet compresses to my head. When I ranted or cried after yet another run-in with my mother, she listened without complaint.

"Maybe you should just tell your mother you love her," she said after a particularly upsetting episode with Charlotte in my junior year of high school, related to my weight gain.

"What?" I said.

"That's what she wants, isn't it? For you to love her."

"I don't think so." I didn't.

"Just try it. What have you got to lose? While she's yelling at you, just say, 'I love you, Mom.' Can you imagine what she'd do if you stood there and told her you loved her? I'd bet anything she'd stop yelling at you."

I never put Julie's theory to the test, but in retrospect, of course, it was an extraordinary idea for a sixteen-year-old mind to come up with. But then, Julie was an extraordinary person.

eight

The short course. The next morning I made my way down to the MRI department again, this time without an official transport and without Sam.

He explained again. "It's too much," he said. "My son's brain? I just can't."

"*Our* son," I said.

The receptionist told me to wait for the doctor in the waiting room. I sat down, leaned my head against the wall, and closed my eyes. A new vision collected around me like water.

I am standing with Sam in a hospital room, not the NAR. Not even in the PICU. This is a regular hospital room, with a window. Outside, trees are flowering. It is no longer winter. A doctor we have never met comes halfway in, draws the curtain behind him. Tall, very thin and pale, back sagging.

"I'm Dr. Angus, Mr. and Mrs. Galligan. I read the MRI." He shifts from one foot to the other. "There is nothing normal in your son's brain."

"But Dr. Moore . . ." Sam's voice cracks. ". . . said Elijah's MRI looked normal."

"Sometimes it takes time for cellular damage to show up in the tissue so that it can be seen in an MRI. I'm sorry."

That was what Dr. Jonas said.

"How long will he live?" Sammy asks.

"It's difficult to know. Theoretically, years."

My mind has been wiped clean as a spotless counter.

"How many years?"

"Well. It depends on how aggressive you want to be."

"What does that mean?"

I already know what it means. I have been reading books on the subject. Grief has deprived me of the ability to read a magazine, a nursery rhyme, or a headline, but I can read articles with titles like "Ethical Decisions on the Removal of Life Support Systems in Encephalopathy."

"Children in this kind of situation develop other problems," Dr. Angus says. "Secondary infections, for instance. We can treat them with antibiotics. Or not."

"So what do we do now?" Sammy asks. "Send him to rehabilitation?"

"There is nothing to rehab. I'm very sorry." The doctor sighs. "You could send him to a long-term chronic care facility. There's a good one in Connecticut. Isn't that where you're from? The Laurel Institute."

And this too I already know.

"If Elijah were your child?"

"I can't really tell you that, Mr. Galligan. I can tell you this. He's in a persistent vegetative state. He has no awareness of who he is or that you are here. He doesn't feel pain, not in the sense of consciously feeling it. All that's functioning is the brain stem, the most primitive part of the brain, the part that controls the autonomic functions, like heartbeat, respiration. But even that has been damaged severely, which is why we haven't been able to wean him from the respirator."

"Is removing it legal?" Sam's eyes are fixed on Elijah, transfixed.

"There is ample precedent. You would not be pioneers."

"Would he die then, if we removed the respirator?"

"He hasn't done well the times we tried to wean him from it."

"But—no, stop," Sam says. "I can't talk about this anymore right now."

"Mr. and Mrs. Galligan?" I opened my eyes and was right back in the waiting room outside the MRI department. A doctor I had never met was standing over me, holding a thick sleeve of MRI photographs. He was tall, pale, his back sagged. "I'm Dr. Angus. I'll be on rotation for the next few days."

My tongue felt as thick as a slab of putty.

The doctor took me into a small room, where he placed several large sheets of film on the light boxes mounted on the wall. Each photograph showed an individual slice of my son's brain. I stood mute, while he explained about gray matter, and white matter, and light spaces, and dark.

"It's a good sign that it looks normal, Mrs. Galligan," the doctor assured me.

When I got back upstairs, Dr. Jonas was in the room examining Elijah on his morning rounds. When he left, Sam left, too. For a run, Sam said. Every day he ran, even here, even now. How could he carry on as if nothing had happened? I almost expected him to announce that he was going to drive up to Westport to play in his usual weekly tennis game with Becky's husband. Wouldn't surprise me. He wouldn't want to miss a week, might lose his competitive edge, get out of shape.

Half an hour later, I saw him come back into the PICU, sweating, holding a box of donuts. I knew him. He was going to leave it for the staff and other parents. How could he still be so friendly when I was marinating in bitterness? For me, Big Time Grief would be a total eclipse, opaque, blocking out everything but itself. I would only be able to see the inside of my own skin, which would be ugly, ugly, and oozing rancor. Grief support? Hah!

I watched him pass by Dr. Jonas, who was standing with Jimmy's father and mother in a huddle near the other NAR. He walked right past them and placed the donuts next to the coffee machine, then stood there for a moment, his head bowed.

He came to the NAR doorway and stopped, his face ashen. "Oh. My God," he said softly. "When I walked by Dr. Jonas, I heard him say to Jimmy's parents, 'I'm afraid there's nothing more we can do. I'm very sorry.'" He dropped into the chair next to Elijah's bed. Softer still: "Good thing I didn't interrupt for donuts."

The next time I looked out I noticed that the door to the other NAR was open. The curtains were pulled back, the bed had been stripped, and the machines were resting comfortably.

"Did you see it? Did you see it?"

The ghost was perched on top of the Coke machine, legs dangling over the edge, guitar on his lap. He seemed more substantial now, the edges of him more defined, more solid. His skin even seemed less pink, though it was still more the color of cotton candy than flesh. Gone were the bell-bottoms. Gone was the doctor garb. Now he was playing patient. Of course, the effect was marred somewhat by muddy boots and by the leather jacket he had on over his speckled hospital gown. Planted next to the Coke machine was a rolling IV pole with a tube that ran from a bottle of pink liquid into the sleeve of his jacket. I didn't look too closely at that pink liquid, which seemed to be moving, very fast.

"Did I see what?"

"The Angel of Death. The Dark One was here this morning. For Jimmy."

"No," I said.

The air bubbled like blisters, and he disappeared from the top of the soda machine. The air beside me percolated, and he reappeared with his guitar right there.

I took a few steps back. Oh, the stink of him, the fetid stench of the grave. He should have looked worse for that smell. And the emanations of heat and cold that swirled around him, that issued from him, the disturbances of atmosphere. It was as if his presence altered the fundamental structure of air.

He strummed a few chords and smiled. "Well, too bad. That one is something to see. Of course, it's just as well you didn't."

"Why?"

"Well, it's obvious, isn't it? Once you see the Angel of Death, that's it for you. It's the eternal dirt nap. The house of perpetual un-motion."

"*You* seem to be kicking around and in motion," I said.

"You think this is *fun?* You try it for a while, let alone forever." He leaned toward me. "Want to trade places?"

"No thanks. How did you know Jimmy was going to die?"

"I already told you. The dead know everything the living don't. If you want to know what I really think, the living are jealous of the dead."

"Why?"

"Because they're always speculating about the dead. *N'est-ce pas?*"

"Why didn't you *do* something for Jimmy? You said you know the secret of how to escape the Angel."

His laugh began as a twittering sound, then escalated, and I heard other sounds, hee-hawing like a donkey, cackling like a coop full of hens. Were those bees buzzing?

"Why would I?"

"Just to be kind."

His eyebrows drew together, and it occurred to me that his changes of expression were more like rearrangements of a still life.

"Kind to who?" he said.

"Kind to Jimmy. To his parents. To his sister."

"Well, aren't *we* the compassionate one?" He made a sound like the clearing of a throat. "Excuse me, kind to whom? That man always corrected him when he made grammatical mistakes."

"What man?"

"The man who was this spirit's father, when the spirit was alive. Oh yes. He was never good enough for his father, but take it from me, this miserable wreck was once a human being—and quite a handsome human being, if I do say so myself. Tempted *all* the young women. They swarmed around him like bees to honey, as a matter of fact." He strutted, holding his arms out, preening like a drag queen.

I stared at him until he stopped and came back.

"Of course, now he's all shriveled and putrid, and he stinks, and all his cavities and organs are positively crawling. *C'est dommage,* his flesh only tempts tiny insects and wriggling creatures now." He wiggled his fingers. "Or, as Baudelaire put it, *de noirs bataillons, de larves,* battalions of black larvae."

Well. I had met up with a ghost who quoted Baudelaire.

"Of course," he said, "all of that is shuttled away in the ground, so the living don't have to witness the processes by which flesh becomes one with the soil."

"That's because it's repulsive," I said.

A shrug, like the winking of air. "Never lost a moment's sleep over it myself."

"Do ghosts sleep?"

"Ho, hum. Oh yes, a permanent siesta, a happy slumber. I only meant it doesn't matter a bit to me, all that crawling putrescence. Would have been a lot easier, though, if I could have used what was left of his body. Of course, then you wouldn't be sitting here talking to me. You'd be regurgitating. Tee, hee."

"Human beings don't want to think about what happens to their bodies after they die. It's too horrible."

"Well, you're going to think about it plenty, Dinah. Mothers can't help it. They think about their babies in the ground all the time. Just remember your Grandmother Elizabeth."

Yes. I remembered.

"Never goes away. Never, never."

"What are you saying?"

"Oh nothing. Nothing. You're not afraid of me, are you?"

"You're nothing in comparison," I told him.

He laughed. "I know, I know. I'm counting on that."

"Wait a minute. *Should* I be afraid of you?"

"Absolutely not." His words rang loud and sonorous. True words or lies?

"Did you ever hear the one about the man who stayed overnight in the cemetery and overheard two ghosts talking—"

"Please. I'm in no mood for jokes."

"This is no joke. It's a story. So the man heard one ghost tell the other that hail would destroy the crops of anyone who sowed at the first rainfall. And so the man went and sowed at the second rainfall, and everyone's crops were destroyed, except his."

"What's the point?"

His face reorganized itself into an expression of disappointment. "I don't know. Does there have to be a point?"

"You're saying I shouldn't be afraid of you. And you can help me. Right?"

"Up to you."

"This *has* to be a dream. How can a dream help me?"

"A dream, is it? 'All my days are trances, and all my nightly dreams'? That's Poe, you know. Well, certainly you know. Poe was one of your favorites, was he not? So. Which part of this is the dream, and which part the trance, and which part the reality?"

"The part where Dr. Angus comes in and says those awful things about Elijah is the dream—the nightmare. The part where my son dies."

"I see."

"So then, you see why I don't need your help," I said. "Because Elijah is going to live. His MRI is normal, the doctors say so."

The ghost nodded. "All the same, I think I'll tell you just one little secret. There are some special exceptions to the rule about the Angel of Death, for mothers. Has to do with the flesh of the flesh, or something like that. If a mother stays very sharp and listens *very hard*, she can hear that monster Angel. She can't see it, but she can hear it. It comes between blinks, you know. Anyone who sees opens his mouth in horror. Which is the exact moment when the Angel unsheathes its sword and drops its poison into the mouth." There was a loud *pinging* sound, and he snapped his long fingers. "Takes less than a nanosecond."

Such things the ghost told me. "How do you know all this? Because the Angel of Death came for you?"

"Well. I wouldn't be wandering around this way if that one had come for me, now would I?"

"But you're dead. Didn't the Angel come for you?"

"Yes. And no."

My ghost talked in riddles, and I was tired of being confused.

"Well, I don't have to worry about that," I said. "Because it's not going to happen. Not to Elijah."

"I know, I know, because you've seen your son at eight. In the Great Barrier Reef."

The ghost took one hand off his guitar for a moment, and something materialized between his long fingers. What was that? Fat, small, brown. It was a cigar. He brought the thing to his black lips and drew inward, or seemed to draw inward anyway, as if he were drawing smoke into lungs that breathed. I even thought I could smell the cigar. The tip turned hot red, and smoke curled out of it and seemed to drift toward the ceiling.

"*Cohiba,*" he said, leaning back, eyeing me. "Finest there is. Want one?"

My Grandpa Eli had said those same words to my father once, a very long time ago.

The ghost put the cigar into his mouth again and drew inward again. He exhaled, and smoked languidly for a while. After a few more puffs, he leaned toward me, strummed a few strings with his other hand, this time a discordant sound.

"Well, Dinah, you may have had a dream, as you so quaintly call it, of your baby in the Great Barrier Reef, but you've also had a dream of your precious baby in his hospital bed, one of several where he might be spending the rest of his abbreviated life. What did you think that was? Chopped liver?"

"No, I just—"

"Perhaps we should continue to review your life," he said, taking a contemptuous puff on the cigar, "to see which you deserve, door number one, or door number two."

nine

Grandpa Eli was a huge man, totally bald, and the day I met him he was holding an enormous cigar between two of the largest, fattest fingers I'd ever seen. He greeted us in the marble front hall of the faux Tara-style mansion outside Atlanta where my mother had actually grown up. I was seven, my brother twelve.

He kissed my mother on the cheek, shook all of our hands, apologized for not having had a chance to get out of his golf clothes, asked my dad about the plane ride. Dad said we got a little rambunctious (meaning me), and I wondered why Dan got away with only saying hello, while my mother had been nervously preparing me for this first-ever visit to her family for weeks.

Grandpa Eli bent over and breathed in my face, suffocation by cigar breath. "Well, my, my, my, you must be Dinah. Aren't you the cutest thing? I'm your Grandpa Eli."

But I wasn't a cute thing, I was fat, my brother called me Tubby Turd. And my mother called Grandpa Eli "the Bull." I'd heard her talking to my father in their bedroom. "If the Bull starts something, Martin," she'd said, "we're leaving."

"Calm down, Charlotte," Dad said.

Now that I'd finally met him, I wasn't sure whether he was a bull or not. He wore big, black glasses, but he had a twinkle in his eyes. His voice boomed, but the features on his wide face were so cherubic, the skin on his bald dome of a skull so smooth that I thought he looked like a giant over-stuffed infant. On the other hand, *everything* was weird here. Everyone talked slow and easy like my mother when she wasn't mad, all of them purring contentedly like sunning cats with all the time in the world. The trees were different, a big black convertible with a driver had come to get us, it was warm in the middle of December, and this house was not a house but a castle.

"Hello, Grandpa Eli, nice to meet you." It was what my mother had told me to say.

"Very nice, Charlotte," her father said, as if my mother had said it. "But you don't have to wind the child up like she's meeting the big, bad wolf."

My mother took off her sunglasses. "I know, Daddy." That was what she called him to his face, Daddy. She looked around. "Where's Mother?"

Grandmother Elizabeth. I knew she existed, but my mother hadn't talked about her at all, the way she had about her three brothers, Bernard, Marshall, and Lee.

Grandpa Eli's nostrils flared as he puffed on his cigar. "Your mother is having a headache."

"Naturally," Mom said, with a look at her father that I didn't understand.

"Your mother's *fine,* Charlotte," Grandpa Eli said.

She just gave him that mysterious look again.

I realized that he had an even odder accent than the stewardesses who'd served the soda and peanuts on the plane. Looked like E.G. Marshall, talked like Khrushchev.

"You sound funny," I said.

My mother put her hand on my shoulder. "We don't tell people any old thought just because it happens to jump into our head, Dinah."

"Don't reprimand her, Charlotte," Grandpa Eli said. "She's a spirited little thing. Takes after her mother."

She didn't smile at that. "Your grandfather is from a place called Russia," she said. "Very far away. That's why he talks like that."

"Farther than New York?"

Grandpa Eli put his whole body into his laugh, and flashed big yellow teeth. "Oh, much farther. But my mama and papa brought me and my sister on a big ocean ship. It took days and days, and I was just a little boy and I was sick the whole time."

I tried to picture this ancient, balding man who already looked like an infant as a little boy, throwing up over the side of a boat.

"Is Lee here yet?" my father asked.

"Bernard and Marshall arrived this morning. Lee phoned to say he wasn't coming, after all. Of course, *you'd* already know that, wouldn't you, Charlotte?"

What was going on here? I loved Uncle Lee. He was the only uncle of the three who visited us, a slightly built man who laughed a lot and had a high-pitched voice. We shared a love of books and sometimes played a game where he'd start a story and I'd have to continue it, then he'd pick it up, then me. Usually by the end it was so silly that we both collapsed with laughter.

My mother took a step backward. "Daddy, how can you resent that I keep in touch with Lee?"

He put his hand on her shoulder. "You're right, Charlotte. What do you say we start again?"

My mother stared at him, again. Wait a minute. Those were tears in her eyes, something I'd seen only when she was furious and hysterical. She had in fact gotten furious at me just a few days ago. She'd been telling me how, when she was growing up, her father had sent her to a place called Miss Funk's where such things as wearing white gloves, curtseying, and the proper selection of silverware were drilled into her head. "I hated it," she said. I agreed it sounded awful, and asked why she bothered to teach *me* to use the right fork. She said she wanted her father to know she'd raised a good girl.

"Why do you care if a bull thinks I'm a good girl?" I asked her.

Charlotte stared. "You *listened* to my private conversations with your father. How dare you!" Her face had flushed, a mottled purple. She was shaking with rage, and I had the idea that her head would explode. She'd never hit me before, and it was only a push, but it was the first time. She called me a sneak and a liar, and spilled venom: "Do you know what happens to little girls who listen to other people's private conversations? They grow great big ears so they look like Dumbo the elephant. And that's what you're going to look like, Dinah. Great big fat Dumbo the elephant."

Sometimes my mother seemed like two different people. On the airplane, she'd reprimanded me quietly. "I reckon there's no need to tell everyone you meet what you got for Hanukkah."

"Why not?" Well, I hadn't informed *every* passenger that I'd gotten three new Barbie dolls, just those sitting near us.

She glanced at my father, who was reading the paper, then looked back at me. I wondered if she was going to start screaming, then decided she wouldn't in front of all these strangers whisking through the sky.

"Oh, Dinah," she said with a sigh. "You are just such an exasperating girl. We don't tell people we celebrate Hanukkah, honey. It's nobody's business but ours."

I was exasperating? Grown-ups, especially my mother, were so impossible and full of contradictions. Why then was she bringing an enormous suitcase stuffed with Hanukkah presents? Why then had she been complaining for weeks that we were going to have to sit around their Christmas tree like we weren't even Jewish, those hypocrites? Why was she going in the first place, to see someone called the Bull?

Now, with this discussion about Uncle Lee, I saw there were grown-up secrets here in Atlanta that I didn't know anything about.

Grandpa Eli held out the cigar, toward my father. "*Cohiba,*" he said. "Finest there is. Like one?"

"Maybe a little later," my father said.

"How about you, my boy?" This to my brother Dan, who shook his head as his eyes widened. Grandpa Eli laughed and patted his head.

A bunch of grown-ups appeared, along with a toddler and an infant. I didn't even try to keep the names straight as we were introduced all around; then a tiny, pale girl about my own age and a boy about my brother's age came bounding down the stairs.

"You must be Dinah," the girl said. Her face reminded me of a ferret. "I'm your first cousin Mebane Ruth. Uncle Bernard's daughter." She pointed to the grown-up who looked like a younger, thinner version of Grandpa, then to the boy. "And that's Cook."

"Mebane?"

"Mama and Daddy named me Mebane because that's my mother's last name. Martha Mebane. I mean it was Martha Mebane before she married Uncle Bernard; now she's Martha Mebane Blake." She seemed to have jumping beans in her pants.

"Well," Grandpa Eli said, grandly, "what're we all standin' round here for? Let's all go into the living room."

"Grandpa Eli," Mebane Ruth said, "can't we show our cousins the house?"

"Why, sure, Mebane," he said. Then, walking with my father, he led the adults toward an adjoining room. I could hear him asking my father about his law practice.

"I've decided I've had it," Dad said. "I'm going in with Charlotte."

"So, then. Your stores are doing well, Charlotte. How many now? Five?"

"I didn't know you kept count, Daddy."

All very interesting—my parents had been poring over papers every night at the dining room table for weeks—but we were off, tearing through a palatial house filled with carved, dark wood furniture. After exploring an immense hall called the game room, which had a pool table, two pinball machines, and a real soda fountain behind the bar, we went outside to a field in back of the house. In the crook of a huge oak tree was a tree house, with windows and a real door. The door opened and a head came out. "Halt! What's the password?"

"They don't know the password, stupid," Cook said. "They just got here."

He climbed up the ladder, and Mebane, Dan, and I followed. When I got to the top and peered over the edge of the platform, Mebane, already sitting cross-legged on the floor next to Cook, introduced us to Ashlin, Richard Andrew, Ross, and Reynolds.

Reynolds? Everybody I'd met had a name I'd never heard before, or two first names, or a first name that sounded like a last name. But after hearing the explanation of "Mebane Ruth," I wasn't about to ask Reynolds why her parents gave her a boy's name. I settled myself down next to my brother. Though there was a slight chill in the air, and we were all wearing jackets, it was beautiful in the heart of that tree in the middle of winter.

"What *is* the password, anyway?" Dan asked.

"It's a secret, can't tell you," Ross said.

"We should tell them," Cook said. "They *are* our cousins."

"Oh, all right." Richard Andrew leaned toward me. "It's 'pig breath.'"

It struck me as a stupid password, but I didn't say so. My brother did.

"Oh yeah?" Richard Andrew said. "What would your password be?"

Dan whispered something into Cook's ear. Cook laughed, too loudly and long.

"Tell us!" Richard Andrew demanded.

"Can't," Dan said. "You're too young. Right, Cook?"

I groaned. My brother was being a jerk, as usual. But then so was Cook, who said "Right." Maybe being a jerk was a twelve-year-old boy thing.

"Come on, let's show them everything." Mebane Ruth was already on her feet, scrambling back down the ladder, followed by the boys, and Reynolds and me. We saw the weeping willow tree that got rot last year but was saved. And the bubbling brook, and Grandpa's putting green, and a vast rectangular garden filled with roselike white flowers, one of the most awesome sights I'd ever laid eyes on. And blooming in the winter!

"They're camellias," Mebane whispered. "That's where the pool used to be."

"Grandma went bonkers, and had it filled in," Richard Andrew said.

"Why in the world would anyone who had a pool in their backyard fill it in and plant stupid *flowers* there?" Dan asked.

"Because of Charlie," Ashlin said. She too was whispering.

"Who's Charlie?" I asked.

"He was our cousin," said Richard Andrew. "He drowned."

"Right in there." Cook pointed to the strange and amazing garden. "And he wasn't our cousin, he was our uncle."

"You mean uncle like Uncle Bernard?" I said. "So that means Charlie was our mother's brother too, right?" She'd never mentioned another brother.

They all nodded.

"He drowned years ago, like when he was four," Mebane Ruth said. "But my mama says Grandma never got over it, so we gotta have sympathy."

"You better not say anything about it," said Ross, "because my mama says we're not allowed to talk about Charlie in front of Grandma. It makes her even more bonkers."

"What about Grandpa Eli? Can you talk about Charlie in front of him?"

They all shook their heads. "No, him neither," said Cook.

Soon we went back inside the house, into the huge, elaborate living room. My mother's Hanukkah presents were going to stand out like blue and silver thumbs amidst the piles of presents wrapped in red and gold and green Christmas paper, arranged under a tall evergreen decorated with beautiful glass ornaments and twinkling lights.

"We're not allowed to have a Christmas tree," I said, trying to exude conviction. "Our mother says you can't be Christian and Jewish at the same time."

"That's stupid," Ross said. "*We're* Jewish and *we* have a tree."

"Well, we only light the Hanukkah candles, and my mother gives us presents every night of Hanukkah. I like it that way."

My cousins exchanged glances but didn't say anything, just moved us over to the collection of old photographs hanging on a far wall. I was particularly interested in a group shot in a gold leaf frame showing a thinner Grandpa Eli, a woman holding a baby, and two toddlers at her feet. The woman's face was quite pretty but pale and peculiar, really—blank somehow, almost as if the photograph had failed to register her. Standing on the other side of Grandpa Eli was a pudgy, pretty little girl of about eleven in a white, ruffled dress, her mountain of curls done up with a big white ribbon on top, white-gloved hands folded in her lap. My mother *fat?*

I looked again. "Is one of these Uncle Lee? And Charlie?"

"*Shhhh,*" Mebane said. "We told you not to talk about it. That's Uncle Lee, he talks like a girl. Charlie was already drowned. And that one's our daddy." She pointed to one of the toddlers.

"And ours," said Reynolds, pointing to the baby.

We moved on to another photograph in which a slim and unsmiling, now teenaged Charlotte stared out at me, wearing a white strapless tulle gown, with a cinched waist and full skirt. She had been truly, breathtakingly beautiful.

"Looks like a wedding dress." I knew it wasn't. In the picture at home of my mother and father on their wedding day, my mother was wearing a white suit and a tiny veiled hat that dipped down smartly over one eye.

"Oh, don't you know?" Mebane Ruth said, then explained debutantes, and the country club, and the Ballyhoo ball—none of which seemed interesting to me, and I said so.

"We found a bullfrog in the pool last month," Reynolds said when we were back under the Willow Tree That Got Rot Last Year, sipping lemonades.

"The day my best friend Julie met me she brought over a frog," I said.

"You have frogs in New York?" Richard Andrew said.

"Yeah, except our frogs have purple polka dots and yellow feet." I smiled.

"She's full of it," Dan said. "She's always that way."

"You are so full of it," Richard Andrew said.

"No I'm not. We put the frog in my mother's car, too. It hopped right onto her head."

"She's always getting into trouble," Dan said.

"Does it snow a lot in New York?" Ross pronounced the state like "New Yawk."

I nodded. "Sometimes it gets so high you can't get out the doors. And it's not New *Yawk*. That's not how we talk."

"Is too," Ross said.

"Is not," I said.

Maybe never getting to see my cousins wasn't such a bad thing after all.

"Well, my mother says your mother is the black sheep of this whole family," Mebane Ruth said. "I heard her talking on the phone to Aunt Lucinda, and my mama said there was bad blood between Grandpa Eli and Grandma Elizabeth and your mama."

"What's bad blood?"

She shrugged. "Don't know, maybe like blood that turns black."

"Blood can't turn black," said my brother, who even as a child had no imagination.

"Maybe bad blood is when you have melancholy, like Grandma," Ross said.

"Is melancholy like bonkers?" I asked.

Ross nodded. "Just like it. It's because she always stays in her room, crying."

"And because she drinks gin," Cook said. "She goes through a whole quart of gin every day, our daddy says."

I had no idea if he was exaggerating. My father had an occasional drink, but my mother never drank liquor.

"Grandma always talks about Charlie, too," Mebane said. "Like he was still alive only he's been dead, like hundreds of years."

"She had to be put away because of melancholy, you know," Ross said.

"Put away where?" Now that sounded really bad.

"Someplace where they put you when you have it. She was only there for a little while, but they obviously didn't get rid of it for her because she still has it."

Mebane Ruth shook her head. "We weren't talkin' about melancholy, Ross, we were talking about bad blood."

Ross seemed to know the most about melancholy, while Mebane Ruth was the expert on bad blood and black sheep.

I stood up. "Yeah, well, I heard my mother say Grandpa Eli was a bull."

Now they all gasped.

"What'd you tell them *that* for?" Dan said.

I didn't know where I was going, I just ran—right into my mother and father, who were strolling along a brick walkway at the side of the house. Their heads were close to each other, which meant they were talking about something interesting, which meant I wasn't supposed to hear. I tried to run in the other direction, but Dad grabbed me by the arm. "Whoa, Dinah, where are you going?"

"My cousins are mean. They called Mommy a black sheep."

My mother started to laugh, a loud and bitter laugh. "Well, isn't that just hunky-dory, *I'm* the black sheep," she said.

"Charlotte, they're just kids," Dad said.

"Kids repeating what the adults around them say."

"We are going to try," my father said. "*Right?*" Very forceful for Dad.

She shrugged.

"What does that mean, black sheep?" I asked.

She sighed loudly. "It's just that I . . . well, I don't get along so well with Grandpa Eli and Grandma Elizabeth. That's all. Grandpa Eli decided I couldn't take over his business, so I went to New York to make my own way. I'm happy for it now. Believe me, it turned out to be for the best."

"But he let Uncle Bernard and Uncle Marshall into his business, why not you?"

"Because I'm a woman. By all rights, I should be running this business when Grandpa retires, which he probably never will. They're going to have to cart him out of that office in a casket. I am the eldest child, Bernard is seven years younger than I am."

"Then why?"

She leaned down toward me, cupped her hand over her mouth. "It certainly isn't because of his brains."

I giggled. Uncle Bernard was Mebane Ruth's father.

"Remember," Charlotte said, "you can do anything you want, Dinah. Anything. Women are strong and smart and coming into their own, no matter what Grandpa Eli says. His ideas are a *lot* older than he is."

It was 1962. My mother was way ahead of her time.

That night, in the bed next to Mebane Ruth, I couldn't fall asleep for the longest time. I tossed and turned, then woke up again in the middle of a dream where I was stuck in that tree house. My brother had taken away the ladder and I couldn't get down.

Moonlight was streaming in through the sheer curtains at the window. I went over to the window, drew aside the curtain, and looked out over the expanse of lawns and fields. The willow tree was a tall hulking form against a brilliant dark sky, its branches swaying and bowing gracefully in the night breeze, a full moon illuminating the scene. My eyes scanned the field and sky and gardens, lingering on the rectangular camellia garden. It was pretty, but it seemed so weird—to fill in a pool and plant a garden. Such a big space, and all of it planted with the same species of flower, row after row of camellias—

I blinked. I noticed then there was a very old woman standing at the side of that garden, ghostly and pale in the moonlight. Partly hidden in the shadow of a tree, almost indistinguishable from the white expanse of flowers, she was wearing a white bathrobe, white ankles poking out of the robe, white feet on the grass. Her robe was made of some silky material, rippling like water in the breeze.

With her head bowed that way, it looked like she was praying.

Grandma Elizabeth finally made an actual appearance, toward the end of breakfast the next day. We were eating formally, in the dining room on the gold-rimmed white china. The minute she came in I knew this was the woman who'd been standing by the camellia garden the night before. My grandmother was a tall and thin woman, with dull, gray hair she wore in a loose knot. Her dress had a large stain at the bosom and her mouth had these little ridges around it, as if she had pursed her lips and her face got stuck that way. Her eyes were deep-set, and so light they seemed almost clear. She held herself rigidly straight, as if she had a steel bar holding up her back, and stumbled a bit as she walked. Her arms and hands didn't seem to move with her when she moved, either, and anyway she moved as slowly as anyone could unless they were standing still. She didn't look solid somehow, even standing right there.

"Hello, Mother." Grandma Elizabeth bent down to kiss my mother but was left kissing air because my mother turned her cheek away. "And Martin. How nice to see you. So very nice." Her speech had a vapid, singsong cadence.

"Yes, Liz, it's nice to see you again."

Grandpa Eli asked Bernard to introduce me and Dan to our grandma. She bent down slowly, one inch at a time, and kissed me on the cheek. "And you must be Dinah. How nice to meet you."

I winced. Her breath was sour. "Nice to meet you, Grandma."

"You look like your mother did at your age."

Charlotte was watching us intently from her place at the other table. I knew it wasn't true. After all, I was Tubby Turd and my mother had been thin and perfect and beautiful. No. Wait. She was chubby when she was a girl, just like me.

Uncle Bernard drew Grandma Elizabeth on to my brother. Dan held out his hand.

"Oh." She seemed flustered but held out her own hand. I thought my brother's vigorous handshake would knock her over. She already looked like she might blow away.

She closed her eyes and when she opened them she suddenly gripped my brother's hand and held on tight, for the longest time. I thought she'd never let go, but then she let his hand drop and used hers to smooth his hair several times. Tears came to her eyes.

Finally she said, "I had a little boy once. His name was Charlie. You look just like Charlie." A smile flashed across her face.

"Elizabeth, *shut up.*" Grandpa Eli's voice was even uglier than his words. His teeth were clenched and a vein stood out on his neck. "The boy does *not* look like Charlie."

"Of course he does, Eli." She glared at him. He glared right back. How could this be? Grandpa Eli had seemed almost jolly before. How could they live together in this house and look at each other with such hate? I often saw hair-trigger changes in my mother, but it seemed different with a mother and a kid. And maybe Grandma Elizabeth was right. Maybe Charlie, like my brother, had dark skin and hair that really stood out in this family with so many redheaded, light-skinned children.

"Go upstairs, Elizabeth," Grandpa Eli said. "Don't spoil it for everyone."

Grandma Elizabeth brought her index finger to her lips and said, "Shhhh. I'm not allowed to *ever* speak of the dead in this house. It's forbidden by the *master.*" The way she said that word chilled me.

She sat down at the adult table, and everyone went back to eating. But when I happened to look again about ten minutes later she was gone. She only came down once again, on Christmas morning. Busy opening presents, including a beautiful locket from Grandpa Eli, I noticed that she kept sneaking looks at my brother, as if she were expecting him to get up and do something amazing.

"Stop it, Mother!" My mother must have noticed it, too. She was mad, I certainly knew her mad look.

Grandma Elizabeth just got up and shuffled and stumbled out of the room. I saw her only a few more times in my life, as the Christmas visit to Atlanta became a despised yearly event, one that was always strained and difficult for my mother (which meant it was horrible for me). The grandparents and cousins came north for Dan's Bar Mitzvah, but that was it. The last time I saw her, all of them, was at Grandpa Eli's funeral when I was fifteen. I didn't want to be there, standing at the grave, a light cool drizzle sprinkling on my arms under a gunmetal sky, as gray as my grandmother's hair.

I was thin and fidgety and jazzed up on black beauties, and it was obvious my cousins didn't want me in Atlanta any more than I wanted to be there. The rabbi was reciting the prayers, and I was thinking that I hadn't even known my grandfather, though I would have liked to, and suddenly I noticed Grandma Elizabeth staring at my brother again. She was swaying—by then I understood that she was drunk—although no one seemed to notice it, or never said so if they did. My mother, on the other hand, often made embittered comments about her lush of a mother. I wondered how my grandmother could think my brother looked like her dead child.

He'd drowned when he was four, it had to have been more than fifty years ago, my brother was now twenty years old. What a weird old lady. So transfixed by her loony fantasies about my brother that she didn't even notice when the rabbi handed her the shovel to toss the dirt on the casket after it had been lowered into the ground.

That night I stood in the hallway of the big house in Atlanta and listened to private conversations.

"What is *wrong* with you, Mother?" Charlotte said. "My son's name is Daniel."

There were some exchanges too low for me to get, then I heard Grandma scream at the top of her lungs: "Go *home,* Charlotte! I don't want you here, I never want to see you again."

I felt nothing for my mother, for the pain she must have felt, being screamed at and summarily dismissed by my grandmother. I loathed my mother. I was jazzed.

My grandmother died the year I turned sixteen, and none of us went to her funeral.

ten

I did not see the ghost again until several days after Jimmy died. I tried to soothe myself by conjuring up the vision of my son as an eight-year-old, an Elijah who could express ideas and wonder about God, an Elijah who wasn't afraid of water. I attempted to recapture the image of the two of us on a boat in a great azure sea, but by the end of the second week that rapturous vision was getting fainter and smaller, no bigger than a distant point on the horizon. It was the others—the horrors—that now loomed huge.

I could understand my grandmother's melancholy now. She was pitiable because she was filled with relentless sorrow, and wretched because she was angry, and couldn't help herself. Her grief weighed hundreds of pounds and sat like a monster on her shoulders. She'd never been able to cast out the monster, or even tame it—it had poisoned her marriage and the rest of her life. I'd never thought about her compassionately, about the pain of losing a child, what it does to you. I'd treated grieving mothers, of course. Had I believed sitting with all the pain prepared me for feeling it?

I kept whispering in my son's ear: "Wake up, Elijah! You have to come back to your Mommy because there's so much more to live. You have to dance to Elvis. You have to look at me through your glasses, give me the best hugs. You have to learn to swim, to tie your shoes! You have to come back because I can't survive without you, I would miss you too much, the monster grief will sit on my shoulders and haunt me for the rest of my life."

If Life rejected me, hell, I would reject Life right back, surrender my own life to the sulking, hulking monster Big Time Grief, just like Grandma Elizabeth.

After I told Elijah all that, I stopped and waited and listened, but there was no sound from my son, no sign from God, not even a word from my ghost, nothing from anything except the *whoosh*-pumping machine. And time was running short. Even Moore seemed less convinced Elijah was going to wake up soon, though he never said so. He never said anything directly.

Just before the rest of the family arrived that evening, Uncle Lee showed up. My brother had yet to make an appearance. He'd called from Ohio and asked if I wanted him to fly in because he might be able to find something out from the doctors that I couldn't—he was, after all, one of them. I managed to say he could come if he wanted to, and not hang up on him. Uncle Lee had flown in all the way from San Francisco, still a slight man, now sixty-two, who still somehow looked boyish.

He hugged me for a long time, then bent down over Elijah and hugged him, whispered something in his ear while Sam and I watched. Elijah just lay there.

He stood up again. "George came, too, Dinah," he said.

I nodded. George and Lee had been together for twenty-five years.

"He's waiting outside, he didn't feel it was his place to come in. But he's praying, Dinah. He's praying for Elijah. And for you and Sam."

Lee put both hands on my shoulders, leaned in. "This story has a good ending, Dinah."

I remembered one we made up when I was about twelve and we were playing "Pass the Story." I'd just finished reading *Little Women,* and we had great fun coming up with a new ending: Jo decides the Professor isn't for her, runs off to Japan to become a famous geisha, then meets a Japanese man named Chang (a Chinese name but who cared?) whose magic carpet transports them all around the world having adventures. The carpet, I decided, should land on Marmee's head, suffocating her just as she's making one of her annoying little cheer-up speeches to the other sisters. "Oh, my girls, you must not despond but hope and keep happy." *Splat.*

In a few minutes the rest of the family arrived. After everyone hugged and kissed, and looked at each other with meaningful silences, they made some small talk, just as they always did, these two incongruous in-law couples, with the added presence of Uncle Lee. My father asked Sam's father about the lumber business, in which he had no interest. Charlotte asked Lee how his antiques business was going. Charlotte and Sam's mother talked about how much traffic there had been coming into the city that night, how cold it was that winter.

"I brought the Elvis CD," Kate said, pulling it from her backpack. We closed the door to the NAR, put the CD player next to Elijah's ear, and switched it on, loud. "Hound Dog" blared in Elijah's ear, bright parallel lines formed inch by inch on the monitor, but he slept on, unmoved. Come on, Elijah. Get mad. How dare we tie your wrists to the side of the bed! What if you want to get up and dance?

My daughter finally switched off the CD.

"Tomorrow," Sam said.

I stared at this stranger I'd been married to for all these years, studied his face carefully, his pale skin, his out-of-style glasses, the slant of his square jaw.

"Admit it! You hate him!" A disembodied whisper, a sibilant sound, a hiss.

I flicked at my ear, and the ghost materialized at the ceiling, right inside the NAR now. He was getting closer.

No, I didn't hate Sam. I loved him. Didn't I? What was it I loved about him? If someone had asked me that before all this, I might have reviewed the facts of Sam, his likes and dislikes: loves a good joke; hates spinach and adores pumpkin pie; doesn't like me to wear makeup, he says, because I'm so naturally beautiful. Or his qualities: does this thing with his mouth when he's amused, a wry half-smile with dimples; incredibly affectionate and incurably boyish, still leaves me little love notes after all these years; disciplined, dutiful, and easy to please; and considerate, too. For example, adores rock music but pretends to prefer jazz when my father is around because my father does.

"I have a lot of homework," Alex said.

"I'm sure they'll understand, " I said, taking rapid breaths.

"How long do you expect them to cut me some slack?"

"I don't know, Alex." I didn't. Why was he angry at *me?* I leaned over and pressed my lips to Elijah's cheek. His skin felt warm.

"Why are his wrists tied like that?" Charlotte asked.

"So he doesn't fall off the bed when he wakes up," Sam said.

"Did the doctor say when he was going to wake up?" his father asked.

"Any day now," Sam said. "Any day."

"*Fool!*" the ghost said, lying back now, floating on an invisible settee.

"He's not a fool," I told the ghost. "Sam just thinks of the glass as half full."

"A regular Pollyanna," the ghost said, nasally, floating down toward me, passing over and through my family.

"A positive outlook," I countered.

"Complacent and self-satisfied."

"Hopeful."

"Unrealistic."

"Faithful and loving."

"So's a Boy Scout."

"Ethical."

Mocking laughter. "An ethical ad man? *Puh*-lease."

There were those who might describe Sam's career as pushing unnecessary stuff on people who couldn't afford it. I thought of all the clients Sam had worked with over the years, a list which included corporations that had surely engaged in child slave labor in foreign countries, a pharmaceutical manufacturer hawking medications that had serious health risks, a tobacco company. And those were just the obvious ones. But wasn't that the way life was? You made compromises. *I* made therapeutic alliances with all kinds of people, too, counseled wife abusers, once treated a pedophile.

"Doesn't sweat the small stuff."

"And the big stuff?" The ghost, who was now beside me, cast a glance at Elijah, who was still lying there with his wrists tied to the bed.

My face felt as if it might collapse, my bones seemed to be turning to paste. The ghost was making animal sounds, snorting like a pig, braying like a mule, bellowing like a cow.

I closed my eyes. How did the ghost *know?* Yes. I hated my husband. And not just Sam. I hated everyone. I loathed every doctor in that hospital. Dr. Jonas and his blandness; Dr. Moore and his darting lying eyes; Dr. Reichert with his schoolboy innocence; Dr. Williston of the owl face; that resident, Dr. Laurentin, who was so far up the ass of Dr. Moore you could barely see his face for all the shit.

I hated every nurse, too, these women who left their healthy children at home and came in here and hovered and thought, thank God this isn't me. And I hated my own parents, and Sam's parents. My mother was impossible, so what else was new? And Mary Galligan, the way she clutched her rosary, as if that might help, and talked in her chirping brogue, and Tom with his alcohol buzz. Even Lee, who'd come all this way. Even my other children. I was Elijah's mother! My grief was greater than any of theirs. My grief could swallow all their griefs put together, and still have room for a thousand more griefs.

I reached over to untie Elijah's wrists.

"I didn't mean you should go against the doctor's orders, Dinah."

I uncoiled to face my mother. "Then what *did* you mean?"

"I just meant it doesn't seem right."

"Might as well untie them," the ghost whispered.

"Me cousin Caleb Coyle's son had something like this," Mary said, "and he's just fine now."

"Well, aren't *we* full of good cheer," the ghost said.

I stared at Mary. Something like what? They hadn't even made a diagnosis. They didn't know what the hell was the matter with Elijah.

"Caleb Coyle's son is a drunk," Sam's father said.

"Well, Thomas Galligan, that's got nothing to do with the sickness. Nothing t'all." Mary had looked up from a pillowcase she was cross-stitching to make these pronouncements. She leaned over Elijah and gently rubbed her palm on his forehead. "There, there, wee man. Mother-o-God, he feels warm." She looked over at me, as if she expected me to know what to do about it.

Both Mary and my mother had always been in denial about Elijah's problems, each in her own way. When Mary came to the hospital to see our newly born Elijah, tiny, sickly, skin loose on his bones, Sam had said, "Did you see our little plucked chicken, Mom?" Mary Galligan didn't even crack a smile. "Oh, my good Lord Jesus, Sam, he's not a chicken, he's just a mite skinny, that's all. A beautiful wee boy."

Elijah *was* a beautiful little boy, who in time would be physically beautiful, but at that moment he looked like a plucked chicken. "It was just a joke, Mom," Sammy said. "Of course it was, dearie," Mary said. "I know."

Charlotte was touching Elijah's head now, too. "He does feel warm."

"His temperature has been going up and down," the nurse said. "I'm going to give him some Tylenol."

"*Why* is his temperature going up and down?"

The nurse shrugged. "I don't really know."

"Liar!" the ghost said. "She knows. She's heard of cases like this. She's just never seen one. It's his central temperature, gone kerflooey!"

"Central temperature? What's that?"

"Just the mechanism that controls human body temperature around ninety-eight point six," the ghost said. "It's already starting to fail. And once it does, only the more primitive temperature regulator will keep working, the one from deeper in the brain, so that his body will stay cold, like a reptile."

"*Reptile?* What are you talking about?"

The nurse was ripping a plastic tab from a medicine tube, pouring a clear liquid into the IV. My son got everything through tubes. Air through the tube in his throat, food through a tube in his nose, medicine through the tube in his arm.

"Can't take it, can you?" the ghost said. "It's simple biology, that's all."

Kate, standing next to Mary, had started to cry.

Mary hugged her. "There, there, my girl. It'll be fine. Everyone is praying for him."

"Yes, we're all praying," Charlotte chimed in.

Well, didn't everything always come out fine when people prayed?

Now came the infectious disease doctor, again. Dr. Williston. She nodded, Kate backed up like a car in reverse, my mother hovered. I wanted Sam to tell her to stop, but Sam didn't understand anything I thought or said; Sam was a stranger.

The doctor listened to Elijah's heart and lungs, touched her hand to his forehead, looked in his ears. Elijah lay there like Sleeping Beauty, with the machine suck-*hissing* away while my hope was dying a cold death in my head.

"Did you get the cultures back?" I asked the question every time I saw her. They hadn't yet ruled out meningitis; Elijah had some white cells in his lumbar, which meant he could have meningitis or even encephalitis. They'd done bacteriological studies, all of which had turned up negative. They'd sent other blood cultures to faraway labs to test for rare viruses, but those hadn't yet come back.

"This seizure *must* have had something to do with all his problems," Charlotte said.

My mother said this as if it explained something. She'd been saying this sort of thing forever, when she wasn't saying things that made it sound like she blamed me for all his problems. I remember once we went to a picnic in Sam's parents' small house in Fort Lee, New Jersey. We were all sitting around after the barbecue when Elijah began to make clicking noises with his tongue.

"What *is* that?" my mother said.

Kate said, "That's Elijah's clicking noise."

My mother's upper lip pulled slightly upward, as if she'd just gotten a taste of something bad in her mouth. How could such a thing happen? How could a grandson of hers have such problems?

"He's just a little weird," Alex said.

"He is not weird, Alex," I said. "He's just different."

"There is nothing different about him," Sam's mother said. "Our wee boy is just fine. More dessert?"

Now Dr. Williston said, "We have no evidence that any of this is connected to his previous problems." She took the earpieces of the stethoscope out of her ears and draped the thing over her neck in that one swift motion all doctors have mastered.

"But it just makes sense that all of his problems and this . . . situation are related, doesn't it?" This was Charlotte? Challenging a doctor? My mother has always clung to the now arcane notion of doctors as gods. She has to cling. My brother Dan, blessed be he, is a doctor, an oncologist in Cincinnati. (Oh, please let *these* doctors be gods.)

The owl just shrugged. Her glasses were even thicker than Elijah's.

My mother did have a point. "But how can you say it isn't related?" I asked.

"I just said we had no evidence for it."

"But he's always had neurological problems, he—"

"Dinah!" Charlotte snapped. "I'm *sure* the doctor knows."

Oh. Now she was back to doctors as gods.

Sam put his hand on my shoulder, the ghost nudged me forward.

"Go ahead," he said. "She deserves it, the bitch."

"You could be right, Mrs. Galligan," the doctor said on her way out of the room.

"Here's some cards you got, Mom." Kate handed them to me. I opened them, then handed them to Sam. He sorted through them, announcing out loud who had sent each card, supplying us with a running commentary that drew a lot of "Oh, isn't that nice?" and "Isn't she sweet?" responses from his mother.

"This one's from Sue Barson, she's a neighbor. Two doors down—you remember, Mom? You met her last summer when we went for a walk. She was out hosing her lawn."

"Oh, yes," Mary said. "How lovely she was."

"And here's one from Ellen Shoenfeld. Who's that?"

"Someone in my writing class," I said. "Let me have it back." This one I forced myself to read.

Dear Dinah,

I just wanted you to know that although I have been unable to bring myself to pray for many years, I pray for your son. I hope he will be well soon. There. I wrote something.

Best regards,
Ellen Shoenfeld.

I smiled in spite of myself.

"Look, Di," Sam said. "Here's one from Tammy Pearl."

"Why the hell is *she* writing you a note?" the ghost said. "Her kid was too good to be in a playgroup with him, now she's writing sympathy notes?"

"What the hell does Tammy Pearl want?" I said.

Mary said, "Gracious Jesus, Dinah, she's only trying to be nice, I'm sure."

"Tell her to shut up." Now the ghost was reclining near the ceiling, smoking a cigar.

"What do you know about it, Mary?"

"Dinah, please," Sam said.

"How *could* you have married him?" Zip, back down to me again, and whispering in my ear, a cold exhalation.

"I already told you, I loved him."

He took a puff on the cigar, blew smoke out of his mouth, gazed down at me. "What about your best friend Julie?"

I felt as if I were choking, a fish sucking air. "Stop talking about Julie!"

"Who's Julie, Mom?" It was Kate.

Had I blurted out Julie's name?

"Julie was an old friend of your mother's, Kate." Sam glanced over at me. We never spoke about Julie. This was so typical of Sam, out of sight, out of mind, speak of nothing that causes discomfort. When I told him about my patients and their problems sometimes, he listened, but it never affected him. What was I *doing* with someone like him?

"Oh. I never heard you mention her," Kate said.

Kate was sitting by Elijah, stroking his hair. Alex was curled up in a corner, knees drawn up, staring out at the NAR where Jimmy had died. Now there was a teenage boy in there about Alex's age, a hemophiliac with AIDS, the result of a blood transfusion. I wanted to ask his mother how she went on living, knowing her son was going to die. Maybe there was some secret to this that I didn't know. Alex looked up.

"She was your mom's best friend," Sam said, as if he and Julie hadn't ever met.

I cut him off. "I haven't seen her in over twenty years."

Kate shrugged. "Some best friend, if you haven't seen her in twenty years."

"Please, Kate. I can't talk about this now."

Kate went back to stroking Elijah's hair. Elijah slept on.

"I suppose by now it has occurred to you, Dinah," the ghost said, "that this is all your fault."

"I've tried to be a good person. I love my children, I love my husband."

"Oh. Do you really?"

"I try to help people in my work."

"Well now, that last one is a total crock of elephant dung. You're a head-shrinker because your own head needs shrinking." For a moment I thought I saw his head shrivel and blacken, but I blinked, and he was back to the way he had been.

"There is nothing you can hide from me, Dinah."

I became afraid of him then, as he looked at me with eyes as black as a pair of tar pools and cooed, "Maybe your great and good God is punishing you after all."

"For *what*? Please!"

"Well," the ghost said, moving his mouth so that I could see the blackness within, "you did almost do away with your son once."

I stared at him. Now very afraid.

"But I wasn't going to do it. I was just thinking."

"Thinking about aborting him? You didn't want him if he wasn't perfect."

"What I wanted was for him to be healthy. I didn't want him to suffer."

"You can't con me, Dinah," the ghost said. "Just like you couldn't con Julie."

Poof. He was gone.

eleven

Why had I let them drag me downstairs to the cafeteria? Sammy and Kate were still upstairs with Elijah, but there I was, sitting at a cozy table for nine in the hospital basement, a regular interfaith gathering. Marty and Charlotte, Mary and Tom, Alex, Uncle Lee and his partner George, and Dinah. And one ghost, lolling in an imaginary chair just behind Charlotte, patting the top of her head.

"Stop that," I said.

"Why should I?" said the ghost, who had leaned toward my mother, who of course didn't notice a thing.

"Stop what?" Alex.

"I was just thinking out loud. Sorry." And to the ghost: "Why does this keep happening, sometimes they hear me?"

"How the *hell* should I know?"

The ghost kept on patting, patting. I found myself remembering the first time I brought Sam home to meet my parents, something I hadn't done in the whole year we'd been seeing each other.

"Galligan? That's an Irish name," Charlotte said after an excruciatingly long dinner only partially redeemed by the sight of my usually wisecracking fiancé offering some serious veneration to my mother, who presided over the meal in a way that reminded me of Amanda in *The Glass Menagerie.* My father had taken Sam upstairs to see his collection of thirties and forties jazz records, and Sam, I supposed, was going to take the opportunity to ask him for my hand. "Anyone who's going to get *me* for a son-in-law," he'd said with a grin, on the way driving up from D.C., "has a right to at least be given the chance to say, 'Get out of here, you bum.'"

"He seems a very nice boy," Charlotte said. "But darling, he isn't Jewish."

"Well, thank you," I said. "I didn't know that."

"There's no need to be sarcastic, Dinah. There might be problems, that's all. You're not going to kneel before a priest, are you?"

"We'll probably have a justice of the peace. Or maybe a rabbi and a priest."

"You know, Dinah," she said, with a sigh, "life is full of unexpected difficulties. Things happen that you'd never expect. Not in a million years. Now you think you can handle anything, but when two people come to very difficult problems with different viewpoints—"

"What different viewpoints? Neither of us are religious."

"You don't have children yet, Dinah."

"Well, Charlotte, to suddenly get religion just because you have children strikes me as pretty hypocritical."

"All I'm saying is that life is so much more complicated when you come at things from different ways of thinking. There might come a time when you want a man who can really understand the most basic things about you."

Right, like you're an out-of-control screamer and Dad's a silent stone. But she wasn't screaming now. She was talking about this calmly.

"Judaism isn't what's basic about me," I said. "Judaism isn't even basic about you."

"You're wrong, Dinah. You think it isn't basic, but it is. Remember, this is an anti-Semitic world, and we're a hated people."

"So?"

"So when people fight, and married people do, sometimes you get so low, so out of control that you can forget yourself, and when that happens you might suddenly hear your husband say something you never thought he'd ever say—or even think, for that matter."

I thought she was being one of those Jews who believe history teaches us nothing if not that anti-Semites lurk behind every door. As far as I was concerned, she was ambivalent at best about being Jewish. For example, she hadn't wanted me to have a prominent nose, even though it hadn't been all that prominent, which made her a hypocrite in my nineteen-year-old eyes.

"I can't see anything like that happening to us," I said. "Sam doesn't have a mean bone in his body, let alone an anti-Semitic one. I love him."

She sat back. "I know you do, Dinah. I can see that. It's just . . . well, sometimes love isn't enough."

I didn't pursue it. I just wanted to get the weekend over with.

And the next, which we spent *chez* Galligan, in a small crowded house with a cross over Sam's parents' bed, and religious art on the walls, about one step more sophisticated than Jesus on black velvet. Dinner was boisterous and homemade and plain, Irish soda bread, and corned beef and cabbage, and beer, lots of it. Sam winked at me during grace before the meal, and he called his father "Da," and it was obvious to me that Sam, the youngest in the family, was the golden boy, in fact the only one who'd made it through college, paid for mostly by a swimming scholarship. Sam's sister Anne was a hairdresser; Aiden worked in their father's lumberyard; and Tim, who'd started college, then quit and joined the marines, had survived a tour in Vietnam, gone back to a community college, and now worked in the lumberyard, too. Still, I never considered for a moment that this third-generation Jewish girl and this second-generation Irish boy were going to make it.

"So, what did she say about me?" I asked that first night when Sam came creeping into the little bedroom Mary had assigned me, off the kitchen.

"'Ah, Sammy, what a lovely girl. Lovely. Just grand.'"

"She called me grand, that's nice," I said.

"You're sure you want to hear this?"

"Every word."

"So she said, 'Well, gracious, Sammy, she isn't Catholic, what about the children?' Then she cups her hand over her mouth as if she's telling me a secret she doesn't want anyone to hear, even God, and you know God hears everything, and she says, 'The Jewish people—they're fine people, absolutely fine, but they don't believe in Our Lord.'" His imitation of Mary Galligan's accent and mannerisms had me stifling giggles lest my future mother-in-law hear them.

"So Aiden says, 'Mom! Give it a rest.' And then I dropped the bombshell. 'I'm not sure I do either, Mom.' So she says, 'Oh, don't you be silly, now.'" He looked at me. "This isn't a subject you can discuss with my mother, you know what I mean?"

"I'm getting the picture." How could I not, when he was doing such a terrific job of enlightening me.

"So now she tells me, 'They don't baptize their children.' I said I thought she was getting a little serious, but she wouldn't hear that, and she said, 'What about their *souls?*'"

"What about them?"

He laughed. "Dinah, I'm no priest, but I went to mass and Sunday school forever, and it seems to me the Jews get some sort of special dispensation. Anyway, it doesn't matter to me. Really. Whatever you want to do, we'll do. Our kids can be Jewish, if you want. It'll hurt my mom, a lot, if we don't baptize the children. But it is my life, right? And, you know, even she picks and chooses, though she'd never admit it. I mean, she didn't have thirteen children, only four of us, and I know they have an active sex life, this is a very small house. You figure it out. As far as I'm concerned, Catholic and Jewish, it's the same cake with different flavor icing. Can we have Christmas, though? I'd miss that, I have to admit."

I said Christmas would be fine and told him what my mother had said—and we felt even closer for having had essentially the same conversation with our two mothers.

"You won't make me kneel before a cross or a priest at our wedding, will you?" I whispered, kissing him lightly on the lips.

He laughed. "No. But you'll have to kneel before me every night."

"Anything you say," I told him.

We looked into each other's eyes. Thus ended the most serious conversation we'd ever had on the subject, for in seconds we were making love.

"Are you okay, Dinah?" Charlotte asked now in the cafeteria. A pair of doctors were walking by the table, carrying trays, and I was hearing her warning in my head: Things happen that you never expect.

No. I wasn't okay. Who would have ever thought *this* would happen? It had happened to Charlotte's mother, but that was a different time, and that was a different place, and that wasn't me. Who would have thought anything could hurt so much?

"Dinah?"

I pushed chicken and rice around on my plate. Why had I gotten this? Maybe something dry, something like crackers, or plain bread. "I'm all right."

But I wasn't all right. I was so muddled I couldn't determine whether the breach between Sam and me had anything to do with our two different religions, with two different viewpoints, as Charlotte had suggested all those years before, but I certainly couldn't deny that the breach was there. I hated everything Sam said. I even hated *him.* And I hated Charlotte even more, for having been right.

"Dinah?"

The ghost was making lewd gestures in front of my mother's face.

"Please stop."

"Fiddle dee dee." He wagged his finger coquettishly, Vivien Leigh in drag. "You can't stand the woman. There were times when you were a little girl that you wanted to put your little hands around her neck, and squeeze. Still do. Try to deny it. And I'll call you a liar.

"I'm not going to deny it."

"Of course not." The ghost put his face next to my mother's face. My mother brushed away a strand of hair. "You certainly haven't kept that old honor-thy-father-and-mother commandment. Have you now?"

I stared. "Yes but my mother was so difficult, I—"

The ghost wagged a finger in my face again. "Uh, uh, uh. It isn't honor thy mother unless she's difficult, is it now? Why don't you do your Charlotte imitation right now? I'm sure they'd all love to hear it."

"How do you know about that, too?" Even about that.

A whistling noise whizzed out of his mouth. "Well. I'm really getting annoyed. I know because I've seen you do it, babe."

What was he talking about? I had to be going mad. "When?"

"Go ahead, admit it. You despise her."

Obviously I wasn't going to get an explanation. For any of this. For him. "She bothers me less than she used to."

"Liar!"

"Go ahead, Dinah," Charlotte said. "Eat."

"Go ahead, Dinah. Eat." The ghost had her drawl, her tone and mannerisms exactly.

"Go away."

The ghost cooed, "Where would you like me to go?"

I gestured toward an elderly couple and a middle-aged woman sitting at a table nearby. "What about hanging around them for a while?"

He didn't even move his eyes toward them. "I'm only for you, who are they?"

"Dinah doesn't have to eat if she doesn't want to," my father said.

I stared at my father. Was he actually defending me? He never used to defend me, back when I was a child and needed defending. Well, not never. But rarely.

"No, no, of course she doesn't have to eat," Charlotte said.

Silence.

"I'm going to cancel the new store opening," my mother said suddenly. Other women retire at seventy. Charlotte was opening a store in Phoenix. Tears welled up in her eyes. "I don't think I can go through with it."

A very tall doctor carrying a full tray of food jostled the table. The ghost was making lewd gestures again.

"I don't think Dinah cares about that right now, Charlotte," my father said.

My mother put her fork down, pulled a handkerchief out of her pocket, and dabbed at her eyes. "You can't think about it all the time. I know she's upset, Martin. We're all upset. You have to take a break sometime."

"I need to go upstairs," I said. Was she complaining that this was taking too much of her precious time? Was she thinking that she was being forced to support me and I'd be beholden to her forever after?

"I'll go with you," my mother said.

"Please," I said. "I need to be by myself for a little while."

She looked hurt. Which did not surprise me, knowing how insulted my mother becomes at lesser or even imaginary slights. What surprised me was the thought that her hurt was justified. I was being mean. The ghost was wrong. I didn't despise her. I didn't really think she was looking for points for support like she often did, or complaining about the amount of time this was taking. But I couldn't take anyone else's puny little grief just then, least of all Charlotte's. I would have been much better able to handle Charlotte's Wrath.

I left the cafeteria, but not alone. The ghost got on the elevator with me.

"Push the stop button," he said.

I backed into a corner.

"Push it now." Arms crossed over his chest, he glared at me from across the elevator.

I did as he said, and the elevator came to a screeching halt between the second and third floors.

"I am really quite insulted that you don't remember, Dinah. I've gone to a lot of trouble so you would." His eyes bore into me, black and cold. "I thought surely the Julie business would do it, or Mother dearest, but possibly something else is needed to jog your hopeless little memory. Perhaps the name Jay might do it."

"Jay *Salisbury*?"

The elevator vanished. I found myself standing in an attic room full of shadows and slanted light, sunlit slices of dust, a sluice through time—this one backward instead of forward.

The attic is very long and narrow, with a high sloping roof that comes to a peak across the whole length of it and three sections cut by two large dormer windows. In the center section a curved arch cuts into the sloping roof; within the arch a small stained glass window refracts available light like a prism, bathing the room in a dreamlike brilliance. The furnishings are shabby, student furnishings, with a few notable exceptions. A small drawing of an odalisque hanging on a wall in a beautiful frame, the naked woman reclining on her back, one arm draped over the settee on which she's lying. A Tiffany lamp. A mirror, a carved gilt thing.

I was jolted out of the memory and back into the elevator, stalled between the second and third floors. I spent many hours in that attic room. It was home to my first lover. Seth Lucien.

The elevator cabin now seemed unbearably hot and close, and I detected a pungent metallic smell that seemed briefly to overpower the other smells in the airless air. I tried to take a breath, but all I could manage was a series of little gasps. My God! All these years I'd barely thought of Seth, and now I realized that the ghost standing before me was in fact he—or more accurately, an approximation of him. I gripped the metal railing, my knees apparently about to give way. "Seth."

"Well, sort of." The ghost picked up the guitar that had suddenly materialized and strummed a few chords.

Shame rose in my face and my neck like a hot flash. My relationship with Seth Lucien was not a part of my life I cared to remember at any time and was the last thing I wanted to think about here, now. I was all the young things when I met Seth—vulnerable, confused, innocent, desperate for love and affirmation.

"What are you *doing* here?"

"I already told you," the ghost said. "I'm here to help you."

"What happened to your dog?" The immaculately groomed black poodle he called Mephistopheles. His constant companion.

"Not my dog, Seth's dog. In doggie heaven, I suppose."

"Why don't you have him with you?"

A bitter laugh. "You think a ghost gets a companion? Oh, no. I don't think so."

My mind was spilling over with images: Seth's Harley; the click-click of a Smith-Corona typewriter late into the night, Seth at the keys; a back alley theater where the masks of comedy and tragedy are carved over the stage; a rowdy Georgetown bar. And hashish laced with opium, the sweet hot smoke in my lungs. And long nights in bed with Seth. Meeting Sam, whom I knew I loved the first time he smiled at me. And Julie, oh Julie, whose loss of friendship was my biggest regret. And poor Jay Salisbury, whose death I might have prevented, if I hadn't been so self-involved.

The ghost had a kind of smirk on his mouth. I should have seen it right away. A ghost in black leather. A hippie ghost who quoted Shakespeare and Baudelaire. Could Goethe be far behind? Now my mind was suffused with images of riding on Seth's Harley, of mesmerizing speed, of danger. "You were a lunatic on that motorcycle. You always had a death wish."

The ghost laughed. "Well, aren't we the little Freudian mama."

"You almost killed *me* on that motorcycle."

"*Moi?* I didn't do anything. He was the one who did it."

"Whatever. Almost killed is almost killed."

He stared at me for a moment, then said, "Maybe that's why I'm here. To make up for that. And because I feel sorry for you."

"You never felt sorry for anyone in your life."

"Ah," he said, raising a finger, "but I am no longer alive. That tends to change one." He positioned his hands on the guitar and played the first few bars of an old Cat Stevens song, about being followed by moon shadows.

"You are not helping me. You're destroying my hope."

I wanted to see Elijah, needed to see him. I moved toward the button that would start up the elevator again, but was catapulted back by a blast of arctic air. I cowered in a corner.

"The only thing I'm doing, my Dinah, is helping you see the truth. I'm for you, only for you."

He kept saying that. "'Only for me?' What does that mean?"

"It means what it means," the ghost said.

"Please stop telling me riddles."

"Riddles? Here's one. What animal goes on four legs in the morning, two at noon, and three in the evening?"

The Riddle of the Sphinx, solved by Oedipus. Of course it was Seth. "Get out of my way." I moved toward the button again. This time I pressed it, and the elevator lurched upward.

"Some people just can't face the truth, Dinah," the ghost said. "Looks like you're one of them. You and Seth's father." Seth had loathed his father, I knew, though I never found out exactly why, and never met the man. Our relationship hadn't lasted long enough for that.

"The father of Seth Lucien, when he was alive, I mean," the ghost said.

But Seth Lucien stopped being alive more than twenty years ago. What was he doing in the middle of my catastrophe, prattling on, playing tricks with my mind, plunging me into my past, tormenting me with the future?

The elevator door opened. Fourth floor. PICU. Sam was standing there.

The ghost made a little bow. "Ah, the fellow you threw Seth over for," he said.

"Your mom called the desk," Sam said. "She thought you might need me."

"I didn't throw him over for anyone." I stepped out of the elevator. "This is my husband. We've been married for twenty-one years. What's wrong with you?"

"I'm dead," he said. "That's what's *wrong* with me. And the truth is, maybe this really is all your doing."

I froze in mid-stride.

"Dinah?" Sam said.

Maybe the ghost was right. Maybe God was punishing me for the awful things I'd done—and not done—all those years ago, when I was with Seth. And after. Hell on earth for defects of character, mistakes made, foolish choices, selfishness.

I turned around, but the elevator doors had closed behind me, and the ghost was inside.

twelve

I met him in Political Science 100. The professor—Murray Grunwald, of the rancid yellowish hair and matching beard—used no notes and took no questions during his hour-long lectures to three hundred intimidated students, mostly freshmen. Paced back and forth like a caged animal, ticked off points in outline form. Point 1! he'd cry. Then he'd make points 1a through 1g, then move on to point 2, 2a through 2k. And so on.

Point 6p! he cried on a certain late September morning. And from the back of the classroom, a voice, casual and deep: "You were on point 6n, professor."

Everyone turned to look at the young man who'd spoken out.

Including Julie, who sat next to me. "God!" she gasped. "Do you *see* him?"

"Yes!" I whispered back, having by this time stopped thinking about the boy I'd met in the registration line the first week; he hadn't asked me out and I never ran into him again. Besides, this guy was incredible. I'd noticed him at the beginning of class. How had I missed him all these weeks? I'd never seen anyone with such sleek good looks. Such prominent bones, so handsome and dark, with thick black hair and an intense brow, he reminded me of a beautiful animal, a hawk or a panther.

"Thank you. Point 6n," an unfazed Dr. Grunwald said, then resumed pacing without missing a beat.

Seth caught my eye and smiled, and I quickly looked away.

"Did you *see* that?" Julie whispered. "You want him, he's yours. If you don't hurry and find a guy to sleep with, you're going to end up the last virgin on earth."

Practically the first day in the dorm, Julie and I had been issued the Virgin Challenge by one of our roommates, a Pennsylvania congressman's daughter.

"Are you virgins?" she asked.

I didn't know what to say. We both were.

"Are *you?*" Julie struck a pose, one hand on a bony hip.

Janet threw her head back and laughed. "Are you kidding? I've been sleeping with my boyfriend for almost two years." She hesitated, looked from face to face—mine, Sally Weiner's, Julie's. "So . . . are you?"

Julie waited just the right amount of time. "Well, I *really* don't remember."

Nevertheless, she'd spent the first month of college meeting the challenge. She'd been through three boys already, two one-night stands, and an international relations major named Ralph Woo. He never said a word, had a triangular head that reminded me of Fred Flintstone's, and she inexplicably cried for a few weeks when he stopped calling her.

"What in the world would that guy want with me?" I whispered now.

"He is a major hunk," she said. "But have you looked in the mirror lately?"

I blushed. In the last few years I'd undergone something of a transformation, physical and emotional. Trench mouth having cut my speed supply off at sixteen, I'd gained some of the weight back—the reason, Charlotte kept telling me, I didn't have the boyfriends *she'd* had when she was the Jewish belle of Atlanta. "I'm only telling you this for your own good." Right, Charlotte.

Secretly, of course, I longed for the affirmation I thought a boyfriend would bring, while outwardly I began to court Charlotte's Wrath. I ate everything in sight, cultivated a wickedly foul mouth, wore the most ragged, filthy jeans I could find, cut my high school classes, cultivated a nihilist philosophy, and called myself a hippie. My grades plummeted. When Charlotte screamed at me, I said things like, "What's the difference? We all die in the end," or "You don't give a shit about my grades, all you care about is Dan." She decided to take me to a shrink when I told her I didn't even want a boyfriend because I was a lesbian.

Amazing my mother could find one in Nassau County she hadn't yet seen herself, let alone one the caliber of Paula Lowe. Dr. Lowe was patient through the first two months, when I refused to talk. When I finally did, she gradually helped me detach from my mother's craziness and neediness so I could stop playing Charlotte's Game—a strategy that worked well enough to diminish the frequency of our scenes. I was left with a great love for my therapist, the knowledge of what I wanted to do with my life, and the certainty that if I ever had kids, I'd be calm, easy, and giving, the perfect mother, to make up for mine.

Didn't matter. I had the mind-set of the fat girl no one could ever want.

"He's looking at you right now!" My best friend was daring me.

I spent the rest of class trying to think of a clever opening line. I was ready to forget it, but after class, he approached us, flashed his smile, and introduced himself, saying he was a senior. He did look older, twenty-one at least, to my eighteen.

"You'd be perfect to play Gretchen," he said. "I'm in the Playmakers."

"I've heard of you. I mean, them." The Merry Playmakers were one of the drama groups on campus. I'd seen posters tacked on bulletin boards around campus for their production of *Oedipus Rex,* scheduled for December. "Who's Gretchen?"

"A character in Goethe's *Faust.* Ever done any acting?"

"Not really." I was a psych major, and knew next to nothing about Goethe. I hoped I wouldn't have to make a response that branded me a total illiterate.

"Gretchen is the beautiful young woman Faust falls in love with. Seduces. Next semester we're doing *Faust*, but it's going to be my own version."

I was enthralled. Not only had he implied that he thought I was beautiful, he was writing a play that was actually going to be performed. I'd done some writing myself in high school—some self-flagellating poetry, a few pained stories—nothing I'd have ever shown to anyone.

We'd come to the front steps of the building, where Seth's magnificent black poodle was patiently waiting. I'd noticed the dog on the way in. Seth bent down to pet it. "Hey, Meph."

"Meph?"

"Mephistopheles." He tossed his head of glossy black hair that reached midway down his back—his crowning glory. He laughed. "A poodle named Mephistopheles? Don't you think it's funny?"

Julie laughed, too eagerly. "Definitely. Beelzebub would be funny, too." We'd been ignoring her, but I was too intent on him to pull her into our conversation.

Seth eyed her as if she were an insect. Then he patted the puff of orange frizz on her head. "What's *this* called?" He grinned. "Hair?"

Julie stared at him for a moment, said, "See you later, Dinah," and walked away.

"You insulted her," I said.

He reached out and touched my mouth, just for a second. "When I'm in the presence of a beautiful woman, I lose all sense of propriety. Forgive me? I was just kidding."

I was feeling weak in the knees. Well. He *had* smiled when he made the crack about her hair.

"Now where were we?" Seth said. "Oh. Right. When the Devil first appears in the Goethe *Faust,* he appears as a poodle. You'd figure the Devil would be a Doberman or a shepherd. Poodles are a very smart breed, you know." Then: "Sit, Meph."

Meph sat. Meph also walked, stayed, heeled, and shat when Seth Lucien commanded it to. It was the most thoroughly trained dog I've ever seen.

Seth asked if I wanted to see him rehearse, explaining that he would have played Oedipus had he not promised to get a draft of his Faust play to its director by Christmas. I watched all afternoon from the back of the Little Theater, a small, shabby, subterranean auditorium that you entered through an alley, which was only loosely connected to the university. Other than my stint at the age of ten as the mayor of Munchkin Land, and successive Camp Pequot productions, my theater experience had consisted of working lights in my high school production of *Bye Bye Birdie,* where there was a lot of fooling around. The Playmakers were all serious theater types, some of them very talented. Though he was playing a small role, the shepherd who tells Oedipus that he's killed his father and married his mother, Seth was among the most impressive on stage.

Between his scenes he sat next to me and gave me a running commentary on the actors. Gabby Sterling, playing Jocasta, a tall, lithe, ethereal junior, was "a decent actress, but she'll fuck anyone with a prick." She'd played Ophelia in their production of *Hamlet* last year. (Yes, he played the lead.) Patty Garfinkel, in the chorus, was "the best actress in the group, by far, but she needs to lose weight." (Well. I'd certainly never mention all that weight I'd lost, and thank God I'd lost it, because Seth Lucien would never have looked at me if I hadn't.) Jay Salisbury, playing Creon, a slightly built boy with thinning brown hair and wire-rimmed glasses, "does good work, but he needs better direction." Rich Lender, playing Oedipus, was "going to make it as an actor, because if he doesn't, he'll kill himself." Then, with a laugh, "No great loss."

The poodle bounded ahead of us, up four flights in a decrepit building that once must have been a spectacular Washington house. Seth told me to wait outside for a moment, he just wanted to put away a few things before I came in, which I thought was kind of sweet, that he wanted to clean up for me. A minute or so later, he opened the door to his apartment and let me in, then went to the sink to get the dog some water. I just stood there in the long narrow attic room and looked around. His very own place! As a freshman, I had to live in a dorm. I took it all in: the tarnished brass bed; a Tiffany lamp that looked real to me, intricately leaded in a multicolored floral pattern; a large baroque mirror framed in gilt and gracefully carved in a floral-and-grapes motif presided over by two ripe cupids on each side. There was a table with a typewriter on it; an expensive-looking camera on a tripod set up next to a sewing mannequin draped in a purple and black and gold costume; a shelf filled with spools of film; an electric guitar and amp. Actor, photographer, filmmaker, and musician, too.

Seth put an album on the stereo, The Doors' "Strange Days." Morrison's sardonic monotone filled the room as I ventured over to the extraordinary gilt mirror next to the bed and looked at my reflection. I touched one of the gilt Cupids but quickly withdrew my hand, startled by the voluptuousness of the carved figure. I could see the reflection of a smaller mirror strategically hung on the wall on the other side of the bed, and the bed, and myself, repeated over and over, each image a smaller version of the last.

"Nice effect, isn't it?" Seth came up behind me, put his arms around my waist, moved my hair away, kissed the back of my neck. His lips to my skin made me shiver and I pulled away.

"That was funny, what you did in class today."

"I should have told him what I think of him. These socialists are whistling up their asses."

Quite a statement to make on a college campus in the early seventies. "Why?"

"Because there's the matter of the real world to consider. Communism is an idealist's delusion. Only inferior minds think people are good, Dinah. People are greedy, predatory, and egocentric."

"I don't agree," I said. "I think most people try to be good, most of the time. *I* do."

He made a *psshing* sound between his teeth. "I hope you're not one of these so-called radicals we're overflowing with on this campus. Want some wine?"

My mouth and throat were very dry. Radical? Everyone I knew was a radical, or a pseudo-radical, anyway. It was a down-with-the-establishment time. What I wanted was water.

He moved back to the kitchen area, took a bottle of red wine from a cabinet, expertly opened it. He filled two goblets and handed me one. "To us?"

"Sure." No one ever drank to me before, let alone to an "us."

We clinked.

"What beautiful wineglasses," I said. They were. Delicate cut crystal, a swirling design.

"They were my mother's. These wineglasses are about all I have of hers."

"What happened to her?"

"She's dead."

"I'm sorry, Seth. When did she die?"

"I was ten. It was an accident." He took my hand and walked me toward the bed. "Have you ever been with a man before?"

I didn't mind his just assuming that I was going to sleep with him. I was. Even if he didn't use a condom, which he didn't. I'd worry about birth control later.

I didn't answer him. I was quivering, a leaf in a strong wind.

"Come." He led me to the bed, set our goblets on the small chest next to it, sat me down on the edge. He started to kiss me.

"Can we put out the lights?" I could see our reflections in the gilt mirror.

He pulled away. "Dinah, do you have any idea what happens, or should happen, between a man and a woman?"

This seems now the first of many cruelties, to use my inexperience against me, though of course I didn't see it that way at the time. Nor did I laugh, as I should have, when he kept referring to me as a woman. I was barely eighteen. This was calculated flattery on his part.

I nodded. "Of course." I hadn't spent my high school career studying the subject with Julie to not know anything. I'd been pawed at a few times, read Dan's nudie mags, my mother's hidden copy of *Kinsey.*

"I'm not talking about the sexual part of it, babe." He tapped his head. "What's going on up here is far more important. For two people to really love each other, they have to really know each other. Completely. Nothing held back."

I wondered how he already knew he would love me. I wanted him to, so much that I remember thinking, hoping, he'd said that because he already did.

He took two black candles and a pair of wooden candlesticks from a drawer in the little chest by the bed, set them on top, and lit them before switching off the Tiffany lamp. In the trembling light, he began again.

"I can't with him sitting there." I could see the dog next to the bed, watching.

Seth snapped his fingers and pointed. "Meph. Scram."

The dog turned around and walked over to the table, beneath the stained glass window. There it sat through my entire deflowering.

In the coming days, the dog quickly became a point of contention between us. It gave me the creeps to have it watching that way, but Seth refused to put it out. He commanded it to sit under the window, but it still watched, never lay down and fell asleep, moved closer and closer. There were times when it would actually rest its long, sharp muzzle on the edge of the mattress before Seth commanded it to move again. Perhaps he had trained it to do this, I do not know. In any case, sometimes, even as I saw our bodies reflected in the mirror, over and over and over, framed by those two little Cupids, I would feel that dog's hot breath on my bare skin.

Afterward, Seth sat up against the brass headboard. Beautiful and sleek as he was, I'd noticed that his left foot was badly scarred. Ugly white welts encircled the ankle, snaked over the top of his foot, around the arch and the toes, as if his foot had been mangled and sewn back together again. He also had a small star-shaped tattoo under his left nipple. I asked about that.

He shrugged as he lit a cigarette. "Just something stupid I did when I was younger."

I took the cigarette he held out to me. And coughed.

He took it back. "Never let it be said that I corrupted you."

And back I grabbed it. "Too late. Besides, I smoke once in a while." Julie and I had tried smoking cigarettes when we were fifteen. Her asthma stopped her cold, and since we did everything together, I didn't continue. Now I took to it like an addict in training.

"You didn't enjoy the sex," he said, watching me smoke.

I covered myself with the blanket and sat up next to him, against the headboard. Not inhaling, so I wouldn't cough.

"No . . . it was fine." Actually, it hurt, but not very much, less than I'd expected.

He lit a cigarette for himself and inhaled deeply, blew a curl of smoke out of his mouth that wafted up around us in a lazy spiral. "I know when people are lying, Dinah. I have a sense about it."

"Okay. It was my first time. I'm sorry you didn't have fun."

He assured me he had, then kissed my neck, took the cover down and moved his lips to my breasts. When his head came back up, I covered myself.

"Looking at your body gives me pleasure, Dinah, you know. You've got a lot to learn about pleasure." He took the blanket down again. "You know what I think? You're afraid of revealing too much to me. You didn't want to admit that you have no experience because you were afraid I'd think less of you. Right?"

I shrugged. His intuitiveness was disconcerting, to say the least.

"You think I care you're a virgin? What I care about is honesty. A man and a woman must be totally honest to truly love each other. So now, tell me something important about yourself." He took another drag.

"You tell me something first." Suddenly bold, I traced a fingertip along that ugly bas-relief on his foot. "What happened to your foot?"

He stared at me for a moment, then smiled. "You know, the Devil has a mark on his foot."

"Be serious," I said.

He took another drag on his cigarette. "Look it up if you don't believe me. In any book on the history of Christianity."

I knew nothing about the history of Christianity, or Judaism, for that matter. "Come on, tell me what happened."

"I was in a plane crash." He said it casually, as if it were something you heard every day. "I was ten years old. We were heading for Los Angeles. Crashed in a cornfield over Kansas."

"Did people die?"

He stubbed his cigarette out in the ashtray. "On impact, the plane cracked into two pieces. We'd been sitting in row five. Everyone in the back died, everyone up front who survived was in really bad shape. I was wedged underneath a section of the wreckage with a piece of jagged metal cutting into my foot. Took them hours to free me."

"My God, Seth. The pain must have been incredible. What did you do?"

"Lay there in incredible pain." He played with a dribble of wax from the half-burnt candle.

"How many died?"

"If you include the people who died later in the hospital, fifty-four. Including my mother. My father was in the hospital for months."

I took the odd, almost boastful, way he told this story as a stoicism to be admired. "My God, Seth. I'm so sorry. You were lucky to have survived such a thing."

He tipped his head as if my sympathy puzzled him. "I never think about it anymore." He smiled. "Now tell me what *you've* learned to live with."

"I don't have anything like that."

"Way of the world, Dinah. Quid pro quo. I give you, you give me. Any old deep dark secret will do. Doesn't have to be as dramatic as mine."

Without realizing it, I was already beginning to be alarmed by his sangfroid in such matters, even while his overall demeanor was edgy, almost agitated. I gave him the safest deep dark secret I could come up with. "I feel kind of bad saying this since you lost your mother, but I can't stand mine." I stopped. But he said nothing, so I went on. "I used to think it was my fault she screamed at me all the time, and hated me, but she sent me to this psychologist who helped me see it's her problem, not mine."

Seth giggled. "Ah, so *that's* why you want to be a psychologist. All right then, if psychology explains everything, and Mama Rosenberg is a sadist, why aren't *you* a sadist? Or perhaps you are."

"Ha, ha. Very funny. I didn't say she was a sadist. I just think she can't control her anger. It's probably something in her upbringing that made her this way."

"So then her parents are terrible people?"

"They seemed fine." I wasn't about to tell him my grandmother had been a little strange, not to mention a drunk, and that she and my grandfather seemed to hate each other.

"There goes the upbringing theory," Seth said, leaning back against the headboard, his hands behind his head. "Take my father, for example. The asshole."

"You don't get along with him?"

He touched my nose. "Understatement of the year, babe. Of course he didn't bring me up, anyway. I brought myself up."

"It's also possible people have chemical things, or genetic things," I said earnestly. "There are physiological causes for behavior, you know." I told him about my intro psych course. The professor had lectured on nature and nurture that very day.

"Did you discuss the issue of evil?" he asked.

Now I giggled. "Evil isn't in the syllabus, as far as I know." I was making a joke, but he didn't laugh, so I kept talking. "If you're talking about the Holocaust, say, or Adolph Hitler, maybe psychology alone can't explain it."

"Which proves my point. In that case you've got history, and politics, and economics, and, most of all, religion. At the heart of Christianity—at the heart of European culture—you've got two thousand years of the charge that the Jews killed Jesus. But even with all that, it doesn't explain what happened in Europe in the 1930s and forties. Only a concept like evil would come close."

Anne Frank's diary had piqued my interest in the subject when I was about thirteen, and I'd read other books after that, books that described the horrors of the concentration camps, some in excruciating detail. Ghost stories had been supplanted by real, true evil.

"Well," I said, "it seems to me that blaming evil acts on some sort of evil force—on the Devil, which seems to be where you're going—is a way of not taking responsibility for your actions."

"Personally," he said, "I see two possible explanations for the presence of evil in the world. One, the existence of evil negates even the possibility of a benevolent God. And two, there's a force of evil separate from God, maybe greater than God. Simple as that."

"Greater? No way. I vote for number one. Because no truly good God could allow horrible things to occur, like the Holocaust, or the Inquisition."

"Atheist, are you? The existence of the Devil doesn't nullify your psychological argument, it just explains the supremacy of evil, and fills in holes that psychology, genetics, and history can't."

The Devil again. A subject with which Seth Lucien seemed obsessed. That night, and nights to come, he lectured me on the subject—its origins, the difference between Jewish and Christian concepts of Satan, and so on—as if I were his student. Given his fascination with evil, what amounted to a theological *belief* in evil, I doubt he accepted the dry historical facts he spouted. I was certain even then that his attraction to Satan was helped along by his having read that the Devil's foot is marked. He'd interpreted his injury as distinguishing him in some way. And it was pillow talk like none I'd ever heard of. Not that I had a concept of pillow talk at the time.

But that night he lifted his glass in the flickering light of black candles. "How about we drink to the blossoming of Dinah?"

I resolved in my mind to be more uninhibited with him, clinked with him again, too hard, and the two goblets shattered, spilling onto the bed and our laps. His mother's goblets, for God's sake. "I'm so sorry, I—"

"Wait, don't move. You're bleeding." He took my finger and put his mouth to the cut and kissed it, then gave it a few strokes with his tongue. "Let me get you a bandage." He brought the bandage back to the bed and wrapped my finger in it, kissed my finger again. "You know what this means? I've tasted your blood." He smiled. "That means you're mine forever."

It seemed over the top, even at the time, but I loved it.

During the next few weeks, I hardly ever went back to my dorm room. I did my homework in Seth's attic while he worked on his play or practiced with his band, Death Trip. I watched his rehearsals, hung out with his actor friends, though I was completely left out of their conversations, ate my meals with him, slept in his bed, discussed philosophy and religion, his brand of it, as best I could. He was constantly quoting this or that—long soliloquies of Shakespeare, multiple lines from Hermann Hesse, stanzas of Tennyson or Goethe. I was fascinated with his recall, which truly was remarkable, but I mistakenly interpreted a pathological need to show off for something else entirely, a love of literature itself. I even changed my way of dressing for him. He favored black, of course, black jeans, tight tops, boots. He introduced me to marijuana and hashish, and we listened constantly to The Doors. Jim Morrison was already dead, and his records were all Seth ever listened to, other than his own band's music. One time I brought over a few of my own albums, James Taylor, Cat Stevens, and he called them "old lady music."

Weekends, we went for long rides on his big motorcycle and hung out at the grungy little club where Death Trip had a gig. He played lead guitar without a shirt, holding his electric Fender in front of his groin, his hair hanging sweat-soaked and stringy in his eyes. Seth loved being up there, having all those adoring girls watching him. When we got home he was insatiable in bed, he wanted to do it all night.

The afternoon of Halloween, Julie and I left our lit class on Shakespeare together. "What are you and Seth doing tonight?" she asked.

"I'm not sure," I lied. Once, just after we met Seth, I'd invited her to hear his band. Everyone got stoned first; Julie refused because of her asthma, and Seth had been calling her Weezer Geezer Girl ever since. That night we were going to a costume party, and Seth had told me not to invite her, because she was a drag. My contact with Julie had dwindled to our two classes together, including poli-sci, which Seth was also taking, and my occasional trip back to the dorm for new clothes. I still loved Julie, but I was hooked on Seth.

thirteen

The company was off-book, and the theater had been darkened for the rehearsal of the now familiar *Oedipus Rex.* I made my way down the creaky wooden floor to a front-row seat next to the aisle, stepping over Seth's dog, which as always was lying down quietly waiting. Seth, on stage with Rich Lipton doing a scene near the end, was saying his lines:

For if you are what this man says you are,
No man living is more wretched than Oedipus.

I was sitting there waiting for Seth to finish, when Jay Salisbury sat down next to me. He had a short break between his Creon scenes. He leaned over and whispered, "Lucien's good, don't you think?"

I nodded. He was. Not so Rich, who in my opinion overacted. At the moment, he was overweeping:

I, Oedipus,
Oedipus, damned in his birth, in his marriage damned,
Damned in the blood he shed with his own hand!

As the chorus went into the Ode, Jay leaned over and whispered, "I like you, Dinah."

"I like you too, Jay." I did, I liked him the best of the whole group.

"I wasn't looking for a compliment," he said. "I just wanted to give you some advice. Be careful with Lucien. "

"Why?"

His eyes were kind, concerned. "Just be careful."

"Hey, you can't say something like that and not tell me why."

Jay sighed. "I know Seth Lucien about as well as anyone does. I'm not trying to ruin a good thing with you, if it is. Maybe you'll be good for him. It's just that he scares me sometimes, and if you know him well at all by now, he ought to scare you, too. He doesn't care, Dinah."

"About me?" I picked at a rip in the red velvet fabric of the seat arm.

"About anything."

"But I think he does, Jay. Underneath."

Jay folded his hands in front of his face, and gazed up at Seth. "No, Dinah. I don't think so." This mild-mannered boy with thinning chestnut-colored hair was very serious. "Can you honestly say he doesn't scare you? Ever?"

I couldn't. "I think you're wrong about him, Jay," I said. "He's just troubled. He and his father don't get along so well."

"Hey, my relationship with my old man isn't wonderful, either. That's no excuse."

"He also lost his mother very young. Don't forget that."

Jay shrugged. "Shit. He doesn't care about that."

"See. That's where you're wrong." I knew Seth cared, I was certain of it.

"You think you can rescue him. Love of a good woman?"

"Rescue him? From what?"

Jay's face was flushed. "Look, I've seen him do things that would really scare you, Dinah, all right. I mean it."

"Like?"

He wiped his palms on his pants, flicked a glance at Seth on stage, then looked back at me and took a deep breath. He leaned in closer, practically whispering now. "After *Hamlet* last year, we were out drinking, over on M

Street, and he and I met this girl. The three of us got a little bombed, I'll give you that, but when we went back to Seth's place he started fooling around with his camera. At first the girl was into it, but then she got cold feet. She started to cry and beg and he wouldn't stop, he wouldn't stop—" Jay cut himself off, looked over at me. "Some people may be beyond rescuing, Dinah."

My heart was thudding. I wanted to know the rest of it. "But he did stop. Right?"

Jay sighed. "Only because I was there."

"But he did."

He nodded, and we went back to watching the scene on stage.

"Hey, what do I know?" Jay said, after a few minutes. "I'm stoned all the time. He's stoned all the time. For that matter, we're all stoned all the time." He laughed. "Maybe she was into it, and I just misunderstood."

When Jay went back up on stage for his last scene, Seth sat down in the seat he'd left empty. "I thought Rich was going to drown me in spit. What were you two talking about?"

My heart started to pound again. "Why? What's the difference?"

"Jay's been trying to get into your pants since I introduced you, babe. I see the way he looks at you."

"Seth, he doesn't look at me like anything."

"Don't be naive."

"I am not." A boy. Jealous of *me*. How about that, Charlotte?

He gripped my arm. "What did he say?"

"We talked about how much you hate your father." I was afraid to tell him I brought it up, and I wasn't even sure why I was afraid.

Seth glared at me for a moment, breathing hard, a flush rising in his neck and face. At first I thought I was seeing him embarrassed for the first time since I'd known him. Then I realized he was boiling mad.

"Big fucking deal, *I* told you that." He glared up on the stage at Jay, who caught his eye, then looked away.

"We should talk about it more, Seth. Maybe I could help."

He began to laugh. "You want to help me? Well, now, that *is* cute." His laughter became so loud that the actors on stage heard it. A few of them glared at him.

The director called out, "Get it together, Lucien." Why did everyone call him Lucien?

He stopped laughing. "Sorry, Allison." Back to me. "Help?" he whispered. "How about I bring you home, and my old man'll give you a good fuck."

"Seth!"

"Think I'm being crude?" he whispered. "He just got married, you know. Third time. She's only three years older than you are, he's pushing fifty, just loves the young flesh, younger the better. I figure my next step-mother will be maybe fourteen."

I had never heard such lethal bitterness.

He leaned over and began to kiss me, hard. I could feel the teeth of his fury, and I thought he was going to swallow me.

"Allison, would you *do* something!" Gabby stood glaring as we pulled apart. "Do you think you can ask our first-row lovers to give us just a little break?"

"Lucien, you are on thin ice!" Allison said. "A little professionalism, please."

I jumped up and started to collect my things. "I'll just go, anyway."

He caught hold of my arm. "They're all bullshit, sit down, for Christ's sake."

I shrank into my seat, not wanting to extend the spectacle any longer. Seth leaned over and whispered in my ear, "Oh, yeah, Allison. This dinky college bullshit is *real* professional. Might as well be Broadway."

The party was already in full swing. All manner of ghosts and witches were jammed up against each other on every floor of the narrow Georgetown house, along with one Einstein, two Beatles, four Marx Brothers, including Zeppo, and at least five Nixons. One showoff was naked, sucking on a baby bottle, and wearing only a sheet drawn up between his legs and fastened around his waist with huge blue safety pins. I thought I saw another, bigger baby, this one in red Dr. Denton's with feet, but then I saw him toss three red balls into the air and heard him refer to himself as a Juggler Vein.

Seth came dressed as Mephistopheles, of course. Though he never would have admitted it, he was very into his good looks, always took a lot of time in the bathroom, getting dressed, brushing his long silky hair. That night he took extra care. Horns, a false goatee, hair streaming down his back, red cape, the whole bit. He also brought his movie camera with him that night. As Lachesis, the Fate who measures off people's lives, I wore a gown of black silk Seth had borrowed from the Playmakers, and carried a rope and a scissors. I was self-conscious in the gown, but got into my part. Seth followed me around, filming, as I made pronouncements: "Patty, you will have a long and happy life, and marry a doctor from Chevy Chase. And you, Rich, won't last the night."

There was dancing, drinking, marijuana. We made our way to the second floor of the house, where furniture had been pushed aside to make room for dancing. Seth took his camera into the middle of the dance floor to film the action, leaving me alone with Jay.

"You haven't told me my fate," Jay said.

I said he would meet a mysterious woman and live to the ripe old age of ninety-one.

He laughed. "I shouldn't have told you what I told you this afternoon. It's really not my business, Dinah." Then he moved away.

Around midnight, our group, Jay, Patty, Gabby, Seth, Rich, a few others from the Playmakers, and two Georgetown students I didn't know ended up in a large open sitting room on the top floor of the house. Jefferson Airplane was blaring from one of the rooms below us, and Gabby and one of the Georgetown men were really going at it on the sofa. Gabby was Aphrodite, in a lavender gown threaded with gold. Her date was a pirate in purple balloon pants, naked from the waist up. At the moment, they were writhing around on the sofa, his hands under her gown.

"I think the goddess of love is about to get screwed," Jay said.

Seth jumped to his feet. He never relaxed, he was like a wind-up toy. "So. Who wants something to drink? Dinah?"

Everyone was watching the pair on the sofa. Gabby's gown was now bunched up at her hip, revealing nearly all of one long, pale leg. Seth and Patty went to get the drinks, and eventually came back with a tray of glasses filled with the fruit punch that had been on a table downstairs. The goddess of love and her pirate had retired to a bedroom.

"I'm afraid we've gone to a commercial," Jay said.

"Too bad." Seth set the tray on the table in front of us. Rich had lit some incense, cinnamon. The punch was spiked, it was hard to tell what with. I was already very stoned so I didn't want to drink too much, but my mouth was dry. I took a few sips, then a few more.

Jay gulped his down and sat back in the chair. "Update, Lucien. How's *Faust* coming along?"

Day after day I'd been watching Seth pounding away at his typewriter, only to crumple the pages into little balls and toss them at the wastebasket. The dog kept picking up the balls that missed in its mouth and bringing them back to Seth. I thought this was funny. Seth did not.

"I'm working on it," he said. Then: "I understand you've been trying to get into Dinah's pants."

"That's bullshit, Lucien." Jay started to get up, then fell back. "I feel a little funny."

I felt a lot funny myself. The feeling was more intense than being stoned, and it was building, from my belly into my head, like a seismic tremor. I blinked. Pin-bright lights twinkled in front of my eyes, a dizzy sparkler. The walls and ceiling and floor seemed made of something gelatinous that expanded and contracted. The room began to rock, at first slowly, then faster and faster until it was rising and falling like a roller coaster. Then I was looking into a camera lens. I saw my own distorted reflection.

A huge monster got on top of me, pawing at me, and my stomach, my whole body, was lurching out of control. I realized it was Seth. I was incapable of making out, or anything else. A large hulking form appeared at the far end of the room, on the sofa, opened its mouth in a great yawning chasm, and inside it I saw intense fire, spewing earthquakes, and people fleeing in terror. I blacked out.

The next thing I knew I was in Seth's attic room, in bed beside him. I was naked. It was still night. I remembered a dream, a dragon. I remembered Jay saying, "Man, there must have been something in that punch," then dropping like a stone. I slogged through a surging universe, fighting to get control of my body, my mind, finally getting my ear to Jay's chest. I listened for a heartbeat, put my fingertip to his neck, closed his eyes.

But it was only a dream. I burrowed into the covers and fell asleep again.

In the morning I told Seth about the nightmare.

He was mopping up syrup with a hunk of the unbeautiful pancakes he'd insisted I make him. "Don't you remember? Jay passed out and we took him to the hospital. Someone spiked the punch. Everybody who drank the stuff went on some wild trip—you saw dragons, sounded like. Quite a scene. Someone said it was Sunshine, but who knows?" He wolfed down the last few bites.

"So he's all right?"

"They kept him overnight, for observation. Probably be out today."

I started to remember. I'd waited in the car, fearing the hospital might call the police, or my parents. Charlotte would have gone nuts on me.

I looked at the lopsided, soggy pancakes on my plate and pushed it away. "Thank God," I said.

"Why are you thanking God? Jay's a shit. He wouldn't do shit for me."

"Oh, come on, Seth. Yes he would. He's your friend."

"You are so naive, Dinah. He's just like everyone else, out for themselves. Self-interest is all there is, the rest is self-delusion. Period. If you and I capsized in the ocean, and there was only room for one on our rescue boat, you'd do anything to keep me from taking your space. You'd even kill me. And I'd kill you."

"We're not on a boat."

He eyed me. "But we are. It just depends on how you define your self-interest. Every moment we live, we have to prepare for that one moment when our time comes. Looking forward you have a whole lifetime before you, looking back it's only an instant. And when it comes, there's only one person, wanting to live another day or moment. Then you start looking for the God of Desperation to help you, the atheist in the foxhole with the guns blazing all around. Might as well forget it then. It's too late."

"Too late for what?"

"To back the right horse."

What was he talking about?

Laughing, he picked up our plates, dumped my pancakes into the garbage, and dropped the plates into the sink with a clatter. He leaned back against the sink.

"Have you ever seen anyone dead, Dinah?"

"Jewish people don't have open caskets."

"At least you don't paint on these masks of peace at funerals, like the Christians do. They had this open casket for my mother, everybody standing around and saying, 'Oh, doesn't she look so nice and peaceful.' Bullshit. The dead's eyes are open and their mouths are open and they've shit their pants. My mother lying there with her hands clasped together, her face all beautiful and peaceful again. Bullshit."

I got up and tried to put my arms around him. He pulled away.

"Please," he said. "Spare me. I can take care of myself, always have. You should stop walking around in a fantasy. Case in point, Jay. He doesn't give a shit that I'm with you, he's trying to get in your pants."

"He *isn't*."

"You still haven't told me what he said to you, besides talking about my father—which, I might add, he has no right to do. He doesn't know shit about the bastard."

"Why do you hate him so much? Because he likes young women?"

"Not women, Dinah. *Girls.* I'll tell you what I'll do. You tell me what Jay said that you don't want me to know, and I'll tell you why I hate my father."

Why couldn't he just talk to me without bargaining for information in return? And why did I continue to tell him? He was like a corkscrew, digging deeper and deeper inside me. "He said you went too far with some girl you met in a bar." As soon as I'd blurted it out, I wanted to take it back.

He tried to laugh but it came out something between a snort and a cough. "Oh Christ, that! What a pig she was, a real whore."

I stared. "And what am I?"

He touched my nose. "A virgin can't be a whore, babe."

"But I'm no longer a virgin."

He laughed. "Don't be ridiculous. I love you. Best thing that ever happened to me in my whole fucking life."

I was still stuck on "I love you." "Jay said I should be careful of you."

Now he did laugh, loudly. "He's trying to get into your pants behind my back, and you should be careful of *me?*"

Jay died. He had a massive stroke early that morning in the hospital. We gathered to cry at the Little Theater, where two D.C. homicide detectives interviewed everyone, confiscated Seth's film. It turned out the camera hadn't been working, and with more than a hundred people in attendance and an open front door, the investigation never turned up a viable suspect. Jay had, for some unknown reason, reacted fatally to the horse tranquilizer and LSD someone had spiked the punch with. At one point, I asked Seth if he was sorry about the things he'd said about Jay. "I'm sorry he's dead," he said. "It doesn't change the fact that he was a shit. Out for himself, just like everyone else. If you weren't so naive—"

"I'm not naive, just because I don't think everyone is selfish and cruel and evil, the way you do."

"What I said was people *can* be evil and cruel, given the right circumstances," Seth said. "If you're going to quote me, get it right."

"Well, I can't imagine myself doing something I knew was evil." I was thinking about the Milgram Experiment, which I'd just read about in psych class. Subjects were placed in front of a machine and told they could inflict shocks on someone in the next room, and that the purpose of the experiment was to test the efficiency of using pain to increase memory. A huge percentage of people shocked people up to levels where the guy in the next room screamed in apparent pain. Very few refused to participate, even though there was nearly no motive to do so, except wanting to please the experimenter, the authority figure. Now there was a commentary on evil and cruelty, and sadly, it seemed to fit with Seth's analysis.

"You're not imagining very well, babe. What about your so-called best friend Julie? As far as I can tell, you lie to her all the time."

I made myself look at him. "If I've lied to her," I said, "it's because I was trying to spare her feelings."

"That's what people always tell themselves. But it's bullshit. I thought you were more honest than that, Dinah."

"I've only lied to her because I know you don't like her. There. That's honest."

But the truth was I was afraid he'd think less of me for still wanting to be her friend.

"Seth doesn't like me, does he?" Julie asked on the train ride home at the beginning of Christmas vacation.

"What makes you say that?" I hadn't mentioned that, in addition to the books I needed to study for finals, I was lugging in my suitcase a pile of books Seth had given me that he said I *had* to read right away, including an 1808 translation of Goethe's *Faust.* The only decent translation, he said. As if he could read German, which I suspected he couldn't.

She sighed. "This is me, Dinah. Do you suddenly think I got stupid? Look, I'm not saying I want to tag along every time, but he's a really cool guy, and his friends are really cool, too. You *could* invite me to some of the parties."

"I'm sorry," I said. "Consider it done."

When I showed up back at Seth's place after Christmas break, having slogged my way through *Faust* (I had to eventually get a different translation to make heads or tails of it), there were two copies of his play on the kitchen table. The title page:

THE DEVIL'S BARGAIN

A THEATRICAL EXPERIENCE

by Seth Lucien

"It's only the first two acts," he said.

He wanted me to read with him, so he could hear what the dialogue sounded like aloud. But first he said he wanted to try out a new photographic technique. We smoked a bowl of hash, then he had me take off my clothes and he draped me in a very sheer piece of white material he got from the Playmakers. Arranging me on the stool in front of the camera, he then produced a ruby-colored glass stone on a chain, which he fastened around my neck.

He turned the brass floor lamp off and the Tiffany lamp on, then snapped a few pictures. He put on the overhead light, a black light, stood back to assess the effect, tried the Tiffany with the black light. Finally he switched on every light in the room and moved around just like a prowling panther, snapping away.

"You are very beautiful," he said when he was finished.

I loved it when he told me I was beautiful. I felt vindicated somehow.

After I got dressed again we read the play, a modernized version that took place on a college campus he called Walpurgis University, with a professor named George Faust, and a female student named Gretchen. I took the parts of God, Faust, and Gretchen; Seth read Mephistopheles' part. His play began like Goethe's, with a prologue in heaven, where God and the Devil are betting over whether Faust can be tempted to sell his soul. Some of the first part took its inspiration from Goethe also, with Satan appearing first as a poodle. Seth snapped his fingers and Meph trotted over, prepared as always to do his master's bidding, even to act.

Two evenings later, we went to see the only movie we ever saw together, *The Exorcist,* which had opened that Christmas. I thought all that head spinning and green vomit was a little hokey, but Seth loved it. When we got back, Seth presented me with his photographs. I sat at his kitchen table and began to look through the set of 8x10 black-and-whites.

"My God," I said, "I can't believe I posed this way."

He smiled. "Relax. Your body is exquisite."

At first I didn't catch it, but by the fourth or fifth photo I was noticing subtle changes in my face. By mid-stack I knew that whatever the technique was, it was aging me. Lines materialized, then deepened, around my eyes and mouth. I saw my hair go gray, my jaw line start to slacken, my neck and waist and hips thicken, my breasts sag, and sag, and sag. And in the very last I saw myself as an old, old woman. Practically a crone.

"Pretty cool technique," Seth said. "Don't you think?"

"Seth, what is *wrong* with you?" The photographs disgusted me. I got up to go.

"Hey." He reached out. "I was just experimenting. I'll rip them up if they bother you so much."

He picked up several photographs and with a flourish ripped them in two. Then ripped these pieces in four, in eight, in sixteen, and threw them in the wastebasket. He picked up another stack and began the same process. And another. Until the wastebasket was full.

The Merry Playmakers opened *Oedipus Rex* in February, with Allison announcing before each performance that the production was dedicated to Jay. After the final curtain the cast went to a bar on M Street, with a blaring jukebox and a roomful of boisterous, drunken students. I invited Julie along. No one seemed to mind having her except Seth, who wouldn't look at either of us. All evening long, whenever someone mentioned Jay it would spark a round of remembrances, toasts, tears, then back to less emotional topics until somebody else said, "Let's drink to Jay."

"Lucien is very sexy, isn't he?" Gabby said when Seth headed off to buy the next round of beers. "But then, so are you, Di-nah." She said it directly to me, but loud enough for everyone to hear.

Everyone at the table started to laugh except Julie. I studied her pale freckled face. She was a butterfly in that brood of scorpions, holding a mirror up to my face.

Rich, who was very drunk, began to pound his empty beer glass on the table. "Sex-Y, Sex-*Y!*" The others joined in. "Sex-Y! Sex-Y! Sex-Y!"

People in the bar turned to look, but not for long. There was too much noise in the place for anyone to concentrate on us.

Seth returned to the chorus of chants. "What's this?"

Rich stopped banging. "Gabby says she thinks you're sexy."

"She does, does she?" Seth put the beer steins down on the table, leaned over, and kissed Gabby on the lips. It was a long, sexual kiss, their mouths open, tongues exploring while the others yelped encouragement. It seemed to go on forever. "Go, go, go!" Rich shouted. "Instant replay. *Hamlet!*"

What was he talking about? I wanted to slink away and take Julie with me.

Then Seth was back in his chair. "Seize on my heart, sweet fever of love," he said, inflecting Goethe's words with sarcasm so heavy the couplet sounded nasty. Gabby made a show of wiping her mouth with the back of her hand.

"Don't mind Lucien, Gabby," Rich said, "He's obsessed with his *Faust.*"

"If he were that obsessed," said Tom, "he'd be done with it already."

"I'm getting there, *Mein Direktor,*" Seth said. "Right, Dinah?"

I hated him.

"What I've seen is very strong," Tom said, "but two acts do not a *Faust* make."

"Well, I think we should do something else, anyway," Gabby said. "We could do *Lysistrata.* That would bring the audience in. What we need is lots of sex."

"I agree," Allison said. "This is the 1970s, no one cares about the Devil anymore. Except Seth, of course. What's all that moaning about knowledge and fallen women?"

"We could do *Lear,*" Rich suggested. "People love a good crazy."

"We did do really well with all Shakespeare last year," Allison said.

"*Lysistrata.* Sex beats madness any day," Gabby said. "Shit."

"Gabby," Tom said, "sex is all you ever think about."

"Well, you're *all* a bunch of assholes." Seth stood up. "When you read my *Faust,* you'll see. It has lots of sex. I'm working on a seduction scene that'll kill you. Can you picture it?" He spread his arms out dramatically, hovering over us, as he did when he took the floor, which was often. "Gretchen's virgin bed. We dress her in white, Faust gives her jewels, offers her immortality." He sat back down, laughing. "Then he fucks the shit out of her. Balls her till she screams for mercy."

I was squirming in my seat. I couldn't look at Julie.

"Lucien," Rich said, "people don't care about virginity anymore."

"You're an asshole, Rich," Seth said. "Virginity is practically an archetype."

"I agree with Seth," Patty said. "For sure, every girl remembers her first."

"Every girl except Gabby." Seth was laughing again. "Because *she* can't remember back that far."

"Oh, I remember," Gabby said, fixing him with a narrow-eyed stare. "You don't forget fucking a viper."

I realized then that Seth had bedded Gabby, and probably Patty, and maybe Allison, too. There was a chorus of "Oooooh's," and "Now that's hitting below the belt."

Seth was laughing, too. "Don't forget, Gabby, vipers eat insects. For snacks. They're attracted by the *smell.*" He made a leering face and did something disgusting with his tongue.

Everyone stared at him for a minute and then at Gabby, who turned to me.

"Watch out, Dinah. You might get a disease."

Seth leaned over close to me. "Why don't we just ask our Gretchen whether she'd rather do *Faust* or *Lysistrata?*"

I just stared at him. He could as easily humiliate me as he had Gabby. She was clearly willing to engage with him in cruel displays like the one we had all just witnessed, but I wanted nothing to do with it anymore. Any of it.

I got up and left, taking Julie with me.

Seth called the dorm later that night. I hung up on him. He called the next day. I told the girl who answered the phone to tell him I didn't want to talk to him. He sent roses. He wrote me a letter, said he was sorry, said he loved me. Julie said he wasn't capable of love. "I was totally wrong about him."

I held out for a whole week, then I received what I mistook for a love poem:

Barroom intoxication is no companion
next to Dinah in my room.
Booze, reefer, others
who are not you,
who are nothing but jesters,
donning cap and bells
Nothing but fools and jokers,
next to Dinah in my room.
Beauty pale as a bride's veil.
My mouth thirsts for you there,
Dinah, I am as dry as ale
without you.
I forsake all spirits but you now.
Let me drink you (and only you).
Intoxicate me, Dinah.
Together we will drink forever,
Eternity for two.

We left D.C. on the motorcycle about noon that Saturday, heading into Virginia, on a cold winter day. He kept bearing down on the accelerator. I was utterly terrified, he always drove fast, but never *this* fast. I kept begging him to slow down, he kept making whooping and howling noises, hypnotized by the speed, or by the danger, or perhaps both. "What a rush." He wasn't wearing a helmet. He never did. "What's the point if you can't feel the wind in your hair?" he said. And, when I insisted on wearing one: "What're you practicing for, middle age?"

Around two, he finally stopped next to a reservoir and lit a joint. I didn't want to smoke pot with him anymore, I just wanted to go home and never see him again. But I'd suddenly realized that I was afraid of how he might react to that, so I told him I felt sick. He agreed to head home, and we got back on the bike as soon as he finished his joint.

We were somewhere near Reston when I saw a truck approaching in the distance, battling over the crest of an oncoming hill. I looked at the speedometer, which was hovering around 100. Did he think he could survive anything?

"Slow down!" I screamed.

He took his eyes off the road, looked around. "*Pray,* Dinah. *Pray* for your life."

"*Slow down!*" I screamed. But my voice was swallowed by the wind, the roar of the bike engine, and the engine of the truck coming closer, closer. I did pray. Please, let me live through this, God. I'll do anything. Please.

And then the behemoth was upon us, huge, bearing down.

Seth swerved to the right. I heard the screech of a skid. In the silence that followed I seemed to be floating, soaring soundless through the cool air.

The next moment or the next hour, I lay breathless in the dirt at the side of the road, tall trees rising over the asphalt, a gothic arch of bare-branched trees, the motorcycle on its side near me. I moved my legs, my arms. Everything worked. Everything hurt.

I took off my helmet, looked over for Seth. He was lying flat on his back a few feet away, his face turned toward the sky, his eyes closed.

"Seth?" I struggled to all fours and crawled toward him. A pool of blood, dark and thick, was widening around his head. *"Seth?"*

fourteen

After the hospital elevator doors closed with the ghost inside, I returned to the NAR with Sam. Kate was sitting next to Elijah. She was singing.

And some folks thought 'twas a dream they'd dreamed
Of sailing that beautiful sea—

She stopped singing as I walked in. "Maybe he'd wake up if I played my flute for him, Mom." Sam looked at me, as if he expected me to know how to comfort her. As if I should want to.

"Katie." I put my hand on her back. I couldn't bring myself to tell her everything would be all right, wouldn't be starry-eyed and unrealistic, like Sam. I needed to be prepared, to run in place just to keep up, yet I could barely move my limbs. I sat down in the chair next to the bed and held my daughter, tried (and failed) not to cry. All the while thoughts and questions spiraled through my mind, stabbing at me like polished blades. Should I have told the police Seth had been jealous and angry toward Jay, rather than tell myself lies about its relevance? *Was* my son sick because I was lacking in character, after all? Had I been something more sinister than young and foolish back then? Worse, had surviving that motorcycle crash used up my ration of God's mercy?

"Mom!" Kate pulled away. Once unleashed, my crying had turned into howling. And the ghost who called himself Seth Lucien was there, patting me on the back. "There, there," he said. "There, there."

Elijah slept.

Alex, my parents, and Sam's parents all came up from the hospital cafeteria about ten minutes later. Sam went home with the children that night, for the first time. In the quiet hours after everyone left, I held Elijah's hand and began to pray, more formally now. The only actual prayer I could remember was a psalm, and only a line or two near the beginning. I went out to the desk, asked for a Bible, and found the psalm. "My help cometh from the Lord, who made heaven and earth. He will not suffer thy foot to be moved . . ." I read Psalm 121 over and over, while the ghost of Seth Lucien whispered savage words he delivered in his inflectionless, affected coo. This I heard in my ear for hours on end, but I wouldn't look at him, and I kept reciting the psalm. "He that keepeth Israel shall neither slumber nor sleep."

"Speaking of sleep, my Dinah, you really should be grateful the kid's unconscious. Think of all those who die in pain, imploring God to intercede. Think, Dinah! It could be so much worse. He could be conscious and looking at you with pleading eyes."

I turned away, I prayed and listened for the sound of God's glorious, booming voice, or His still, small voice, or any voice discernible over Seth's sibilant murmurs.

"What's wrong with you, Dinah? A decent mother would have taken her child to the hospital."

I tried to defend myself. "The doctor didn't act like it was any big deal."

"Don't these doctors make all sorts of pronouncements, and aren't they always so sure? Weren't they sure when they gave those pregnant women thalidomide in the fifties?" He bent his arms at the elbow and began to flap them like flippers. "Well, weren't they? Of course they were. And you believed every single one of Elijah's doctors, like a submissive child, no matter what they told you to do for him, or not do. Truth is, you should have let Elijah be. You got him too many doctors in the first place."

"But I had to! He had so many problems."

"That's a pile of dog turds if I ever heard one. You were trying to make him over in your own image. You're just like your mother, much as you deny it. You were embarrassed he was your son. You wanted him to be smart like you! Smart, smart, smart."

"I wasn't. I didn't. I wanted him to be happier. Less frustrated." It was my mother who wanted him to be smart, wasn't it? It was Sam who couldn't face his handicaps. Not me.

"You were never even there. You were out working all the time, trying to fix everyone but you."

I got off the bed, walked over to the glass wall, drew back the curtain and looked out. A lone resident was sitting at the central desk.

"Leave me alone, Seth. I beg you."

"Beg?" The ghost began to pant like a dog, and the face distended and lengthened and darkened, and the nose became a snout. For a moment I saw a black poodle, then the ghost was back, zipping up to the ceiling. "I *will* leave you alone if you don't stop calling me by that name."

I turned. "What *is* your name?"

A whisper. "I have no name."

No name? "You told me you were Seth."

"So I did, my Dinah." In an instant he was beside me, as if the air had slurped him there.

"Stop calling me that. I'm not your Dinah. I never was."

"Oh, but Seth loved you."

"Seth? Love? They don't belong in the same sentence."

He stamped his foot. "He *did*."

"I don't care. It was almost twenty-five years ago."

"But a passing moment for me, my Dinah. A passing moment—and an eternity."

I took a step backward. "Who are you, really?"

"I already told you. A kind of a ghost."

"What kind?"

"Think of me as the Angel of the PICU."

"How can a ghost be an angel?"

"How the *hell* would I know?"

"What kind of angel? Are there different kinds?"

He spread out his hands. The air in the darkened room shimmered and moved, undulated like an exotic dancer. "I'm a specialist."

"What do you specialize in?"

"Being a nuisance." He grinned. "Some of us hang around questioning God's judgments. Some of us think God may make some mistakes." He clamped his hand over his mouth and drew in air like a siphon. "Oops." He leaned toward me. "After all, who would question God? Right?"

"I do. I question God." I went back over to sit on the bed with Elijah, took his hand.

"Well. Any mother would in your situation. Remember Job?"

"Of course."

"Then you remember how the angels all are sitting around, and one of them suggests to God that this fellow Job who lives in the land of Uz so happily and prosperously really doesn't deserve such protection—"

"Wait a minute. You're *Satan?*"

He laughed, and his laugh bounced around the NAR, glass wall, floor, ceiling, Mylar balloons in the corner. "I can assure you that I'm not Satan. I'm just a poor misbegotten ghost. The spirit of your former paramour, Seth Lucien, to be sure. But you've already figured that out. Finally."

Now he seemed to be contradicting himself again. Was he lying? Maybe he was both Seth's spirit and Satan, too. Maybe neither. Maybe everything he told me was a lie.

"But I didn't love Seth. If he hadn't died in that crash, I never would have wanted to see him again."

He clapped his blood-dark hand over his mouth. "Well, you really know how to hurt a ghost. Tee hee hee."

"Go away. Why am I bothering with you?"

"You are bothering with me, dear Dinah, because I am the only game in town." He gestured around the room. "You see anyone else around here telling you the truth? Anyway, Moore's the only doctor who's saying he's going to wake up, babe, but Moore's your basic eye-darter. Some doctors are like him, too bad for you. Haven't got a clue how to deal with patients, or with parents of patients, for that matter. Moore has trouble dealing with all women, you know. His own mother was cold, cold, cold. Poor L'il Abner, never got anything lower than an A in school, and never got a bit of praise. Here he is, the big-cheese doctor, national reputation, and he's still never been good enough for that woman. Never will—she's dead, of course."

"Doesn't he have any children?"

"Four, poor things. Nothing they ever do is good enough for cold cold Abner." He chuckled. "You, unfortunately, are stuck with him just as much as they are. And he's stuck with you. And he figures you don't want the truth, if it's bad news."

He took up his guitar and plucked at the strings, picking out the beginning of a flamenco tune. He took a couple of steps toward Elijah's bed, stamping his feet in a fast, flamenco-type rhythm.

"Stay away from him." I moved between the ghost and my son.

He held up his hands. "Relax, I'm not going near him. Not until you want me to. Not until you beg. And you will, my Dinah, before this is over."

"I do want the truth." The words seemed launched from my mind like a fired rocket.

"Ah. The truth. I shall oblige." He began to dance, to twitch his hips, and I saw a new guitar, this one a white Fender electric, the wire plugged into a place in the air. He played and twanged: "You ain't nothin' but a hound dog," doing a fair imitation of Elvis. Then he stopped singing and put down the guitar.

"Might as well untie those hands, Dinah," the ghost said. "He's finished dancing."

"You are *lying!*"

"You say you want the truth, and when I tell it to you, you accuse me of lying? Fine, no problem, I'll just leave right now." He started to shimmer like a mirage.

"No. Wait. *I have to know*."

He solidified again and settled into the air. "The truth is, on the twenty-second day, Elijah will open his eyes."

"But that's good, isn't that good? That he opens his eyes?"

"No. It's bad. Very bad." The ghost made a wounded sigh. "He'll open his eyes, Dinah, but there'll be no one there. Behold."

I looked over at my baby, lying on the bed with his eyes closed, and had another vision then, a momentary ripple in sight and in time, an image.

Elijah's eyes flutter open before me. I see my son's blue eyes staring at nothing, at no one. Something else happens, too. His eyes begin to move.

I watch the irises and pupils of my son's eyes revolving around and around in their sockets. They begin at the right side, and both eyes jerk left in tandem until they get to the other side of the eye socket, then they reappear and begin again back at the other side, as if they have gone all the way around the back. The movement isn't smooth like the natural movement of eyes focusing or tracking or really looking at something. It's a tick-tick-ticking; like the mindless ticking of the second hand of a clock, as if a machine is putting Elijah's eyes through paces.

He was doing this, my vicious ghost, he was making me see my son with his eyes rotating tick tick tick in his head.

"The doctors have a medical name for it," the ghost said casually. "Nystagmus."

The night nurse came in, a kind, gray-haired woman. "Mrs. Galligan?"

I was crying. "Please go away," I said to her.

She nodded and backed out the door.

"No one there, Dinah," the ghost said. "Nothing behind the eyes. Even Moore will stop telling you Elijah's going to wake up anytime soon, but he still won't tell the truth."

"Why not?"

"Well, now that's a good question. Because he thinks he can fix anything. He is, after all, such a genius. He'll still come in every day, and every day he'll shout Elijah's name and pound at his chest. He'll act as if there's a point to doing this. And he'll pay a lot of attention to Elijah's heels and ankles, but he won't tell you why. But *I'll* tell you. Elijah's toes will already be starting to point downward. An early sign of brain damage."

"He's going to be *brain damaged?*"

The ghost nodded solemnly. "Afraid so. Remember when Angus came and told you it was hopeless, he was vegetative? There was nothing normal in there."

"But that was just a dream."

"Well. I see I shall have to spell it out for you. We're not talking a few little neuroglitches, like he had before. We're talking profound brain damage. I'm talking vegetable, babe. Do you know what that means?"

I only knew from my visions. Tears were slipping down my cheeks. I held Elijah's hand to my cheek.

"What about the Great Barrier Reef? Why this future, why not that one? Which future is the truth?"

"You gone deaf or something? Or just dumb. Haven't you been listening to anything I'm saying?"

I got myself to my feet and began walking away from him, I knew how to put one foot in front of the other. The ghost came along with me as I plodded out of the NAR. It was the middle of the night, a pall and the hush of darkness lay over the PICU. A resident-on-duty looked up from the desk as I passed but said nothing. Outside in the corridor by the Coke machine, I stopped. I could still hear the beat of the respirator in my head, a whoosh, click, pump, pump march, John Philip Sousa in my head, even though I'd left the room. I tried to get my bearings, then went into the bathroom, the ghost behind me, with his accusing, cooing tirade. I looked into the mirror and gasped. All I could see was the reflected doors of the stalls in the mirror and my own face, which was haggard beyond description, blotchy and bloated. I reeled around.

He was there, of course. Leaning against the tiled wall. Black jacket, black eyes. He flapped his black lips like a whinnying horse. "What kind of mother doesn't set an alarm and go into her son's bedroom and check on him in the middle of the night when he's sick?"

"He didn't seem that sick!"

"Well, too bad. Now his brain has been oxygen-starved. He's never going to wake up."

I clapped my hands over my ears and pivoted around to look into the ghostless reflection in the mirror, preferring that to him. I *had* to be going mad. Maybe I was, maybe I wanted to slide into oblivion, emptiness, delusion, pain. Not the pain I was feeling now, this fear and grief for my son. Any *other* pain. Would I trade my sanity for my son's life, then? Consent to go stark raving mad? Walk into it with both eyes open?

"I don't know. Would you?"

I pivoted around slowly, the earth turned on its axis. He was there, leaning back against the tiles, just as he had been before. "Would I what?"

"Trade your sanity for your son? Consent to go mad to save your son's life? That was your question, was it not?" He seemed amused.

Now I couldn't turn away.

"Well. Finally, we're getting somewhere," the ghost said. "Of course you'd trade your sanity, what mother wouldn't? How about the famous sense of humor, or your career? What about your marriage, would you trade that? Your so-called morality? Let's be a little creative, shall we? How about your ability to love? Would you go through life without that? You'd have your living child, but you couldn't love him. Hmm."

I took a breath from deep in my diaphragm. "You're finishing the *Faust* right here."

The ghost clapped his hands together, but the sound was muffled, like a faraway slap of thunder, or a bluster of wind. "Maybe you're finishing it for him."

I stared. "But it doesn't work this way. You can't bargain with God."

"You see God here? You see anyone here but little ol' me?" He moved toward me, the air gurgled and boiled. "So what about it? Maybe we should try the negative formulation. What *wouldn't* you exchange for your son? What about your life?"

The ghost tittered, snapped his fingers like a performing magician, and disappeared.

The next morning after Moore came for his rounds, I wandered out of Elijah's room while Sam's sister Anne was visiting. Dr. Jonas was sitting at the desk, working on one of the computers. He looked up as I approached. I asked him if I could have saved Elijah the night he had the seizure by sitting up with him and watching him all night.

"He was sick," I said. "I should have been with him."

The young doctor sighed. "All the signs are positive. Try not to blame yourself, Mrs. Galligan."

Right.

The doctor put his hand on my shoulder, then went to attend the Spanish child in the silver blanket, whose monitor alarm was beeping, whose mother was screaming something that sounded like "*Socorro!*" Help! sounds the same in any mother's language. As for me, I was standing at the desk in the center of the PICU, and I was sucked into a horrendous vision of what I was now convinced was my future. I was cornered and chained and caged.

Morning. A conference room, a large oval table. A white coat convention, formal this time, hands folded neatly. Dr. Moore, his third partner, Dr. Lambert, the head of nursing on the pediatric floor, the pediatric social worker, the chief resident, the chief surgical resident, Sam, and me. Table for eight. No Dr. Angus.

"Gastrostomy and fundoplication," Moore says, dart-dart. "It's a simple procedure. We insert a tube into the stomach for the feed. And the stomach will have to be moved, and we have to put a special flap in the esophagus. Takes about three hours."

Sam draws a deep breath. "Why do you want to do this?"

Moore glances down at the papers in front of him, as if to check for the reason. "Because he's been vomiting his feed."

We already know this, of course. Every time a nurse fills the tube in Elijah's nose with the white liquid they call "feed," it comes back up again, out of his mouth.

"If you just insert the feeding tube into his stomach, will that stop the vomiting?" Sam asks.

"Probably not."

"But what's the point of *doing* it, for God's sake? Dr. Angus described Elijah as hopeless. And now you're proposing to do a complicated three-hour operation to rearrange his organs? If Elijah can't keep that stuff down, maybe his body is telling us something."

"It's not complicated at all. The surgical staff does that operation all the time."

"Are you saying now it's *not* hopeless?"

I close my eyes to block it all out, but shutting my eyes does no good, none at all. I still see the bright lines galloping across the monitors, I still hear the whoosh and pump of the respirator. And I can hear a phone ringing somewhere, the beep of a patient call button, the rattle of a cart, the nurses chatting at their station, their laughter. I noticed a cake when I walked in the corridor before. People do have birthdays.

"No," Moore says.

"No, it's not hopeless?"

I open my eyes in time to see Moore hide his hands under the table. "There are chronic care hospitals." He looks at Dr. Lambert. "What about Laurel?"

"This morning I spoke to admissions there," the social worker says. "They won't take him with a nasal tube. The tube has to be put into his stomach. That's their rule."

"But you said the other day they would." My voice is hoarse, a croak, as if I have been talking for days. "That's why we made the appointment."

Dr. Moore has a hint of a smile. "So he'll have to have the operation after all."

Sam has his head in his hands. "What about hospice?" He looks at the social worker, who suggested this only yesterday.

"Hospice won't take patients with respirators," the social worker says. "It goes against their philosophy."

And this, too, we know. All extraordinary means of keeping a patient alive must be removed for them to be admitted to a hospice facility.

"And the order to remove has to come from this hospital," Moore says. "Look, these things are very complicated ethical decisions that people have argued about for many years. These are decisions not to be taken lightly."

"*Lightly?*" I can see the pulse throbbing at Sam's temple. "How dare you! You don't know anything about us—"

I place my hand on top of Sam's. Don't get him mad at us, Sammy. We're at his mercy. But oh, I want to tell this arrogant man how much we love our son, how hard we've tried for him, how—

"Just because a child is handicapped doesn't mean you kill him," Moore says.

Kill him?

The social worker and the head nurse exchange glances. Is he saying removal of Elijah's life support would be like murder? But his colleague said it was an option.

"*Handicapped?*" Sam says, rising from the chair. "Handicapped is a person in a wheelchair, handicapped is a child with some kind of palsy, handicapped is retarded. A handicapped person has limitations but he knows you are there, knows *he* is there, can communicate in some way. How can you call our son handicapped when he has no brain left? Your own colleague said there is nothing left in his brain that's normal. He cannot possibly have any consciousness. He can't even feel pain."

Dart-dart. "We don't know that."

Dr. Lambert shifts position in her seat. She does not volunteer her own opinion as to Elijah's capacity to feel pain. No one suggests that he can feel anything *except* pain. Seems to me I read in one of those books I'm always looking at that pain is the last sense to go. Or is it smell? But Elijah doesn't smell anything, either. Could he be smelling and just not able to show it?

"Dr. Angus said we should consider removing the respirator," Sam says.

I realize that Sam has come to a decision: He wants to remove it. I haven't even begun to think about that, I'll need a thousand years to think about it.

There could be a miracle, couldn't there? Maybe Dr. Angus is wrong. No. Destroyed Brain Tissue Doesn't Grow Back. Even Moore isn't saying it can do that. But why not, why not? What about the Dead Sea Parting, the

Fishes into Loaves? No. I don't believe in that. But Sam is Catholic, he should believe in fishes into loaves.

Wheels within wheels, within wheels. I have to stop this, I have to pull this plug, but if I pull the plug he won't be alive anymore, but so what, he's not alive now, so I need to pull this plug, but how can I assume that responsibility, but if not me, then who?

Not to decide is in itself a decision. Don't decide and your son spends his life lying there because you keep forcing air into his lungs. And what if he's crying to go, what if his soul is hovering right in the corner of his room, hovering and saying, "Set me free."

"Well," Sam says. "I guess we're stuck, then. He can't go to hospice with the respirator, and we have to give consent for the doctors to do this operation here if we want them to take him at Laurel. So what happens if we don't give consent?"

Dr. Lambert shrugs. "He'll stay here. We can't release him unless we release him to somewhere."

Ah. Catch 44.

"Look," Dr. Moore says, "all I'm saying is that you should wait. You don't yet know what the outcome will be. He could regain some function, with time."

"Please, Sam, we have to let them do the operation," I say. I wonder if they give a vegetative child who can't feel any pain an anesthetic when they operate on him. And when they finish, do they come out and assure you the operation went just fine?

"You think I haunt you," the ghost said now, as I came out of the abominable imagining. "Abner Moore will haunt you the rest of your ruined life."

I realized that, lost in my future, I had unknowingly strayed over to the Spanish child's bed in the far corner of the PICU. I was just standing there, with the ever-present ghost beside me. No one seemed to notice me, they were busy working on the child, and the mother was standing off to the sidelines with her eyes closed. Her hands clasped in front of her, she was making short high-pitched shrieks and rocking herself back and forth like a praying *Hassid.*

I turned and started walking back toward the NAR. The ghost came with me, flitting hither and yon.

"This is all your fault, Di-nah."

"Please. I'm just a human being."

"Poor excuse for a human being, if you ask me."

"And what were you? You were a horrible human being."

Smile, colossal. "Well, I'm a much better ghost. Don't you think?"

I thought he was a vicious, tormenting ghost.

"My sister had to go. Where were you?" It was Sam, coming up behind me. I walked on and we were a threesome. I could see through the glass that the room was empty. Even the nurse wasn't there. I started to boil. How could Sam have left Elijah alone?

When we got inside the NAR, Sam pulled a little envelope out of his shirt pocket. "I called the doctor and got these for you." Opened the envelope, handed me two little white pills. "Take them, Dinah."

The ghost had floated up to the ceiling. His smile had become huge, one end of the ceiling to the other. "Get a grip, Di-nah."

I swallowed the pills with the water Sam gave me.

"Look at your husband, Dinah," the ghost ordered.

I did as he commanded, I was already well within his spell. Sam was sitting beside Elijah's bed, just staring blankly at him.

"Prepare for the future I show you," the ghost said. "There will be a day when you get a call on the phone. 'Is this the mother of Alexander Galligan?' " A new voice emerged from deep within the ghost's throat. " 'Mrs. Galligan, this is Sergeant Dominetti, Bronx Police Department. We have your husband, Samuel Galligan, down at the station on a DWI. He's unable to drive, we'll be keeping him overnight. But we'd like you to come and pick up your son, who was in the car.' "

DWI with my son in the car? "He isn't . . .?"

"Oh, Alex will be not be hurt," the ghost said. "But you and Sam? You will not survive this together. It was a ludicrous marriage, anyway, a marriage built on deceit and betrayal. Remember?"

fifteen

I sat beside Seth's body on the side of that lonely Virginia road for a long time. I didn't touch him, I was in shock. The smell of blood and death was everywhere. All I could hear was the sound of my own breathing, and the wind whispering through the naked trees.

Finally, just as the sun was beginning to set, a car came along and pulled over. A man wearing a business suit and dress coat got out. "My God, are you all right?"

I nodded. I was sore and sticky with sweat, and bruised and scratched, but, amazingly, otherwise unharmed.

"He's dead, isn't he?" He didn't go near the body. The pool of blood around Seth's head was immense.

I nodded, and started to blubber. "We had an accident, he was going too fast, there was a truck, I *thought* there was a truck, maybe there wasn't . . ."

Another car came along soon, followed by a squadron of police, then the paramedics, who covered the body with a sheet, and looked at my cuts and bruises.

"You were wearing that?" One of the paramedics motioned to the helmet, which was still lying on the grass.

I nodded.

"Smart girl," he said, then looked at my hands and my lip again. "None of this looks too serious. But you really have to go to the hospital. You might have internal injuries."

"Please, I just want to go home." Mostly I didn't want them to call my parents.

They insisted I go, and they put me into the ambulance to take me to a local hospital, where a balding doctor who reminded me of my grandfather examined me, put a stitch in my lip, then called my parents, after all. I listened while he told them what had happened. He assured them I was okay, then handed the phone to me.

Charlotte was hysterical, ready to drop everything and come.

"Please, I'm fine. Julie will take care of me, I only have a few cuts and bruises. One stitch on my lip. Don't come."

After the concern came the questions. "What were you doing on a motorcycle? Why were you going so fast? Don't you have any sense? Are you stupid?"

I agreed with everything Charlotte said, including the part about being stupid, and managed to convince her that I'd learned some kind of a lesson and wouldn't do it again. When I hung up, the same policeman came in and questioned me again about the accident, then drove me back to campus. It was almost ten o'clock by the time we got to the dorm.

Julie and Angela were sitting on Julie's bed, playing chess, the Beatles' "White Album" blasting on the stereo. As far as Julie was concerned, the "White Album" was the most important music ever composed. Listening to "While My Guitar Gently Weeps" was a religious experience for her.

"Dinah! What happened?"

I started to cry. Julie turned the stereo down and rushed over. She hugged me—gently. Angela got a cold compress, and Julie patted my face with it.

Julie and I had argued about Seth that morning. I told her about the poem he'd sent, though I didn't let her read it. Poetry or not, she said, there was something seriously wrong with him.

"He *died,* Jules. He died."

She held me in her arms and tried to soothe me.

Now, between sobs, I explained what had happened, while she sat with me on my bed.

"Sounds to me like he was trying to kill you *both,* Dinah." She had her arm around me.

"No, I don't believe that. Why would he do that?"

"Because he was a sick son of a bitch."

The next day a D.C. policeman came to see me in my dorm room. He asked me how long I'd been seeing Seth Lucien, then said, "We checked with the university registrar. He was never registered in school here."

"I don't understand," I said. "What about his classes?"

"Did he go to classes?"

Had he? I always assumed he had a full load of classes. But I'd never actually seen him walk into any class except Grunwald's. And now that I thought about it, I'd never seen him write a paper, or study for a test, or even refer to another class. All he ever did was read—maybe not for class, after all—and write.

"Last semester he was in my poli-sci class. With Professor Murray Grunwald."

"He wasn't registered for it," the policeman said. "He wasn't carrying anything that would help us get in touch with his relatives, there's nothing in his apartment. Didn't even have driver's license. Do you have any idea where he was from?"

I told them I didn't have a clue.

The police came back one more time a week later. They couldn't identify him, they said, and since no one had come forward to claim the body, they asked if I wanted to take possession of it for burial. I told them I was sorry, I couldn't.

I spent the rest of the school year in a major depression, but I didn't want to call Dr. Lowe because then I'd have to tell my parents, since I didn't have any money to pay her. I finally went to the school counseling office, where I saw a tall, hulking young graduate student named Lloyd, who tried, though we never really made a connection. Nevertheless, I somehow managed not to flunk out.

My spirits began to lift a bit that summer, when Julie and I got jobs at Camp Pequot. I didn't go near a male all summer long, but in the fall of our sophomore year I started dating a pre-med student named David Lester. He was a redhead, too, strapping, serious, rather sweet, and kind of dull. And Julie fell in love.

He was the perfect guy, she kept telling me and our sophomore roommates, Sally Weiner and Alicia Parker. "Adorable, really. Fun and funny, and he isn't always stoned." She looked meaningfully at me. "He doesn't have to smoke pot to have a good time. And he respects the fact that I can't." There was just one problem. "My mother's gonna kill me if I marry an Irish Catholic." She was already thinking marriage.

Oh, and he was sexy, too, an amazing kisser. And a great body, he was an athlete, a swimmer.

I didn't meet this paragon until she'd been dating him for a month. She brought him to a bar on M Street one night, to a table where I was sitting with Sally and David. Julie had her arm draped around his waist. He *was* adorable. And I recognized him.

"Hey, didn't we meet once last year?" he said when she introduced him.

"In line at registration."

He nodded, flashing his contagious smile. "I remember. You were dropping things, I was doing my Sir Galahad routine. How'd I do?"

"For a male chauvinist, you got an A."

The smile again, this time with dimples. "That's fantastic. Brings up the old GPA. Definitely in need of some help in that department." He shook David's hand and helped Julie find a seat.

"Isn't he the greatest?" Julie said when Sam and David went for a round of beers.

He was.

Over the Christmas break, Julie and Sam, David and I drove up to Killington, Vermont, for a skiing week with Sally and her boyfriend Greg. The six of us rented a cabin. Sam was the only real skier among us. Tom Galligan had taught Sam and his brothers and sister to ski when they were just toddlers, and had taken them skiing five or six times a year since then.

Sam skied with us in the mornings, then went off by himself to do more challenging terrain after lunch. Early in the afternoon of the second day, I made a wrong turn off the Great Eastern run and ended up at the bottom of the Needle's Eye run. Sam was in the lift line.

"Where's everybody, Dinah?"

"I lost them, I'm afraid."

"Needle's Eye is perfect today. Want to try it?"

"I can't ski with you," I said. "I'm practically still snowplowing. You're an expert."

"Expert compared to what? Besides, I saw you ski and you've got great potential. Sounds to me like those guys told you I was a bully. Not guilty!" He pulled his ski hat down over his eyes, made a dopey lopsided face with his lips.

I laughed.

"See. I'm perfectly harmless."

I looked up at the steep intermediate run.

"It's really not that hard," Sam said. "And it's nice and wide. I can give you lots of pointers. I'm very good on giving pointers, just not so good on getting them."

We took the lift up together. He skied in front of me, sometimes backward, coaxing, helping me with my form. About midway down I started to feel comfortable and picked up speed, cruising at a faster clip than I'd ever gone before.

He was waiting for me as I passed by. "See, I told you! Dinah Rosenberg wins the gold."

That was when I hit a patch of ice, lost my balance, and went down. I thought I would never stop tumbling down that hill. Worse, for some reason my ski didn't release. Over and over I went, my leg and foot twisting around at unnatural angles, until I finally landed in a heap about twenty feet farther down the slope, my right ski still attached to my boot.

Then Sam was bending over me. "Dinah, I'm so sorry."

"It's not your fault, I'm the one who fell." I was trying not to cry, my ankle was throbbing cruelly but I didn't want him to think I was a baby. I started to get up but the pain was unbearable. I groaned.

He put his hand on my shoulder. "You're not going to move until the ski patrol gets here." While I rocked and groaned, he released the binding on my ski and crossed the pair upright in the snow so no one would plow into us.

He sat down beside me in the snow. "Maybe I should do penance for this. My mother would be ashamed of me if I didn't, considering it was my fault."

I looked at him. "Your mother's religious, is she?"

He slapped his thigh and laughed. "Religious? My mother could teach the Pope a thing or two. Her parents didn't name her Mary for nothing."

"Well, go ahead. I've never seen anyone do penance before."

"You're kidding."

"You're talking about a formal prayer, like with a rosary? I'm afraid rosaries were in short supply in my house. Charlotte had pearls."

He cocked his eyebrows. "You call your mother Charlotte?"

"It's a long story."

"Well, all the same, I'd better get this penance right if you've never heard one before. 'HailMaryfullofgrace . . .'" He said the words of the prayer faster than I'd ever heard anyone say anything.

"Sounds like you've said that a few times."

"A few million. I was always fast, but my brother Aiden, now I once clocked him at two seconds on my Spiderman watch. Look, my penance did do something."

"What?"

He smiled. "Got you to stop moaning."

Eventually the ski patrol put me on a gurney and wrapped me in a blanket to take me to the bottom. Sam skied down alongside this embarrassing little procession, went with me to the hospital, waited with me for the X rays. He kept telling me stories and jokes while we sat in the waiting room, got me laughing until my side hurt more than my ankle. Finally the doctor came over and told me it was just a sprain.

"Boy, don't I feel stupid," I said.

"I'm afraid I have the lock on that department," Sam said, making a sheepish face.

I had to have a cast anyway. And for the next few days I sat immobilized in the lodge or in the cabin feeling sorry for myself even though everyone, particularly Sam, made it a point to spend at least a little time with me, and waited on me hand and foot. Sam brought me a little gold statue he'd found in one of the novelty shops. "Ski Bunny of the Year." Along with that I received a Sam Galligan original, penned in his freewheeling hand: "Roses are red, violets are purple, I'll take my forty lashes now, with a wet nurdle."

On New Year's Eve we all went out to a bar called The Wobbly Barn. They had a live band that night, very good, very loud, and we were all having a great, raucous time, laughing and talking and dancing. David loved to dance, and I was on crutches, and that left Sam and me sitting alone together whenever David and Julie were dancing. Every time I caught Sam looking at me across the table, I looked away. Every time I looked at him, he did the same.

Being with Sam made me feel clean again, happy, hopeful—and smitten. I tried to tell myself I was mistaken, it was just the good time, a few drinks, but I knew I was lying to myself. I also knew my friendship with Julie wouldn't survive a second crisis.

"I'd like to sign your cast, Dinah," he said.

I lifted up my leg and put it on his knee. "Go ahead, everyone else has." I fished a pen out of my bag.

He rolled up the sleeves of his sun-faded flannel shirt and started to make a production out of signing, cracking his wrists, his hand poised over the cast. Then he looked up, straight into my eyes, and said, "I can't."

"Why not?"

"I'd have to write something no one else could see. It would have to be only for you."

"I don't think that's a good idea."

He handed me the pen.

I couldn't resist asking. "What would you have written, Sammy?" No one else called him Sammy. I started to right then.

He looked into my eyes. "Remember that old John Sebastian song? 'Do You Believe in Magic?' "

"Where are you, Dinah?" David asked me at some point during a bout of clumsy sex that night. "I'm here," I said. But I was thinking about Sam, wanting to make love with him, wanting to feel his lean body, his skin, him. I knew it would be slow, and tender, and passionate.

The next day, New Year's Day, I went back to sleep after everyone went out to hit the slopes.

"Dinah?"

Sam's voice. I opened my eyes. He was standing in the doorway, still wearing his parka.

He took a deep breath. "I should have asked you out last year," he said. "Then we wouldn't be in this mess."

Oh, God. If he'd asked me out then, he would have been my first and only. I'd never even have met Seth Lucien.

"What mess?"

He looked at me for a long time. "You know exactly what I'm talking about, Dinah," he said, and he came in.

That first time *was* passionate and tender, and thrilling, and full of sweet, dizzying joy. It was also dangerous. We knew we might be discovered at any moment, which made it twice as sexy, and I had that cast, which made it funny and awkward, too.

"I never knew," I said.

"Knew what?"

I kissed him. "How great, how intense, how . . ."

"Magical?"

"Yes." I laughed. "Magical. And fun—nobody ever even told me sex could be fun."

He nuzzled into my neck. "I love your neck, Dinah. Has anyone ever told you how beautiful it is? Just like a swan."

Well, no.

We laughed a lot, and we kept remarking on how we'd both known almost from the first moment at that bar on M Street. I didn't mention Seth Lucien, I didn't mention the accident. I never wanted to think about any of that again. And the wrenching subject of Julie? When it came up, and it did that morning, we were already dressed.

"What are we going to do?" he said.

"I don't know," I said. "I don't know."

I broke up with David as soon as we got back, and Sam broke up with Julie. She came back to the dorm after he told her and slammed her books down.

"How could he *do* this? Damn him!" She started to cry. "I was sure he liked me, I thought we would . . . Now I've been dropped—he thinks I'm getting too serious about him. Oh, Dinah, I can't unlove him."

"It *has* only been two months," I said weakly.

"I know, but he's the first guy who's ever made me feel . . . I mean, who treated me like a human being. How could he do this, Dinah? I felt so comfortable with him."

I stared at her. For me, it was far more than comfort. For me, being with Sam was like coming home.

"At least he's not in my class this semester," Julie said, "so I don't have to look at him every day." At least.

Sam and I had vowed to stay away from each other until Julie felt better and started dating again. We'd meet surreptitiously, but never anyplace where we were alone, much less where there was a bed. My desire to be with him burned brighter and hotter with each passing day.

About a month later, on a cold February day, we spent a few hours together, poking around Georgetown, our conversation returning again and again to Julie. "Maybe if I just tell her I want to go out with you casually," I said, "like it's no big deal, she might be able to accept it that way."

"I have a feeling no matter what you do it's going to turn out badly, Dinah."

I huddled into my coat. "If I handle it right, maybe it won't."

"Maybe *I* should talk to her again," he said. "Don't think you're the only one who feels guilty about this. And stupid, too." He grinned. "Never thought of myself as a heartbreaker."

Without breaking stride, I linked my arm through his, leaned over and kissed him. "Well, you are."

Julie did seem to be calming down. She'd even had a few dates. That night, I cornered her as she came into the dorm room.

"I ran into Sam today."

"You did?" Her pale eyes blazed hopeful. "What did he say?"

"We had a cup of coffee."

"And?"

"And nothing. He's a nice guy."

"Did you tell him how upset I am?"

"Seems like you're starting to get over it."

"Do you think . . . does he still have feelings for me?"

"He feels terrible that he hurt your feelings."

She put her books down, took off her coat and pitched it at her desk. "Big deal, he feels terrible. Time to get out my violin."

I took a breath. "Jules? Would you mind terribly if I went out with him? As a friend, I mean."

She stared at me for a long moment, studying my face. "What?" she said finally.

"You know. Like a friend." I sounded less convincing by the second.

"This is me, Dinah. Julie." She dropped down on her bed. "I don't believe this."

"We couldn't help it, Julie. I never meant for this to happen." I started to cry, and sat down on my own bed.

"Dinah!" She glared at me from across the room. "You are such a devious shit. How could you do this?"

"You're so important to me, Julie, you're the last person on earth I want to hurt. You've been my friend through everything."

"You know what, Dinah?" She came over to my bed and hovered, her pale, freckled complexion mottled with rage. "I've been your friend, but you have never been mine. Not since high school, maybe not even before that."

"That's not true, I love you."

"Oh, right. Seth Lucien comes along, and it's bye-bye, Julie. So then I finally meet someone really great, someone I really fall for, and along comes Dinah, and it's bye-bye, Julie again, tough shit, Jules. Never mind that we've known each other since we were six years old. Never mind that it was your idea that we go to the same university. If this is your idea of friendship, I feel sorry for your friends."

"I'm sorry, I'm sorry. I'd never do this if it weren't so . . . it's just that what Sam and I have is . . . a once-in-a-lifetime thing." I wasn't sure it *was* a lifetime thing. I thought it was. I hoped.

"Once in a lifetime? Excuse me? You've already been to bed with him, haven't you?" Her eyes were on fire, as hot as her hair.

I got up, I couldn't bear it.

"When? Tell me *when.*"

"Only once. What's the difference?"

"You know what?" she said. "You're right. There *is* no difference."

Our third roommate, Sally, had walked in during this last round. Only a few weeks ago she'd been devastated by a breakup herself. Julie looked at Sally, then back at me.

"I just hope you know who not to go to when he drops you, too, and moves on to the next." She walked out, and Sally followed her.

Julie stopped speaking to me. Sally wouldn't speak to me, either, and she told everybody who'd listen what a shit I was. As soon as the university found me a new room, which seemed to take forever, I moved to another dorm, Sam's dorm, in fact, and we were together constantly from then on. Whenever I ran into Julie on campus she turned away. Our college graduation was the last time I laid eyes on her.

Sam had graduated the previous year and gotten a job with a D.C. political ad agency. He and I were already engaged and, much to my parents' consternation, living together in blatant sin (as often as possible) in a small Washington apartment.

After the graduation ceremony, Sam, my brother, my parents, and I, in my cap and gown, were walking out of the stadium when we passed Julie with her parents and brother, posing for photographs in her cap and gown. It was a hot day, and Julie's hair was longer and wilder than ever, two fire and frizz puffs sticking out of either side of the mortar cap. Working up my nerve, I moved toward her to wish her good luck, but she saw me coming and spun around, giving us all a full view of her back. This little interchange didn't escape Charlotte's rapier eye.

"What in the world is wrong between you two?" Charlotte asked. My father, with his sixth sense for trouble between my mother and me, retreated, mumbling something about confirming our restaurant reservation.

I wasn't about to tell my mother that I'd betrayed and hurt the most important person in the world to me. "I don't want to talk about it, Charlotte."

"I was just asking. You and she were always as thick as thieves." She sighed. "Well, I guess that's what happens when you fall in love."

Now this was a typical Charlotte comment. My childhood had been punctuated by a litany of her clichés: "You don't wear white before June or after September"; "Men don't buy the milk if they can get the cow free"; and "Fabrics should be natural." (Except in recent years she'd amended it to "—unless they're one of those new *fabulous* polyesters.")

I would never have thought Charlotte might be right about one of my life's turns, certainly not about anything important, but I knew that Julie and I would never see each other again, and it *was* all because I had fallen in love.

I made a choice between my best friend and the man I hoped would be my husband. For all these years, it had seemed like the right choice.

sixteen

"The children need you," Sam said when he came back to the hospital. He was sitting in the chair next to me. He'd slept at home, and I'd folded up the reclining chair when the clock told me it was morning.

"You missed Kate's recital. They need you now. Alex and Kate."

"I know their names, Sam."

He looked over at Elijah. "I meant if you just go home for one night, it might reassure them. And you need to get out of here."

"Why?"

"Because you've been sitting here for seventeen days."

Seventeen days. The ghost's deadline was approaching.

"Do you think God is watching this, Sam?"

He shook his head, then lowered it, eyes closed. "I don't know."

"Are you praying?"

He sighed. "My mother's doing enough praying for everyone. I really think tonight you should go home. I'll stay here with our little guy."

I hadn't the will to say no.

I got home about 7:15 that evening. Poppy greeted me at the door, panting and jumping. My in-laws and my parents and Alex and Kate were already in the dining room. My mother-in-law had set the table with the tapestry mats and the good white china, as if by making my homecoming a festive occasion she could wipe out the reason I hadn't been coming home. Mary had also made a lamb roast, one of her specialties.

"We're so glad you're here," Tom said.

Charlotte kissed me. "You needed a break."

Is that what they thought this was? I kissed Alex and Kate, gave each of them a long hug. That was what I'd come home for, wasn't it?

"Sit down, sit down," Dad said. "Have something to eat."

I sat down in the empty chair, since Mary was in my seat. She spooned a serving of lamb onto my plate, smothered it with sauce, and reached over to set it in front of me. Poppy sat at my feet, looking at my plate with soulful eyes. I looked from the dog to my plate heaped with food and fought the urge to slip Poppy every bit of it.

"How is he?" It was Tom who finally asked.

"He's the same," I said.

Everyone was silent, even Mary. Except Tom, who kept asking Alex questions. "What sport are you playing, Alex?" Shrug. Basketball. "What position?" Shrug. Forward. "You like it?" Grunt. It's okay . . . "I hear you like math." Shrug. Teacher's an asshole. "I hear you're quite the baseball player." Frown. Shrug. Who cares?

Tom started in on Kate. "So, you scored thirteen hundred on the PSAT. That's quite a score."

Kate shrugged—was it catching?

We'd been waiting for her scores. I tried to be happy for her, I said I was proud of her. It sounded incredibly phony. I was no good to Alex and Kate without Elijah.

"Let's talk about something else," Kate said.

But we didn't. We went through the rest of the meal in virtual silence, forks clinking against the good china plates. I felt as if I had entered an alternate universe. Hospitals are so insulated and isolated and self-contained you can forget the rhythm of the outside world. You know only the hospital, only those walls, only this room and these doctors, nurses, machines. After a while you begin to feel the hospital's rhythm inside you like a new pulse beat, like a new heart. Being at home with my children was no longer normal. It was odd.

After dinner I tried to look over the mail but couldn't focus, then wandered from room to room and stood for a while in each of them, looking around. Den, dining room, living room. Finally I went into the kitchen, where Charlotte and Mary seemed to be engaged in a contest to see who could be the most helpful. I appreciated it. But Charlotte, doing dishes?

Indeed. She was standing at the sink, swirling water with a vegetable brush. "Oh, there you are, Dinah." She turned off the faucet, stripped off the Playtex gloves, dried her hands, then moved toward me, blood-red nails touching wisps of auburn hair at her neck. She seemed to have touched up the gray roots since I saw her the last time.

"Want some coffee?" She put her arm around me.

"No thanks." Charlotte hugging me? I pulled away.

She took a few steps back and began burrowing into a cabinet, straightening the spices. Charlotte, who barely knows nutmeg from a double boiler.

Mary filled me in on the status of the laundry, then moved on to who had called lately. Sam's boss, who'd visited a few days before. Friends. A few colleagues. Miss Stanakowski, Elijah's teacher. She and the children were making a card, she was praying for him every day.

I heard a tinny sound, a beat, from somewhere deep in the house. Probably Alex, holed up in his room with his earphones on.

I made my way through the front hall and stood at the foot of the staircase, listening. I realized I was standing just below the worn place in the carpet on the third step, the spot from which Alex used to jump until he was about seven, the spot from which he taught Elijah to jump. Elijah jumped down and down and down, over and over and over, until even Alex couldn't stand it anymore.

I climbed the stairs and stood in front of my son's door for a moment, looking at the poster of the skull and crossbones he had tacked on the door. It said, DO NOT ENTER UNDER PENALTY OF DEATH. HUMAN LIFE INSIDE. I wondered who makes all this paraphernalia of pop culture that takes death so casually, that plays so easily to the cynicism of teenagers, even teenagers seriously in danger of losing someone they love.

I knocked, and knocked again. Finally I turned the knob and opened the door. Poppy greeted me, panting and jumping. My son, all five feet eleven inches, one hundred forty-five pounds of him, was lying flat out on his bed, eyes closed, earphones on. There was a tinny beat, Nine Inch Nails at full volume, filtered through headphones.

I stepped over piles of clothing and sneakers and books, picking my way to his bed, then tapped him on the shoulder. He sat up, leaned over, and pressed the pause button on his CD player. "Don't you knock, Mom?"

I put my hands together to try to still them. How could I do this, deal with a son who despite everything was still what he was, a teenager?

"I did knock."

He shrugged. "Didn't hear you."

"How was your day? Did you take the bus home?"

He moved away from me. "We played basketball after school." He flipped the off button, took out the Nine Inch Nails CD and placed it in its jacket, thumbed through the CD wallet on his desk. Names like Megadeth, Narcotic Gypsies, and Metallica flashed by along with pictures of the performers, whose skin tended to be littered with demonic tattoos not unlike Seth's pentagram.

"You don't have to do this, Mom."

I willed my eyes to stop filling up. "Do what?"

"Keep up this front. Acting like everything's fine."

Would you like me to do what I really want to do, Alex? Shall I howl?

"I just wanted to come home to check up on you guys. That's all."

He shot me a sharp look. "Dad told you to come home. You wanted to be *there*."

"I want to be there when Elijah wakes up, yes. But I also wanted to make sure you guys are okay." Steady. Calm. He needed to think I was okay, then he'd be okay. But what if Elijah didn't make it? There'd be no making Alex think I was okay, because I wouldn't be okay. I wasn't okay now. The walking dead are not okay.

He pulled a Metallica CD out of the stack and popped it into the player, slammed it shut, and sank down onto the bed.

"Are you angry, Alex?"

His eyes filled with tears and he stood up again and moved over to his desk, stepping over piles. "Why the hell should I be angry?"

I felt so very tired. "Please, Alex." How could I handle this now?

"Please come here, Alex."

He looked at me for a moment through teary eyes, then he came over to the bed and sat down, allowed me to take his hands and sit down next to him.

"I'm angry, Alex. I guess you must be, too."

He looked at me, then the tears spilled over. "Dad keeps saying he's going to wake up, Mom. And the doctors. Everybody keeps saying it, but Elijah keeps not waking up."

I hugged him, patted his back. "I know, honey, I know." I was offering comfort on automatic pilot. There was nothing genuine about it.

When the moment was over, I knew I needed to sleep. I managed to tell him I loved him. As I left the room he put on his earphones, plopped back down on his bed, closed his eyes, and began tapping his feet and moving his hands as if he were playing the drums, all to some rhythm he alone heard.

I got in bed but couldn't sleep. How would I live in this house if Elijah died? What would I do with his books, and his Barney blanket, and his Sesame Street bedspread? And the purple Smurf boots from three sizes ago that I saw in the cubbies in the mudroom, and Addie's hand-painted chest? What would I do with his room, hack it off the house like the tough end of a stalk of asparagus?

Around three A.M. I got up and wandered around the house in my pajamas. I went into Alex's room. The quilt had fallen onto the floor and he was lying sprawled out across his bed. I listened. My son was breathing regularly, evenly. He was all right.

He drew a deep, satisfied breath in his sleep, some dream of love perhaps. Almost a year ago he'd abandoned pajamas for jockeys and a T-shirt. His legs were skinny, though just lately I could see that they were filling out a little. One thin arm cradled his head, the other hung down off the bed, fingertips brushing the floor.

His face was turned toward the window, hidden in shadow; a wedge of moonlight streamed across his torso. Someday the feel of that lanky body would give a young woman pleasure, just as his father's had given me, and that young woman would wind herself around my son and cling to him and hope and trust that he would be able to make everything all right. Until something like this. No. There was nothing like this.

Alex rolled over now on his side and drew his knees up to his chest, the floor and bed creaking under his weight. Without his blanket he looked skinny and adolescent and cold. I moved to cover him with the quilt but was stopped by a new vision.

I am sitting in the kitchen. It is morning. I am still in my bathrobe, drinking coffee. Alex appears in the doorway. He is several years older, he has filled out, he looks more like his father than ever. "When is it going to get better, Mom?"

"When is what going to get better?"

He shrugs. He turns away.

"You know when it'll get better, Alex?" I say. "It'll get better when I'm dead, too."

I say things like this, even to my son. I seek out the drop in the jaw, the white-lipped stare, need people's shock and dismay. I want them to have just the tiniest glimmer of this grief. Martyr. Martyr. Sam is sick to death of me. So am I.

"Mom!" In his room, back in the present, Alex sat up in his bed. "What are you doing?"

"Watching you sleep." Checking for life in the middle of the night. Imagining inconsolable grief.

"That is weird, Mom. Very weird."

I ended up sitting on the floor in the den, going through picture albums. I'd already gotten through most of them when I decided to put together an album of Elijah's life. Yes. I'd bring it to the hospital. If the nurses and the doctors had some idea of the way his smile lit up a whole room, maybe they'd try harder.

I took all but three baby pictures out of his album, which had red and green and blue blocks painted on the cover and *ELIJAH* stamped underneath the blocks. It held only twenty pictures, and I chose the remaining seventeen carefully: Elijah sitting on Alex's shoulders in front of Lake Winnipesaukee; Elijah standing in front of the piano, banging away; Elijah with his pants bunched around his ankles—he was two, he hadn't noticed his pants had fallen down.

I took the album to Elijah's room, sat in the rocking chair, and rocked and cried. Eventually I slept, in the same bed where I had found my son seizing. Someone had changed the sheets, Mary probably.

When I awoke, I went into my bedroom, opened the overnight bag, took out the last batch of clothing Kate had brought to the hospital, replaced it with clean things. It occurred to me that I had not washed my hair in seventeen days, though I'd used the shower in the parents' room outside the PICU. Now I got in my own shower and washed my hair. When I came out, the phone was ringing. I grabbed a towel and looked at the bedside clock. Seven A.M.

"Dinah? This is Lucia Orsini. Your daughter has been part of some gang behavior I think you ought to know about."

"Kate?"

"Yesterday morning, one of the girls threw a bucket of water in Allison's locker and soaked her gym clothes."

"*Kate* did this?"

"One of them did."

"I'll talk to her, Lucia. But maybe the kids should work things out for themselves. They're almost sixteen."

"Dinah, this is gang behavior. Last week they all threw snowballs at Allison."

"Maybe she's been doing something the others haven't liked."

"Allison would never do anything unless someone did it to her first. Allison is *always* telling me about something Kate did to her."

"Like what?" My knees gave out from under me and I sank into a chair.

"Like Kate is always calling to get homework from Allison. Then one time Allison called Kate for homework."

"Allison always calls here, Lucia."

"Not for homework. And this one time Kate gives her the homework, and then she says, 'You owe me big time.'"

I waited for a punch line that didn't come. "All the kids talk that way," I said finally.

"Well, *we* don't talk that way in *my* house."

What universe was she living in?

"Lucia," I said, "do you have any idea what's going on in my life?"

"Yes. Well, I'm very sorry about your son. But I thought you'd like to know."

"Fuck you, lady." I slammed the phone down.

"Mom, who was that?" Kate was standing in the bedroom doorway.

I couldn't handle this now. I just couldn't. "Wrong number."

"Oh. Is Elijah all right?"

"He's the same, Kate. I'm going back now. I'll see you tonight when you come."

"I was thinking of not coming tonight. Is that okay?"

She hadn't last night or the night before, either. Didn't she care? Of course she cared, she loved her little brother like crazy.

"Whatever you want, Kate. Come. Or don't come. Just tell Grandma and Grandpa."

"Which one?"

"Take your pick. Say goodbye to Alex for me, will you?"

I kissed her goodbye, hugged her, scooped up my dirty clothes, laid them on top of the washing machine, and left.

"Imagine it, Dinah." The ghost leaned forward from the backseat as I pulled out of my driveway. "You think it's going to get any easier? I don't *think* so. Imagine your life when your son is a vegetable. It goes on and on, the grief forever.

"Your practice is finished, your column over, your friends avert their eyes when they see you, they even cross the street. You're up every hour or so during the nights, thinking of your son lying there with his eyes that way. You get out of bed every morning at six. The last thing Sam says to you before he leaves for work is, 'When will it end, Dinah?' He thinks it's up to you. You give the children breakfast. No conversation—there never is."

"You are lying. All of this is a lie." My protests sounded weaker, even to me.

"Lying, am I? Why don't you drive up to Laurel and see it for yourself? Do it right now. Elijah's not going anywhere. Take Interstate 95 north instead of south."

I did as he said and went north. The ghost told me where to go.

"You do this drive daily for years and years. You have to follow the directions over and over before you can follow them without looking. Eventually, you will know every curve, tree, sign on the route. You play the same tape in the car during the ride, over and over. The voice on the tape is high and clear and the singer asks who will warm her soul. This music is undemanding, melodious, very beautiful actually. Not as beautiful as my own music, of course. Becky gave you the tape, and it's the only music you're capable of listening to. You play it when Sam drives there with you on the weekends.

"You have a lot of time to think in the car, and when the music can't stop the thoughts, you do sums to keep from thinking. You count hours. It's nearly a two-hour ride each way. You have been in the car a total of 4,337 hours, six minutes, forty-three seconds.

"You never look at the other children as you come into the main ward. They have their own mothers, even though you have never seen them. This is the twelve hundredth time you've been here, you tell Jane, the doctor. You visit. You stay for four hours each day. You go home and your other children are there."

"Alex and Kate!" I said. "They have names."

"You barely remember their names, you barely know they're alive. That's what they think. Alex never speaks a word, he loathes you, he goes off with his low-life friends to do drugs, anything he can get his hands on. Kate goes off to college in two years, relieved to go, but Alex will never go to college. Sam stays with you, tries to make up for you with the kids, pretends this is life. He finds what he can in affairs."

"Affairs?"

"Honey, you are whistling 'Dixie' if you think a man is going to put up with this for *years.*" He whistled to emphasize the point.

"Sam will."

"Well, now, let's just wait and see." His laugh bounced around the car.

I looked in the rearview mirror, but I saw only the reflection of the road disappearing behind me. I looked away.

"Why are you so cruel?"

I could feel him move closer to me, murmur into my ear. "When you are getting ready for bed every night, Sam asks, 'How was he today?' He no longer speaks your son's name, this husband of yours. You detest the sight of him. The feeling is mutual."

I knew this hating had already begun.

"Every night, you look at the clock. It is 11:10 P.M. You will be lying beside Sam for five hours, fifty minutes . . . three hundred fifty minutes . . . twenty-one thousand seconds. This is the way your mind has to work. If you don't count numbers, you'll get your thoughts stuck in a circle again, start praying for miracles again. The circles drive you mad."

We had arrived. I'd expected a kind of asylum: old brick, gothic spires, a huge foreboding place set high on a hill with small narrow windows. As I pulled to a stop, I saw it was nothing like that. This flat red brick structure with its multitude of huge windows was so new that the construction trailer was still on the property. A stand of laurel surrounded a small monument in the center of the driveway.

I got out of the car, walked past a receptionist, followed the arrows to pediatrics. There were two sides to the common area, each with a row of beds, and in each of the beds some mother's nightmare. Most of the children seemed to be at least somewhat conscious. About half had tubes running into their stomachs or noses. Some were sitting up.

"But I thought if Elijah didn't get the tube in his stomach they wouldn't take him."

"Too bad, someone made a mistake," the ghost said.

I walked through, heard their stories from the ghost: Suzie had been hit by a car, her eyes followed as we passed; Chris had a degenerative disorder, he gave us a weak smile. And in the corner, we came to TJ, who had drowned, and Louisa, who had seizures. It was hard to tell how old they were, propped up in their wheelchairs, limbs twisted inward, eyes bulging, rotating tick tick tick, bodies puffy and bloated. Immobile as rocks. Stone children.

"This is what happens after a very long time when people are in a true vegetative state, Dinah. They all start to look the same."

I looked from one to the other, TJ to Louisa. He was right, they did look the same.

"In the morning the staff moves TJ and Louisa from the bed to the bean bag in front of the television. This is called playtime. At noon they have a bath. Then they move them into the sunlight, not that they can feel the sun on their faces. Oh yes. The staff takes very good care of them. Exercises their limbs and creams their skin and massages their muscles, so they won't be too atrophied, so they won't get sores. They look pretty good, too. They look more alive than me, don't you think?" He puffed himself out, imitating them. "Pretty lifelike, wouldn't you say? Considering TJ's been here for six years, and Louisa's been here for eight. You say *I'm* cruel."

A small picture of a toddler was tacked on a bulletin board in back of TJ. "But why don't they turn off the machines?"

"Watch that loose talk, Dinah. Will *you?* Summer will turn into fall and winter and spring and then fall will come again. And again. And again."

"How long?" I whispered.

"Eight years," he said.

I recoiled in the definitive wake of this. A sound came from my mouth, half moan, half gasp, as I tried to make myself comprehend it. No. I could not listen for another moment to my future laid out like this. I retreated back toward the entrance.

On the way out, I passed by a bed where a tiny woman in a white hospital coat, with dark hair cut boyishly short, was tending a young Down syndrome boy with a breathing problem. I froze in mid-stride, unable to turn away as she adjusted his breathing machine, stroked his forehead, touched that boy with those tiny hands, as tenderly as if he were her own child. After a few moments, he began breathing more easily, and she stood up. She saw me then, an anonymous voyeur in the place where they send you when there's nothing left to do with you.

"I'm Dr. Jane. Can I help you?" Her voice was high-pitched, like a child's voice. "That's what everyone calls me, anyway. You're not one of our parents, are you?"

"No, I—"

"Do I know you?" She looked at me as if she thought she should.

I shook my head and fled.

seventeen

From then on, the ghost was in the NAR with me every minute, night and day, lounging, strumming, taunting. "You're running out of time," he kept saying. "The Angel is coming. Can't you hear it, Dinah?"

Once, out of the corner of my eye, I thought I saw something hovering over another child's bed, but when I looked directly at it there was nothing to see but air.

Becky had come faithfully almost every afternoon, but her husband, Mark, had visited only once, and stayed for only a few minutes. He wouldn't look at Elijah, his eyes dart-darted, just the way Dr. Moore's did. I wondered about some of our other friends, the Magills, the Stuarts. They'd called, sent food over to the house, but they hadn't come. By the twentieth day, Becky, Addie, and a friend and colleague named Grace Atkinson were the only friends of mine who'd actually shown up in person. I'd missed a lunch date with Grace, which prompted her to call. During her visit, she said things therapists say, words meant to be empathetic and validating. I was glad when she left.

"No one cares," the ghost said. " That's why none of your other friends have come."

"They just can't take it, they don't want to intrude."

"Poor, deluded Dinah. Haven't I already shown you it's *you?*"

But Becky came, handed me the music tape I expected her to give me, some notes and letters she'd picked up at the house that I shuffled through as if they were playing cards. I couldn't read them, but one letter caught my eye when I saw the return address. As soon as Becky left, I opened the letter.

Julie Bronstein Lasker
142 Bolinger Road
Slatesville, New York

Mrs. Dinah Rosenberg Galligan
c/o Connecticut *Star*

Dear Dinah,

Last week my mom ran into Lillian Chumley at a movie theater in Ft. Lauderdale. Remember Lillian? She used to work at your mother's first shop in Great Neck. Remember, she replaced Bea Stern, the one you got fired? My mother knew Lillian too, from a bridge game they both played in before my parents moved to Florida. You know how people always pass on bad news. So I heard that your son is very ill.

Dinah, I know we haven't seen each other in over twenty years, more than half our lives. I was nineteen and hurt over a boy—what can I say? But I just wanted to let you know now that my heart aches for you and I haven't been able to stop thinking about this since I heard, even though I don't know anything about what happened to your son. All Lillian knew was that he's five and it's very serious. She didn't even know his name.

I've thought about you all these years, not just now. Once I realized how unimportant what happened between us turned out to be in my own life, and how important it was in yours, I thought about calling you but always put it off. I was afraid it would be awkward and you'd be angry that I let it end what would have been a lifelong friendship between us. I know you didn't mean to hurt me. I sort of admire you for being so certain about *anything* back then.

In my own way I've kept in touch. And the last few years, my brother, who lives in Connecticut, too, sent me your columns from the Connecticut *Star.* It doesn't surprise me that you became a writer. I loved the columns, Dinah, they were just as I remember you: funny and cynical and incisive, sometimes even wise.

I didn't want to call your mother, which is why I sent this letter through the newspaper offices. They wouldn't give me your address but said they'd forward it. I'm not exactly sure what I want to say except that I hope your son gets well very soon. I am praying for you, and for him. And, too, I hope that you have many caring, giving people all around you, and that Sammy is everything you wanted him to be, even through this. I hope your other child (or children) are some comfort. I know you have at least one other child, a girl, because of the column "Sock Monsters and other Female Problems," where you mentioned her. I hope especially that you have at least a few extraordinary friends, women (or men) of depth and honesty who are worthy of you, who are capable of real compassion, and who aren't failing you.

I hope all this for you, Dinah. My son Robert had to have a heart operation when he was an infant. Those few weeks when I thought I might lose him were unspeakable. Please forgive me for not being there for you when you may need me. I think about calling all the time now.

I lost my dad a few years ago. I grieved deeply, and I miss him very much, but I know that losing one of my children . . . well, I can only imagine how you're suffering. My children's names are Robert, Melissa, and Lauren. They are the light of my life. I've missed you and I want to know about everything: your work, your marriage, your friends, your children, what you think, what you've learned, and most especially, how you are coping.

It makes me sad, Dinah, that you have a son and you're in danger of losing him already, and that I don't even know his name.

With all my love,
Julie

Elijah, I whispered into Elijah's ear, my lips to his fragile skin. His name is Elijah, Julie.

"Who's that from, Dinah?" Charlotte had shown up with Dad after Becky left. Now they were back after getting a cup of coffee downstairs.

"Julie." I folded up the letter. "Her mother ran into Lillian Chumley, who told her about Elijah. Bad news travels fast."

"Dinah, you've got to try to be as optimistic as you can."

"Why?"

"I'm sure she was just trying to be supportive, Dinah. You two were practically glued together as kids. I always liked her."

No, she hadn't. She always said Julie was a bad influence on me, though it was more the other way around. But it didn't surprise me she remembered it this way. Anyway, that was another lifetime. I leaned over and put my cheek to Elijah's hand.

"It was a long time ago," I said, but I slept for an hour or so that night, clutching Julie's letter, hoping to dream of forgiveness, dreaming only of pain.

"I have to get out of here for a little while," Sam said the next morning, shortly after he got back from his run.

Where else was there to go?

"Just to the office for an hour or so," he said.

"The office, the moon, the office, the moon," the ghost whispered, making a noise like the clanking of bones.

"What about Elijah's EEG?" He'd already had two EEGs.

"It's scheduled for this afternoon. I'll be back before then."

The EEG technician was a tall, muscular black man wearing blue, a blue coat, blue cap. He attached electrodes to Elijah's head, smeared the red curls with goop he squeezed out of a tube, all the while sighing and shaking his head, then he went back into his booth and turned on the machine.

I heard it humming, electronic noises, bells and gongs. I saw the light switch on and off. Elijah lay there, still, silent, gooped, illuminated.

I looked through the window of the technician's little booth and thought I saw him sigh. Turning off his machine, he began to check the readout, folding page over page, neatly. I stood up, went into his booth, and looked over his shoulder at the continuous black line, dipping and cresting across the long page. Were the peaks and valleys still too shallow for a normal EEG?

"What does this mean?" I asked him.

The technician ripped the page from the machine. "I'm sorry. You have to discuss it with the doctor."

"Well, you know what *that* means," the ghost said.

Did I? Could the technician be just following the damned rules? No. No one could be that cruel, not to reassure me if it were normal. I tried to bypass the ghost and speak directly to God. Don't You see this? Don't You see what's going on? Can't You do something? I'll be good, I promise. I'll be good.

But I didn't hear God respond.

"You're running out of time," said my demon ghost.

Back in Elijah's room, the social worker poked her head in the door.

"May I come in?" She closed the door softly behind her, and went to Elijah's bed. She took his hand and began to stroke it.

"How is he?"

"No change," I said.

"Where's your husband?"

"He said he was going to the office." I laughed.

She said, "Be gentle with each other, Mrs. Galligan. Men and women cope very differently."

What language was she speaking?

I took the elevator to the ground floor and headed for the little shop in the lobby, scanned the array of Mars bars, Twinkies, T-shirts, paperback books, and magazines, a shelf sparsely stocked with an assortment of medicines, a middle-aged woman clerk. It could have been any shop anywhere except for the glass display case of flower arrangements in the corner, and my ghost, hovering above the stuffed animals, flapping huge wings—he had assumed the shape and color of one of the animals in the display, Big Bird. Long yellow feathers ruffling, long orange beak opening and closing.

"Miss? Can I help you?"

Miss? She did not realize how old I was. I was old, very old. I asked for the brand of cigarettes I'd smoked before quitting seventeen years ago. I had definitely come a long way, baby.

"I'm sorry. We don't sell cigarettes. It's a hospital."

Oh. Right.

I headed out to the street entrance. I didn't have a coat. I'd forgotten it was winter.

Everything seemed to be going so fast out here, cars whizzing by, people rushing along. I looked around. Two hospital workers in blue coats were standing under the awning, smoking. I extracted a cigarette from one of them, who seemed vaguely annoyed that I needed a light, too. I retreated to the other side of the doors, closed my eyes, and inhaled until it hurt my lungs, and I felt woozy. When I opened my eyes, the ghost was next to me in the cold, back to Seth, in jeans, leather jacket, boots. He was smoking his own cigarette. He cast no shadow on the ground.

"Listen," he said. "Look. And see the end."

I am in that place again, the Laurel Institute, with the bright cheery walls and the tender Dr. Jane. I have been coming here daily for years. I am sitting on the bed next to Elijah. He is bigger now, taller at least, quiet and stiff, back arched, mouth open. His eyes are quivering in their sockets. I look at the respirator, watch the bulb inside the tube inflate, deflate.

Whoosh and pump. I want to take the loathsome machine apart, piece by piece, the bulb and the tube, every gear, crank, and computer chip, and smash them all, grind it all into dust.

I notice there's a second IV line. I hear a whistling sound from Elijah's chest.

Jane comes in. Elijah needs a dressing, he needs to be turned, he needs an adjustment of the feed, he needs. It takes so much effort to keep him alive.

She moves Tuddy to the bottom of the bed, places her palm with its tiny fingers on his forehead, smoothes back his hair, the silk that has now turned to straw, touches his other hand, holds it. His hands are now rigid, like claws. She listens to his lungs.

"What's this?" I point to the second line. My voice is altered. I sound like a machine when I speak, and I cannot speak louder than a whisper.

"He's got pneumonia again, Dinah. I can start him on another course of antibiotics, if you want me to."

With her tiny hands she keeps doing my bidding, saving him. "I guess I should call Sam." She stands aside while I go to the phone.

"Why are you asking me, Dinah?" Sam says. "You know what I think."

"I hate you, Sam." I hang up and turn to face Jane. "Give him the antibiotics."

I go back to him, sit down in the rocking chair, and watch while she sets up the new medicine. "It's amazing that you can come in here and grieve the way you do," she says.

Grieve? This is not grieving, this is atonement (for what I cannot even remember), this is hell, the living death. I have no more tears, I am sick to death of my tears, of my own skin. My eyes are as dry as bones. And Jane is just trying to be nice. No one can be nice to me. I hate them for being nice.

"Most of our parents don't ever come," she says.

"Why not?"

Jane sighs. "People deal with tragedies like this in different ways. For some people the only way they can deal with it is not to deal with it."

"What about the two in the corner? TJ and Louisa."

"I really can't talk about individual patients, Dinah," she says.

Right. At Easter there's always something of a crowd. Perhaps they expect resurrection. "Then why . . . I mean, they just leave them here?"

"Some of our parents say their religion won't let them turn off the machines."

"Is it up to the parents?"

She sighs. "Who else?"

Who else, indeed?

"I can tell you this, Dinah," Jane says. "I have not seen Elijah make any responses that are purposeful. His brain stem is functional, barely, and that's about all. My opinion is he's vegetative. We can keep him alive, for some period of time, I don't know how much longer, but he will never recover, never be any different than he is right now."

I cannot even look at him anymore. She has not said this so directly before.

"I'm sorry," she says. "Would you like another doctor's opinion?"

The vision moves forward: Now I am in my own bedroom, getting ready for bed. Sam, naked, is pulling on his pajama bottoms. We have not made love in years.

"I went to see Father Tamari this morning," I say. I'd sat with him on a pew in front of a huge gory crucifix; he gave me a booklet about the five stages of grief.

"What for?"

"I just wanted to see what the Catholic Church would say. Don't you even want to know? You were raised in it."

Sam picks up the glass of scotch he's been nursing from the night table, and shakes the glass so that the ice tinkles. Tinkle Tinkle. Oh. Those chimes.

"So what did he say?"

"I talked to him for an hour or so. He was very nice, very sympathetic."

Sam takes another gulp. "Big deal."

"He said the Church believes in the sanctity of life."

He looks at me. "Yeah, this is *real* sanctified, Dinah. You suddenly planning to become a priest? Look. Dr. Angus said it. We are not pioneers here."

Wrong. I feel like a woman who's set out in a covered wagon with her young husband, looking for a place to call her own, bearing her children along the way, and burying them along the way, too. That woman would not have had to make this choice. Her choice would have been already made.

"I know."

Sam moves to wrap his arms around me. I cannot bear it and I duck so that he is left reaching for air.

"Dinah, we have to do this," he says. "You went to see Rabbi Leiberman last week. He supported it."

Temple Beth Elohim. The rabbi's office so cozy and lined with books, so many books, and the rabbi, with his glasses and neatly trimmed beard. "Not *every* rabbi would support it," I say.

"Suddenly you're worried about what the ultra-Orthodox would say?" He sighs, and sits down on the bed. "You can't expect that everyone in the world would support this, Dinah. But Jane supports it. This new neurologist supports it. The courts would support it. When, Dinah? Two more years? Five?"

In two more years I will have bought Elijah two new sets of clothes, in five years, five new sets. They dress the stone children every day, they pretend this is life. In two years he will be twelve, fifteen, then twenty. I will be fifty-one, fifty-four, then fifty-nine.

"Dinah, you have to let go," Sam says. "He's almost ten years old now. This is killing us. This is killing *you*."

"Fine. Maybe that's for the best. But that's no reason to kill *him*." I am the living dead.

"*Kill him*? I'd like to kill that Moore for saying that. Besides, all he meant was that we should wait. We waited. As far as I'm concerned, there is no other moral decision, Dinah. We can't just leave him there like this forever."

I look down at my hands. "He's my son. You haven't read a single book on the subject."

"He's my son, too. You've read a hundred and you still can't bring yourself to do what needs to be done." He shakes the glass again, looks down into it. "I just can't be in this every minute of every day the way you are."

It's the only way I can be.

He downs the rest of the scotch and says into the glass, "Someone has to pay the bills."

"Are you saying you think I should go back to work?" My work isn't like his work. The living dead don't have great stores of wisdom to dish out to patients. I can't write really amusing little columns about my vegetable son.

"I want you to do whatever you feel you can," Sam says, and stands up again.

"He doesn't mean it," the ghost says, his voice drifting like ether into the vision. "He's sick to death of you. He's got a new girlfriend. He's thinking of leaving you."

"If we went back to Moore now, even he'd agree. Even your mother and father—"

"You talked about this with Charlotte?"

"Dinah, I'm sorry, your mother only wants what's best."

"Yeah, well, it's not up to her. *Your* mother wouldn't support it."

"I haven't asked her, Dinah. I don't care what she thinks, I know what's right. And you won't make a decision, you won't be logical."

"I don't want to be logical. I want my son back." I turn away, not wanting him to see the tears that are always a surprise when they come.

Round and round. Usually when I cry, Sam puts his arms around me, or tries to. This time, he stands with his arms at his sides. He reaches for his drink again. "Yeah, well, that isn't your son. And you can't have him back. It's time enough. You've got to face it. We've both got to face it. Dinah, what he is now isn't living. It isn't right. It's crazy. Let him go."

Forward, this accursed vision: Elijah is thirteen years old. His body is drenched in sweat and again raging with fever. I am standing by his bed, watching Jane and the nurses huddle over him, suction him, adjust all the tubes and machines. I can hear the rattle in his throat, in his chest. The machine pump-whooshes, pump-whooshes, and still his color is bluish. He isn't getting enough air, and the machine is at full throttle.

"His lungs are failing." Jane is very calm. She is tap-tapping his skin, looking for another vein to put back the IV antibiotic drip.

"*Turn it off,*" I whisper. "Turn it off."

Jane withdraws the tube from his mouth, then herself from the room.

I am surprised by the moment of death. I expect something very different, maybe that he will look at peace, finally. He doesn't look at peace. Elijah breathes for a moment, then opens his mouth for the next breath, and then he stops. It is quick. His mouth goes slack. His arms are curled in like claws and his head is grotesque.

Sam goes out to tell them. Jane comes in and examines him and says it's over. She hugs each of us. "You did everything you could," she says.

Oh yes.

The hospital chaplain comes into the room and we all hold hands around his bed over his body, and she says words and thanks God for Elijah's life. But words mean nothing to me. Words are no comfort, none at all.

They leave us alone with him again. I place my face next to his face, my cheek to his cheek, I lift his shirt, touch the skin on his belly with my fingertips. I touch his fingers, his feet, his toes, and I stay with him long after his skin has turned cold, fighting to remember his smell. There was once a time when he smelled like a little boy, not like this. I can't even conjure up the memory of that.

Sam touches my arm. I know he is trying to offer solace, but he cannot. No one can. To all would-be comforters I retort: *I am a clobbered egg, ex-orb exploded, white shard in your eye. It hurts, there there. This once perfect sweet rot threaded with bloodeous black. Glutinous maximus, dripping all over the imported linen, sticky on the gold-rimmed china. Soiled with eight years of the grotesque, now with the muck of my child's grave. There with my child, so cold. I sweat this stuff in your face, placid and complacent as a baby's toes. I yield up nothing you want. No angel wings, no down for your bed, no meat.*

I was vacuum-zipped and whisked back into the circle in front of the hospital, where the ghost stood puffing on a cigarette, a rolling IV pole standing at his shoulder like a guard. He was wearing his patient getup: speckled hospital gown, black leather jacket over it, and mud-caked boots. Those stick-thin legs seemed made of something aeons old and rubbed smooth. And every exposed inch of skin, from brooding brow to pink knees, was tinged with mold.

"Have drip, will travel." He smirked, glanced at the site where the IV tube disappeared in the sleeve of his jacket. He inhaled on his cigarette, then waved it toward mine. "We're the last of a dying breed. Ha. Ha. Ha." He threw it on the ground, where it disappeared.

I threw my own cigarette down and ground it out.

A flame flared from his finger, and he used it to light another cigarette. "Without me," he said, "Elijah's a goner, you know. You might as well face it. Years of visits to that place, you a martyr, the suffering saint. Then, like I said, the eternal dirt nap. The house of perpetual un-motion."

I was trying to think, but my mind was a fog, and he was way ahead of me.

"On the other hand, such a good little guy, such an innocent little guy. He'll surely be sitting at the right hand of God for all eternity after he dies. Maybe you should just tell me to take a hike."

"No."

"Then let him die."

"No. I want him with me."

He crossed his arms, and I could see things moving, squirming in the sallow pink liquid in the IV tube. "You want to deprive him of the chance to be with God? And for such a selfish reason, just so you can keep him with you?" He made a *tsk tsk* sound. "I'd say that was very cruel."

"How do you know he's going to die? How can anyone know?"

"Everyone knows, except you. Despite my best efforts." He said it loudly, so loudly, and his voice did drown out the roar of a God I could no longer even listen for. "Did you get a load of that EEG? You think someone's *home* in there?"

I stood there and I looked at him and I forced myself to speak the words at last.

"Yes," I said. "Help me. Please help me."

He smiled and I could see his teeth, the blackness in his ghost mouth.

"Well, now. There's a good girl. Now let me see. Changing the name of the doomed can sometimes fool the Angel. But things are pretty far gone for that kind of simple trick."

"So you *can't* help me?"

"Beg." He pointed to the ground. "On your knees."

"Please."

"Okay, fine, we'll do it without begging." He was like a petulant child, my ghost. "Of course, there is a catch, as I've told you. Just a slight one, to be sure."

"But you said—"

"We've been talking about you. All this time, we haven't said squat about me. It's really quite simple. A simple bargain. If I make sure the Angel of Death can't find your son, you have to let me inside you."

"*What*?"

He started to laugh. "What a dirty little mind you have. All I want is just a little warmth. I'm so cold all the time. That's all."

"That's all?"

"Nothing to it. I'm not so bad, really, once you get to know me."

"For how long?"

"Forever, of course."

"Inside me? What does that mean?"

"What do you think it means?" He crossed several arms over his chest.

I tried to imagine it. Could not. "What will it feel like, with you inside me?"

"Look. Do you want your son to wake up, or do you want vegetable city?"

"What about my other children?"

The ghost cocked his head. "What about them?"

"*All* my children would have to be safe."

He stamped his foot. "I hardly think you're in any position to start setting conditions. Look, we're not talking immortality here. This is a one-time deal. And you'd better think about it fast, babe, because there really isn't much time *left.* Listen."

I listened, but I heard nothing.

"Listen hard, Dinah. Listen now."

All I heard was street noise, traffic noise. But then I did hear something else, a syncopated rhythm, a *boom*-scraping, *boom*-scraping beat. This I knew was the Angel of Death, searching for the doomed with its eyes seeing everything, and whispering my son's name like a lover, like the hiss of a steam engine. *Elijah, Elijah.*

"Coward!" the demon said, chuckling.

Yes I am. I would refuse to turn off the machines, insist on saving him any way I could. And I would be obliged because they have the technology to do it, and because I am, after all, the mother, and that is my wish. But Death would always be there, poised with its poisoned sword over Elijah's mouth, just waiting. Eight years Death would wait, and I would watch an Elijah unaware, vegetative, growing taller, limbs hardening, curling inward, terrible mouth opening and closing like a fish, hooked, brain gray, arching in death throws. These years I would watch him breathing, day in and day out, in and out *whoosh*-pump

he would not watch me watch him

he would not be watching

he would not be

Elijah.

Finally I would agree to turn off the machines, and then, only then, would my boy die, be taken in the arms of the Master Angel of Death.

"Murderer," said the demon, sniggering, as darkness descended over the earth.

Yes.

I stopped and I turned in the shadow of Death. The demon cocked its evil head and strummed a chord on a guitar. "You'll be damned anyway. Might as well take my offer. Best one you're gonna get. Quickly now. Do we have a deal?"

I could not watch my son die. "Yes," I said. "We have a deal."

The ghost smiled and stubbed out his cigarette. "Go now, Dinah," he said, but I could barely hear it over the *boom*-scraping noise.

"What about you?"

"I'll be along."

I pushed my way through the revolving door and got on the elevator. There was a very old man standing inside, as gnarled and bent as an ancient oak tree. He was leaning on a walking stick, carved at the top with the head of a lion.

He smiled. "What floor?"

I couldn't think clearly, still heard the beat of the Angel of Death, closer now, as close as the pumping of my own heart within my chest.

"PICU," I croaked.

He pushed the floor for me. I leaned back against the elevator wall, closed my eyes. I heard the gears engage, and we ascended.

"This is it," the old man said.

I opened my eyes and stumbled out into the corridor. I heard him step out behind me as I went left, then I found myself in a wing with no children. I kept walking, still hearing the *boom*-scraping pulse. Finally, blundering forward, I saw a sign I recognized. PICU. And an arrow.

As I drew near to my son's room, I could hear Sam crying from way outside, over the hubbub of the PICU. Over the praying mothers, the humming machines. My husband must have come back, finally. And now he was wailing and moaning.

"All *right,*" I whispered, then walked into my son's room. Behind me, over me, around me, I heard the ghost's sepulchral voice, this voice of the grave, of torments and darkness: "Will you give me what I want? Will you be with me always?"

Everything. Anything.

Sam stopped moaning and looked up, mumbled something about being sorry he'd missed the EEG, he got stuck in a meeting, traffic coming uptown was awful. The nurse was refilling the feeding tube, and I could still hear the *boom*-scraping rumble of the beast making its way to my son, closer, always closer. But when the nurse withdrew, I began to hear something else. The lullaby. What a glorious sound, and the ghost emerged next to Elijah's bed.

I held my breath as he sat down on the bed and leaned over my son. He played his guitar, some simple chords, and sang his song, just a little demon lullaby.

So open your eyes while your mother sings
Of wonderful sights that be.

I looked outside into the PICU. The old man I'd seen in the elevator was hobbling in. I blinked. How odd. And I could still hear the syncopated death rhythm that I knew would take my son.

"Do something!" I shouted with my mouth.

Sam turned. "Dinah?"

The ghost stopped singing and gazed at me. "Be patient, my Dinah. I am doing something. The beast hates music. Makes it lose its way. Not too bright, that one." He started playing the song again, and he sang:

And you shall see the beautiful things
As you rock in the misty sea,
Where the old shoe rocked the fishermen three:
Wynken, Blynken, and Nod.

I listened, I watched him, until the verses were done. And only then did I realize that I no longer heard the rhythm of the Angel of Death. Only the machines of the PICU.

Elijah opened his eyes then, saved.

Demon

eighteen

I hold my breath and brace myself, but it's impossible to prepare. It slips its arms around my body, clamps its hand over my mouth, crushes my sides like a vise, holding me captive and mute. It places its cold lips at my neck and slides them over my skin, searching, searching for an opening. Its lips become fumes that enter my mouth and throat and nostrils, flooding every cavity. There is a sucking sound in my ears and in my head, a throbbing against the cortex of my brain that drowns out all hearing. Fumes alter into liquid rage, which fills my larynx like strong liquor, so I cannot speak, then travel downward, flowing into my chest and belly, my groin, finally moving out to the tips of my fingers and toes, replacing flesh and tissue with itself. My body is plunged into absolute zero, my insides churn like an arctic sea.

Now fumes become like saltwater lashing, corrosive as acid, hollowing out my chest cavity, eroding the tissue in my belly, licking the inside of my groin. At last I am beginning to understand the fate and the longing of this unquiet soul. This soul is made of rage and arrogance and sorrow and loneliness, striated with history and pain and regret. I feel a profound sadness, a sadness beyond hope, without flesh to make amends.

I know this is a fierce intelligence that exists not to create but only to plan in the service of its master, this is hunger without love, bitter fruit without end, utter desolation. I had not even imagined the swarming I would feel within me, the buzzing sounds in my ears and my head, as if I have swallowed a hive of frantic bees. Eternity is alone, suffering, ranting, raging against God, regretting each moment. Looking for release. And thinking I am its salvation.

My own vision begins to dim as I look out through its eyes. I see dark shapes rising before me, a landscape gray on gray, a jumbled procession of tormented souls, each going its own way, carrying its own burden, counting and cursing its fate, without even each other for company. Only the buzzing of a thousand wasps, within and without.

I cannot hear my son, but I am not yet blind, some part of me sees Elijah's sweet mouth move, and sees him try to reach out for me.

I totter on the edge of possession, of perfect suction, of becoming what *it* is at last, and I begin to understand what it wants from me. It wants to be *with* me and inside me, to feel the boundaries of my flesh, the heat of my body. To live through me. But can I still live then? Will Dinah not be obliterated?

My God, my God, what have I promised?

"E-li-jah?" I was lost in a dark, whipping vortex, but I could see Elijah crying out, struggling against the restraints, and could not leave him there without me. Somehow I croaked out the syllables of the name I gave to my child, his name like a prayer or benediction.

The spirit fled from my body then, out through my mouth as I spoke my son's name, and love and joy refilled the places where it had violated and stung and begun to annihilate me. "Baby?" I moved toward him.

He was twisting and turning his arms, his whole body, trying to get free just as Dr. Moore had said he would. He was tied down and fighting, hopping mad.

The nurse on duty pressed the alarm for the doctor.

"Wait, Dinah!" Sam said.

But I already had Elijah half out of the restraints. By the time Dr. Jonas arrived, all three of us were holding his hands because he was trying to grab at the intubation tube and we needed Jonas for that. And there he was. He withdrew the ventilator from Elijah's throat, which left him sputtering for breath and sputtering mad, but he calmed down as Sam and I hugged him and covered him in kisses and tears. We sat down on the bed, one on either side of him.

"Elijah?" Dr. Jonas said, touching his arm. "Can you hear me?"

I held my breath as Elijah turned his head to look at the doctor, then nodded, slowly.

I gasped. He understood. He was awake and alert.

"Could you take off that white coat?" I said. "He hates white coats."

Dr. Jonas took off the coat and laid it on the table by the bed. He was wearing a polo shirt, and looked even younger without it. "Now, you can't expect him to start talking right away," he warned.

"We understand," Sam said.

I realized that Dr. Jonas had not really met him. "This is Dr. Jonas, Elijah," I said.

"How do you do, Elijah?" Dr. Jonas said, putting his hand on Elijah's shoulder.

"How . . . do . . . I . . . do?" Elijah said, his voice as husky as a cough.

The young doctor looked utterly stunned.

Elijah just gave him a big smile, as if he'd never even been afraid of doctors. There were Sam's dimples. I hugged my son again.

"You were sleeping," I told him, burying myself in his hair, breathing his smell, his skin as tender as a newborn.

"Night, night," Elijah said.

Now Dr. Moore joined us, eyes dart-darting, his mouth proclaiming he had been right all along. A massive drug cocktail had caused the coma.

"I heard singing," Elijah said after a while. His voice was as raspy as sandpaper, and he was speaking tediously and with great effort, but he was speaking.

"Singing?" Sam said.

He looked up at me with his bright blue eyes. "Lullaby."

"Who was singing?" Sam asked.

Elijah closed his eyes, then quickly opened them again. He shrugged both shoulders. "Someone."

"It seems like a miracle," I told Dr. Moore when I met with him a few days later. They had moved Elijah to the regular pediatric floor, and we were standing outside the playroom, looking in through the glass window. Elijah was sitting on the blue rug, playing with one of the female therapists.

"People do come out of comas," Moore said. "Especially young children. Even after twenty-two days. His MRI is normal. It's not all that unusual."

"But look at him," I said. "Look at the way he's playing with that puzzle." Elijah was, indeed, attempting to put together a ten-piece farm animal puzzle. Not only would he have been unable to work it before, he would have lost interest long ago. Now, slowly but surely, he was getting it. I wanted Sam to be there to see it, but Sam had gone into the office that day for a meeting, his agency's biggest account. He said he was going to get fired if he didn't start showing up again. (That couldn't be true. His boss, Ed Larobina, had come to visit several times. Ed understood.)

"It's almost as if he's—I mean, doesn't the patient usually need to do some relearning?" I knew *that* much.

"After brain trauma, the patient is often left with some lasting effect." Dart-dart. "Motor or speech dysfunction, memory losses, hearing, sight. Not always."

"Is it possible the seizure altered some original miswiring of his synapses or something, the ones that were responsible for his developmental deficits?" Not to mention that he used to be able to smell a doctor at fifty yards and he was walking around here like he owned the place.

"I doubt it." He moved toward the door. I stared after this man, this neurologist, who showed not the slightest curiosity about Elijah's new capabilities, then I followed him into the playroom. Once inside, he curtly dismissed the therapist, who said goodbye to Elijah and walked out. Elijah waved to her, smiled, then waved to me, and went back to the puzzle.

"Well," I said. "Elijah seems like a miracle to me."

The doctor glanced out the window at a nurse passing by in the corridor. "I have no problem with that."

I stared.

The doctor looked back at me, but even then he wasn't really looking at me. His eyes were dart-darting all over the place. "After three weeks is when we might have started to worry."

Why hadn't he told me that before, this Dr. Narcissus? All I wanted was not to be condescended to.

Elijah suddenly jumped up, and dashed over to stand between the doctor and me. There. His new talents were just like *that.* Everywhere Abner Moore's eyes darted, Elijah's eyes followed. Wall. Glass window. Ceiling. Floor. At first Moore seemed confused, but then he realized that Elijah was mimicking him. He cleared his throat and flushed as red as a beet.

Elijah remained in the hospital for two more weeks while they did tests. Given the intensity of the seizure and duration of the coma, Moore said, it was likely that the fever had unmasked some underlying seizure disorder—even if there was no evidence of seizure in their tests, at least none that he mentioned. He put Elijah on an anticonvulsant, and on a snowy mid-February morning they sent us home.

There were already five or six inches of snow on the ground by the time Sam and Elijah and I pulled up our driveway. Though I'd come home once during the hideous episode, I felt as if I hadn't really been home then. Only now did I remember how much I loved the house, which we'd painted mustard yellow last year, with black shutters. Originally built as a farmhouse in the 1890s, it retained a quaint charm, with cozy nooks, uneven wide plank floors, a porch in front, and an eclectic floor plan. We'd found it through Becky, which was how I'd met her.

Kate came running out without a coat to greet us, her arms outstretched. Alex was behind her, just as enthusiastic though trying not to show it. Kate scooped Elijah out of his car seat. He held on to Tuddy while his big sister hugged him, and Alex kissed him, then Kate scooted him off into the house. By the time I got inside, she already had Elijah down on the floor. He had Tuddy on his lap and the two of them started playing a hand-slapping game. Alex watched from the sofa. I noticed he was sporting a pierced earring.

"When did you have that done?"

"Last week. Dad said I could."

Before I could respond to that, Elijah erupted in laughter. Kate was tickling him.

"Maybe you'd better not get him all excited," I said.

"Oh, Mom," Alex said, "you're such a worrier."

Worrier?

"I think your mom's right," Sam said. "Let's just give him a chance to settle in. Then we can tickle him all we want. Right, Elijah?" He reached over and tickled Elijah, who giggled happily and climbed onto his lap.

Before long, we had a family Monopoly game going that continued into the night by candlelight, because the power went off just after dinner, as the blizzard got worse and worse.

In the morning, the world was white-hushed and beautiful. There wasn't a sound outside except for an occasional tree branch cracking under the weight of all that snow. A street plow had deposited a mountain of snow in front of our driveway, blocking it. The schools were closed but Sam insisted he had to go to work, and spent an hour digging out.

"Guess I can skip the run today," he said, standing in the doorway of the kitchen, wiping his steamy glasses with a tissue. He'd worked up quite a sweat.

"You couldn't skip the run when Elijah was in the hospital." I was immediately sorry I'd said it.

He frowned. "You handled it your way, and I handled it mine."

I put the coffeepot down. "I'm sorry, that was a stupid thing to say."

"Don't be absurd," he said. "If you were keeping count of every stupid thing I've ever said, we'd be in big trouble. Remember volleyball?"

The summer after Elijah was born, when Alex and Kate were ten and eleven, we'd rented a charming Victorian house on Cape Cod for a week, with Mark and Becky and their kids, and Jim and Pam Magill and theirs. Every day, when we got back from the beach, we all played volleyball in the backyard, even me, when I could coax the fretful Elijah to take a nap. Sam has always been quite competitive, a real jock. He went a little overboard that week, with his cutthroat play and constant instructions. Two days before the end of the vacation, Alex missed an easy serve from Jim and Pam's twelve-year-old daughter, and Sam blurted out, "What's *wrong* with you, Alex?" "I'm stupid and clumsy and I can't do anything right!" Alex said, and he stomped off.

Sam and I had one of our few actual fights ever that night. I told him he'd been completely out of line and he needed to give our kids a break. Sam countered that I was a pushover, I was constantly catering to them, and if I didn't stop it I was going to turn them into spoiled brats. When we made up two days later, we each admitted the other had been partly right.

"Still, I'm sorry," I said now in the kitchen. I moved toward him, holding out my arms, and we embraced for a long time, he in his parka, me in my bathrobe.

He burrowed into my neck, and his kiss was sweaty and salty, but it felt good to be in his arms again.

"We are very lucky," he whispered.

"Yes," I said. "We are."

After he showered, I drove him in the four-wheel drive over to the train station, then hurried back to find Kate and Elijah making homemade waffles and a mess in the kitchen. Alex was upstairs celebrating the closing of school with his new pastime, lying on his bed and listening to savage music, loud. In the kitchen, Kate abandoned ship before cleanup, but Elijah helped, then I put him in his snow pants and he played in the snow while I shoveled the rest of the walk. In the late morning, we all built two snowmen on the front lawn, right next to each other.

That afternoon, Elijah and I ventured out to the supermarket. He'd always ridden in the cart but this time he wanted to walk alongside me, which he did in his awkward gait. When we came to the cereal aisle he walked right up to a tall, obviously pregnant black woman looking at the cereal boxes.

"I like Sugar Pops," he told her. "What does your son like?"

She looked down at him and smiled. "I don't have a son."

"Yes, you do." He pointed to her belly. "He's in there."

She stared at him for a moment, then looked at me and laughed. "He's right. The doctor told me last week I'm having a boy."

When we got to the meat aisle, Elijah wanted to ride in the cart. I got him settled in, then noticed Tammy Pearl, selecting a chicken. She turned away.

"Hello, Tammy," I said.

"Oh, hi. Did you get my card?"

"Yes, thanks."

"Hi, Elijah. I'm so glad you're better." She patted him on the head.

He patted her on her arm. "Are *you* better?"

She looked puzzled. "I wasn't sick."

Elijah closed his eyes.

"Is he all *right?*"

"He's fine, Tammy." I moved past her, sorry I'd even said hello. "What are you doing, Elijah?"

He didn't respond, kept his eyes squeezed shut.

"Elijah?"

Finally he opened his eyes. "I close my eyes, Mommy."

"I know you closed your eyes. Why?"

He turned to the case full of shrink-wrapped meats and pointed.

"What?"

He kept pointing.

"What in the world are you pointing at, Elijah? The steaks?"

He nodded and closed his eyes again.

Oh. Once they'd weaned him back to real food at the hospital, beginning with Jell-O and liquids and finally working up to meat patties and chicken stew, he'd refused to eat any kind of meat at all. Back home, he ate everything else but kept leaving his portion of meat untouched on the plate. "Doesn't taste good," he said when I'd asked him why.

The following week, Elijah went back to Miss Stanakowski's class, and I resumed my practice. Before Elijah got sick I had a nice part-time practice, thirty patients, including the seven women in my Tuesday night women's group. By the time I came back to work after a hiatus of nearly six weeks, I'd lost five. Two decided to terminate, two decided they liked the colleagues I'd referred them to better than me, and Danielle O'Connor, the new referral whose husband was using her as a punching bag, never called Grace, the colleague I had referred her to, and never called me back either.

When I got to my office, I reviewed my notes for the morning's patients, called Danielle and left a message letting her know I was back at work if she wasn't seeing anyone else. When I hung up, I felt better than I had in a long time.

My first patient arrived right on time, Zandra Leeward, a comically exotic name for a stocky college dropout now working as a secretary in a local law firm. Her problem, she told me during our first session, was that a paralegal in the office was sexually harassing her. Her definition of harassment? He'd brought her a rose on her birthday and asked her out to lunch.

It turned out that Zandra had never had a relationship with a man, sexual or otherwise. "It's not for me," she said. When I asked her why, she said, "Well, just look at me. I'm uglier than homemade sin." She certainly wasn't pretty, but uglier than sin was a little strong.

I was not surprised to learn that the source of this wretched self-image was dear old mom, a beautiful, successful fashion model, now dead. The interactions she described with her mother were so harsh they almost made Charlotte look good. When Zandra told me back in December that I didn't look anything like her mother, I knew she was beginning to trust me. That was where we had left it before my world stopped.

In for our first session after my hiatus, Zandra seemed angry and I finally asked if she was angry with me. She denied it at first, but about midway through the fifty minutes she said I had left her "high and dry." I usually got this reaction from patients once a year, around vacation time. But my absence had come as a surprise to Zandra, without warning.

"I'm very sorry," I told her. "It couldn't be helped."

"Where *were* you?" She started to cry. "I needed you. Ray Johnson called me at home. He asked me out on a *date!*"

Back when I was a new therapist, I found this very hard to deal with, having people so dependent on me, when I barely knew what I was doing. Unfortunately, it's not until you have a better idea what you're doing that you begin to get used to the dependence.

"One of my children was very sick, Zandra. He's all right now, but I had to take the leave of absence. I'm really sorry. It just couldn't be helped."

She seemed puzzled for a moment, then said, "It seems so weird that I come in here and tell you everything about myself and I know nothing about you. I didn't even know you had children."

I nodded. "Yes. I do."

"Well, I'm glad he's okay," she said. "How old is he?"

I folded my hands on my lap. "He's five. But I really don't feel it's a good idea to tell my patients a whole lot about myself, Zandra. It can interfere with what we're doing together. I also really don't feel it's right to talk about myself or my son on your nickel."

She sighed. "I suppose not."

"You were saying you were angry that I wasn't there for you, weren't you? Can you tell me more about that? What happens when you get angry?"

She described tightening feelings in her stomach and throat, then started to cry, and we spent the rest of the session talking about when she first felt that way.

It felt right and good to be back at work. What had happened to me during those unutterable weeks had been a kind of madness, a fugue state or a psychosis of some type. Temporary, and now over.

The last week in February, a massive nor'easter swept into a region already suffering through the worst winter anyone could remember. That morning, after I got the kids off to school, the snow began with a few flakes that steadily progressed into another blizzard, piling yet more new snow on top of old. I was working on the essay with which I would reintroduce my column. I was going to call it "Film Noir Housewife":

> If I could be anyone in the world, I'd want to be one of those blond film noir women. Lauren Bacall, in *To Have and Have Not.* Veronica Lake in anything. I'd even settle for the more recent crop of film noir stars, like Kathleen Turner, in *Body Heat.* I admit I sometimes dream about this at night. There are no children in these dreams, no homework, no hemorrhoids, no husbands. There are only dark men involved in shady deals whose lips tighten with lust when they look at my blond hair, which dips seductively over one half-closed eye, or hear my voice, which is three octaves lower than possible for female Homo sapiens. I wear a khaki trench coat sashed over a body men would die or kill for. I am dangerous and I always carry my piece in my trench coat pocket. I wake up, alas, and realize I have to pick up dinner. Much to my surprise, my local Stop & Shop is filled with dangerous blondes. Dangerous blondes everywhere, squeezing cantaloupes, testing tomatoes, drawing their pieces on the butcher: "Hey, I want my meat prime!"

Satisfied with the first two hundred words, I turned on the radio to see if the schools were shutting down early. They were. Again. I decided to pick up Elijah early enough so I could observe him in class. The roads were a slippery mess already. Once I got there I stood in the corridor with another mother looking in through the window. The runoff from snow melting on our coats and boots made two widening puddles on the floor.

"What's the latest?" I said. "One foot or two?"

"Two, I think." She smiled. Late twenties. She was pretty, but she had that look so many mothers of special-needs children have. Overwhelmed and exhausted.

"Which one's yours?" the young mother asked. Then, when I pointed him out, "Oh, he's adorable."

Elijah was staring at an oversized book on marine life Miss Stanakowski was holding up to the class. She had the book resting on her pregnant stomach, which had grown a lot bigger in the six-week absence. Page after page filled with incredible color photographs of sea plants, coral, brilliantly colored fish, lobsters, dolphins.

"Whale," she said, pointing to a picture of a whale.

Some of the children repeated, "Whale." Some couldn't speak, some couldn't pay attention. Elijah? He seemed too enthralled to say anything.

"Which one's yours?" I asked the young mother.

"Frederick." She pointed. "He's sitting right next to Elijah."

I looked at the little boy on the floor with Elijah. He seemed to have some sort of palsy. His head lolled to one side, his mouth drooped.

I tried to keep my voice steady. "How's he doing?"

"Okay." She hesitated. "I heard Elijah was in the hospital. Is he better now?"

"He seems to be doing fine. And Frederick?" He'd been in the hospital just about eight months ago, I'd heard. Some of these kids went to the hospital like other kids went to camp.

"Oh, yes, he's fine. He has to go for an operation every few years." Her face was very tired.

"Octopus," Miss Stanakowski said, and some of the children repeated it. Elijah sat and gazed at the pictures, until Miss Stanakowski told the class to get ready to go. "Can I see?" Elijah asked.

Miss Stanakowski smiled and handed him the book. By now several other mothers had arrived, and we all went in to help sort out coats and knapsacks and boots. Elijah was still sitting on the floor, oblivious to the hubbub around him, slowly turning the pages of the picture book with his pudgy fingers the way he always did.

I bent down. "That's a beautiful book, isn't it, Elijah?"

He gave me a hug and a big smile, then went back to the book. I tried to coax him into his snow pants, but he wouldn't budge. The other kids were already starting to clear out. Miss Stanakowski said goodbye to the last little girl, then came over to us.

"I doubt we'll have school tomorrow," she said, glancing out the window at the whirling snow. "Or the next day."

I stood up. "That'll be a break for you."

"Enough is enough already. I love my class. I wouldn't exchange these for any kids on earth." She looked at Elijah and smiled. "It was his idea that I show this book to the class at story time, you know. He found it in the book corner this morning. Right, Elijah?"

He nodded without looking up, and his fingers turned over another page.

"Okay, little guy," I said. "Why don't we go now before the snow is up to our ears?"

Reluctantly, he closed the book and stood up, still clutching it.

"I think we have to leave the book here, honey."

He pushed out his lower lip.

"That's all right," Miss Stanakowski said. "He can have it."

The last thing I wanted was a tantrum. "You're sure?"

"Of course."

I started to help him get into his snowsuit.

"You know what he said to me today when we were having our snack?" the teacher said. "I spread peanut butter on his cracker, and he told me I looked like an angel."

I zipped up his hood, looked him in the eyes. "Where did you hear that word, Elijah?"

He pushed his glasses up on his nose. "From you, Mommy."

But I had never mentioned angels to him, any more than I had ever said anything to him about babies in stomachs.

"What does an angel look like?" I asked him.

He laughed and pointed to Miss Stanakowski.

"Miss Stanakowski *is* an angel. But don't angels have wings?"

He nodded. "Some have lots of wings."

I stared. "Did you see a picture of an angel with lots of wings?"

He shook his head no. "Some angels are teachers and some angels make you forget." He pointed at Miss Stanakowski's bulging stomach. "She knows."

What in the world was he talking about?

"And some angels scare Mommy," he said, gazing up at me.

I glanced at Miss Stanakowski, who seemed only perplexed by all this, but I was suddenly, staggeringly frightened.

Then Elijah, just as suddenly, threw his arms around me and gave me his Schwarzenegger hug, and I put it out of my mind.

nineteen

The first Monday in March was unbelievably cold, and set a record for the date. That night, as a wicked and bitter wind whipped around the house, sending snowflakes dancing across the yard, Sam came up behind me. I was fixing dinner.

"Hey, honey." He kissed my neck. "You put out for strangers?" It was a familiar routine for us, and it went both ways. We put out for horny bastards, lizards (lounge and otherwise), floozies, turkeys, nerds, etc. It was "strangers" tonight because we hadn't made love in almost two months, a record for us.

"Only for strangers I love," I said.

"Later, baby."

"Later, stranger."

Back to our normal routine, we all ate dinner together as a family that night, filling each other in on the day's events and the next day's plans. Elijah had shown us his *Creatures of the Deep* book every night since he got it, and now he showed it again.

I announced that I was planning to go back to my writing class at the Jewish Community Center the next day, ignored Alex's comment about geezer day camp. Sam said he'd struggled all day to come up with a campaign concept for a new lemon-lime soft drink.

Kate suggested calling it Lemonitious. "Then you could do a jingle using words that rhyme with that. Delicious. Nutritious. Scrumptitious. Like that." She started to sing a tune, using the words.

" 'Scrumptitious' isn't a word, asshole," Alex said, frowning.

"Alex, must you use that kind of talk," Sam said.

"Don't even pay any attention to him," Kate said. "Using 'scrumptitious' would be like artistic license. Right, Dad?"

Sam agreed it would, except that soda wasn't exactly nutritious. Still, it wasn't a bad idea, he said. "Maybe you'll follow dear old Dad into advertising," he said.

"Mrs. Kotchkins said she thinks I should really pursue music."

"Well, whatever makes you happy, Kate," I said, thinking that I really should talk to her about the conversation I'd had with Lucia Orsini during Elijah's illness, about Kate and some of her friends picking on Allison.

Even Alex participated in our daily dinner ritual, telling us that he was planning to try out for the junior varsity baseball team.

After dinner, Sam retired to the home office we shared to work on his concept. I went into Kate's room, where I found her on the phone, as usual. I motioned for her to get off, then waited while she finished and sat down on the bed. She took it pretty well.

"You're right, Mom," she said. "Allison is a pain in the ass, nobody can stand her, but I feel kind of sorry for her. I already apologized. It was stupid and mean."

I gave her arm a little squeeze. "I'm proud of you, Kate."

She leaned back against her wicker headboard and crossed her arms in back of her head. "Yeah, ain't I the greatest?"

I told her to come down and say good night when she'd finished her homework, then played with Elijah for a while before I helped him get washed up and into his pajamas. We looked at his *Creatures of the Deep* book together, and I sang him his lullaby, then I waited until Alex and Kate were settled in bed before going into our bedroom, Sam's and mine, and setting the stage for romance. I lit a phalanx of candles, found a soft jazz station on the radio, and slipped into a slinky negligee. Sam seemed surprised when I came to him in the office as he was shutting down the computer.

"What's this?" he said.

"This was your idea. Stranger."

He followed me into the bedroom.

I spent a few hours the next morning working on a column I was going to call "Diets for the New Age." There was the Whole Book Diet ("You don't read the Whole Book Diet, you eat it. One page at a time. Made of edible reconstituted protein . . ."); the Astral Projection Diet ("Project your pinchable midriff onto Brooke Shields, your flabby thighs onto Jane Fonda. And Heather Locklear gets your rear end!"); and the Time Machine Diet ("Travel back in time to when buxom and round was all the rage. Keep the same old body, but now everyone will consider you a prize instead of a cow . . .").

I dropped the column off at the newspaper offices and rushed over to the Jewish Community Center. They all seemed glad to see me and I thanked them for their cards and prayers while Elijah was sick. They remembered him from the day he'd had to leave Sue Weinberg's art class, and in response to their concern I told them a little about his experience in the hospital. That led to a half-hour discussion about illnesses and hospitals and doctors, a favorite subject of the over-seventy set. We heard about Pearl Ott's back pain and arthritis and polyps. (Her rheumatist was an absolute genius, in case we were wondering.) We heard about Rose Felber's daughter Belle, who had meningitis when she was very small, but was fine in the end, thank God, though blind in one eye. (Which was nothing, everyone agreed.) We even heard from Abe Modell about why he became a dentist instead of a medical doctor ("Dentistry! Now there's something you can really sink your teeth into!").

"You're a little long in the tooth for that kind of story, Abe," said Carl Moskovitz.

"Ha, ha, ha, Carl!" said Pearl Ott, who didn't appreciate their brand of humor. Pearl wasn't my favorite of the bunch.

For their next class project I suggested they write about what they most regret, and they seemed to like the idea.

I asked Ellen to stay after class. "I was very moved by your card, Ellen," I told her loudly. "It was generous of you."

She eyed me with those trenchant eyes. "Generous?"

"I mean because of what you must have been through yourself."

"You think I can't wish good things for others because I've been to hell myself? Because I live in hell?"

"Is that how it feels, like hell?"

"That was how it was, that is how it feels. I lost my whole family, you know. Both my mother and my father."

"I'm sorry."

"*Ja.* I mean, yes. I never like to speak that language. I *spit* on that language."

I closed my eyes.

"And my sister, and my brother," she said. "And my first husband, and my daughter. My baby. "

When I opened my eyes I expected to see tears in her eyes. But Ellen Shoenfeld's eyes were clear and dry. I put my hand on her shoulder. "Why don't you try the regrets assignment?"

She waved me away and took her pocketbook on her arm. "*Nein. Nein. Nein.*"

That night, still safe in my complacency, in the comfort of my quotidian days, I dream I am on the motorcycle with Seth, my arms around his waist, my legs encircling his thighs, the leather of his jacket cool against my cheek.

He bears down harder and harder on the accelerator.

"This isn't real," I tell myself. I can't die because I'm not here.

But he is going faster, still faster. The wind lashes at my face. I see a truck in the distance. The road is too narrow, winding. Wait. No. Stop. This is his death, not mine.

I hear the sickening, screeching skid. I am soaring soundless through the cool air.

I search for Seth in the failing light. He is lying flat on his back a few feet away, face turned toward the sky, eyes closed. His jacket is covered with bits of leaves, his boots full of mud.

"Seth?" I struggle to all fours and crawl toward him.

He lifts his head and smiles. "Fooled you, didn't I?"

I awakened with a jolt and looked over at Sam, sleeping peacefully, snoring slightly. Breathing, breathing, I took inventory of my bedroom in the dark. The clock (2:30 A.M.), the novel I'd just begun on my night table, bottle of moisturizing lotion to cure alligator skin, the hulking furniture shadows—two overstuffed plaid chairs we got on sale at Ethan Allen, television set on its stand, armoire, dresser. Dog curled up in his usual place in the corner.

I told myself it had only been a dream. Like all dreams, it had been constructed of bits of my psyche, pieces of wishes and fears and guilt and life—*my* life.

It was just a dream, I told myself, and I even tried to believe it.

twenty

The next day I had a lunch date with Becky. I had decided to tell her the story of what had happened to me in my first year of college. Becky and I had confessed to each other practically everything else. Well, nearly everything. Maybe telling her would get it out of my mind, maybe she would reassure me that it wasn't my fault. Maybe I could then put it to rest. I had never even told Sam about Seth.

I couldn't bring it up because she brought someone along, as it turned out a delightful seventy-nine-year-old dowager whose house had provided her with her only sale of the year thus far. Mrs. Mitzi Hertzl had a sweet face with a tiny, perfectly painted rosebud mouth. She must have been very beautiful once, in a Lillian Gish sort of way.

"Buried two husbands, divorced two," she said as she took bird-sized bites of her ravioli. "Ready, willing, and able for number five."

I told her about my writing class and the four widowers in it, then invited her to join us.

"Sounds like fun," she said. "What are we working on?"

I told her.

"I know exactly what I'll write about. During the war, when I was in the WACs, I met the handsomest Englishman. I think he's what I regret."

"Why so?" Becky asked.

"He became my first lover."

We both leaned in.

"I wanted to marry him, but my mother, well, you know."

"Well," I said, "if that's what you regret, then that's what you should write about. I can't wait to read it."

On the way out of the restaurant, Mitzi Hertzl stopped, looked me up and down, following the line of my legs with her cane. "Good legs," she said. Meaning, if I ever found myself in need of a man, this news about my anatomy would come in handy. She was adorable.

When I got to the little conference room the following Thursday, Mitzi Hertzl was waiting for me just outside the door. I brought her in and introduced her to the class.

"Come sit by me," Abe said. "I'm Abe Modell." He patted the empty chair next to him. Abe always had a twinkle in his eye when he said anything to a woman.

Mitzi sat down next to him, smiling, then pulled out of her purse several pages torn from a legal pad and densely covered with writing. She unfolded the pages, smoothed them out, and squared them just so on the table in front of her.

"I'm glad you gave our regrets assignment a try," I said

"It's probably not very good."

"We're not into good or bad here," I told her. "We're into self-expression."

"WHAT?" Ellen Shoenfeld said.

"SELF-EXPRESSION."

She nodded, then smiled at Mitzi. I wondered again if she heard anything at all when it was spoken in a normal voice.

"So. Who wants to begin?"

Pearl Ott. She cleared her voice, rustled her papers, began to read: "My sister was a very jealous woman, angry all the time, very wrapped up in herself. Her name was Rebecca . . ."

Whatever the original cause of the break between them, it was so serious that when her sister died the two had not spoken to each other for fifteen years. That wasn't what Pearl regretted, though. Her great regret was having kept the birthday gift Rebecca sent at one point during the silence between them. "I wore that scarf and I hated wearing it," Pearl read from her essay. "What I should have done was send it back."

I was feeling a twinge of remorse, thinking about Julie, my long separation from her. I resolved I would call her, this time for real.

Mitzi Hertzl went next. I settled into my chair, expecting to hear about her first lover.

"It was June of 1928, and I was ten years old, when the sheriff told my mother and sister and brother and me that we had to leave our home. It wasn't much of a home, just three small rooms over our tiny candy store, but it was all we knew. I hadn't seen my father in over a year. He had a disease no one wanted to talk about while he was still alive.

"The first time I heard the word 'tuberculosis' was when he died in a sanitarium somewhere out west. I didn't know the name of the sanitarium. All I knew was that there were bills due. That was what my mother kept saying. And now this man was here to make us leave our home. We had spent the last two days packing our meager belongings, and the bags and boxes were stacked by the door, right in front of all the bins where we kept the candies . . ."

Mitzi read to us from her handwritten yellow pages in a strong, clear voice. What did she regret, even after all those years? The sheriff ("a huge man who took up most of the doorway") had patted her on the head and said, "I'm sorry, girlie." She'd wanted to stomp on his foot, and didn't.

"That was wonderful, Mitzi," I said when she finished.

"Thank you."

"Maybe you can add a few details."

"Like what?"

I asked her what kind of candies they sold in the store.

She smiled. "Oh. Well. Jelly beans, all different colors, like a rainbow, and licorice whips and little sucking candies. The licorice was always my favorite."

"Me too," I said. "What did they smell like?"

She smiled. "They smelled like home."

Of course they did.

I talked about point of view for a little while, then suggested that for next week they might try writing something from another person's perspective.

"If you're a man," I said, "maybe try something from a woman's point of view."

"Impossible!" Abe Modell said. "Who could understand a woman's point of view?"

"Very funny, Abe," Pearl Ott said. Then, to me, "But I don't get it, either."

"For example, you could try the essay you read to us today about your disagreement with your sister from her point of view."

"My sister's dead." Her jaw was loose, her expression flat.

"Of course she's dead, Pearl," Lucy said. "Dinah wants you to do it as if she's alive."

Pearl shook her head and started packing up her things. "Nah. Not for me."

"Why not?" Carl said. "I like the idea. Be a good sport, Pearl."

"I've never been a bad sport in my life! What do you know? You have no idea how my sister hurt me—"

"It's all right, Pearl," I said. "It's a suggestion, not an assignment. You don't have to do it." I looked out over the class. "I have another idea, some of you may like it better. Try writing up the funniest experience you've ever had."

Even Ellen Shoenberg tried that one. The following week she shocked me by coming in with a short, hilarious piece about her granddaughter's Bat Mitzvah. At least my own sense of humor seemed to have returned. The baker delivered a cake that said, "Happy 80th Birthday, Sadie," the cantor tripped on the *bimah,* and when they did the candle lighting ceremony at the reception, the tablecloth caught fire.

I wondered, not for the first time, why it had taken her so long to participate.

"Sounds like a fun time," Carl Moskovitz said. "I'll go next."

My best writer did not disappoint me:

"At three o'clock in the afternoon of March 1, 1979, three baboons got together and ate the vinyl roof of my brand-new Grand Prix with the sunroof and the power windows."

Carl and his wife had ridden through one of those wild animal parks in Florida, uneventfully until they got to the baboon section, separated from the rest of the park by a high wooden fence. An attendant stopped them and said they couldn't proceed unless they signed a release. He pointed to a sign on the fence: NO CONVERTIBLES ALLOWED. BABOONS MAY DAMAGE VINYL ROOFS. It was a very small sign and there were a lot of signatures on the release form, so Carl overrode his wife's qualms and signed.

"I told my wife they didn't mean brand new vinyl roofs, they meant old dilapidated vinyl roofs. Well, those baboons saw us coming in our brand-new Grand Prix and they were licking their chops. The minute that gate clanged shut, they came at us from every direction, from behind every tree. Baboons are really nasty animals. Who knew?

"They surrounded us, hopped on top of the car, and started dancing around like it was a party, all the time making baboon noises, squawking and squealing, hooting and egging each other on. As they started to claw at the roof, my wife said, 'Carl.' Whenever Sally was angry or upset, she always said my name as if it had two syllables. Car-el.

" 'I mean, Death by Baboon?' I said. 'Come on, Sally.'" He began to rock the car, shifting between reverse and forward gears, trying to make the baboons fall or jump off. "But they were too busy eating my roof. And my wife was busy saying, 'I told you not to sign that release.' I had visions of us heading out to the highway, riding down Interstate 95 to Miami with the baboons still hanging on."

Eventually the attendant at the other end of the section poked the baboons off with a long cattle prod. He had a smirk on his face.

And Carl had all of us laughing out loud. Usually, after they heard each other's stories, they'd say things like "My daughter got married in a New York hotel, too," or "Oh. Then you're from Pennsylvania, like me." Then they wanted to know if it was their turn next. But that day for a brief moment Carl had all of them wanting to listen, rather than tell. Maybe it was the way he dropped his deadpan delivery, and began to choke up as he ended the story:

"Of course it wasn't so funny then, but Sally and I laughed about it for years afterwards. Looking back on it now, I can only think one thing, how I'd love to hear my wife say, 'Car-el.' With those two syllables, the way she used to say it when she was upset or mad at me."

"CARRRR-ELLLL."

I looked around the room. "What?"

"CARRR-EL."

No one had spoken.

"Is something *wrong*, Dinah?" Abe Modell said. My face must have drained of color.

"CARRR-EL."

I managed, "I'm all right."

But I wasn't all right. I had heard an old woman's voice, abrasive and rather whiny but all around me, emanating from nowhere and everywhere. My blood froze in my bones.

When I finally fall asleep that night, I have a degrading little playlet of a dream.

Sam and I are walking down the aisle of a packed movie theater, where every seat seems to be filled with someone I know. People I know from my past, people I have in my present: Gabby Sterling, Jay Salisbury, Mark Sullivan, Becky, Tammy Pearl, my grandfather Eli, smoking a cigar. He has an expression on his face I can't understand. Is he leering?

We sit down in the only empty seats in the front row, then the lights dim, the curtains open, and I can hear the gritty whir of a projector. A movie begins with a hand-lettered title, white on a black background.

THE DEVIL'S BARGAIN

A Film by Seth Lucien

Cut to a room with a peaked ceiling, an attic. Crudely filmed. Stationary camera. Black-and-white images. Familiar. Another black title card now:

PART ONE

INNOCENCE SURRENDERED

Cut back to the attic. A poodle bounds in and out of the camera's field as a young man and woman walk to the bed. The man leaves the shot for a few seconds; the young woman stands there, looking around nervously, admiring a beautiful carved mirror on the wall. The man returns, stands behind her, puts his arms around her waist, kisses her. She pulls away. He leads her to the bed, where, in a queer tremble of black and white light, he begins to kiss her again.

But wait. A protest. Their lips move but there is no sound. The young woman motions toward the dog, who is resting its long, sharp muzzle at the edge of the mattress. The man points, the dog retreats, then the couple begins to make love. There is an odd kind of staged quality about the scene, though the actors are convincing. First some foreplay; then, as the man thrusts his hips a few times, pain shows in her face, followed by an easing of tension, followed by what could be pleasure. The actress's facial expression, mouth open teeth apart, is so similar to her expression at the previous moment of penetration that it might still be pain she's feeling rather than pleasure.

Of course. The expression *is* pain. The actress is me.

I hear noises all around, gasps and sighs. I turn to Sam, sitting in the next seat, and I see that he is gaping back at me, his expression a mixture of revulsion and anger.

As I awakened from the dream, I remembered an event I had long buried: Early in the morning after the motorcycle accident that killed

Seth, I realized that his dog had been alone in his apartment for the entire day and night. I rang his landlady's apartment. She was a heavyset woman with bleached blond hair and black roots, who reeked of perfume, even in the morning when she was wearing her ratty bathrobe. She was none too pleased at being awakened. I told her what had happened.

"What a shame," she said, pulling her robe closed over her massive breasts. "No wonder that dog was barking all night. Had to take him out myself. Damned animal did his business on my floor."

I convinced her that I needed to collect some of my belongings from Seth's apartment, and she took me upstairs, complaining that it was prime D.C. real estate and that Seth owed her three months' rent. We could hear the dog growling behind the closed door. She unlocked it and stood back while I went in. I could smell dog shit. Meph stopped growling and trotted over to me. The landlady came in and looked around while I collected my books, which I'd left on the table in the kitchen area.

"You want the dog?"

"I can't have a dog in my dormitory." Even if I could have, I didn't want him.

"Well, I guess the police will take him away, when they come." She'd moved in front of the gilt mirror. She was touching it. "I think before the police get here, I'm going to hold on to this little item of his to pay for what he owes me." She shoved the dresser out of the way so she could get to the mirror, which she managed to lift up and away from the wall.

"That is one heavy mother," she said, setting it down on the floor. "Bet it's worth three months' rent. You want any of the rest of his stuff?" She gestured toward the purple costume. "Like that Halloween getup? If the cops don't take all this away, it's going in the Goodwill dumpster."

"I don't want it." I was looking at something mounted on the wall, just above where the mirror had been. Good God! It was a camera lens. A wire snaked from the lens to the floor to the molding it was tacked to for about ten feet. I'd never noticed it, hidden behind the mirror and dresser, painted white to blend into the wall. Now I followed the wire to where it disappeared under the door of a small closet next to the kitchen. I opened the door. The wire led directly to Seth's 8mm camera.

I looked at the lens mounted where the mirror had been. A bird's-eye view of the bed. He'd *filmed* Sexuality 101.

My face heated with humiliation. I fumbled with the camera until I finally got it open. There was a spool of film inside. I grabbed that. I took every last spool of film there was in that closet, and on the shelves, and got out of there as fast as I could.

Now in my bedroom, I blinked. The room seemed so oddly bright. What a queer light, had I forgotten to turn off the reading lamp next to the chair? I looked.

The ghost was *there,* perched on the arm of the chair, and I was catapulted once and for all out of my complacency.

A shrill sound emerged from my mouth. This *entity,* this demon or spirit or ghost (I wasn't sure what to call it anymore), which had identified itself as Seth Lucien, looked entirely different now. Now it wasn't anything resembling human, it had black eyes and teeth but was blinding white, as if all the light in the world had congealed in a single place, collected and contained within a membrane as thin as a soap bubble. Squinting, I could actually see through it to the plaid on the chair's fabric.

"Howdy do." The voice was the same, though, still the insinuating, intimate murmur.

"Why are you doing this to me?" I whispered.

"Doing what?" It smiled. I knew I'd seen teeth.

It got up from the chair, luminous and white, advanced and descended onto the bed, wagged a hand—no, a claw—in my face. It even smelled different now, a metallic odor, like a tin can left out in the rain, rusted and rank.

"You should have watched the film when you had the chance." It stroked my cheek with its cold white claw-hand, stained with something dark and clotted. Yes. I never watched it. I'd thrown every roll of film Seth had into a dumpster and never told a living soul, I was too ashamed. And I had successfully put it out of my mind all these years.

I shrank back against the headboard, glanced over at Sam, who was sleeping comfortably.

I turned back. "Why *did* you film it?" I couldn't help myself. I wanted to know.

The white mass that seemed to be its head moved downward, as if it were taking a bow. "Not me, dimwit. The filmmaker was Seth."

"You made me the unwitting participant in a pornographic film."

Now it laughed, a chorus of cackling crows. "I'm afraid so. But not me, *him.* Can you get that through your head?" Why was this distinction so important to the demon? I had felt it inside me, and I still didn't know.

"All right. Him."

"That's better. And what do you mean, unwitting? You knew what was going on."

"Liar. I knew nothing. I was a naive young girl."

"No point in arguing. I'll leave you your little self-deceptions. It's quite a piece of work, you know. If Seth hadn't been stupid, he would have made a mint with it." It leaned toward me. A movement suggesting a swagger. "Want to see the rest?"

"No thank you. It's beyond rape."

"Oh, *psssh.* Do you have to be so dramatic about everything? Could have been a lot worse. You could have been Jay."

Sam made a little sound in his sleep, and I got out of bed, moved away from it, over by my dresser. "Seth killed him. Didn't he?"

"Well, duh." It was beside me in an instant, a winking of air. "Everyone tripped. Just a little extra in Jay's glass. The pièce de résistance."

"But why?"

"Let's see, now. He was consumed with jealousy?"

"Seth didn't love me, he wouldn't have cared if I were with Jay."

"Ah, but you're wrong. Seth did love you."

The demon didn't know the difference between love and hate. And neither had Seth.

"Even if he did love me, that's not why he killed Jay. Tell me why."

The demon gazed at me. Its eyes turned as white as the rest of it, and seemed to disappear. "I don't remember."

"Was it because Jay told me what happened with that girl you picked up?" Seth had called that girl a whore, right to my face, and I had ignored it.

"Can't remember," it purred, eyes blackening again.

How sad. It couldn't remember why it had committed murder. Unless Seth *hadn't* committed murder and it was lying. Why would it want to take credit for that?

"Are you sorry for killing Jay now?"

"Why should I be sorry for him? He isn't sorry for me."

"Maybe he is."

"He's dead. How can he be sorry for me? Would you have refused to make our bargain if you'd known Seth had killed Jay?"

No, I would have made the deal no matter what. "You told me being dead changes you."

"I lied."

"My God." I moved away, toward the door. The thing drifted with me.

"Surely you don't think I offered you my help because I took pity on you and your boy. Surely not."

I was cornered against the door, my back against the cold knob. "Why, then?"

"I came to you because I knew you would be willing to do what I asked."

"But you said anyone in my position would do what I did."

It began to laugh, and I could hear others laughing, tittering in the background. Then it stroked my face. " 'He's mad that trusts in the tameness of a wolf, a horse's health, a boy's love, or a whore's oath.' "

Shakespeare again, perhaps *Lear.* I closed my eyes to it, but even with my eyes closed I could still see it, and still smell the odor of wet metal, corroded and corrupt.

"Now you want to weasel out of the deal," it said. "Not a chance."

"What is it you want me to do?"

"At last a good question. Now we're getting down to it."

"What do you *want?*" I tried to duck around it.

"You know what I want. You've already given it. You will take me inside you."

I tried again to get away, but it was blocking me there by the door. "I've done that, I've done it. I fulfilled my end of the bargain."

The thing's eyes blackened and bore into me. "You fought against it."

"I didn't," I said. Yet I wasn't sure what had happened. Through demon-dimmed eyes I'd seen Elijah struggling. And I now realized why it had vacated me. At least I thought I did.

"You can't stand that I love Elijah," I said.

The demon moved forward, crushing me closer to the door, the knob jammed against the small of my back.

I gathered myself. "That's it. You can't stand it. Can you?"

"We shall try again," it said, not answering the question.

"I'm right, aren't I? You want me all for yourself."

"Did we or did we not make a deal? "

"Under duress. This isn't fair."

"Who said anything about fair? A deal is a deal. Let me be with you."

I felt something encircle my neck.

"And if I don't?" Somehow I managed to escape around it.

It made a shruglike motion, a shifting of whites, plane against plane, a shoulder, an arm.

"Not an option," the demon whispered. "You'll see." And then it faded away.

The next day I went to my office, but I was nervous and jumpy and full of dread. Still, I sat through my sessions, conducting the work competently if not well. The last patient of the day was Zandra Leeward. She had seemed to be making some progress, connecting her rejection of men to the abandonment she'd felt as a young child, related to her mother's rejection of her. The session began well, but about halfway into it I began to feel chilled. I buttoned my jacket, I was looking for a draft. Zandra was talking about her mother.

"She said she didn't ever want to look at me again. She locked me in my room and refused to let me come out for dinner."

It reminded me of scenes between another daughter, another mother. "That must have been very painful for you," I said in my best mode-neutral psychologist tone, but I was beginning to shiver. The window wasn't open but it needed caulking. It *was* still winter.

"My mother never liked any of my friends," she said.

I realized I was feeling more than cold, way more. There was that change in the atmosphere, emanations of heat and cold, and the pervasive odor of metal corroded with rust, corrupt in my nostrils. I sat up straight in my chair.

"I don't know," Zandra was saying. "It's not like Ray's ever done anything mean or bad . . . What do you think I should do now?"

"What do you want to do, Zandra?" Automatic pilot.

She frowned. "I hate it when you say that."

"What feelings does it—"

I froze. The demon had materialized, standing between Zandra and me. Right there. But it wasn't a monster, or a formless mass, or a skeleton or a pink hippie, or something gooey from the grave, or even something white and luminous. Oh, no. It had emerged as a tall, elegant woman with long, lovely legs, deep red lips, painted fingernails, and a mass of auburn hair.

"Charlotte!" I jumped to my feet.

"Dr. Galligan?" Zandra said.

The demon began to laugh in my mother's voice, and I sat down.

"Is something wrong, Dr. Galligan? Who's Charlotte?"

Never mind, dear. Countertransference to the max.

I closed my eyes, I'd pull it together, I'd go on with the session, I'd—

"Spread those legs, honey, because you're never going to get another chance, a dog like you." Bark, bark.

"Damn you!" I screamed. "We're talking about *her* mother, not *mine.*"

The she-demon mother with the red lips and the red hair stood over me and laughed.

Zandra stood up. "I think I'd better leave."

In a moment, my patient was gone.

"*Why?*" I asked.

The demon just hooted. "Because I saved him, and you are mine." The demon moved very close, so close, I could feel the touch of its cold and slick membrane on my skin again. "It can still happen, you know."

I was paralyzed.

"Oh yes. The brain is quite a little mystery. Even Moore told you it was possible he could have another seizure."

That was true, even though I gave him his anticonvulsant every day.

"You humans are so fragile. One little blood vessel, boom! Do you think because the lullaby blinded the Angel's eyes for a moment, it can't return? I can make sure it does."

"Leave Elijah alone." I was quaking and rolling. Could it really do that?

"Leave Elijah alone, leave Elijah alone . . ." it echoed. The words got softer and softer, and the demon faded and shut into itself, leaving just the faintest whiff of metal in the room after it completely disappeared.

twenty-one

For the next few weeks, I tried to go on as usual, teaching my class, writing my column, seeing patients, cooking dinner, attending to my mothering tasks. Over-attending, I suppose you could say. I had an idea that if I maintained a constant vigilance over Elijah, I could protect him, and spent most nights sleeping fitfully on the floor by his bed, until one morning Sam found me there, curled up next to Elijah's *Creatures of the Deep* book. Elijah wanted me to look at the book with him constantly, and it was starting to get a little beat-up from so much attention. I'd made a mental note to replace Miss Stanakowski's copy.

"Dinah," Sam said, standing in the doorway, "he's going to get a complex if you don't stop hovering over him this way."

"*Shhh.* Don't wake him." I got to my feet and pushed past him.

"Dinah?" He started to follow me.

I waved him off. "Leave me alone."

That night, I was pretending to read in bed, while Sam got undressed and got in beside me, wearing only his pajama bottoms. "I'm sorry about this morning, Di."

I put my book down on the night table. "It's okay, Sam." I turned off the light and rolled over on my side, away from him.

Sam nestled in closer, spooning me. He wanted to make love.

How could I when that damnable thing could show up *anywhere, anytime?*

Sam was kissing my neck. I had always loved it when he did that.

"Wait," he said softly, then grabbed the pack of matches we keep by the bed and lit our scented candles. Sweet incense, the smell of vanilla, filled the air. I turned to him, and for a time I allowed myself the familiar comfort of my husband's body.

After Sam had fallen asleep, the demon appeared in a flicker of many candlelights, a halo of golden fire. I saw it crouched in a corner of the bedroom, I saw its bright white body bowed like a crescent moon. It gazed at me with two eyes as dead as black granite, as immutable as primordial stone, a fossil that once lived many aeons ago but could never live again. And sang:

The lady weeps tears of glass,
stone tears.
The lady weeps snakes.
The lady betrays.

The dog, curled up in the opposite corner, looked up and yawned, then went back to sleep.

"Betrays?" I said.

"The lady is *mine,*" it sang. Then it disappeared with a breath of chill winter wind. And when I finally slept, I dreamed I was looking for Elijah.

In the dream, I am walking down Main Street, behind a couple in front holding the hand of a five- or six-year-old boy with hair the color of a robin's breast. I have to get a look at the child's face, see that face and compare it to Elijah's. Only then can I say to myself, No, this face is thinner, this boy's eyes are brown, not blue, this one doesn't have Elijah's dimples or the cleft in his chin just like Sam's. None of the little boys I see compare. None of them are my son.

But this boy does resemble Elijah. He even wears glasses.

"Look," I say, pulling a picture of Elijah out of my purse. "Oh, look, your son looks just like mine. Do you see the resemblance to this picture of my dead son, or is it my imagination?"

The couple stare at me, their jaws dropping. I seek out the white-lipped stare in my grief, I want everyone, anyone, to share my ruination.

I shove the photograph in their faces. "Look! Don't you *see* the resemblance?"

"Dinah?"

Sam was shaking me. I looked at the clock: 6:30 A.M.

"Dinah, you were saying something in your sleep. Something about a picture."

I sat up. "I had a dream that I had this photograph, and I was showing it to this couple on the street. And I kept insisting that their son looked just like my dead son."

Sam stared at me. "God, Dinah. Why would you dream about that? It's awful."

I wanted to tell him then, but I was afraid. Afraid he wouldn't believe me, afraid he'd think I was insane, afraid of what the demon would do.

"I can't help my dreams, Sam."

"No. I guess you can't. But, honey? Maybe you should see a psychologist yourself."

I started to cry.

He put his arm on my back. "I mean because you're so tense all the time. Wound up as tight as a drum. Is it me? Am I doing something to upset you?"

"Oh, aren't *we* Mr. Sensitivity," the demon said. It was at the foot of the bed.

I tried to avert my eyes, to look only at Sam. "It's not you, Sam. I guess I'm terrified that Elijah isn't all right, that this isn't over, I'm afraid something will happen to Alex, that Kate's going to get in an accident when she learns to drive this summer, I'm just afraid."

"But they're fine. And Elijah's better than fine, he's better than he ever was. You know what he said to me yesterday? He said he could see God. Have you been talking to him about God?"

"No. Have you?"

He shook his head.

"So what did you tell him?"

"I told him we can't see God. He said, 'Yes, you can. If you close your eyes and listen.'"

"Listen?"

"Maybe we should take the little guy to a church, if he's interested." He hopped out of bed, grabbed his robe and tied the sash. "Or a synagogue."

"If he can see God when he closes his eyes, maybe he doesn't need a church or a synagogue."

Sam leaned over and kissed the top of my head. "You know, Dinah, that's why I love you."

"Why?"

"Because you say stuff like that. I admire you. The way your mind works. It's so . . . I don't know, different. I really admire it, kiddo."

I hugged him around his waist. "Well, thanks for the compliment, I think."

"You're welcome, I think."

It was one of the few conversations we'd had since it all began that we seemed like our old selves. An amazing feat, since I was already walking through my days as well as my nights in a constant state of panic.

I took a deep breath and clasped my hands together. "Elijah *is* incredible, isn't he?" I said. If I could keep my focus on my daily concerns, and on Elijah, I could manage to sound pretty normal. "But Moore did say he still may have a seizure disorder."

"I'd say it's hard to see how that's possible, given how well he's doing. And after all, they've got him on that medication."

"You're so optimistic, Sam."

"You're so pessimistic, Dinah."

A familiar exchange.

"I'm not pessimistic, I'm realistic. I think you assume these doctors know everything. Know what they're doing. Despite evidence to the contrary."

"What evidence?"

"I don't think they really know what happened to Elijah."

He sighed. "If you're so concerned, we'll get another opinion."

"Maybe that's a good idea. Maybe at one of the other big hospitals down in New York."

"Tell you what. I'll ask Ed Larobina. He's really well connected, he'll know who besides Moore is good. And he's been really nice through this whole thing."

"Okay."

"Good. And promise me you'll consider seeing someone yourself. Okay?"

"I'll consider it," I said.

"I'll consider it." I had almost forgotten the demon was there, and now I turned and it was gone. Where was the sibilant voice coming from?

Sam looked at the clock: nearly seven now. "I really have to get going, I have a nine o'clock meeting down on Wall Street." He grinned. "Last night was great."

It was.

He leaned over and kissed me again. "I've missed you. Hey, what do you say we do it again tonight?"

The demon emerged beside me, under the quilt, sliding claws as cold as the fingers of death beneath my nightgown. It touched my body, my belly, my breasts, it felt like paper rubbing against paper, like rusted metal between my thighs. It had no weight, but I felt its fingers there on my skin. It did not attempt to possess me then, but pinned me there until Sam had gone into the bathroom.

"Tonight you are *mine,*" it cooed, and disappeared.

I had just gotten out of the shower when I heard a noise from the attic. I put on my robe and made my way through the hallway and up the creaky stairs.

Elijah was sitting on the floor with Kate, she in her nightgown, he in his Big Bird pajamas, Tuddy between his legs. They were looking through one of the boxes of old pictures I kept up there, Elijah peering at them through his Coke-bottle glasses. Kate has a great sense of history; she loves to look through pictures. Most of the photos were rejects, the doubles and near-doubles, the ones of such poor quality or taste that they'd never make it into one of the albums. There were photos where my mother Charlotte looked a hundred and fifty years old (a serious affront to a woman who still plucks her eyebrows and dyes her hair red at the age of seventy); where Alex was blurry and the top of Sam's head was cut off; where Elijah looked particularly odd, the reflection of his glasses obscuring everything. He was a beautiful child, but only from some angles. From other angles he looked peculiar, with his wide-spaced eyes and the bulge in his forehead and his thick glasses.

More than a few were pictures of Sam and me as children and teenagers and young adults, the fifties, sixties, and early seventies versions of the prized collection I kept in the albums downstairs. In becoming a parent your own life is eclipsed, subsumed within your children's lives, downgraded, in this case to a box in a dusty attic.

Once, when she was in fifth grade, I tried to tell Kate about this process, this shift in which *I* becomes *I and my daughter and my son and my son.* The day she came home crying because Vanessa Van Dorn had told everyone she had bad breath.

I said, "Let me smell." She breathed in my face. "Sweet as springtime," I said.

She didn't believe me. Why should she? I'm her mother.

"Are you sure?"

I hugged her. "Positive."

She started to cry. "Then why did Vanessa say that?"

"She probably thinks that if she says bad things about you, everybody will like her instead." I leaked a few tears myself. Kate saw them.

"Why are *you* crying? I'm the one Vanessa said has bad breath."

"What makes you sad makes me sad."

"Why is that?"

"Your children are part of you." I moved her bangs off her forehead. "It's in the cells, in the molecules."

"What's a molecule?"

"The smallest, tiniest piece of something."

"What about all those bad mothers?"

"Their children are in their cells, too, they just don't know the right way to show it."

Now Elijah reached into the box and hauled out a handful of photos he promptly tossed up in the air like confetti. He laughed as the pictures floated down and scattered across the floor around them.

"Don't do that, little guy," Kate said, "you'll make a mess."

They did not see me, standing there. Elijah turned around to peer at Kate through his glasses, then moved in for a second handful.

"No. No, I'm serious now," Kate said. "Help me pick these up."

For a minute I thought he was going to have a tantrum. He didn't. He seemed so much happier and more content than he used to be, so much less frustrated. He picked Tuddy up and pressed him into Kate's face, with a little dancing turn of his wrist. She laughed, then sighed deeply. Her expression turned serious.

"Elijah?"

Sitting amidst the litter of photos, he looked up at her.

"When you were sleeping in the hospital? Do you remember?"

He nodded, slowly.

"Did you know we were there?"

He didn't respond, just stared at her with a cocked head and a puzzled expression.

"Were you scared?"

He raised his eyebrows. "Scared like on the merry-go?"

When he was three, Sam, Kate, and I took him on a Saturday outing to a local amusement park. He loved the place; he loved just *looking.* When Sam took him on the carousel, he loved it for about one revolution, then started to scream bloody murder. The operator had to stop the thing.

"Yes, like that."

"I like to go on the merry-go. Round and round. I like the blue sky and the horsies. And the song. I really like the song."

She looked at him for a moment, then she reached over and wrapped her arms around him, drew him to her chest. "Listen, little guy, you scared me. Much worse than the merry-go. Don't do that again. Okay?"

"Okay, Kate," Elijah said, his voice muffled by her fuzzy robe. She wiped her eyes and kissed the top of his head.

"It'll be okay, Kate," Elijah said.

"Yes, of course it will. And we're not scared, right?" She took a deep breath. "Well, that sure is good news. Now, what do you say we—you, me, and Tuddy—pick up these pictures?" She showed him how Tuddy could help pick up the photographs, too. With Tuddy helping they put all the photos back except for one I saw Kate slip into a pocket of her robe, then she closed the box, and they started downstairs.

"Mom! How long have you been standing there?"

"Long enough to see how much I love you both."

Later, when I was making breakfast, she showed me the photograph she'd pocketed. It had been taken at Killington, Vermont, the day before Sam and I made love for the first time. I am nineteen years old in the snapshot, and my leg is in a cast. Sam is just twenty. He and I are lying on a sofa, our heads at either end. Sam has no shirt on; his body is lanky, boyish, not so different than it is now, all these years later. I am wearing a peasant blouse with crudely stitched red embroidery edging around a scoop neck. Sam has his head resting on the side arm but he is looking at me, only at me. Our bare feet are touching, one of his to my one good foot; we are playing footsie. We were already in love, though we didn't yet know it. We had yet to make love, but we had to touch each other in any way we could, hands, feet, bodies; it was as necessary as breathing.

A doorway leads into a kitchen, where you can see a tall slim girl with a mass of frizzy red hair tending something on the stove. Julie. On the coffee table in front of the sofa are three burning candles, an ashtray full of cigarettes, a water pipe. Some of our group, including Sam and me, had been smoking just before the photograph was taken; you can just make out a faint white trail of smoke rising from the bowl. Julie had been steaming mad, at both of us.

"Well, hey, man," I said, trying to make light of the evidence of drug use, "we really were groovy, your father and me!"

"The grooviest," she said.

I handed the picture back to her.

"Who's the girl in the kitchen?"

"Oh, that's Julie," I said.

"The friend you mentioned. Where is she now?"

I did not want to tell her.

"*Tell* her!" the demon whispered.

"I haven't seen or heard from her in twenty-two years."

"But Dad said she and you were best friends."

"We were, Kate," I said. "When we were six, she showed up at my door with a frog she'd found under her house. We put it in Grandma's car."

My daughter giggled. "Wish I could have seen it. Grandma Charlotte trapped in a car with a frog!" Then, "So what happened with you two? You just drifted apart?"

"It's a long story, Kate. I'm not exactly proud of it."

"Why?"

"Well, if you must know, Julie had dated your father first."

She stared at me. "You stole him away from her?"

"Well, they had broken up recently. But I suppose you could look at it that way."

"I'll bet Julie did."

I started to defend myself. "Your father used to hang around a lot. We started getting to know each other. Julie and some other friends and I all went on a ski trip. I ended up skiing with your father, only I fell, and sprained my ankle. He took me to the hospital. We couldn't help it."

"Jennifer Megan did that to Lisa Pell a few weeks ago. Lisa and Gary Rothman had a date for a concert, but Lisa had to go to her grandma's house that night, and she told Gary to take Jennifer. So now Jennifer's dating Gary, and no one's talking to her."

I hugged her. Well, it was something like that.

"You know what your father said to me when we realized what was happening between us?" I was still defending myself. "He said that even if Julie forced me to make a choice between him and her, I should trust him. Because he just knew we were each other's one."

My daughter stared at me for a few seconds. Then she said, "That's the most romantic thing I've ever heard, Mom."

The demon made a *psshing* noise in my ear. "Romance?" it said, as it shimmered into the room. "I could take you right now."

Oh, please. Not again. Please not again.

Elijah walked into the kitchen just then, dragging Tuddy. He stopped, blinked.

"I gotta get to school," Kate said, grabbing her book bag from the kitchen chair. "See you later." She kissed me, kissed Elijah, and left.

I heard the door slam, Elijah was sniffing at the air. The demon moved toward him, laughing.

"Stay away from him," I said.

Elijah was staring right at the place in the kitchen where the demon occupied space.

The demon just went right on laughing. "Who are *you* to make demands?" it said to me. "You are nothing, you are no one, you are *mine*."

Elijah blinked rapidly, several times in succession. Then he wrinkled up his nose, and sniffed again. Was it possible he was seeing the demon?

"Elijah? Do you see something?"

The demon disappeared, instantly vanished like smoke in a gale.

Elijah stood there for a moment without speaking. I noticed that his eyes seemed particularly crossed, the right eye looking in an entirely different direction than the left. He pushed his glasses up on his nose, and that seemed to help him focus better.

"Did you see something there?" I pointed to the place where the demon had been standing.

He smiled. "He doesn't see me."

"*Who* doesn't see you?"

He put his chubby finger in front of Tuddy's mouth and said, "*Shhh.* Zipped lips."

Zipped lips? Where in the world had he heard such an expression? It certainly wasn't something *I* would ever say. Miss Stanakowski? Not with a classroom full of handicapped children, some of whom could barely talk.

"Where did you hear that saying, Elijah? Zipped lips."

He pursed his lips together and made a fish face. "I'm a fish, Mommy. Look at my lips." He pursed his lips again, released them, then pursed, then released. Again and again. I couldn't help laughing at his antics, and I dropped the subject of lips—fish lips, zipped lips, any kind of lips.

The demon didn't return that night, as promised, and I half-wondered whether Elijah had somehow scared it away.

twenty-two

"Mommy, can I have a pet fish?" Elijah asked. It was the day after the zipped lips incident. I tried to discourage him on the grounds that his hamster and Poppy might not like it, but Elijah said they needed some friends. So two days later, fish having become Topic #1, we went to the Everything Under One Woof Pet Shop to check out the fish.

Elijah marched up to the tank full of brilliant orange fish, took his glasses off, leaving them dangling on his chest, and pressed his nose to the glass. He stared into the tank for several minutes then pulled away, leaving little breath marks on the glass, tiny pearls, delicate as bubbles. He pursed and relaxed his lips, pursed and relaxed, pursed and relaxed, laughed at his own clowning, and moved on to the next tank. Finally, when he had finished looking into every single tank, he went back and pointed to the tanks where he'd seen a fish he particularly liked. This one. That one. And that one.

"But that's a tropical fish," the salesman said. "And it can only live in freshwater. And that one's a saltwater fish. And that one can only live in brackish water. You can't put them together."

Elijah put his glasses back on and stared up at the man. "Why?"

It was his favorite new word.

"Because you can't." The salesman looked at me.

"Because the freshwater fish doesn't like salt," I said.

Elijah shrugged. "He would if you gave him a chance."

"Look," the salesman said to me. "Why don't you just start out with a ten-gallon tank and a few small tropical fish? Just to get the hang of it. It's a little tricky to get the chemicals right in a saltwater tank."

"I like that one best." Elijah pointed to the large blue fish with the long nose, a saltwater variety.

We ended up with the saltwater tank, the blue fish with the long nose, and a yellow striped companion.

Sam's boss, Ed Larobina, had a friend with an epileptic daughter whose parents swore by her doctor, Dr. David Selson, of the Manhattan Medical Center.

"I called Selson's office and told them a little bit about Elijah," Sam said. "They said he'd be glad to give a second opinion. It's even covered by our insurance."

Elijah's hospitalization and follow-up had cost more than $250,000.

"Would we have to see Selson first?" We were scheduled for Moore's EEG the next day.

"No, but of course Selson's office could do the EEG, too. Or we can just take them the results."

"We might as well go ahead with Moore."

"Whatever you think." He came closer, put his hand on my shoulder. "Feel better?"

No.

"Where is everyone?"

"Alex and Kate are doing their homework. Elijah is fish watching."

"What's that?"

"You know how he's been bugging me to get him a fish. Well, we took the plunge, so to speak, this afternoon. We set the tank up in the dining room, and he's been in there ever since."

I followed Sam in. The lights were all off and the tank gave off an eerie blue glow.

"Well, now," Sam said, "those certainly are some beautiful fish." He switched on the light.

"Hi, Daddy." Elijah didn't turn around.

Sam leaned over and kissed his cheek. "Do they have names?"

Elijah shook his head and kept on staring into the tank.

"Look at that blue one," Sam said. "Wiggles his tail like he's dancing. You could always call him Elvis."

Elijah turned around and laughed. "Elvis," he said, and went back to fish watching.

"Dinner'll be ready in about twenty minutes," I said. "If Elijah can tear himself away."

I kissed him and he giggled.

The next morning Sam and I drove Elijah down to the hospital for his EEG. I was nervous about it, unsure how he'd react to being tethered by his head to a machine for twenty-four hours.

Elijah walked between Sam and me, holding our hands as we took him up to the pedi-floor, where they gave us a room for the night. He didn't seem to mind the ordeal, even when they gooped up his head. He sat quietly while they hooked him up and even laughed when he saw himself in a mirror a little later.

We had brought along games and toys to keep him amused, but mostly he wanted to walk around and talk to the nurses and doctors, show off Tuddy and his *Creatures of the Deep* book. He had become so friendly and interested, not afraid of anything, even hallways full of white coats. The machine was portable, and we wheeled it around with us.

Just before they brought Elijah his dinner, Sam went home. Elijah ate everything on his plate except the hot dog, then we—Elijah (and Tuddy and the book), me, and the electroencephalographic machine—went into the little playroom. A girl of about eight was already in the room, playing listlessly with a Barbie doll. Her bloated little face was as pale as dough and she was nearly bald, with just a few wispy clumps of fluff on her head, like duck fuzz. I nodded at the mother hovering over her, a woman nearly as pale as her daughter, with deep raccoon-like circles under her eyes.

"This is Margaret," the woman said softly. "We call her Maggie."

"Elijah," I said.

My son sat down next to Maggie and opened his book.

The little girl smiled, widening her chipmunk cheeks. "Do you want me to read that to you?" Her voice was barely audible, and scratchy.

Elijah nodded.

She took the book. "What happened to your head?"

Elijah smiled, then leaned over and whispered something in her ear. Maggie smiled back. Then she took my son's hand, and both of them closed their eyes. They stayed that way for a long while, holding hands, eyes closed.

Maggie's mother and I just watched. Neither of us made a sound.

After a few minutes the two children opened their eyes, and Maggie began reading the book to Elijah, and they looked at the pictures together. She seemed to love all the pretty fish, too. When she was finished, her mother said it was time for her to sleep, she had a big day tomorrow.

I slept on a cot next to Elijah's bed, and in the morning it was over, twenty-four hours of observation. There was no sign of any seizure activity, not a trace. But when Moore came in, he still said he wanted to keep Elijah on the medication, at least for another few months. Reason enough to get another opinion.

As I was packing up to leave, Maggie's mother came to the doorway. "Can I talk to you?"

"Sure."

I told Elijah I'd be right back, then went out to join her in the corridor.

"I asked Maggie why she and your son did that," she said. "I mean, closed their eyes."

I nodded but didn't say anything. Just held my breath.

"She just finished another round of chemotherapy, you know. Now they're talking about a bone marrow transplant. I mean, if we can find a match."

I put my hand on her arm. "I hope you can."

She sighed—a great, exhausted sigh. "My daughter is so, so sick. They're not even sure she's going to make it now." The woman's voice was full of tears. "She was in remission for a while, but it was during the winter, and she was sick again when summer came. She used to love summers, because she could swim. She hasn't been swimming in three years. Her father taught her when she was four and she was good at it until, well, until all this." Another sigh. "Her father and I are divorced now."

"I'm sorry."

She looked bewildered. "Can you imagine? A man walking out on a daughter so sick. He moved to New Jersey. He has a new wife now, hardly ever comes to see Maggie. I'm here all the time. He just couldn't take it, I guess. Sometimes I can't take it, either. I don't know. How could I have married someone who would do that? I'm sorry, I shouldn't be telling you this—"

"It's all right. Really."

She wiped her eyes. "Anyway, do you know what she told me she saw when she closed her eyes? She said they were swimming."

"Swimming?" I wanted to run away, I didn't want to hear it and I wasn't even sure why.

"She and your son," Maggie's mother continued. "She said the water was warm like a bath, and as clear as the air. Clear as the air, that's just what she said. And she said the sunlight was shining right through from the sky. And there were so many fish, she said, all bright colors." She hesitated. "She said swimming with Elijah was so much fun. And . . . well, I just wanted to tell you that. That she had fun. Maggie's so scared all the time. She never even smiles anymore. And she's so sick, and so tired of it all, and sometimes I think she wants to just give up. But last night when we got back to her room, she laughed when she told me about swimming. I'm not sure I understand it, how she could be swimming by just closing her eyes. But I do know she was laughing about it, giggling. It was so good to see her giggle again. Know what I mean?"

I did.

When Sam and I were getting ready for bed that night, I told him about Elijah and Maggie. Then I told him about my Great Barrier Reef vision, the azure water, the limitless ocean, though I referred to it as a dream.

Sam seemed barely interested. "And?"

"Isn't that sort of strange? That Elijah and Maggie were swimming like that? It's just like the dream. Like we shared a dream, or had the same vision, or something."

"You mean like a religious vision?"

My husband was a good man, a moral and charitable man, but his view of the world didn't include religious visions any more than it included ghosts.

"I don't know, Sam. Are there any other kind?"

"You're not a religious person."

"You mean because I haven't insisted on doing rituals?" We had tried to follow the most important customs in both religions. Sam took the kids to mass with him on Christmas, we lit Hanukkah lights, and had a little Passover Seder every year. Our children made out like bandits in December.

"Are you saying you wanted to do the rituals," he said, "and I was holding you back?"

How in the world had this turned into a fight? I just wanted him to understand.

"No, no."

"So what is it? My mother was holding you back?"

Each grandchild's birth had created a crisis between Sam and his mother. Mary Galligan always said she didn't care what we did about religion, so long as we baptized the children. Sam refused. Though he never told his mother why, he'd told me that he had no respect for any belief that a baby would be deprived of heaven, or whatever it was, just because the child wasn't baptized. Mary always let the matter drop until the next child was about to be born, at which point she'd start working on him again.

"Sam, no. I just want you so see that something extraordinary is happening, something—"

"So they pretended they were swimming," he said. "They're kids."

But he hadn't *seen* it.

A few weeks later, in early April, I have a new dream.

Elijah is lying on the bed, hooked up to suck-*hissing* machines. I am standing beside him with Charlotte, who pulls a small scissors and an envelope out of her purse. She has prepared for this, she has brought things with her. And she takes in her fingertips an inch-long curl of Elijah's hair, now brittle as dull red straw. There is so much hair. The body without consciousness is on mechanical grow mode, the bones lengthen, puberty arrives, the hair gets longer, parched and wild as an untended garden.

Snip-snip.

She slips the lock of hair into the envelope, tucks the envelope and the scissors back into her purse. She doesn't look at me, because she thinks I am upset by what she's done. I am not upset, the living dead have no emotions. But I'm still plenty smart, I know why she has done this. My mother has taken his hair so that she'll have it when he's gone. And he will be gone, I know that, though I don't know when. I realize then that taking a lock of Elijah's hair might be something I want to do, too. Then I'll always have it, even when I have no way to get to him, even when he's in his grave.

I opened my eyes, awake in the middle of the night again, buffeted back and forth by the twin winds, fear and hope. The demon, who played with time like it was bouncing a ball back and forth, back and forth, had been watching me sleep.

"What kind of woman are you? So ungrateful."

I got up and went into the bathroom to pee. I had taken to doing that, ignoring it as best I could.

It stood there while I did my business at the toilet. "You know, I will possess you again." It never raised its voice. Never seemed angry. It murmured, it whispered, it insinuated. I hated that.

"Rape, you mean."

It leaned against the back of the sink, crossed its limbs over its midsection, and smiled sardonically, a cartoon devil. I blinked and I could see the heavy black boots again, caked with mud. Just for a moment back to Seth. I blinked and he was gone.

"I can see your body beneath that nightgown," it told me.

I stood and pulled up my panties. "I'm a middle-aged woman. Find someone young and supple."

It laughed, and I could see its teeth. "You would wish me on a mere babe?"

"Go away." I tried to pretend it didn't scare me, a useless deception.

"Oh, zip your lips," it said.

Zipped lips?

"You stay away from my son."

"Your son?" It was behind me, hissing like a steam engine in my ear. "Breathe deeply, Dinah. Shall I tell you what might have happened to your son were it not for me, what still could happen?"

No.

Yes.

Night. A luminous full moon bathes row upon row of identical stones in a pale light. The air feels like late autumn, gusty with a chill wind. The wind whips at my nightgown; the leaves dance in the air, skate over the stones, make scraping noises like scratching animals. I am old, very old, my flesh has begun to sag.

The demon ghost takes my hand and we walk among those stones, over the graves. I see dark shapes shuffling here and there, a netherworld of lost souls.

"There." It points with a ghost finger in the moonlight. "There it is."

I look. Carved into the headstone are the words: *Elijah Rosenberg Galligan. Beloved Son, Grandson, and Brother.*

I kneel down at my son's grave and trace the letters with my fingers. Those few words are not enough for a life, not for my son's life.

"He would have made it to twelve, Dinah. Just imagine that party. Carry the kid and roll his machines with him, put him in the beanbag with his machines, bend him in the middle, arrange him in a sitting-up pose, if you have the strength to move the steel-hard limbs, and light some candles. Happy Birthday, Elijah.

"Think of it, Dinah. Your child's smell is the last thing you'd ever think about, but you think about it now. You know what it's like to live with its loss every day."

Oh, my demon is right. I would be so grateful for a fleeting whiff, oh, my sweet little boy's smell, the smell of his hair, the back of his neck, behind his ear, his arm. Oh, if only I had kept his Tuddy instead of burying it with him in this ground. It will be a very long time before his smell disappears from that fuzzy turtle. Turtle fuzz isn't like flesh, it *might* still smell like Elijah, even though I am old myself now. If I had Tuddy now, I could have Elijah anytime I wanted. But Tuddy is in the ground beneath me, clutched in a corpse's arms.

"You really *are* a selfish bitch, aren't you?" the demon says. "All this pretense of being a good person. The kid needs comfort from his Tuddy, and you would take that away from him?"

"If he's dead he's with God," I say. "Surely God is enough comfort that he doesn't need his turtle, too. So I could have kept the turtle for my own consolation."

The ghost makes a mocking, whistling sound that the wind carries away.

"Please, I want the turtle," I say. "Can't we open Elijah's grave?"

"Of course," the demon says.

Shovel and shovel, a pile of dirt. It opens the vault, lifts the lid, tosses it aside as if the lid weighs nothing, and then we can see the casket within. It lifts this second, smaller lid. I close my eyes to the sight of decaying flesh. But then I grow bolder and withdraw the turtle from the blackened little hand and from under the arm, that Tuddy cloth that does not decay like flesh. And then I hold the turtle to my breast, and smell that smell, ignoring the other smells that cling to it now. Yes. Faint, but there. I can still smell my son. Now that I have Tuddy back, I'll be able to smell my son in the turtle for a very long time until all trace of the smell finally vanishes. It is all I have left, and I whisper, "Elijah."

"Ah," the demon says. "You would be quite mad with grief."

I look it in the eye, or rather the two black beads that pretend to be eyes. "I am mad now."

It places its outer membrane against my cheek, the cold seems to pass right through me. "It doesn't have to be this way, my Dinah. We can be together."

"Please, please." I weep.

"Go ahead, cry then. In the end, you will love me. And you will beg me to come to you. You will beg!"

The demon not only wants to possess me, it wants me to desire possession.

"Please. I cannot bear it again." No. I cannot. Not the metal hunger, the stinging wind, the eternal emptiness and wanting of release.

The ghost demon pulls me to my feet. "Come, Dinah. You must find some small stones."

"Stones?"

"Your people's custom? An old Jewish custom. What's wrong with you, don't you even know that? They leave a permanent record of your visit. You must leave them every time you come."

"But this isn't real," I say, my voice a gulp, a burp, in the whipping wind.

The demon regards me with great solemnity. "It might be real, Dinah. Perhaps it is." It touches me with its glacial talons. It moves to me and presses itself against me again. I feel the cold beneath that flimsy nightgown.

I withdraw, kneel down over the grave again, weep again. "My son. My son."

"Oh, stop that whining," the demon intones. "How do I bear it anymore? Women lose children. Always have, always will. Everyone has tragedies. You think life is a party? When Seth was alive, he lost his mother. He was only ten."

"Did it hurt you, when you lost your mother?"

It makes a shrugging movement, and its eyes go all white, and it rises above me, floating for a moment, its form fading away. You can see right through it to the dancing leaves, to the stars and moon.

"Nothing hurts me. I am a ghost," it whispers. "The stones, Dinah. You must leave the stones."

"Why?"

Back beside me again, just as it was, its teeth gleam in the moonlight. "Your ancestors piled stones on graves. To keep the spirits down, keep them from getting out and roaming the earth."

"Like you? You roam the earth."

"Like me." It kneels down beside me. "Be with me now."

"Be with you? I hate you."

Its laugh bounces off the moon and stars.

"Then wash the guilt from your hands," it says.

I was back in my bathroom, and the demon was gone, and my hands were covered with blood. I began to rub at my skin, at the dark stains on my fingers and my dusky palms, to scour and massage, but no matter how hard I rubbed, the blood remained.

"Dinah?" Sam was standing in the doorway. "It's three o'clock in the morning and you're standing here, rubbing at your hands like Lady Macbeth."

I burst into tears. The demon had done it on purpose. It wanted me to tell Sam.

"What is it, Di? What is going on?"

I stared at the man I'd been married to for half my life. I had to tell him.

"Are you sure you want to know?"

He nodded. I wiped my eyes and took a breath. "Do you remember when I said I heard singing in the hospital?"

Another nod.

"It was Elijah's lullaby. 'Wynken, Blynken, and Nod.' Someone was singing it."

"What does that have to do with this?"

"Listen to me, Sam." I clasped my hands together. "I kept hearing the song. And hearing it. And hearing it. So I went out into the corridor. I saw a ghost, Sam."

"You saw a ghost." His voice was flat, without inflection. It was not a question, not even a statement, just words strung together.

"Or a demon, I'm not sure which."

He studied my face for a long time. "Oh God, Dinah," he said finally. "You're serious."

"Very serious."

He rubbed both palms against his cheeks, then said, "I think I need a drink."

I stared. "Since when do you drink in the middle of the night?"

He pulled on his robe. "Only when my wife tells me she saw a ghost."

"Sam, you *know* me." I followed him into the living room. "You know I'm not the kind of person who'd imagine something like this. You know that."

He went to the bar and poured himself a stiff drink—scotch, yet. Then sat down on one of the sofas and took a swallow. "I don't know, Dinah. I mean, Elijah's been sick, and you've been worried, and under a lot of pressure."

"Sam, please. Elijah said he heard his lullaby. Remember?"

"But he could have heard you, or Kate was singing. He was in a coma, after all. They say people hear others talking sometimes around them when they're in a coma."

"And he could have heard what I heard, Sam."

He sighed and took another swallow. "All right, tell me. You saw a ghost."

"There was this being, in the corridor. Just sitting on the bench, playing a guitar."

"A guitar-playing being? But this was a ghost. Dead. Right?"

"That's right."

"And did it speak—did this ghost speak to you?"

I started to laugh. "Speak? God, yes. Hours and hours, it spoke. Day and night. This ghost has verbal diarrhea."

He sighed. "Dinah, Dinah . . . You're the psychologist. Anyone can snap."

"Please, Sam. I'm trying to tell you this. It's hard enough."

"I'm sorry. What did the being look like?"

"Pink. Like it was made out of cotton candy. And it was wearing muddy boots and bell-bottom jeans and a black leather jacket. It looked like a hippie." I took another deep breath. "Sam, you know I had a lover before you."

"I should think you had several. Who cares?"

"Well, he obviously does."

"Who?"

"Seth does. Seth Lucien, my first lover. That's who it is."

"Dinah, please, I'm trying here. That's who *what* is? There's this ghost, there's your lover—your lover before we married, right? What's he got to do with your ghost?"

"He *is* the ghost. He says he's the ghost of Seth Lucien, who was my lover before you."

"What about David?"

"Before him."

Sam got up, paced around a few minutes, sat back down on the sofa. Heavily. "So you're being haunted. By the ghost of a dead lover."

"I know how nutty it sounds, Sam."

He stared at me. "*Nutty?* Dinah, this is way, way beyond nutty."

"Don't you think I know that?"

He got up and began pacing again, holding his drink in his hand, the ice tinkling in the glass. "Dinah, you really have to get some help."

"Listen to me, Sam. In the hospital I kept seeing this ghost, and seeing him, and he kept tormenting me."

"How could you be any more tormented?"

"He destroyed my hope."

"Hope is what you have inside, you're in charge of it, Dinah. That makes no sense."

"He showed me, Sam. Somehow he showed me what could happen,

the worst that could happen. He's still doing it. Were you always so sure Elijah was going to make it?"

Sam sighed. "I don't know, I tried to be sure."

"In a way, at first, he gave me some comfort. I was petrified, Sam. I still am."

"But why?"

"You weren't petrified?"

"Of course I was. But I didn't manufacture a ghost to comfort me."

What did comfort you then, Sam? Your relentless optimism, your unrealistic sanguinity? "You think I'm making this up."

He took a sip of his drink. "Making it up? No. I think you must believe what you're telling me. And I may have been petrified, but I'm not *still* petrified."

"I haven't made this up, Sam. And I am still petrified."

"Why didn't you come to me before? Then?"

"I wasn't capable of coming to anyone with anything at the time. I could barely take my next breath. Anyway, you would have said the same thing you're saying now. That it's crazy. That I'd snapped under the emotional strain."

"Dinah, I don't believe in such things." He sat down on the sofa again, took my hands in his. "Neither do you."

I sat down next to him. "I never did before. Now I have no choice but to believe." I started to take a calming breath, then I got a whiff of it. The metallic smell, the odor of empty damp metal. "It's here, Sam. Right now."

Sam's upper lip was raised at one side and quivering. It was as if he were trying, unsuccessfully, to keep his face from registering distaste, from showing any emotion at all.

"I don't see anything."

The demon laughed and mocked. "What, will these hands ne'er be clean?"

"But you do," Sam said.

"I don't see it right now, either."

"But sometimes you do."

"It comes to me in my dreams, in visions, it appears in our bedroom, in my office. It won't leave me alone. It kept telling me that Elijah was going to die. It said it could help me. It said it could show me how to escape the Angel of Death."

"The *what?*"

"They say that when a person dies they breathe their last breath when the Angel of Death drips a drop of poison from his sword into their mouth."

He was up again. "Who says? Some *Hassid* with sidecurls? Some Christian fanatic? Who?"

"It's an old, old tale. The ghost said he could help me save Elijah. Escape the angel. I made a deal with it, Sam."

"For our son's life?" His eyes, oh, his eyes.

"Yes."

"Dinah, wait a minute. This is too much." He closed his eyes for a moment, then opened them and looked right into mine. "What was the deal?"

"In return, I have to be with it."

"What? What does that mean, Dinah?"

"It means I have to let it inside of me."

Sam's square jaw was clenched, like a fist. He took off his glasses and rubbed his eyes.

"Dinah, that is disgusting."

"It's not sexual, Sam."

"What the hell is it?"

"It enters by . . . I mean, through . . ." I stopped. How could I describe such a thing to him?

"Well, whatever it is, Dinah, it's still disgusting. And it's also nuts. I'm going to bed."

He had no idea how disgusting or nuts. Not even a clue.

twenty-three

"Morning, Mom. Morning, Elijah."

Alex walked into the kitchen on a warm spring morning, wearing a black Megadeth T-shirt stamped with a cartoon of a huge skull. Inside its open mouth was a girl drawn with big cartoon breasts, wearing a few white lines intended to depict a skimpy bikini. Sam had left early for an out-of-town trip, leaving me to deal with the offensive sartorial display on my own, before my second cup of coffee, yet. Elijah was eating pancakes in his pajamas, swinging his feet back and forth under the table, face full of syrup.

"Morning, Alex. What do you want for breakfast?"

"No time." He opened the fridge, peered inside, then closed it.

"Have some juice." We had this same conversation every day.

"Okay."

I handed him the juice. "I hate to say it, Alex, but that is one god-awful shirt."

He downed a gulp. My fourteen-year-old seemed taller and more handsome every day, despite the attire. No wonder girls were constantly calling him, trying to be casual in their polite, earnest voices: "Hello, Mrs. Galligan, can I speak to Alex?"

"I like this shirt," Alex said.

"It ought to come with a rating. PG for Probably Gruesome. Or maybe DV. For Definitely Vulgar."

"You're not going to tell me I can't wear it." Another gulp.

"No, I'm not. But what is it about misogynist art that appeals to you?"

"I don't even know what that means, Mom." He sat down next to Elijah and snatched a piece of pancake from his plate.

Elijah giggled, reached for it just before it disappeared into Alex's mouth. "Hey!"

"Mom's right, Alex." Kate came into the kitchen, dressed as usual in baggy jeans ripped practically front to back at both knees. "That shirt has got to go. Seriously."

"I only bought it last week," Alex said.

"And the store, I'm sure, is forever grateful that you took it off their hands," I said.

He rolled his eyes. "Give me a break, Mom."

"It's not just the shirt, it's what's *on* the shirt."

"And the music, and the earring, right? So you tell everyone."

The "Agitated Observer" piece I called "Generation Gap" had run just a few days ago. I hadn't mentioned Alex by name but I'd used his newfound interests as a way into my own musings on the moment of truth in life when you suddenly realize your complaints about your children sound just like your parents' complaints about you sounded.

"I thought you didn't even read my column, Alex."

"I didn't need to read it. Adam showed it to me."

I sighed. "I'm sorry if it embarrassed you, Alex."

He shrugged. "It didn't. Anyway, what about *her?"* He pointed at his sister, who was pouring herself some juice. "What about those jeans?"

I hadn't meant to start World War III.

"This is just a style, Alex." Kate put her hand on her hip. "But when you're a little punk I guess the only way you can prove what a big man you are is to wear a shirt like that with a naked woman on it."

"She's not naked," my son said. "Get a life, babe."

My palms went damp.

Kate was frowning. "Babe? Excuse me?"

"Where'd you hear that expression, Alex?" I asked.

"All his friends talk that way, Mom," Kate said. "It makes them feel like big men."

"Kate's mad," Elijah said.

"No, I'm not, little guy." She kissed Elijah on the cheek, then moved past Alex. "Gotta go. 'Bye."

" 'Bye, Kate," Elijah said.

She grabbed her book bag and was gone. I turned back to Alex. "I really am sorry about the column."

He shrugged.

"Don't be mad at Mommy," Elijah said.

"It's all right, Elijah. He's allowed to be mad."

"I'm not really mad." Alex was pouring himself more juice. "It's no big deal."

"How about if I never mention I have a son in print again?"

"Everybody knows now. What's the point of never mentioning it again?"

I poured myself another cup of coffee, took it over to the table, and sat down next to Elijah. I took a sip.

"Mommy loves you, too, Alex," Elijah said.

Alex stared at him for a moment, then turned to me. "I'm sorry, Mom. I think your column is cool. It's just a shirt. I'm just expressing myself." His look of amusement reminded me of his father, though lately Sam was more upset and wary than amused.

"Some forms of expression are better than others." I wiped Elijah's face. He sputtered.

Alex sighed. "Don't worry so much, Mom. I'm fine. When I start flunking out of school, then you can worry." He came over and kissed me on the forehead. "See you later."

"Do you like that shirt, Elijah?" I said when Alex had gone, slamming the door behind him.

He shook his head. "It's ugly."

"I'm with you, kiddo."

Holding his fork in a meaty grip, Elijah took the last bite of his pancake. "Don't be mad."

I wiped his mouth again. "Why's that?"

"Because then *he'll* be mad. He'll change his mind."

"How do you know that?"

Elijah took a sip of his orange juice. "He will."

"How the hell does *he* know?"

I jumped. The demon was sitting on top of the counter, dangling its boots.

"Know what?"

"Know that Alex will change his mind."

"You did this to Alex."

Its eyes quivered. "Lady, you have really lost it. You think I can haunt two people at once? You think this is easy?"

I moved in front of him, to block his view of Elijah. "Stay away from my children."

It feigned a look of indignation. "After all I did, I should expect a little appreciation—"

"Stay away."

"Make me." It sniggered and disappeared.

I had no patients that day, was coming up on deadline, had not a germ of an idea for the next column, and was so jumpy that concentration was hopeless. Knowing the potential consequences of using either of my teenage children as fodder didn't help.

I turned on my computer, and for two hours sat with an empty screen and an even emptier head.

Sam called around noon. "Hi, Di. Here I am in beautiful downtown Milwaukee."

I'd been so preoccupied I didn't even remember where he said he was going.

When he asked me how the kids were, I told him about the Megadeth T-shirt incident.

"I really don't think you should make such a big deal about this stuff."

This from the man who'd said the lyrics to Alex's music were sadistic? "The shirt doesn't bother you, Sam?"

My husband was silent.

"Sam?"

"Dinah, I think . . . I mean, I really think you should worry about yourself right now."

"Sam, I am not crazy."

He sighed. "I just think you should talk to somebody besides me."

"I don't need a psychiatrist."

"Dinah, I'm sorry, but I think you do. You tell me you're being haunted by a ghost, and you expect me to just believe you?"

"Maybe it's you who needs the psychiatrist, Sam. You are so intent on calling me crazy, you don't even see what's been happening with your son."

"Which son?" I could hear phones ringing in the background. Must be calling me from his client's office.

"Elijah. How can you not have noticed the things he says, what he's suddenly interested in. It's like something's changed in him."

"He's happier, less scared of the world. Smarter, maybe. What's bad about that?"

"How can you be so complacent? Sam, you told me yourself he said he could see God by listening for Him."

"So? Kids say all kinds of things. And what does this have to do with this ghost you're telling me about, anyway?"

"I don't really know, Sam. I just thought you would help me."

"Help you? I don't know what to do."

"Neither do I, Sam."

"So maybe you should talk to someone who does."

Who? Ghostbusters? "I'll see you tonight, Sam. When do you get in?"

"I land at six. I'll be there around seven. We have the party, remember?"

Right. I'd completely forgotten Becky and Mark had invited us to Mark's forty-seventh birthday party that night.

"I remember." I hung up before he could tell me he loved me, which I didn't want to hear.

As we were dressing for the party that evening, he brought up the psychiatrist again.

"You know, Sam," I said, slipping a silk blouse over my head, "your concern about my seeing a doctor is touching, but you haven't even asked if I've called David Selson for Elijah."

He was pulling on a pair of pants. "You're the one who wanted a second opinion."

"You don't?"

"Frankly, I trust Moore. I think he's being cautious, and that's probably good." He began buttoning his shirt.

"And you like him?"

"Not particularly. He's not the friendliest guy in the world, but who cares? Besides, we have opinions from Moore and both of his colleagues."

"How do you know they even agree?"

Sam's hands dropped to his sides. "What makes you think they don't?"

It wasn't something I could explain to him. "Well," I said, "if they don't agree, they're discussing their disagreement behind closed doors. And we'll never know. Will we?"

"I think you think too much, Dinah."

I thought the way my mind worked was part of what he loved about me.

"You want everything in life to be perfect," my husband said, "including the people in it. Including yourself. And if it isn't perfect, you think you can will it to be perfect. Or analyze it into perfection."

I grabbed my purse. "I just want my baby to be okay."

He grabbed my shoulders, looked me square in the face. "Elijah is fine."

"Who wants everything perfect now? Pretending doesn't make it so."

"Dinah, I just think this ghost business is coming from deep in your mind, maybe as a way to help you find a reason for your continued pain. Anxiety. Whatever it is."

"Please, Sam. Spare me the amateur analysis, would you? We could lose him, and you seem entirely too complacent about it."

"And you seem entirely too hysterical. We are not going to lose him."

Becky greeted us at the door of her dramatic, contemporary home. She was wearing drama, too, deep red lipstick, pale white makeup that set off her shining black hair. And the black slip dress from Henry Lehr.

"Come in, come in." She kissed us and I looked through the two-story foyer into the living room, to a party already well under way. She had lit candles everywhere, adding to the romance and atmosphere. I was in no mood for a party.

"You look wonderful, honey," Becky said.

"Thanks." I didn't feel wonderful.

"Hey, what about me?" Sam whipped off his glasses and struck a pose. "Don't I look wonderful, too?"

She sidled up to him, batted her eyes. "Baby, do you."

This little pseudoflirtatious exchange was typical for the two of them, but that night it irritated me. Maybe it was because Sam was so damned self-possessed. After all, we'd just had an argument that for us was major, and arguments were getting to be a habit.

I was determined to act uncrazy. I kissed Mark when he came over, vowing that I would never say a word about his failure to show up at the hospital except that one brief uncomfortable time, instead talked to him about a case he was working on. I took Sam's arm as we moved toward the Magills and the Sterns. Talked with the Magills about their daughter's college choice, listened while they said they had meant to come to the hospital but just couldn't make it, heard more than I could ever have wanted to know about the Purcells' $60,000-over-budget, six-months-overdue addition.

"How's the job hunt going?" I asked Addie, who'd faithfully visited, who'd painted the beautiful dinosaur chest in Elijah's room. Only last month, she'd lost her job with a New York publisher when a European conglomerate purchased the company.

"I've decided I'm not going to get another job," she said. "Paul and I decided we can afford for me to take a break. Twenty-two years I've been working, commuting. I'm going to take it easy for a while."

"Sounds good to me," I said. "You can always go into business painting furniture."

She smiled. "Actually, I'm not going to be a total lug. I'm going to teach the nursery art class at the Jewish Community Center this summer. Thursday afternoons. Hey, maybe Elijah could come."

"I tried putting him in that class once, Addie. Last year, when Sue Weinberg taught it. It didn't work out too well."

"Oh, I didn't know."

"Of course, he's doing so incredibly well now, he might be okay."

She touched my shoulder. "Well, I'd say we ought to give Elijah another try at art. We start in a couple of weeks. What do you say?"

I mingled and chatted and smiled until just after the cake was served.

"I heard your son was sick, Dinah," said Ann Louise Remson, a real-estate colleague of Becky's. A wiry blond woman, she always dressed in conservative knit suits, stockings, and pumps, as if she'd just stepped out of the Talbots catalogue. She had a clipped way of talking, and an abrupt manner that always made me think she bestowed time by assessing what any particular person could do for her. A local shrink wasn't on her radar.

"Is he all right now?" she asked, looking past me to a group over by the piano that included the Magills and the Lawrences. According to the gossip from Becky, Bill Lawrence had made a fortune in computers over the last few years. Maybe Ann Louise was zeroing in on them, in case they bought a bigger house anytime soon.

"Yes, he's fine," Sam said. "Thanks."

"It's wonderful that you're here tonight."

I looked at her.

She sighed. "I mean . . . I don't know. If my Patty or Louis got sick like that, I swear, I don't think I could ever leave them again. Not for a minute."

Becky was staring at me, I could feel the heat of her eyes. I didn't care.

"You know what, Ann Louise?" I said. "You're a jerk."

Her mouth opened wide enough to catch a squadron of flies.

I turned to go. "I'm sorry, Becky, Mark. Sam, I need to go now."

As I headed for my wrap I could hear them making apologies for me, explaining that I'd been under a lot of strain lately. And Sam and I had yet another confrontation when we got home, this one silent and full of accusatory stares.

I needed a diversion, and the best I could come up with was a Wednesday matinee. The Art House is the kind of place you don't see much anymore, at least outside of New York City, since they've all been turned into twelve-screen movie parks. At the Art House you get serious films and foreign films, beautiful, slow-moving films about small, poignant moments. The kind of films Sam, whose favorite movie is *The Terminator,* fell asleep watching, always insisting afterward that he'd seen every frame. My testing him after a foreign movie was one of our running jokes. When I woke him up at the end of *Babette's Feast,* he said, "Loved it!" "Oh yeah? What was it about?" He grinned and said, "Let's eat."

They were already showing the trailers when I pushed open the doors to the theater that afternoon. The whole space pulsed with the light and noise of car crashes, gunshots, helicopter rotors, explosions, and shrieks. Why were they showing a triple-testosterone trailer at the beginning of a movie like *Il Postino?*

I began to walk down the wide aisle. When the trailer ended and the screen went dark for a few seconds, I swayed.

"Whoa. You all right?" The voice was male. He caught my arm.

I turned around but could make out only a broad black shape. "I'm okay, thanks."

Now a voiceover and a second trailer were heralding, ta-da!, the ultimate in action and adventure.

"What do you think they'll say after everything's been called the ultimate?"

"What?" I looked back at the dark figure again, just as a white flash from the screen illuminated his features for maybe half a second. He was handsome, about forty-five or fifty, tall, broad. You don't have to study a face at length to recognize handsome and guess an age.

I smiled. "I guess they'll just have to come up with ever greater superlatives."

He smiled back. "And I'm sure they will."

I chose a seat in the middle of the nearly empty theater. The coming attractions ended, finally. The lights dimmed, the credits began. A clarinet, high and plaintive. A charming Italian town. You could tell this wasn't an American film by the look of the actors, who resembled regular people, except for the woman the postman loved, dark-skinned and breathtakingly beautiful. When I see women who look like that playing such roles, I always think, For God's sake, all your character has to do to get out of that life is head for Eileen Ford. Oh, honey, are we going to make you a star.

Every image on the screen seemed to have been tipped in gold, perhaps by a filter over the camera. The poet was thoughtful and noble, the postman simple and wise. The camera movements were languid, the Capri vistas sweeping.

"Are you all right?"

I turned. The same man was sitting in the row behind me, just a few seats over. The last credits were rolling. I had slipped into another daydream, I think, yet another imagining of a dreaded future. I'd been so caught up in my own suffering that I hadn't even realized I'd been sobbing. He must have heard me.

"I'm fine. Thank you." I took the handkerchief the man held out. "Just a sentimental fool, I guess."

"Me too."

"Oh. Were you crying, too?" I handed back the handkerchief.

"Only on the inside," he said.

We both started moving out of our rows.

"Did you like the film?" he asked.

"I liked it." I'd been watching without taking much in. Poetry and love. Great scenery.

"I used to write poetry," he said. "To my ex-wife, before we were married. After we were married a few years . . . well, you know you're in trouble when your wife starts criticizing your love poems. Even when they're written for her."

I laughed. "I guess that's why she's your ex."

We had reached the end of the rows and started up the aisle together.

"One of the whys. But do you think life is like the film? That people from such different places can affect each other so profoundly like that?"

"I'm not sure."

"I'm probably bothering you. Sorry."

"I'm probably being rude," I said, stopping for a moment as we got to the lobby, redolent with popcorn.

"Why shouldn't you be rude? I could be a serial killer, for all you know."

I laughed and started walking again. "Are you?"

He laughed and guided me around a group of people blocking the entrance. People were trickling in for the next screening. "Definitely not," he said. "Ask my patients, any of them."

I stared.

"I'm a physician."

"Really." I said this evenly, as if it were neutral information for me. We had come out of the front doors and were standing on the sidewalk in front of the theater now, in the glare of a sunny afternoon. I fished my sunglasses out of my bag.

He nodded. "Wednesday's my day off. I like movies. We surgeons need our downtime, too."

I put my sunglasses on my face. "Surgeon, huh?"

"You have something against surgeons?"

"Well, you know what they say about surgeons."

"That our egotism is exceeded only by our arrogance?"

I smiled. "Something like that."

"That there's only one thing we think is larger than our own importance?"

"Something like that, too." I realized I was blushing.

"Oh, yeah? Well, who are they? Can you get them here? I'd at least like the opportunity to defend myself and my ego, which is actually on the puny side."

The guy was charming. "I'm sorry. Someday I'll learn to keep my big mouth shut."

"No need to apologize. I'm the one who spelled it out, anyway. And whoever they are, they're probably right." He smiled and extended his hand. "I'm Peter St. Clair."

I shook his hand. "Dinah Galligan."

He stared at me for a moment, then said, "You write the humor column for the Connecticut *Star?* The 'Agitated Observer'?"

"Guilty as charged. Assuming I can come up with an idea for my next one—I'm stuck, which is why I went to the movies. Diversion."

"Your column is the best thing in that rag," he said. "Didn't see it for a while. I really got a laugh out of 'Film Noir Housewife.' "

"Thanks."

"But why do you give the impression in the piece that you're a housewife when you're not?"

"Why do you read the paper if you think it's such a rag?"

He notched a finger up in the air. "One for you. Oh, just to keep up on the local and state news. And because of your column, of course." Smile. "You live here in Norwalk?"

We were standing on the sidewalk now. "Westport. How about you?"

"Fairfield," he said. "You like writing the column? Must be fun."

Well, I used to like it, used to like a lot of things. "Actually, the column is a sideline. I'm really a psychologist. We aren't exactly known for our humility, either."

"Psychologist and columnist. I'm impressed. You have a practice around here?"

"Westport. You?"

"Fairfield. Neurosurgery."

I couldn't help myself. "You know Abner Moore?"

"Not personally, but I heard him speak at a conference last year."

"Really. What was the topic?" And did Moore's eyes dart-dart when he spoke to a crowd, or did that only happen one-on-one?

"He's doing some interesting research on prenatal neurological development."

"He should stick to research. His bedside manner leaves a lot to be desired."

"Did he treat you for something?"

"Look, Peter, I—"

"I'm sorry. I don't mean to pry."

"I'm sorry, too. I'm the one who brought it up." And shouldn't have.

Peter St. Clair hesitated for a moment, rubbing the palm of his left hand over his mouth and chin. He had fine hands, strong but elegant, graceful, with scrupulously clean nails. A surgeon's hands.

"Would you like to have a cup of coffee with me, Dinah?" He glanced at his watch. "I haven't got anything to do all afternoon. It's my day off."

"I'm married, Peter. I have three children."

He threw his head back and laughed. "I have two kids myself. It's just a cup of coffee. I'd like to hear why you think Moore should stick to research."

"I really don't think so, Peter. But thanks, anyway."

Sam got home very late that night. He spent a little time with the children, I did some paperwork at my desk and racked my brain for an idea. When we went up to bed, the first words out of his mouth were, "Did you call yet?"

He meant a psychiatrist, not Dr. Selson.

Heidi Victoria Vasquez. She was my first new patient in months. I was losing patients, not gaining, down to fifteen at that point.

The only other patient of the day came just before her, Danielle O'Connor, who had finally told her mother the truth about her husband, that all those bruises she had all over her all the time weren't the result of myopia or clumsiness. Her mother accused her of lying. When Danielle convinced her she wasn't, her mother started to make a list of her failings: She'd gained some weight; she did smart-mouth her husband; she was too lenient with the children. "I'm sure he'll stop if you would just work on those things. He's such a good father."

I asked her if she thought that was true.

She started to cry. "He's hit me in front of my daughter. Would a good father do that?"

It was a long way from leaving him, but it was a start. Maybe I could, at least, hold on to her.

The new patient was twenty-six years old and had legs that went on forever, blond hair, and boobs the size of twin peaks. Perky, pretty, wearing an outfit that was just a hair too sexy for work, the skirt a little too high and the blouse a little low-cut.

I introduced myself and let her settle in, then asked why she'd come.

"It's my boyfriend. Larry." Her voice was throaty, sexy.

"What about him?"

She crossed her legs. The skirt really was short. I actually caught a glimpse of underwear. "Well, he knows I'm in love with him, and he's in love with me. But he won't leave his wife. I know he wants to, but he feels . . . I don't know, loyal."

"Loyal?" I said. "You say it as if it were a dirty word." I was being more confrontational than usual, but it wasn't a bad question.

She laughed, showing a mouthful of straight white teeth. "Well, the woman's not any kind of a wife to him, I can tell you that. She's a nag, she pays no attention to him, he really ought to leave her. He'd be much better off. I mean, don't you think women like that should just give it up, instead of clinging and clinging?"

"I thought you said she pays no attention to him."

She lowered her eyes. "As a woman, I mean."

"I see. Why don't we talk about you for a while?"

She crossed her legs the other way. "Men respond to me. I don't know why, they just always have. All ages—Larry's a lot older than I am."

"How old is he?"

She shrugged. "Forty-four."

"Sam is forty-four," came a hiss in my ear.

Damn. What now?

"Married a long time?"

"Forever." She groaned. "Twenty-one years."

"Just like you." Another hiss.

Damn. Damn. Damn.

"So," I asked my patient, "he hasn't told her you're in the picture?"

"He said he would but then he didn't. And that was two months ago."

She expected him to leave his wife of all those years after a few months with her? We definitely had some narcissism going here, unrealistic expectations, a touch of grandiosity. I did my standard intake, we made an appointment for the following week, and I walked her to the door, thankful the demon sabotage had been limited to whispers and suggestions. The receptionist handed me a stack of mail and gestured toward a small, brown stuffed bear that was sitting upright at one end of the desk.

"That came for you too, Dr. Galligan." She smiled.

Cute. The bear had on a little white coat, and spectacles, and a stethoscope around its neck. A card was pinned to the coat. I took it back into my office and opened it:

Dear Dinah,

I hope you don't mind that I looked up the address of your office. I think I offended you yesterday, and I wanted to apologize. I'm sure my behavior did nothing to change your assessment of physicians as arrogant egotists. But really. Moore notwithstanding, some of us are really nice guys.

Best,
Peter St. Clair

P.S.: The picture above your byline doesn't do you justice.

I laughed. To tell the truth, I looked like hell. Lack of sleep had etched black circles under my eyes, I had hollows in my cheeks. Still, it was nice to hear. And actually I hadn't said anything about doctors and their egos. He had.

I laid the card on a bookshelf in my office and put the little doctor bear on top of it.

That night I managed to fall asleep for a few hours, but I woke up every half hour or so beginning at midnight, until three A.M. when I finally gave up. I went in to check on Elijah, then went down the hallway to my office, where that afternoon I'd been playing around with a piece whose idea had been inspired by Peter St. Clair's little joke about being a "serial killer, for all you know." I'd always been interested in serious pathology myself, but in addition to nonfiction books on the subject, I used to read novels about serial killers, too. Those can-you-top-this-depravity contests, where the writer comes up with an incredibly sadistic and unheard of method of inflicting fatal damage on the human body, usually a female body, and then describes each successive murder in excruciating detail. I swore off them when I read that the number of serial-killer novels published each year is several times greater than the estimated number of actual serial killers on the loose. That can't be good, can it?

I'd written a draft of my piece from the viewpoint of an alien on a fact-finding mission who happens to crash-land his ship on earth at a mall. He goes in and stops in front of the best-seller rack, where each featured serial killer is billed as the most vicious, the most demonic, the most methodical killer ever. "Ah, so this is what these beings are all about. But how do they survive?" I thought I'd call it: "Take Me to Your . . . Gulp . . . Leader!"

My study was dark except for the small lamp I'd left on. I turned on my computer and monitor, which added another element of light in the room, bluish.

The screen should have been blank until I called up the serial-killer file. But it wasn't. There were words flickering on the screen. They were in the font I used, and they were words I had perhaps thought once, but they were not words I had ever typed in:

These years I would watch him breathing,
day in and day out, in and out *whoosh*-pump

he would not watch me watch him
he would not be watching
he would not be
Elijah

I swallowed a scream, clamped my hand over my mouth.

"Mommy?"

Turning, I saw Elijah standing there in his canary-yellow Big Bird pajamas. He was holding Tuddy and *Creatures of the Deep.*

Quickly, I shut off the computer. Elijah was a long way from being able to read, but these days he was full of surprises. The screen turned black and the words disappeared, just as if they had never existed.

Elijah didn't seem the least bit interested in what was or wasn't on the screen. He climbed up on my lap and opened his book. He began turning the pages until he got to something he wanted to show me, the extraordinary two-page photograph of sea turtles.

"I dreamed," he said, pointing.

"Of the turtles?" I could smell the sweetness in his skin. I drank it in, tried to think of a word to describe it, a way to always have it with me.

He nodded. "I want my lullaby, Mommy," he said.

I sighed, picked him up in my arms, and carried him to his bed. Covering him with his quilt, I began to sing. I sang softly, trying not to cry:

Wynken and Blynken are two little eyes,
And Nod is a little head,
And the wooden shoe that sailed the skies
Is a wee one's trundle-bed.

When I was through, he insisted I sing it to him again, and again. His eyes were shining in the dark. He reached up and wound his arms around my neck.

"Don't be afraid, Mommy."

But I was afraid. Very afraid.

twenty-four

I was really struggling in those last weeks of spring, yet I carried on, even with my work, though I was losing patients, for one reason or another, at the rate of about one a week. I had always written the checks for the household bills so I managed to hide the fact that my income was plummeting rapidly. Sam and I didn't talk much during this period, except about household matters. Didn't make love at all. Once or twice we started to, but the demon hovered behind me, lay beside me, licking its chops. My nakedness in front of my tormentor was a degradation I couldn't bear. It was like spreading my legs before an audience of leering old men. I wanted to cover myself, I wanted to peel out of my filthy skin. Although I tried to go on with it, Sam knew I wasn't there. We'd been married too long for him not to know. Worse, he tried to make a joke out of it, but humor wasn't going to fix this. I knew it, and he knew it. I had the feeling he was always watching me, expecting me to suddenly start foaming at the mouth.

Just as bad as Sam's constant watching was my absolute inability to practice my profession properly. I never knew when the demon would show up in some new form or way to frighten or confuse me. Or would show up just to spew accusations, charge me with taking people's money for nothing, denounce me for charlatanism, wonder how I could listen to my patients' self-deluding blather.

I was unable to separate my own feelings from the demon's screeds at that point. How's this for lack of restraint? I told a patient of four years, a woman who claimed only to want to get married and have some kids, but who dated only married men, that she was being "pretty stupid." Transference? Countertransference? Who knew, who cared? It was as if my patience had dwindled to nil and my tongue was a loose cannon.

I was also losing faith in the therapeutic process itself, in the notion that we can even begin to understand the human mind, in the utter arrogance of diagnoses we presumptuously slap on people, infinitely complicated beings in a universe vast and complex.

How did "personality disorder" explain or describe a mother's capacity to be cruel to her child and not even realize she was being cruel? How did "psychosis" explain why someone believes there are aliens poisoning him, hears voices, thinks himself possessed by the Devil? More important, how did we know there *weren't* voices, and aliens, and devils?

My disillusionment with the profession grew, and I became obsessed with the nerve of it. What validity was there to a "science" where there was no general agreement among its practitioners on even its most basic assumptions? Or guarantee that the practitioners weren't dangerously playing out their own psychic disturbances on their patients?

I even began to dream about this, snappy little nightmares attesting to my own conceit. In one dream, I am sitting in my office behind a desk. In walks a succession of my patients, some I recognize, some I don't. I sit behind my desk and touch each of them on the shoulder with a long wand I hold regally in my hand as they parade by. I even have a crown on my head.

Was I the narcissist? I no longer knew.

I did know I was a fake, and a failure. I should not have continued to practice, and I knew it. And yet I went on.

The day my piece about serial killers ran in the paper, I got a call from Peter. I wasn't surprised at his persistence. Nothing surprised me anymore.

It was just after noon. My last patient of the day, in fact my only patient that day, had departed, and I was still sitting in my chair, sluggishly writing up my session notes. At least I hadn't alienated this one. Not yet, anyway. If I lost Marla Lessing, it would be some kind of a watershed. A phobic so anxious she made me, even now, look calm, Marla had been coming to see me the longest of any patient in my practice, almost eight years. The demon would say she was my cash cow, but so far it hadn't commented. Or maybe it had. As I said, I could no longer separate my own thoughts from the demon.

"Hey, I think you owe me that cup of coffee, after all," Peter said.

"Why's that?" Holding the phone in the crook of my neck, I slid open a drawer to deposit the yellow notepad in the file.

"Well, it seems to me I get coffee for being inspiration."

"Oh, that." I closed the drawer.

"I liked the piece, Dinah."

"Thanks."

"So do I get coffee?"

I sighed. "I really don't think it's a good idea, Peter."

"My intentions are strictly honorable."

Right. "I'm sure."

There was a silence. "Okay, I'll leave you alone. I promise."

Yes. Leave me alone, Peter. "There is one thing you could do for me," I said.

"Sure. What's that?"

"Who's the most respected neurologist in the country?"

"Besides me?" He laughed.

"You're a surgeon, aren't you? If a child of yours needed a neurological nonsurgical evaluation, a second opinion—"

"Is it your child, Dinah?"

I took a deep breath and sat down again. "My son Elijah was in a coma for three weeks, in January. Then he woke up."

"Just four months ago. How is he now?"

"He's fine. Great. He's doing better than ever, with his speech, play, everything." I, on the other hand, am a walking disaster.

He hesitated. "That's wonderful. Incredible, really."

"You mean because he should have awakened with brain damage."

"I'm not sure I would have been so blunt. But more often than not there *is* something. But three weeks . . . you're very lucky. *He's* very lucky."

I sighed. "I don't feel lucky. I feel terrified."

"Because you're still afraid you'll lose him?"

"Something like that."

"I can certainly understand."

"No. You really can't."

"Well, if Moore is his doctor, he's one of the most respected neurologists around."

"I know. I'm still thinking about getting a second opinion."

"May I ask why?"

"Because I think it's prudent. Because I don't think he really knows what happened. Because truthfully, I can't stand the guy. He makes me nervous, and he's patronizing, and he lacks compassion."

"He's one of the best."

"I'm not complaining about his skills as a physician."

He sighed. "Sometimes . . ." His voice dropped low, making me wonder where he was calling from. A phone outside the OR? "I'm not trying to make excuses for Moore, I don't even know him. To some degree, you do get used to death and horror. Certain people move you more than others. At least they do me."

"Like?"

"About what you'd expect, I guess. Kids. Maybe people I relate to better. Better educated people. That sounds pretty cold-blooded, doesn't it?"

"Reptilian." At least he was honest. I wondered if he also dated some of his well-heeled successes.

"And kids are the most difficult, of course."

"I just think that when doctors are dealing with situations like ours, they ought to have at least a clue," I said. "Moore doesn't have a clue. I'm not complaining about his skill as a diagnostician, or as a doctor. Only his lack of compassion. And I'm not even complaining, really. My son survived. My son survived brilliantly."

"Sometimes the same skill set isn't possible in the same person."

"These things can be taught. In medical school, if nowhere else."

I heard a little snort. "I think the plan in med school is that if you start out with compassion, you damn well won't finish with any. I'm sorry, I don't mean to be flip." I could hear voices in the background, and another sound. What was that? Wheels on linoleum? Rattling carts? Maybe he was outside the OR, after all. "The way medicine is nowadays, it's easy to forget the reasons we became physicians in the first place."

"Why?"

"Probably some of the same reasons you became a psychologist."

"Let's not idealize our reasons. My reasons, like your reasons, I'm sure, were and are complicated."

"Touché."

"Anyway, Moore has him on phenobarbital. It seems like a judgment call to me, and I was thinking that we need to get a second opinion about that. So I'm asking. If Elijah were your child, and you already had Abner Moore's opinion, who would you go to for a second opinion?"

"I'd go to David Selson, at Manhattan Medical Center. He's chair of the department down there. Many moons ago, he was a professor of mine."

Well, that was two recommendations. Selson it was. I made an appointment.

Two weeks later, I drove Elijah into Manhattan to meet Sam at the Medical Center. He was late, and we waited in the huge glassed lobby. Elijah spent the time toting Tuddy around, peering through the big glass windows at the cars and buses speeding by, peeking around the big desk, engaging the receptionist. I had deliberately left *Creatures of the Deep* at home. He'd taken to carrying the big book around with him all the time, just like he carried Tuddy. Yet I couldn't complain about this new piece of obsessive behavior, not when he seemed so much more sociable, happier, less frustrated. He was still cognitively behind his more normal peers, and awkward and cross-eyed. But he was blossoming like a little flower, gaining in his language and small-motor skills every day, and he had somehow retained the winning enthusiasm that had originally arisen from having to work so hard to learn things. I hadn't seen a tantrum since he came out of the coma. What mother of a child like Elijah wouldn't be overjoyed to see this? I was, and I was also terrified.

Finally, I gave up waiting for Sam, and we got on the elevator. Elijah laughed all the way, all thirty floors. I kept thinking how he might have reacted to the odd feel of the swift rise in the elevator before all this. He might have freaked.

Just as we were ushered in to see the doctor, Sam showed up. No explanation for his lateness, only a hasty, "Sorry."

David Selson was an older man, maybe early sixties, with a full head of white hair, an aristocratic demeanor, and a friendly, calm, easy air about him. He reminded me a little of my writing student Abe Modell. His office was full of toys.

"Who's this?" Dr. Selson said

"Tuddy." Elijah held Tuddy out so that Dr. Selson could see it.

"Oh, Tuddy. I see."

"Elijah takes Tuddy everywhere with him," Sam said.

"Well, I can see why. He certainly is a handsome turtle, isn't he?"

Elijah nodded, then settled into my lap, and settled Tuddy on his own. Selson pulled a Tweety Bird puppet out of his white coat.

"My name's Elijah," he said, moving the puppet's mouth.

Elijah grabbed for the puppet. "My name's Elijah."

"No, mine," the doctor said. "Now just look here." He held the toy up with one hand and shined a pin light into Elijah's eyes with the other.

Elijah, laughing hard, reached for the toy. "Mine!" As he reached he looked into the light. Nice trick. It wouldn't have worked if it weren't for Elijah's newfound friendliness toward doctors, toward everyone, in fact. He no longer seemed so confused by the world or by his own sensory experience, much less frightened by it.

"Mine." Dr. Selson winked at me, then gave Tweety to Elijah. Then pulled something else out of his pocket. A purple dinosaur puppet.

"Look, Mommy," Elijah said.

I had taken Elijah to his first art class at the Jewish Community Center the day before. The kids were going to make simple puppets, and the demonstration puppet Addie had shown the class in the beginning was a purple dinosaur.

"I see. Just like Mrs. Stern's puppet." I wasn't sure if the puppet Elijah had presented me with when I came to get him was supposed to be a bird or a mouse, but it *was* a puppet. Addie said he had concentrated, and listened, and seemed to make friends with a kid named Jason. He'd even used scissors. At this rate, he'd be able to join a regular class next year.

"Barney says Elijah should come over here," Dr. Selson said.

Elijah got off my lap right away and climbed right onto David Selson's lap, and sat there through much of the doctor's examination.

Afterward, in his office, David Selson looked up from the charts and test reports we'd brought.

"I'd say Dr. Moore is following a standard course. I wouldn't change a thing."

"What about all his new talents?" I looked at Elijah, who was sitting on Sam's lap. I expected a self-satisfied "So there!" expression from Sam. No such thing. He was looking at his watch. He'd checked it three times since we'd been in Selson's office. Where did he have to be that was more important than this?

"I suggested to Dr. Moore that maybe the seizure had altered some original miswiring of the synapses or something," I said.

"What'd he say?" the doctor asked.

"He said he doubted it."

David Selson looked at Elijah, then at us. "Well, I suppose it's possible," he said slowly, "but since our measuring tools can only measure what they measure, there's simply no way to tell. A comparison of IQ scores might help but it certainly wouldn't be definitive."

Dr. Selson reached over and tickled Elijah. "Right?"

Elijah jerked his head down once. "Right."

My new patient, Heidi Vasquez, was one tough cookie. I got some very descriptive language about Larry's wife, right out of pop psychology 101. Heidi's rival was frigid, withholding, arrogant, controlling, and middle-aged, not to mention hysterical, shrewish, clinging, and volatile. What a woman. And Heidi had never even met her.

I asked her how she knew all this. "Does Larry complain?"

"Not so much. But I have a special sense about people."

She was special indeed. And if you wanted to know the truth, Larry's wife hated men, and had made Larry's life miserable for years. Of course there were children involved, and Heidi said she felt bad about that, but still, this was the 1990s. Men left their wives all the time. Why, when Larry's wife was so clearly a miserable, unattractive, clinging, man-hating mess, wouldn't he leave her? What was wrong with him that he wouldn't leave such a woman for beautiful, young Heidi?

"Ask her what bar she met Larry in," said the demon. It no longer had to materialize visibly in front of me to turn me to ice. It had only to whisper in my ear.

I already knew what bar. She'd mentioned a place called Thursdays. She had in fact admitted to often picking up men in bars, behavior consistent with my diagnosis of narcissism. There's a certain element of entitlement, of grandiosity, of invulnerability, in reckless behavior. And God knows, Heidi felt entitled. All narcissists do. See. I could still diagnose, slap on a label, play the game.

"Sam goes to Thursdays," the demon said. "It's two blocks from Grand Central Station. Stops in there after work sometimes."

"Dr. Galligan? Did you hear me?"

I was not going to let it take over this session. I asked Heidi what her goals were, other than marrying Larry.

"Grad school," she said. "But I don't know if I can swing it myself. Last year I was accepted in a master's program at Pace, and my parents refused to pay."

"Can they afford it?" I asked.

"They somehow found the money to send me to college," she said sarcastically.

"Had they saved to send you to college?"

She glared at me. "I don't know. I think they saved, and they borrowed some. What's the difference? Last year they took a vacation in Aruba. They have plenty of money. They just don't care about anyone but themselves. Especially me."

A near-perfect narcissistic projection. She was entitled to have them pay for grad school, but they weren't entitled to take a vacation. Never mind that they were probably up to their ears in the debt incurred to pay for her college, or that their generosity and sacrifice had probably never elicited an ounce of appreciation, understanding, or even acknowledgment from their daughter. She was entitled, they were required.

And Larry was required to commit to her, just because she wanted it. Never mind that he'd been married many years and had young children.

I tried a different approach. Steady. Easy. You know how to do this, I told myself. "Instead of focusing on how awful your parents make you feel, how about thinking what steps you could take to get you into grad school?"

"What's the point? My parents won't pay. They paid for a graduate course at NYU two years ago, but I had to drop out in the middle."

Add just one more reason they weren't willing to sacrifice. But Heidi, like all narcissists, simply could not take responsibility for any part it.

"Why did you drop out?" I asked her.

"Because the professor made a pass at me."

Oh, boy. Getting anywhere with her wasn't going to be easy, but if she could learn how to empathize a little bit, see the other point of view, even just a little. I could show her, I could help her. If I could only hold on, maybe I could keep the twelve patients who remained.

"Do you mind if I lie down?" She swung around and stretched herself out, her head at one end of the couch, her feet at the other. "Larry told me last night that his wife made a scene at a party a few weeks ago. The bitch called some woman stupid, right in front of a whole group of people."

"Jerk," the demon whispered.

I closed my eyes and saw Ann Louise Remson's face. At Mark's birthday party, I'd called her a jerk.

"Jerk," the demon said, louder this time.

Heidi was talking on. "Oh, yes," the demon told me. "He met her months ago. They are hot, my Dinah. You don't stand a chance against her. Thy bed is lust-stained."

Othello, now.

The door to my office opens and a man whose face I can't see sweeps in and kneels in front of my young patient. Slowly, very slowly, he opens the buttons on her blouse, and kisses her neck, her breasts, removes her clothes, and then his own, his back still to me. He turns and I see his face, a lascivious expression I have never before seen.

Do I hear the demon laughing? Do I hear a flapping of wings?

"You lie!" I screamed. "This is a lie!"

"Dr. Galligan?"

The vision burst apart like glass, shattered into a thousand tiny pieces.

And the demon was now lounging on my desk. Back to Seth it was, pink skin, black boots, black leather jacket.

"You think I lie?" It raised a long finger and pointed at me. "Ask Sam if he didn't meet her in a bar called Thursdays. Ask him if he isn't fucking her every chance he gets."

"You are trying to destroy me," I screamed with my mouth.

"Destroy you?" Heidi screamed with hers.

"You will see the truth now," the ghost demon said. "There is no one for you but me. You are nothing, you are no one, you are *mine.*"

"Stop it! Please stop." My head was throbbing. I could feel the pulses all over my body.

"Stop what, for Christ's sake?" Heidi jolted to her feet. "What the hell is going on here?"

I told her I was sorry, I was coming down with a migraine.

My patient left, vowing never to come back. Eleven patients now, and falling. That night, as we were getting ready for bed, I asked Sam if he was having an affair.

He had just taken off his shirt. He stopped, turned, and looked at me, holding the shirt in his hand. "Good God, Dinah, why ever would you think such a thing?"

"Why were you so late the other day for Elijah's appointment? You kept looking at your watch."

He threw his shirt at the chair. "What? I was at a meeting that ran long, I had another meeting afterward. What do you think I do all day, play tiddledywinks? Someone has to pay the bills."

I stared. Someone has to pay the bills?

"Do you think I don't know that your financial contribution to this household is shrinking fast?" Still shirtless, he sat down on the bed. "To tell you the truth, Dinah, I think it would be better for you, not to mention for your patients, if you took another leave of absence until you get over this—whatever it is. But why in the world would you think I'm having an affair?"

I sat down in the overstuffed chair. "The demon told me you are." God, what this must sound like to him.

"Dinah. Dinah. You've got to get some help."

"Liar," the demon whispered. "He is a liar. That day he was going to fuck her, right after he finished at the doctor."

"Aren't there pills or something you could take?" Sam said.

I was hating Sam. Hating the sight of him. Everything about him. Even his new glasses I hated. He'd gotten a pair of those tiny wire-rimmed things. A younger, hipper look. Maybe the demon wasn't lying and Sam really was the boyfriend Heidi obsessed about, and *I* was the miserable, clinging wife. Not countertransference, the truth. And maybe he wasn't, maybe I had come to this peculiar conclusion because I was desperate and confused and tired and bedeviled. In any case, Sam didn't seem to be making the least bit of effort to understand what was happening to me. He didn't understand at all.

"There are no pills to get rid of this, Sam," I said.

"Well, you've got to do something. You are starting to really scare me."

twenty-five

My computer was demon-poisoned. Anytime I turned it on I might find a message from my tormenter. Like the one I found on a Thursday morning in mid-June when I sat down to work on my column:

LOVE POTION #66
Extract of romance.
Canned flowers, Valentines, Hallmark.
Pretty poison, potion of his adultery.
Words hang from tree branches by their little necks,
lies like leaves in moonlight,
his lies come back around to haunt her.
Poor Dinah like a tree caught naked and foolish,
with her participles dangling
in the wind.

I stared at the monstrous little sonnet for a moment, wishing Sam were here so that I could show it to him, which would prove I wasn't crazy. My face burned as I thought of when I'd shown him another computer-generated demon screed. He said that I must have done it myself and just not remembered it. "My memory is fine," I assured him. "I remember every moment of every day." (I didn't mention the visions, which came and went in a flash of time, certainly not long enough to run to my computer and write poetry.) "Then in your sleep, maybe," Sam suggested. Right. Maybe in my sleep, if I were sleeping, except I practically hadn't slept in months.

How in the world was I going to write a lighthearted essay every two weeks? What was funny anymore? Clearly the ghost meant to obliterate and mock every single element of my life, everything I loved, everything I held precious. Even my class was beginning to feel like a burden. Not that the demon had done anything since the day it mimicked Carl's wife, but I was always afraid it would. Always the fear, gnawing at my insides.

I decided that I needed to hold on to what wits I still had by concentrating only on what was most important. I would give up my class. I would do it today.

I erased the poem and turned off the computer.

That afternoon, I took Elijah to the Jewish Community Center, dropped him in his art class with Addie, then went to face the music.

Mitzi Hertzl had finally written about her first lover, the romantic Englishman she'd wanted to marry. Her essay was charming, also sexier than I expected from a woman pushing eighty. Not explicit, just sexy.

The group seemed to really like it, even had a discussion about how writers nowadays had to give readers a tour of body parts, spell everything out, and how most of the time less is more.

When the hour ended, I told them I could no longer teach the class.

"You joining the navy?" Abe had a smile on his face.

"No, Abe," Carl said. "*You* joined the navy, and it was fifty years ago."

"I'm really sorry," I said. "I've been finding lately that I can't . . . that I'm too busy."

There was a silence. They stared at me.

"You're abandoning us just as we're getting the hang of it?" Abe was still trying to make a joke out of it.

"What'd she say?" Mrs. Shoenfeld asked Mitzi, who leaned over and loudly told her.

Ellen startled. "Quitting?"

"I'm sorry," I said. "I just have no choice. I'm going to talk to the director. I'm sure he'll be able to find someone else to continue with it."

"What is it, Dinah?" Pearl said. "Maybe we can help."

"Pearl's right, Dinah," Mitzi said. "Maybe we can."

"Is it Elijah?" Ellen Shoenfeld asked, turning her right ear toward me, the way she did when she was trying hard to follow.

"Thanks for asking. No. He's fine. He's taking an art class in the crafts room."

"Then what?" Carl Moskovitz.

"I really can't talk about it. Really."

They packed up their bags and their papers, and they left. I went to get Elijah.

When I came into the crafts room, Addie was just saying goodbye to the other children. Still-wet pictures were tacked up around the room, names scrawled at the bottom of the pages. There were lots of houses on green spiky grass, with a band of blue sky at the top of the page. Lots of stick figures and brown tree trunks with round green foliage blobs. An artist named Jason had painted a purple polka-dot car.

In a corner, Elijah was still painting away, concentrating intently.

"Hi, little guy," I said.

"Hi, Mom." He didn't look up, kept painting.

"Wait till you see Elijah's picture!" Addie said.

I went over to see what he was doing, and stopped. Cold.

The top two-thirds of the large paper was painted a solid powder blue. The bottom third he'd left white. In the blue section were several crudely drawn fish-like figures, rendered in dark blue lines. In the white section was a big pink splotch. Pink.

I stared at the thing, speechless.

"It's pretty, isn't it?" Elijah said.

"I had the kids name their pictures," Addie said. "Tell your mom what you call yours, Elijah."

Elijah smiled. "Angels."

I pointed to one of the dark blue fish figures. "Is that one of the angels?"

He lowered his eyes. "That's Charlie."

Charlie? My knees buckled and I sat down on the table. That was the name of my mother's little brother, the one who drowned in an Atlanta pool. Almost seventy years ago. I closed my eyes.

"That one's Jimmy," Elijah said.

I opened my eyes but I'd begun to tremble. "How do you know about Charlie and Jimmy?"

Elijah smiled up at me. "I see them when I sleep, Mommy. Just like dreaming."

I took his hand and led him out, holding the painting carefully, faceup, in my other hand. We had to pass Ellen Shoenfeld, who was sitting on a bench in front of the building.

"Hello, Elijah," she said. "How are you?"

"Fine." He was staring at her intently.

"Is that your painting?" she asked, pointing to Elijah's picture, turning her head to hear his response.

Elijah nodded. "These are all the angels," he said, pointing to the fish.

"It's a very pretty picture, Elijah. Who were they before they were angels?"

"That's Jimmy. Jimmy was in the hospital."

"When you were there?"

He nodded. "He likes it when his mother gives him apples and honey in the kitchen. When he comes home from school."

"Oh, then Jimmy got well, just like you did?"

Elijah shook his head.

"Jimmy died," I said.

Ellen Shoenfeld gazed at him, one eyebrow raised.

"Do you need a ride?" I asked. "I could drop you."

She shrugged. "My daughter is supposed to be here."

I nodded, turned to go again.

"I think you're making a mistake," she said. "Giving up the class, I mean."

"I'm sorry you feel that way, Mrs. Shoenfeld. But I have to."

She clasped her purse on her lap and looked away. A middle-aged woman pulled up in a Chevy Blazer then.

"There's my daughter now." Ellen got to her feet and shuffled toward the car.

The woman behind the wheel unlatched the passenger door and swung it out. I could see the resemblance to her mother in her face, in the bone structure, the narrowness of the chin.

"This is Dinah Galligan, Anita," Mrs. Shoenfeld said. And to me, "This is my daughter, Anita Braverman. And this is Elijah."

The woman gave me a little smile, and one for Elijah. "Nice to meet you."

Mrs. Shoenfeld was still slowly making her way to the car.

"Come *on,* Mom."

Just as she put her hand out to the door handle, Elijah walked over to her and tugged at her sweater. She stopped. "What is it, Elijah?" He motioned for her to lean down to him, which she did, then he whispered something in her ear.

She straightened herself up and stared at him, then fixed me with a glare I'll never forget. Appalled, awestruck, skeptical, and suspicious, all at once. Finally, she got into the car, which pulled away.

"What did you say to her, Elijah?"

"I told her this one's name. That's all." He pointed to another of the blue figures in his painting. "Gerte."

"Gerte?"

He nodded his head, just once.

When we got home, I tacked his picture up on the door where I always put his drawings, then sat down with him at the kitchen table with a pencil and a pad of paper. I thought if I could calmly be with him, I might be able to ask him how he knew the names he'd never heard of dead people he'd never met.

We worked on his letters for about fifteen minutes. Hunched over the page, nose to paper, forehead scrunched up in concentration, Elijah was gripping the pencil the way he usually did, awkwardly, with the pencil resting in his palm, his fingers clenched around it in a fist. I kept trying to get him to hold the pencil the standard way but he kept going back to his way, until I finally curled my hand around his and made the letters with him. We were up to *j,* our previous attempts strewn all over the table's surface.

"Elijah," I said. "Who's Charlie?"

He smiled without looking at me, and moved his pencil, concentrating hard. "Somebody important to you, Mommy."

To me? I'd never met my mother's brother. He was just a baby when he died, my mother was only a little girl. "How do you know this, Elijah?"

He looked up. "There's a big sun shining in the water, and Charlie is there. Can I go watch TV now?"

I sighed. "Go ahead."

When Sam got home from work a few hours later, he noticed the painting taped on the door and asked Elijah about it. Elijah repeated the angels' names for his father.

Sam stood for a moment looking at his son, then said, "Jimmy?"

Standing by the stove, getting dinner ready, I held my breath.

Elijah nodded. "He died in the hospital."

Sam's expression was indescribable. "How do you know that, Elijah?"

Elijah shrugged. "I don't know, Daddy. I just do." And he took his *Creatures of the Deep* book and Tuddy and left the room.

"Go ahead, Sam," I said, folding my arms in front of me. "Explain that away."

Sam frowned, but then he turned and stood gazing at the picture for a while. For a moment, just for a moment, I thought his infuriating rationality might be beginning to crumble. But then he said, "Do I have time for a swim before dinner?"

Sam often did laps in our small pool after dinner on a warm summer night like this one. In fact, he'd decided that this was the summer Elijah would learn to love the water as much as his father did. He'd enlisted Alex and Kate in his campaign to persuade Elijah into the pool. "He loves to take baths," Sam said. "He loves those fish, for God's sake. He shouldn't have a problem with the pool."

But Elijah did have a problem, the same one he'd always had. He wouldn't even put a toe into the water. And for the first few summer weekends we'd had the spectacle of the three of them standing in the water, coaxing and coaxing Elijah. Even their friends got into the act, Kate's gaggle of giggling teenage girls, and Alex's boundlessly energetic buddies, who spoke mostly in half-sentences and grunts.

I told Sam now that he didn't have time to swim, that I would have dinner on the table in five minutes, and we said nothing more to each other for hours, in fact filtered all of our conversation through the children, even at dinner. After Kate and I had finished the dishes, I went upstairs and turned on my computer. Well, at least I hadn't seen the demon at all that day. Giving up the class was the right thing to do. Now I could concentrate. I sat for a while, trying to come up with a concept for the column. I looked through the newspaper, some magazines.

"Mom?" Alex was standing in the doorway. "Where's Dad? He said after dinner we could talk about me going on that trip with my team." He was wearing the Megadeth T-shirt again. Every time the damn thing showed up in the laundry basket I considered extreme measures. I could shrink it: Oops, sorry, the hot water just turned itself on by accident. I could lose it: Well, the machine ate it; it does eat socks, after all. I could turn it pink, if I could figure out a way to turn black pink. Then he'd *never* wear it.

"Both of us want to talk to you about that." I could hear Kate practicing her flute in her room. I recognized the light trilling melody she was playing but didn't know the name of the piece.

He shrugged. "So you told me."

"And you told me not to worry unless you were flunking out of school."

"For God's sake, I'm not flunking. I just got one C minus. You're always on my case."

Actually he'd finished the year with one C- and a C+, from a kid who used to get only A's and B's. "Alex, you know we're concerned, that's all."

"All right, fine. So we'll talk now. Where is he?"

"I don't know, honey. Somewhere in the house, I guess."

Alex went looking while I put Elijah to bed. "I can't find him," he said when I came downstairs.

"Hmmm. The case of the missing father. Maybe he's taking a swim."

"I looked in the pool," Alex said.

"Maybe he went out." I walked over to the window and peered out through the curtains. No. He hadn't gone out. The car was still there. Wait. Something moved, I could see it through the windshield. Someone was sitting inside the car. *Sam?*

I turned, pushed past my son. "Wait here, Alex."

Down the steps, through the house, out the door. Quietly. Now I saw that he was talking on the car phone.

He saw me and waved. Then hung up, put the phone back, got out. He was wearing a towel wrapped around his waist over his swim trunks.

"Sam, what are you doing?"

"I was on the phone."

"On the car phone?"

"Well, your daughter is always on the house phone." He grinned. "I have to use the car phone or else take a number."

"Our daughter is playing the flute. Who the hell did you need to call that you couldn't wait a few minutes?"

The amusement on his face vanished. "It was a nice night, the car phone was closer."

"Bullshit." He was lying to me. I was convinced of it.

He faced me. "I was talking to Ed about our pitch tomorrow. What are you suggesting?"

"I'm not suggesting anything. I'm saying right out that a man using a car phone in a parked car when there's a perfectly good phone in the house looks suspicious."

"To whom?"

"To me. I'm the only one here."

"Wait a minute. Just what are you accusing me of?"

He already knew what I was accusing him of.

"Dinah, for Christ's sake, I am not having an affair."

"Perhaps he doth protest too much," the demon whispered. "Methinks."

"And I suppose you don't ever go to a bar called Thursdays in the city?"

"Occasionally. So what?"

"You met her there. Her name is Heidi."

"Heidi who?" His incredulous expression struck me as overplayed.

"Heidi-Who-Is-My-Patient. A very beautiful and very young patient, I might add."

"You're accusing me of having an affair with your patient? And just why would I be doing that? Why would *she* be doing that?"

I couldn't think of a reason.

The demon could. "She's checking out the competition, of course."

I repeated what it had told me, what I believed.

Sam stepped around me. "This is ridiculous." He started up the walk.

I caught up with him. "I'm going to ask Kate if she was on the phone. I don't think she was."

He turned on me, mouth open in a grimace. "Don't you *dare* impugn my honesty in front of our daughter." He was angrier than I'd ever seen him before.

I took a step backward in the force of his fury.

"I am not having an affair, Dinah," he said. "But I'll tell you one thing. If you don't get some help soon, I've had it with this marriage." He went inside the house.

"Now, there's a good tactic," the demon said, materializing, white under a clear starry sky. "Make it seem as if you're the one who has the problem, when he's the one fucking a virtual teenager every chance he gets."

It disappeared.

I stood in the driveway for a few minutes, shaking, then went inside the house. The phone was ringing.

I heard Kate's voice. "Mom, it's for you."

I picked up the phone in the mudroom. "Dinah? It's Brian Dawson."

I knew what my editor wanted. I'd missed another deadline.

"Dinah, I hate to lose you, but we can't operate this way."

"I'm really sorry, Brian. I just can't do it anymore. Not right now."

"Is there anything I can do to help?"

"No."

I hung up. I was alone, so alone, and yet I was never alone.

"Dinah?" It was Peter again, phoning again. "Did you see Selson?"

I glanced at the little doctor bear on my shelf. "We were down there a few weeks ago. Thanks. We liked him."

"Good. That's good. What did he say? Did he concur with Moore?"

"He did."

"Has it helped?"

I sighed. "I guess. But I can't help it, I'm still terrified."

"I've been thinking about you a lot, Dinah. What you must be going through."

"No one understands who hasn't been through it." And no one's been through this.

"Of course not. But I can't get it out of my mind. Once, my son Austin fell off his bike and was knocked out, stayed unconscious for nearly eight hours. I think those were the worst few hours of my life, and for months afterward I feared the worst every time he got on that bike. If I ever lost one of my boys I don't know how I'd go on."

We met two days later at a decidedly unchic restaurant on *très chic* Main Street. For coffee and a chat, I told myself. He was better-looking than I remembered from our brief meeting. We talked about the latest White House scandal, Peter's amicable split from his wife, whose name was Vanessa. I pictured a woman with a hard cold mouth who wears a size four, and has tits with little tiny always-erect nipples like pencil erasers that still point skyward even though she's no spring chicken, either, compliments of Peter's colleague Dr. Saul Saperstein, the best boob man this side of Beverly Hills. He told me about Austin and Raymond, whose names were a little highbrow for my tastes and who attended Choate, which I knew was too highbrow for me. Not that we could afford private boarding school. He showed me a picture of two handsome young boys in matching blue jackets, standing one on either side of him.

"It would break my heart to send my children away to boarding school," I said.

He shrugged. "Never thought of it that way. Went to boarding school myself. Besides, if they hadn't gone away they would have lived with her."

Judging by the way he talked about her, I doubted that his split with his wife was all that amicable. Maybe he was amicable since he wanted to leave, or maybe she broke his heart. What we say to one another is only what we choose to present, or what we know, at any given moment.

I told him I didn't really want to talk about my marriage, or my husband. I told him a little about my children. I described Kate, my flute-playing beauty.

"I hate to brag, but her coloring is incredible, auburn hair, blue eyes, real peaches and cream."

"Not unlike her mother's." He smiled.

"Thanks, but at this point I think mine is more cider and milk."

He laughed.

I told him about Alex—the angry, sullen adolescent who in these last months, during Elijah's illness and its aftermath, took the place of a sweet thoughtful boy who used to kiss me goodnight and wanted me to come to his baseball games and cheer.

I told him about Elijah, who'd started in a special summer pre-kindergarten class with a new teacher, Miss Larkin, and was doing remarkably well. He'd mastered the alphabet and was starting to learn how to spell a few words. Last week in Krafty Kids he presented me with a mask made from a mold of his own face. He'd painted it blue and decorated it with white stars. He even came up with a name for it, Blue Elijah.

"Sounds to me like your son Elijah is going to be fine," Peter said. "I know it doesn't help, just saying he's going to be fine. I'm sure everyone says, 'Oh, don't worry. He's going to be fine.' You must want to strangle them."

I stared at him. If I had to name the emotion I was feeling at that moment, it would be relieved. Released, even. It seemed to me as though Peter St. Clair understood me in a way no one had in a very long time. And now my tears were flowing, right in the middle of that delicatessen, and the man I was with reached out and placed his hand over mine.

"I'm sorry, Dinah. I didn't mean to make you think about it, if you weren't thinking about it. "

I tried to stop crying, and couldn't.

"That was probably stupid, too. I'm sure you're always thinking about it."

A young woman at a table nearby was trying not to look. And Peter St. Clair was looking deep into my eyes.

"Do you want to leave?" he said.

I nodded, got up, and headed for the door, stood in the parking lot trying to collect myself until he paid the bill and came out.

"I want to hold you," he said, "but I'm afraid it might complicate things for you."

I laughed, though I was still crying. "Why, because that woman there . . ." I pointed to a woman getting into her car. ". . . probably knows me from the PTA? And that one there could be a patient of mine?" I wiped my eyes. "Or yours."

"We could go to my house, Dinah."

Yes. Without thinking very much about it I said yes.

So. There I was, driving down a long country road in a town about ten miles north of my own town, following the car of a man I liked but about whom I knew next to nothing, with clear intent to take off my clothes and have sex with him. A nooner, they call it.

I turned into a long, winding driveway in backwoods Fairfield, still following him. From what I could see, the man looked pretty comfortable up there in his little black sports car, leaning back, one hand on the wheel. More than I could say for myself.

I could have turned around right there and headed back to the highway. Instead I kept driving, my car close behind his as we passed a gazebo on the left, stark white and quaint, on the rolling lawn behind the border of birch trees. Now his house was coming into view. My stomach started doing somersaults. What in the world was I doing? Was it too late to come to my senses? What did I know about this guy I picked up at the movies?

I knew he was a doctor. I knew he was charming, witty, handsome. I knew he had two sons, an ex-wife named Vanessa, was interested in politics, read a lot, especially history. I knew that, at least for the moment, he was interested in me.

Which was nice.

I knew Peter didn't quicken my heart the way Sammy had. Did. But I'd been eighteen when I met Sam. I was now old, very old. I couldn't expect heart fluttering now.

What was I looking for in this house in the backwoods of Fairfield? I had no idea.

Peter St. Clair's house was all graceful lines, sloping roofs, and tall arched windows, angled planes in the sunlight. Too large for a man living alone, successful surgeon or not. Maybe he wanted room for visits from Austin and Raymond, whose highbrow names could perhaps be blamed on ex-wife Vanessa, she of the warrior boobs.

As I pulled my car to a stop next to his, my stomach felt as though it might lurch right out of my mouth any minute now. My teeth were beginning to chatter. For God's sake, this was the way I felt when I was fourteen and working up to my first kiss. Good God, Dinah, get a grip. You're a grown woman and you are going to do this.

Why? Why was I going to do this?

Now Peter was standing next to the driver's side door of his car, looking hesitant.

What if I couldn't go ahead with the sex? I'd just have to tell him I loved my husband and wasn't even sure what I was doing there. The truth. Except that my husband didn't love me anymore. My husband was ready to leave his crazy wife, my husband was making love to a young thing. Still. I could tell him I'd changed my mind. But what if he refused to accept that?

Who the hell knew what he'd do? For all I knew, Peter St. Clair *was* a serial killer who lured women to his house, raped them, killed them, cut them up in little pieces, and buried the pieces in the woods. For God's sake, he'd read my column on that very subject. Being a surgeon, he probably had a collection of scalpels in a special drawer for occasions like this and used in some sort of twisted ceremony, a compulsion created because his father molested him or because he had too little serotonin in his brain.

I opened the door and stepped out just before he got to it. Now we were both standing up, facing each other next to the car. He looked down at me. Good God. He put his hand under my chin, lifted my head so I would look up into his face.

"You are quite beautiful, Dinah," he said.

Well, come on, Peter, beautiful is going just a little far, don't you think?

But just like that, he wrapped his arms around me and put his mouth to mine, and we were kissing. His lips were warm and soft and urgent, and his extraordinary hands, his graceful fingers, touched me gently, and I thought: Ooooh, this is going to be good.

I had a sense of the power and mass of his body as he pressed himself against me, pulled me even closer with arms that felt solid and strong. I had never been embraced by so big a man, and I wanted it to feel safe. But nothing would ever feel safe.

He stopped kissing me, then took a step back. "You seem tense, Dinah."

"You're not tense?" I managed to say. "Not even a little?"

"Not even a little," he said. He was smiling, tiny wry lines fanning out from the edges of his eyes.

"Pretty sure of yourself, huh?" I raised an eyebrow, tried to be cool. Well, he had less to lose than I, he wasn't married. What did I have to lose, with Sam out screwing a young thing?

"Not all that sure of myself," he said. "But hopeful. Very hopeful."

We made love in a huge bed with a carved wooden headboard and canopy, English colonial style. His bedroom, like the rest of the house, was decorated to the nines and snazzy, and the bed was completely draped in a gauzy fabric that reminded me of mosquito netting, as if we were in the African bush. It created the intended sensual effect, though, and the impression of being in a world apart. Peter was a skillful lover, attentive, generous, and uninhibited. He said all the right things, and afterward, he fell asleep.

I tried to make myself doze, but I heard a sizzling sound and I saw the brightness through the gauze and I heard its voice.

"Well, well, well, aren't we the little whore?"

I sat up, trying to cover myself with the sheet. But I was naked and ashamed and there was no getting away now. The demon possessed me then, came at me and into me like ice sluicing through a warm stream, and I knew then that it wanted me all for itself and that it would allow no one else to have me, not my husband, not even a lover.

I stayed very still as it entered me again, as its vapor filled every cavity of my body, adhering to my organs and the inside of my skin. Very still as it tried to warm itself up in my flesh, sucked the life from my life in the process of possession. My own obliteration.

It celebrated with my body, and I was lost. Whirling, whirling, dancing—exhausting.

twenty-six

The summer evening was a warm one, and when I got home Sam and Alex and Kate were in the pool. Elijah was standing at the pool steps, adorable in his sky-blue swim trunks, adamant in his refusal to budge from the small wood deck. The dog was on its haunches beside him, as if to back him up.

The demon had let me go again, or left me, I wasn't sure which it was. How was I going to clean myself? No amount of washing could clean away this defilement.

"Come on, Elijah," Sam said as I approached the pool from the driveway. "I'll hold you. You know I won't let you go."

I got to the gate in time to see a determined, self-possessed Elijah cross his arms over his chest, lift his chin, and shake his head.

Sam looked over at me and grinned. "Hope springs eternal."

Just seeing Sam after what I'd done left me reeling. I stood outside the fence, keeping my distance. The evening air was fragrant with the scent of English roses. Pink Ruffles. This year I had yet to prune, fertilize, water, spray, or deadhead. Yet the garden had bloomed anyway, gloriously, as if in defiance of my neglect.

Alex splashed water toward Elijah. "Come on, little guy."

Elijah moved back quickly and wiped off his leg, then ran over to me at the fence. I bent down to hug him.

"Come on, it's fun!" Kate's voice rang out with confidence and optimism. She'd announced a few days ago that boys were really okay, if you didn't set the same standards for them as for girls. A good thing, too, because she was wearing a bikini that was going to attract them like flies.

Elijah rested his head against my chest.

"Go for it, Elijah." Alex, whose chest seemed to have filled out over the summer, actually flashed a smile.

"I won't let you go, Elijah." Sam was still holding out his arms. He winked at me.

This man and these children we had made together were the sum and substance and meaning of my life. Everything I was, everything I had done or become in all these years, was part Sam. In the wildest dreams of girlhood I could not have dreamed this, that the years of simply experiencing life together, with our own unique personalities, some might say opposite personalities, would meld us like two blended chunks of clay, a piece of art with no visible seams. Sam was a crucial piece of me, of my molecules, just like Alex and Kate and Elijah. And still we had come to this—I, not he, had come to this utter betrayal, this breach of faith and trust.

What had I wanted from Peter? Had I thought pleasure might rid me of demons, might make me feel understood, might even take my fear and my pain away? But pleasure is so much lighter than pain, lighter than air. Pleasure is ephemeral, illusory as a sunlit slice of dust that bisects the room like solid matter but vanishes like the dust it is when you close the blind.

"Come on, baby," Kate said.

Now it had become a game. Elijah laughed, and wouldn't budge.

"Look how much fun it is to splash Dad," Alex said. He splashed.

"Hey, watch it," Kate said. "You got *me,* Alex."

Elijah shook his head, vehemently. Poppy barked a few times.

Sam took a big soft beach ball from where it was floating in the water, threw it toward Elijah. "Catch!"

Elijah missed, then he and Poppy chased after it, and Elijah brought it back, threw it awkwardly to Sam. They played this game again and again while I stood there and watched. Elijah was happy to play but didn't move a millimeter closer to the water. After a few minutes Alex and Kate gave up, got out of the pool, wrapped themselves in towels, and stood next to me. "Forget it, Dad!" Alex said. But Sam kept throwing and throwing the ball.

Oh, Sammy.

"Let it rest, Sam," I said.

"Rest, Daddy!" Elijah giggled.

"Okay. I give." Sam hoisted himself out of the water with his arms and reached for the towel lying on a lounge chair. "Be a landlubber, Elijah. See if I care!"

Elijah laughed, stretched out his arms, and ran straight into his father's.

"Want a horsy ride?"

"Horsy! Horsy!"

Sam bent down and helped Elijah onto his shoulders. Then he stood up, lifting him high into the air. "Don't let go, now."

Elijah linked his hands around his father's chin.

"Gidd-yup, Daddy!" He squealed with laughter as Sam began making neighing noises and prancing around the yard.

I made love to my husband that night, even with the memory of another man so fresh in my mind. I felt so very awkward at first, embarrassed, but my body soon reacted reflexively. We pleasured each other with great care, and with the tenderness of new young lovers. When we were spent, lying in each other's arms, Sam propped himself on an elbow and looked down into my eyes. "Dinah, I couldn't be with you this way, if I were with someone else. Could I?"

Well. Obviously *I* could. Sex is certainly a gift. But if sex isn't also God's private little joke on us, I don't know what *is.* Just a small joke, for such a very big God.

"I love you, Dinah. You've got to know that. I'm just worried about you, that's all. First you're telling me you're seeing ghosts, then you're accusing me of having an affair."

Looking into my husband's eyes at that moment, I believed in his faithfulness just as certainly as I'd been convinced of his lack of it only hours ago.

"Please, Di," he said. "You've got to get some help."

I began to cry. I told Sam I loved him, I was sorry I'd been scaring him and confusing him. We lay in each other's arms, and eventually Sam fell asleep. I stayed beside him for a long time, listening to the rhythm of his breathing, looking at the ceiling with eyes that wouldn't close.

Finally I got up. I stood for a moment over our bed. Geometry is what I could see in the dim light, intersecting planes and shapes, an arrangement of form as familiar to me as my own breath, my husband's lean spine angled at the hip, a neck, a bent elbow, an arm resting on the sheet where I had lain with him until just a moment ago. His hand was cupped as if he were holding a small object loosely. Under his hand and arm, there was a gentle hollow in our mattress, formed of the weight and shape of me.

I was thinking about the way Peter's hand had felt moving over my skin, the large palm with its smooth, agile fingers, their touch as voluptuous as fine silk, elegant for so big a man. Those facile fingers surely told something about him. Did my own hands tell something about me, too, these skinny fingers and rattled bones?

"Tell him, why don't you?" I felt the cold rush, the presence, turned to the sheath of light that was my demon. "Tell him what a little whore you are."

It followed me into the hallway, into the dining room, into the kitchen. It followed me into the next day, and the next, haranguing and harping, demanding that I reveal my unfaithfulness to Sam.

When Becky told me about her own affair and asked for advice, I told her that if she decided in the end to stay, I thought it would be best to forgo any midnight confession of infidelity. I told her I thought she should just decide, and then get on with it. Because telling Mark would poison their relationship.

The demon's scolding attack lasted for more than a week. Even when I managed to sleep, I could hear the demon's exhortations. I tried to shut my ears, get away from its exhausting diatribe, but where could I go, it was everywhere. Finally, I turned on the demon in the middle of the night. "*You* tell him!"

Sam sat up in bed. "Tell me what?"

"Tell him," it whispered.

Sam reached for his glasses and put them on. "Dinah, who are you talking to?"

I left the room. Sam followed.

"You're talking to hallucinations again, aren't you?"

We were standing now by the bar in the living room. Sam poured himself a scotch. "Dinah, I can't take this anymore. Really."

I followed him into the kitchen, where he plopped ice into the glass, took a sip, and sank into a kitchen chair.

"If you don't call someone to get some help, I just don't know what I'm going to do. Or maybe I'm doing this wrong, maybe I should be calling for you. Maybe I should just put you in the car and take you."

I had to do something. It wouldn't leave me alone, it seemed it would never leave me alone again. It had me, I had made the bargain and I was at its mercy. But maybe I could force it to show itself to Sam, even if he'd hate me in the process. Then at least he'd know I hadn't lost my mind.

"Tell him yourself," I said. "Show yourself to him."

The demon recoiled. "You think you can trick me? Me?" It had stopped cooing, now it was screeching. "Well, you are wrong. You are nothing. You are no one. You are *mine*."

At this familiar refrain, I told Sam.

Sam turned paler than pale. He said not a word to me, just got up from the chair, put his glass down, and walked out of the kitchen. I followed him into the bedroom, watched him put on some clothes and pack a bag.

"Where are you going? Sam, please, I'm sorry."

His eyes narrowed. "You're sorry another man touched you?"

"No. Yes."

"What did you expect, Dinah?"

"I don't know. I just wanted you to . . ."

"To *what?*"

I was frightened now, of his quiet rage, of his being gone.

"I don't know."

"Well, Dinah, I don't know either."

I tried to think what I could say to make him stay. "Please, Sam. It puts ideas in my head. It won't let me—"

"Dinah, stop."

"If I had a mental illness, or if I had cancer and had to have a breast removed, you'd stand by me, Sam. Wouldn't you?"

He stared.

"Wouldn't you, Sam?"

He threw his sneakers into the bag and closed it. "It's hardly the same thing. What is wrong with you?"

I sank into a chair. He picked up the bag and grabbed his wallet from the night table, turned to leave. "I need to go now, Dinah. I just need to go."

I saw the pain in his eyes, heard the determination in his voice, and knew there was nothing I could say or do to stop him.

"What should I tell the children?"

"Tell them I've gone out of town on a business trip. I'll call them as soon as I can."

He was gone, he was gone.

I heard the front door close softly, and I heard the demon's dancing stomping footsteps in the hallway. No sooner had I heard these sounds than it appeared in the corner of my bedroom, preening, victorious. "Payment time."

I started to scream, but it raced to me with light-speed velocity and clamped itself over my mouth. I could still feel the scream in my throat, but my voice was silenced.

"Payment time," it whispered, spurting filth into my ear.

It knew it had won. I lay back against the headboard and pillows. It made me watch while it slithered all over me, its lips on my body, a cold membrane searching, searching. And then it was inside me, swarming.

So be it. My son was after all in his bed down the hall, sleeping peacefully.

In the morning I told the children that their father was away on a business trip, just as he had suggested. I made breakfast, Alex caught the camp bus to his counselor job at a local day camp, I dropped Kate off at CVS for her job, I took Elijah to his nursery school summer program, I went to my office. My practice was practically gone, but I'd been holding on to what was left like a woman clinging by one hand to a twentieth-floor window ledge.

Danielle O'Connor was the first patient of the morning. Halfway through the hour she admitted that although there hadn't been a violent incident in months, she knew it was coming, she felt it.

"How do you know?" I asked.

"I can't really explain. I mean there aren't any words to describe it. There's always a look in his eyes, it's not anger, more like sadness."

"You feel he's sad when he hits you?"

She nodded. "He can't help himself."

"Why do you think that?"

She sighed, folded her hands on her lap. "He just had such a hard time growing up, his father left his mother when he was three, then his stepfather used to beat him and his sister with a leather strap."

"Did Jaime deserve to be beaten that way?"

"No, of course not, he was a little kid."

"Do you?"

She started to cry. "I know I should leave him."

I saw the pain and fear in her face and felt myself tear up. And what was I thinking? I wasn't empathizing, that's for sure. I was thinking that she should just pull herself together and get the hell out of there. I was thinking that her suffering wasn't like mine. My suffering would never leave me.

I looked away from my patient's face, from her tear-filled eyes.

What convinced me finally to give up my practice wasn't that I was afraid the demon would show up, play cheap and nasty tricks, speak in my mother's voice. It was the hard truth that my own pain and fear and self-absorption were too great for me to have room for anything else. Each day my inability to empathize became more overwhelming and obvious.

I told Danielle I was very sorry but I had to take another leave of absence. I hadn't yet alienated her in some way, and so she was shocked. I gave her Grace Atkinson's name. Grace was perfect, I said. She ran a domestic violence group for women every Thursday night, they could do individual, group therapy, a one-stop deal.

When Danielle left, I called Grace. She said she had some free hours, would take as many of my patients as she could, and refer the rest on. She didn't ask too many questions, for which I was thankful. The rest of my paltry patient list I abandoned the cowardly way, by telephone, then left a message with Grace's number on my answering machine.

Peter had called the office several times since our afternoon together. The first message he left had been merely confused: "Dinah, what happened? Please call." I hadn't called him back. The latest, recorded while Danielle was there, represented a new tactic: "Dinah, I'm beginning to worry. At least send smoke signals to let me know you're okay."

I didn't. I took a last look at my office, its shelves stuffed with books, its bright blue walls and comfy couches and box of tissues on the coffee table. Then I turned off the light and closed the door behind me.

I was like one of Pavlov's dogs. I came to know when it was nearby, and would start shivering in the moments just before it appeared, at the smell of it. When I felt the touch of its claw at the curve of my back, at my breast, at my neck and my throat, I would cower and cringe, but I would acquiesce. I was as benumbed as a woman captured in war and brought to the enemy camp for the sport of her captors, so deadened to her own brutalization that she no longer thinks of the body being raped every night as her own and she simply spreads her legs.

Afterward, I felt as if the contents of a grave had been emptied into me, had taken up residence inside my skin. Something always seemed to be crawling inside me, as if maggots were feasting on my organs. Perhaps it thought it could make itself alive again by using my tissue and my flesh as a host, but the opposite was happening. My body was physically deteriorating, food became nauseating, just as it had when Elijah was in the hospital. I had less and less energy each day, felt light-headed and dizzy a lot of the time. It took and it took, and every time it was through with me I was filthy, and there was less of myself. It was as if it were eating away actual pieces of my tissue. Perhaps it was.

When I passed a mirror I seemed less there, seemed to be taking up a smaller amount of space in relation to everything else. My eyes became very light, almost clear, the circles underneath them deep and dark. It was as if I were fading, mixing with background.

The demon had not hesitated to threaten Elijah, and I feared for Alex and Kate. Because of them, I had to let the demon possess me anytime, anywhere—slim protection for my children, or perhaps none, but I saw no other option.

One morning I passed my bedroom mirror and thought I saw the face of Seth Lucien staring back at me from within my own skin. I covered the mirror with a sheet.

"Can you talk?" It was Peter. Six days later, he was calling me at home.

"Is that Daddy?" Over the last few days, Kate had taken to spending a lot more time at the kitchen table, as if she wanted to watch over me, as if she were noticing my deterioration and feared I'd suddenly fade out. I'd also noticed she'd removed her favorite photograph of Sam and me from the collection on her desk, leaving just an empty space in its place. Kate had taken it herself about four years ago. Charlotte had come to baby-sit for Elijah, who was about a year old, and Sam and I were going to a dress-up "do" at a fancy New York hotel, an affair involving one of Sam's clients. I was laughing hysterically in the photograph. Sam was goosing me in my gown.

I covered the mouthpiece of the cordless phone. "No, honey." Into the mouthpiece I said, "Wait a minute."

I took the phone into my bedroom, where the evidence of my nightly exertions was sitting in plain sight—special candles, books, crystals, the covered mirror. In those August weeks, I spent many a morning before I picked up Elijah in the Westport Public Library, reading about demonic possession, looking for exorcism schemes. At night I lit candles in my bedroom and recited incantations and prayers. All kinds of prayers, Catholic, Jewish, New Age, whatever I could find.

None of it helped. The demon appeared night after night, cold and white and laughing. When I felt its presence and then saw it I simply blew out my candles and let it take me, place its cold lips at my neck, slide itself over my skin, searching for its opening. The human body has many, many openings.

Now I quickly shut the door behind me, and apologized to Peter for not calling him back. He said he'd heard the office message.

"Why are you taking a leave of absence?" he asked.

I looked over at the mirror, covered with cloth, then out the window. A brilliant red cardinal was sitting on a low branch of the tree just outside the window. I looked away. I realized I didn't want to share my reasons with this man, even carefully edited reasons. I didn't want to share anything with him. He was a stranger to me, as I was a stranger to me.

"It's not something I want to talk about, Peter."

He was silent for a minute, then said, "What happened, Dinah? I woke up and you were gone."

"I realized that I made a terrible mistake and I needed to leave."

"I see. And now?"

I sighed. "I made a terrible, terrible mistake."

"We could be good together, Dinah," he said softly.

"Please, Peter. Don't call me again."

There was a hesitation, then he said, "Okay, if that's how you want it."

"That's how I want it. I have to go." I hung up the phone, and sat there.

"Mom?" My bedroom door opened. Kate stopped, dead in her tracks. She was staring at the covered mirror. "Mom, what the hell—"

I jumped to my feet. "It's just . . . I . . ." I couldn't think of a single explanation. What was the point of trying to explain anyway?

Kate was looking back and forth from me to the mirror, then she turned and ran.

I heard her feet slapping down the hall, the slam of her bedroom door. Now she would lie down on her bed and cry, under her poster of the latest hot young star whose name I didn't know.

I lay down on my own bed in the dark beside the empty place where my husband belonged. Very soon, I was not alone.

"Daddy?" Kate had answered the phone. I was jumping every time the phone rang, like a hopeful teenager with a new crush. "When are you coming home?"

I was standing on the other side of the kitchen. Alex was sitting with Elijah at the kitchen table, reading him a story about a prince who rescues a princess from the clutches of an ogre. Sam had been gone for almost two weeks. Thirteen days and twelve nights.

"Kevin Sherman asked me out," Kate said into the phone. She listened for another few seconds. "Oh, Daddy!" she said. She listened again, then took the cordless phone out of the room. I heard her ask him if he was going to take her for her driving test.

"Don't hang up, Kate," Alex called after her. "We want to talk to him, too. Right, Elijah?"

"Right." Elijah pointed to the book. They'd come to the part of the story where the ogre tells the prince he'll let the princess go but only if the prince grants him two wishes.

"'I have no power to grant wishes,'" Alex said, reading the prince's words in his own voice. "'Only witches and fairies can grant wishes, I'm just a prince.'"

"'Then I won't let her go,'" said Alex, reading in a low and growling voice, for the ogre. "'She's mine.'"

Elijah listened carefully while Alex finished the story. It ended with the prince returning to the ogre's castle and finally winning the princess with the help of a whole army, slaying the ogre in the bargain.

"He could have just granted the ogre's wish," Elijah said as his brother closed the book.

"How could he do that?"

"He could have if he thought he could," Elijah said.

I turned away. If only that were always true, that you had only to believe in something hard enough to get what you want.

Kate came back and handed the phone to Alex, who talked and listened for a few minutes. "Dad never goes on a business trip for this long," he muttered, handing the phone to Elijah.

"When are you coming home to play horsy?" Elijah said.

At least two of my trio weren't buying the business-trip routine. Elijah? I had no idea what Elijah was thinking anymore. And as much as it hurt, I knew Sam and I were going to have to tell these children something. And soon.

I took the phone into my bedroom. I'd removed the sheet from the mirror after Kate saw it, and just didn't look when I passed.

"Do you want to talk about this, Sam?" I said. "At least talk?"

"I want to come by tomorrow and pick up my gray suit." His voice was shot through with anger, tension, hurt. "I have a meeting on Friday and I need to wear it."

"Of course."

"I'll be there around eleven. Make sure the kids aren't around."

"Sam—"

"I've never gone *near* another woman."

"I know, Sam. I don't know how to—"

He hung up on me before I could finish my sentence.

That night, I heard Alex and Kate whispering in Kate's room, late into the night. I decided Kate had told Sam about the mirror, and was now informing her brother.

On Thursday morning Sam did pick up his gray suit, along with his khaki pants, another pair of sneakers, and enough other items to fill a roomy suitcase. I stood in the doorway and watched him pack, the stone that was my heart sinking lower with every piece of clothing he folded. I was the newscaster, giving him the family bulletin. Since his call, Elijah's class had gone to the zoo, which he'd loved, and Kate had gone out with her new beau, pronounced him hot, though she wouldn't give me an explanation, except to say she was going to go out with him again. Sam looked exhausted, and spoke only to answer my questions. He initiated nothing other than to say he'd taken a monthly lease on an apartment in Manhattan, and didn't want the children to know anything until he'd had more time to think.

I saw some hope in that. Not much.

Three days later, Sam called to say he thought we had to tell the children. I told him I loved him again, but he was unmoved.

We filled in the children together on a Sunday afternoon. We said very little about why we were separating, just that sometimes adults have conflicts that are difficult to resolve. Sam said we felt it best not to share the substance of our conflicts with them because they might feel compelled to take one side or the other, when what we wanted was for them to go on loving both of us. Considering how I'd hurt him, the way Sam handled it made me love him and want him back even more.

"Oh, this is just great, just fine," said Kate. "You guys split up and we don't know why? I suppose you'll tell us when you sign the final papers."

"This is a separation, Kate. It happens." Sam put his arm around her shoulders and drew her in. "I know how hard this must be for you and I'm sorry."

"Sorry?" Alex said. "Our whole lives are changed and you're sorry?"

Sam sighed. "I know it's upsetting. Of course it'll be a change. And of course it's hard for your mother and me, too. But the thing you have to remember, the important thing is, we're both still going to be your parents."

Silence.

"Come on, kids," he said. "What do you say I take you out for some dinner?"

They wanted to go, even Elijah, who seemed more bewildered than angry or sad.

After they left, I sank into the couch.

"Dinah?"

I looked up. Sam was back. "Where are the kids?"

"In the car. Alex wants Chinese, Kate wants Mexican. I told them I'd be right back."

"Sam, I want you to come home."

"Dinah." He sat down next to me. "I don't know if I can ever come back. I've never gone near another woman, not even once—not that I haven't been tempted. I mean, I'm no saint. Last year a woman came on to me at a sales conference. I told her she was very beautiful—which she was—and I was very flattered, but that I was madly in love with my wife. That's what I said. Madly in love."

I couldn't take my eyes away from him.

"So she said that you didn't have to know, it would just be the two of us in that hotel room. I told her that wasn't the point. *I* would know." He looked out the window. "Now I feel like a real schmuck. Or is it schlemiel?"

"I'm sorry, Sam. That's all I can say."

"Please don't. I don't want to hear it. I came back because I wanted to say something else, say it again, even if I'm beating a dead horse. I really think you need to see a psychiatrist. Please. If you won't do it for me, do it for the kids."

"The kids?" My heart started beating fast.

He stood up and walked over toward the window, looked out into the backyard for a moment, then turned. "Dinah, think back to before all this happened. If *I* were all of a sudden talking about a resident demon, ghost, whatever, would *you* feel comfortable leaving me in charge of our children?"

"You want to take the children away from me?"

"Dinah, I just want you to get some help. I think you're having some sort of a breakdown and I just want you to get some help. That's all I want."

I stared at him. The demon was taking everything in return for Elijah—my body, my husband, my work, my self-respect, my *soul*. This, then, was the last thing left, the only thing it had not yet taken, my children. And now, using Sam as its instrument, it would take them, too.

I called a shrink the next day. I decided not to use the psychiatrist I'd referred patients to when they needed medication and got the name of one in Stamford from a colleague in my building. I found it humiliating, more than I had thought possible, that Dinah-with-all-the-answers should have to do this. Worse, I had no conviction whatsoever that seeing a psychiatrist would, or could, help me. But I went.

Dr. Evan Kessler was a large, burly man with a woolly beard who reminded me of a big blond bear. He stood up and shook my hand, then sat back down behind his desk.

I sat down on the couch, trying not to cry, trying not to mind his being behind the desk, a dominant position I'd generally avoided with my own patients.

"I'd feel more comfortable if we could sit here," I said, finally.

"Sure." He stood up without saying a word and sat in one of the two chairs in the corner of his large office. I sat down across from him.

"So. Why are you here?"

I wanted to laugh because it was all so familiar, it comes so easily to the person on the other side of the desk. Had I really felt that way, that it was easy to listen unscathed to another person's pain?

I told Dr. Kessler my story—Elijah's illness, my ghost, all of it. He listened, all the while writing on his notepad, speaking only to ask me a question to clarify a point. I told the story as quickly and economically as I could, as if I were recounting a patient's story. No doubt one of his notes was "flat affect."

When I was through, he sat still for a long time.

I used to do it myself, let the silence speak. Done to me, it felt false and arrogant. "I guess you've got a whole page of notes attesting to my delusions and hallucinations, right?"

He stared at me for a moment, then asked, "What's your profession, Dinah?"

"What's the difference?" I hadn't mentioned it. I was embarrassed to tell him, it seemed like just another of God's little jokes on me, that I should once have been the person to whom others told these kind of stories, to whom people looked for advice and counsel, even, hardest of all, compassion. I had obviously chosen the wrong profession, I had never helped anyone.

"I need to get a history," the doctor said.

I bowed my head. "Psychologist." I looked up, half expecting him to be laughing.

He wasn't. "Dinah," he said, "I was wondering if you feel like you ever deserve to be happy again."

"If Elijah dies . . ." I started to tear up. "I guess I can't even imagine ever being happy again."

"But he's well, you say. What makes you think he's going to die?"

I folded my hands on my lap. "It's as if I have the other outcome in my head, as if the demon put it there, as if I've already lived it. So that I know exactly what would have happened. They have to hook Elijah up to machines to keep him alive, and I cannot let him go, and I—we—go on and on and on that way, for years. My family is destroyed. I am destroyed."

"You feel you're destroyed now, according to what you've told me."

"Yes. I do. In a different way."

"What's different?"

"My son is alive."

"I see. In this other outcome, after you refuse to remove the machine, what happens then?"

I closed my eyes, and an image came into my mind, a pale face, lips stuck in a pursed position, bitterness and anger in the eyes.

"I become like my grandmother."

"What about her?"

"Bitter, hateful, terribly sad."

He made a few more notes, then looked up.

"Do you have any children?" I asked him. I wanted him to be human, to listen to me, to stop making the judgments I knew he was making.

"Two."

"If you lost one, could you imagine ever being happy again?"

He sighed. "Dinah, have you ever treated complicated grief?"

The terms we call it seemed so stupid. Complicated grief—what did that mean, how did that describe the pain of losing a child?

"Yes. But it's just bullshit, everything I did, everything I said, was bullshit. Total bullshit."

He smiled. "Did you think that at the time?"

"No, but I didn't know what it was like, losing a child."

"Dinah, did these bereaved patients walk out your door better able to cope than when they came?"

I shrugged. I had no patients now, of course.

"Did they?"

"I suppose so."

"So then why do you now think that you didn't help them?"

I was crying. "Because I didn't understand."

"Did you have to understand to help? Isn't compassion mostly just a willingness to be close to suffering?" He watched me blow my nose.

I couldn't see it that way anymore. "It's not enough," I said, hiccuping, looking out the window, which had a view of the interstate, where construction and an accident had brought traffic to a dead stop. I'd been stuck in the jam myself on the way down.

"Let's go somewhere else," Kessler said. "Your son lived. Do you have to suffer for that, for happiness?"

"Look. I know what you're going for, you want to talk about my mother and my childhood and show how I've manufactured all this because Charlotte made me feel unworthy when I was a little girl. But even if this demon is composed of my ego deconstructed by grief, it's still real."

He grinned. "I guess I'm going to have to do better if I want to get anywhere with you, huh?"

I offered a smile. "Look, I worked on all that when I was studying for my doctorate and went into therapy myself. I even worked on the issue of my abusive relationship with Seth Lucien"

He stood up and walked over to his mahogany desk, leaned against it. "Maybe you need more work."

"Maybe so," I said. "But how can you say for sure that there aren't entities in this universe that feed on human suffering? Maybe they can even create themselves out of suffering."

He crossed one leg over the other. "I'm sorry, Dinah. I just don't have it in me to believe your story. I believe you're suffering. But you know as well as I do that I can't collude with your hallucinations."

"You'd have done the same thing if it'd been your son." He was trying, and he was as unhelpful as I had been with my own bereaved patients.

twenty-seven

Dinner. I had opened all the cabinets and the refrigerator several times before facing the fact that there was nothing in either that qualified as supper material. I'd given up my practice and my writing class and my column and my marriage and I still couldn't find the time to go shopping. Sam had been sending checks, so I still could go shopping, had I been able to organize myself to do it. Who knew how long Sam's sending checks would last, anyway? One day, any day, he might say he'd only continue to support me if the kids went to live with him. If he took me to court, he'd win.

The phone rang in the other room, and I heard Alex pick it up. "Oh, hi, Grandma."

I hoped it was Sam's mother, calling from New Jersey, and not mine, calling from Long Island. Come to think of it, I wasn't anxious to speak to either. On the other hand, Sam had probably told his parents, while I hadn't mentioned it to mine.

Alex walked into the kitchen, holding the cordless phone under his left ear and chin while he peered into the refrigerator and answered questions. I looked out the window, where the sky had clouded up, as if a storm was coming in. I tried to figure out which grandma it might be from his responses, but the answers to grandmothers' questions are pretty interchangeable. "Yeah, gonna go back to school in three weeks . . . Tenth grade . . . Camp's great, kids are a pain . . . No, I don't know . . . Daddy's hasn't been here for a month, Grandma . . ." He looked at me and frowned.

"I'll take it, Alex." I had to face this sometime.

I took the cordless and walked it out of the room, leaving Alex in the kitchen.

"Dinah? What's wrong?"

I sighed. "Nothing's wrong, Charlotte." Damn. "It's just that Sam and I have split up."

"What do you mean, split up?"

"You know, we used to be together, now we aren't. He's staying in the city."

"That's nothing wrong?"

"All right, Charlotte, it's something wrong." I glanced out the window into the backyard, where I'd set Elijah up with drawing materials earlier at the patio table. He wasn't there anymore. Now he was at the swing set, sitting on top of the sliding board, just staring across the lawn into the cluster of trees that separated our yard from the yard of the house on the next street. The sky had turned dark and threatening. It was going to rain buckets any second.

"You don't have to be sarcastic, Dinah."

My conversations with my mother were always the same. I told her to hold on a moment, and, cradling the phone under my chin, I opened the back door.

"Elijah, come on in. It's going to rain."

He didn't move, just sat up there, staring.

"Elijah?" Was he in some kind of a trance or something? I put the phone down and started out the door.

He turned and waved, then slid down and ran over. He helped me quickly clean up the paper and crayons, we got inside just as the sky opened, and I sent him into the kitchen with his brother.

"Dinah, I was just thinking," my mother said, after Elijah had gone and

I picked up the phone again. "You don't end a twenty-one-year marriage just like that. When the going gets tough, the tough get going, you know. I know you had a hard time when Elijah was sick, but you should be celebrating your good fortune."

"Please stop telling me what I should and shouldn't do, Charlotte."

"You're lucky you have a mother who cares enough about you to tell you anything," she snapped. "Does Sam have . . ." She lowered her voice. "Someone else?"

Of course she would think this. I told her no, and left it at that.

Charlotte was sighing. "Oh, my, my, my. Dinah, honey. When you make a commitment to a marriage, you don't just throw it away."

"This from a woman who discouraged my marriage in the first place."

"My goodness, Dinah. That was so long ago. And I wasn't discouraging. I was just trying to urge you to be cautious. That's a mother's job. I love Sam."

"I just can't talk about this right now," I said. There were tears in my voice, I knew. Hers sounded hurt.

"But I'm your mother, Dinah. Were you *ever* planning on telling me?"

"I was going to, it only happened a few weeks ago. It's just—I just don't want to talk about it."

"Fine, Dinah. You call me when you do." And she hung up.

So. This—like Elijah's illness, like my wedding, like everything—had turned into something about her.

I stood there for a moment, then replaced the phone in its cradle.

"What did Grandma say?" Trying desperately not to care, Alex didn't look up from the newspaper on the kitchen table when I came into the kitchen. Outside, it was night at mid-afternoon, sheets of rain spilling out of a wild sky and slamming against the window. Elijah was sitting on the counter, watching.

I sighed. "She was . . ." My mind raced through various word choices—freaked, mad, upset, appalled, full of reproach, full of advice—and settled on the neutral word so often used by shrinks. "Concerned."

Alex's earring flashed when he nodded, and he still didn't look up. His hair hung in his eyes.

"Look, honey, I know you're upset—" I waited through a near-deafening boom of thunder and the lightning crack that followed it. "Remember what Dad used to say about thunder and lightning?"

When Alex was Elijah's age, he'd been terrified of storms. At four and five he'd appear in our bedroom at night during a thunderstorm, and Sam would take him into our bed and say, "It's only God, blowing His nose." Alex, a born skeptic, would say, "God doesn't have a nose, Daddy." Or, "I'm not a baby, Daddy. Don't make up stories." And Sam would argue back, all the while distracting Alex from his fear. "What do you mean, God doesn't have a nose. Of course He has a nose. How could He smell all His flowers without one? Or what about grass, or the sea? Or waffles? My mother told me God has a nose, and I believe it."

"Mom, will you give me a break?" Alex said now. "Dad isn't here anymore."

I glanced at Elijah, who hadn't asked what his father had told his brother about storms, but sure seemed interested in this one. I sighed. Dinner. I turned my back on my sons to forage for food again, but I felt the older one watching me. Macaroni? Used the last box yesterday. Spaghetti? There was a box in the cabinet, but the leftover sauce in the fridge was growing mold. Cheese casserole? We'd come a long way from chicken Marsala.

"Maybe I should go with Dad," Alex said.

Please, not that, too. I took a deep breath, then turned to face him. Calm, be calm.

"I'd surely miss you, honey."

"I know, but Dad misses me, too."

"Well, maybe after Dad gets settled."

Kate came in just as I said it. "There's no point in going to live with Daddy, Alex. Because they're getting back together."

Alex frowned. "Oh, come on, Kate, that never happens. Don't you know anything?" He glanced out the window at the sheeting, pounding rain, then left the kitchen and headed upstairs.

"Quite a storm, huh, Elijah?" Kate said.

Elijah nodded, without turning away from the window. "It's just like music, Kate," he said.

Kate put her arm around her little brother and looked out the window, where a small maple tree was bending like an old man in the force of the lashing rain and wind. She closed her eyes.

"Yes, I suppose it is like music," she said after a moment.

I looked, too, and listened, but I couldn't hear anything except the sound of rain and thunder. I turned away. In half an hour, I had hot dogs on the table.

The next day Charlotte arrived.

"You look terrible, Dinah." She stood at the front door wearing a long linen sheath, lilac, with a matching jacket, and espadrilles. Her car was parked on the street.

"Thanks." I knew how I looked.

She looked stricken at my sarcastic tone, and apologized. I had no choice, I invited her in.

"Dinah," she said, sitting down at the kitchen table, "you know I'm not the kind of mother who interferes, but I'm not the kind of mother who can just stand by through something as serious as this. I want to help. Now, what's going on between you two?"

This wasn't helping, but I sat down at the kitchen table across from her. "I really don't want to talk about it."

My mother lowered her eyes and folded her hands together. "I always hoped we could have the kind of relationship where we could talk to each other, Dinah."

I stared at her.

Elijah came in then. "Gramma!" His face lit and he stretched out his arms and Grandma Charlotte took him in.

I turned away, I couldn't bear to look, and went to get the mail. The box was stuffed with envelopes. Standing in the driveway, I started to flip through them. All bills. I had no idea how I was going to pay them, since I wasn't working. I was going to have to start figuring out the answers to such practical questions, assuming I could get my mind to focus on anything practical for longer than five seconds. If Sam really wanted this, we were going to have to come up with a plan.

Wait a minute, this one wasn't a bill. Small, fragile letters too small to read easily. The return-address corner had only the street name and zip code, not the sender's name, but I recognized Ellen Shoenfeld's writing from the last note she'd sent me. I opened the envelope. This one was much longer, the whole page covered in tiny script.

6 August

Dear Dinah,

Sleep has always been hard for me, because the nightmares never go away, waking and sleeping. Now I cannot sleep at all, for many weeks. I am eighty years old and this is not a good thing for my health.

They call us survivors but I would say a different term. When we started to get our strength back after we were first liberated, many wanted to tell their story. No one wanted to hear. They did not believe us, or they did not want to know. Now everyone wants to hear. My daughters always urge me to go to the place where the famous movie director is recording our experiences on film. Go there? Tell everything? Bear witness, this is our duty, they say. I lived through what happened to me, that was enough duty. I have not even told my daughters all of these things. Even my husband did not know, although he came out of there too, and he told anyone who asked him. He used to tell how he and his family hid for nine months in a space so small that when one of them shifted positions the rest were forced to do so as well. Many things. I would be angry with him for telling. The response was never enough. It never could be.

In America everyone thinks suffering not shared is not real. All the time on the talk shows I see these people telling about the most personal things, awful things, and the audiences pretend to be sympathetic. It is just an entertainment to them.

My daughters say I should tell for my own sake, because it would make me feel better, and it is probably that you agree since you are a psychologist. What is that, better?

I know you witnessed what Elijah said to me that day, that he had painted a picture of Gerte, and I need to tell you this now. Gerte was the name of my child. There. I wrote this. All these years since she passed away, until this moment, I have kept my vow not to speak her name. This is fifty-one years. 2 January. Not even my daughters have ever heard the name of my child who died, or how she died. I keep it with me always, and I know her name will be the last word I will speak before I die, but I never have spoken it aloud. Fifty-one years.

It is not a common American name, as you know. My Gerte was given a good German name. We were fools, of course. We thought we were Germans, you know.

Dinah, I have not slept. How does your son know this name?

Sincerely,
Ellen Shoenfeld

I folded the paper carefully, put it in my pocket, and whispered, "Ellen, I have no idea." Then I went back into the house, where Elijah and my mother were waiting.

Possession came once again that night, and when the demon was through with me, I took a shower, but I could still smell the metallic odor when I got out. I made my way into the kitchen, unable to bear being in my bedroom anymore. Charlotte was sitting at the table by the window, drinking tea. It was dark, only the single light of the desk lamp illuminated, the room full of shadows, a penumbra of light.

"Oh, it's you, Dinah. You startled me." She took a sip of her tea. Tiny lines encircled her lips, and the light touched her face in unfortunate places. Devoid of cosmetics, the skin was blotchy, the jowls fleshy and full of regret. "I just couldn't sleep."

I had nowhere to go. I pulled my bathrobe closed and retied the sash.

"Is something wrong, Dinah? You look so pale."

I stood there, my arms hanging at my sides.

"Your father is angry at me," Charlotte said. "That's one of the reasons I came. He said I wasn't helpful to you when Elijah was sick. We had a fight. Was he right, Dinah? I didn't mean to say the wrong things, I just felt so useless and terrified. I wanted to be helpful."

My face felt suddenly hot, my palms damp. I didn't want to talk to her about this, it was still about her, always about her. I didn't want to talk to her about anything.

I spun around and started to walk out of the room.

"Dinah, *please* talk to me."

I hesitated, turned, looked at her. My mother had tears in her eyes, she was crying. I stood frozen for a moment in the doorway of the kitchen, my heart full of pain and longing.

"You hurt me," I said finally.

I was mesmerized by her eyes; they had always been a beautiful deep blue, although the color had faded as she aged. It wasn't their color that held me now, it was the way she was looking so directly at me, her eyes full of love and pain. There was no anger there. Her eyes were clear and open and undefended.

"When Elijah was sick, I hurt you?" she asked.

I shook my head. "Always."

She said nothing for a moment, just looked at me. I expected her to defend herself then, tell me she'd never hurt me, and that I didn't know what I was talking about. Or that my skin was too thin. Or some other argument I couldn't even hypothesize. Yes. She would deny what I felt in order to convince me that her own feelings were the only valid ones. It was what she always did.

But this time she didn't do it. Not at all. She pulled a tissue from the pocket of her robe, wiped her eyes, and said, "If I hurt you I'm sorry, Dinah. I didn't mean to."

"It always seemed to me that you did mean to." For the first time in my life, I was telling my mother the truth, how I felt, and I wasn't even sure why I was doing so. Perhaps because I had nothing left to lose.

Her face seemed to collapse, the truth—my truth—was wounding her deeply. "You thought I meant to hurt you." She was making a statement, not asking a question, as if she were repeating my words to try to make herself grasp their meaning.

I nodded, still staking out my territory in the doorway of the kitchen.

"But I love you." Her eyes naked and brimming with tears.

"It never seemed to me you did."

She shook her head. She didn't deny, defend herself, or resist. She simply said, "I'm sorry. Tell me."

I stood very still, and sighed. "There are so many incidents, Charlotte. So much hurt."

She gripped her teacup, her knuckles stretched taut and white. "Maybe if you tell me we could try to understand each other," she said. "We could try to be friends."

Friends. She never had a friend, I don't think. Not like I did. And I did have friends. Good ones. A few in a lifetime is a lot.

My mind was teeming with images and sounds, my mother's face when she was young and beautiful, her gargoyle expression, the vicious names she had sometimes called me, the apparent constancy of her anger. What was the point of telling her these things? She wouldn't get it, she'd remember it differently. Of course she would. I'd given up trying years ago.

"When I was thirteen," I said, "you sent me to that diet doctor. You were always on me for my weight."

"But that was thirty years ago."

"It still hurts."

She nodded and sighed, seemed to shrink back into the kitchen chair. "Yes. I suppose it does."

I took a deep breath and went on. "That man put his hands inside me."

"He *what?*" Her eyes were wide, astonished, repulsed.

"Charlotte. He gave me an internal exam. I was thirteen. He put his hands inside me and I had no one to turn to, no one to tell, and you wouldn't have done anything even if I did tell you."

"Yes I would, of course I would. I would have killed him. I had no idea." Her lower lip was quivering.

"You should have known, I thought so anyway. And then you let him give me those pills, they made me crazy, jazzed. They rotted my teeth. How could you care more about my weight than about me? You were supposed to be my mother."

She clapped her hand over her mouth and stared at me in wide-eyed shock. After a moment, she said softly, "I just wanted everything that was best for you. I wanted you to be beautiful so people would want you."

I suddenly realized that this was how she looked at the world, *had* looked at the world, anyway. I wasn't sure about now.

"Is beauty the only reason people would want a girl? Who told *you* you only had worth because of your beauty?"

She was crying again. "My father, I suppose. My mother."

"I'm sorry," I said.

"I just wanted people to like you." She put her head in her hands.

I stared. Perhaps she had wanted people to like me, but mostly she wanted herself to like me. I was going to be not only beautiful, but compliant and submissive, too. Those were the two qualities she couldn't be, despite her own parents' efforts. I would make everything right for her. Like it or not, I would be a reflection of her, even if it was a false one.

For the first time in my life, I was feeling compassion for her, not for her as my mother, but for Charlotte Blake Rosenberg, for her own hollow places, her longings and regrets and pain and missing pieces. She had looked at the world this way for me because this was the way she looked at the world for herself. She couldn't help it.

My mother nodded, then took a deep breath and stood up. She moved over to the window, looked outside at the dark night for a long moment before turning back.

"My mother hated me, Dinah. Do you know that? My own mother. She couldn't stand the sight of me. She blamed me for Charlie's death. I was only a little girl. Only six years old, and she *assigned* me to watch him. I just went to pick some wildflowers in the field in back of the willow tree and he wandered away. My mother blamed me, do you see? I was only six and my mother took to her bed and she never hugged me again and she never looked at me or loved me again."

My mother's face was contorted with tears, with anguish and weeping.

"I loved you, Dinah. I tried for you. I know I made mistakes. But it wasn't because of you, it was because of me."

Her admission stopped me cold. I stood very still, and then I took a few steps forward, and she took a few steps forward. We had a long way to go, but still, I reached out to my mother, all the way across the miles between us. I moved toward her, and put my arms around her and we embraced, felt our arms around each other for the first time in many, many years.

After a few moments, I told her, "She didn't blame you. I really don't think so. More likely, she blamed herself, and couldn't deal with that, so she projected it onto you." And believed she had failed as a mother for having lost her child, which meant she would ultimately fail with the children she hadn't lost.

"Don't you think I know that?" My mother wiped her eyes and nose with her handkerchief again.

Of course she did. But just knowing didn't help, she would have had to feel it. Only Grandma Elizabeth's effort could have helped make it right. Only the living can make amends, can reconcile with each other, or at least try.

I heard a sizzling noise, and turned. The demon was in a corner of the kitchen, got up in its Seth disguise, black boots, pink skin. It eyed me coldly. But it didn't move, and for once it said nothing. I blinked and it was gone.

I sat with my mother for a while, neither of us speaking, then she said, "I'm sorry, Dinah, I'm keeping you up when you need your rest. Here I've come to try to help you, and I'm the one blubbering like a baby."

"It's all right, Mom." It felt so weird to call her Mom after all these years, but there it was, I was doing it.

I walked her back to the guest room, then I returned to my own bed, where I fell into a deep, uninterrupted sleep, alone for the first time in days. I dreamed.

In the dream, the phone rings, and I pick it up, and I hear the voice of the undertaker. He says, "I'm sorry to bother you now, but I'm preparing your son's body for burial, and I want everything to be right. I have everything I need to dress him—his jeans, his sneakers, his shirt—but I noticed I only have one sock here. Would it be okay if I drive over to pick up another sock?" In the dream, his odd kindness moves me tremendously, and makes me cry.

I opened my eyes in a glorious pink sunrise, realizing that it had been the first dream I'd had since all of this began in which I was able to even take notice of a kindness shown me after the death of my son. For that, it was memorable.

A real phone was ringing, too. Perhaps I wouldn't have even remembered the dream if the phone hadn't wakened me. I glanced at the bedside clock. Nine A.M. I'd slept late. Could it be Sam calling? Oh, Sam.

I fumbled for the receiver. "Hello?"

"Mrs. Galligan?" A woman's voice, familiar somehow. "This is Sarah Gray."

"Who? I'm sorry, I—"

"We met at the hospital. Elijah was having an EEG. I'm Maggie's mother."

"Oh, yes." I got out of bed. "Hello." It was still dark in my bedroom, the shades were drawn. I could hear the children chasing each other, laughing.

"I'm very sorry to bother you, but I just wanted to tell you that my daughter has gone into remission. Maggie's well again."

Why was she calling me? "Well, that's wonderful, Sarah."

"Mrs. Galligan, her white count is just about normal. Miraculously."

"I'm very happy for you."

"Do you understand what I'm saying? The doctors had given my daughter only a few months to live, and now she's completely well. Elijah has the gift." She was speaking so softly that I could hardly hear what she was saying.

"The gift?"

"The gift of healing, Mrs. Galligan. Your son, your little boy, healed my Maggie."

When I came into the kitchen a few minutes later, my mother was standing at the stove, mixing up batter for pancakes. She was wearing a silk robe, and she had put on some makeup.

"Hope you don't mind." She didn't look at me, and I had the impression she was embarrassed about what had happened in the night.

"Of course not, Mom. The kids won't be up for a while yet, though. I'll have to drive them to their stuff."

"Then I think I'll go take my shower now, and put on my face."

It looked already put on to me. "Yes, go ahead."

She took a cup of coffee with her. I poured one for myself.

"Mommy?" Elijah was standing there.

"You woke up by yourself, honey?" I gave him a hug. "Did you and Tuddy sleep well?"

He nodded, then sat at the kitchen table, with Tuddy on his lap, while I cooked and served up some pancakes. I sat down at the table beside him and we both ate without talking for a while. Then I asked him, "Elijah, do you remember Maggie? You met her at the hospital, when you had your test?"

"Maggie." He smiled.

"Can you tell me what happened?"

He placed Tuddy on top of the table and looked at the stuffed creature for a moment before he answered. "I told her about the place where there's music and swimming and she won't be afraid."

"Where is that, honey?"

"I don't know where."

I took a deep breath. "Maggie's well now, Elijah."

He took Tuddy onto his lap. "That's good, Mommy. Her mommy is happy."

"Did you do something to make her well?"

He giggled as if I was tickling him. "Me?"

"You remember how you and she whispered to each other and—"

"God makes people well, Mommy." He scooted over beside me, and gave me a hug. "I think the ghost is making you sick."

I stared at him. "How do you know about the ghost, Elijah?"

"I see him."

"Since when?"

"Since I woke up."

"Why didn't you tell me?"

"I didn't know before. But now I do. He says his name is Seth, but I don't believe him."

"Why not?"

"Because he tells lies. And because the wasps call him another name."

"What name?" I had felt the wasps, the stinging, swirling wind, heard their sounds, but I didn't understand them, their language was unknown to me.

He closed his eyes for a minute, then opened them. "They're always all around him. He's made of them, Mommy."

Yes. I knew this, I had felt it, but I had never named it.

He hugged me again. "Dr. Kessler can't help, Mommy."

How did Elijah even know I'd gone to see the doctor that day?

"He doesn't see the ghost," Elijah said. "He doesn't believe."

twenty-eight

I think it must be said that this was the point when I really started to fight back. I didn't realize at the time that I was at a turning point. I had thought I'd been fighting back all along, though losing. Perhaps I would have died, believing I had given my life for my son's life, believing this was possible.

I left Elijah with my mother while I drove Alex and Kate to their activities for the day. Kate had passed her driving test but we had only one car, as Sam had the other with him.

I drove directly to Temple Beth Elohim, as if by force of physical need. It was a beautiful, modern synagogue with white stucco walls and a soaring octagonal main sanctuary with tall, narrow stained glass windows. I recognized it; I had seen it before in my visions. The rabbi was in; a small hatchback car was parked in the reserved-for-clergy space.

I sat in the car with my eyes closed for a moment, trying to gather myself, my wits, my nerve. Then I opened the door and got out. About halfway up the walk, I turned around and headed back. What in the world would I say?

Feeling woozy, I leaned against my car, closed my eyes, took a few deep breaths.

"Are you all right?"

I opened my eyes. The man approaching me from the woods just beyond the parking lot in a worn tweed jacket, khakis, and sneakers was nice-looking, about my age, with salt-and-pepper hair and a neatly trimmed beard.

I knew him, too. I pulled a tissue out of my pocket. "Rabbi Leiberman."

He blinked. "Have we met? You're not a temple member, I know that. Are you all right?"

"Yes, yes, I just felt a little faint. I'm fine now."

He was staring into my face intently. Obviously I didn't look fine. I looked terrible, my mother had said so.

"Were you coming to see me?"

I stammered something unintelligible.

"You just came to faint in my parking lot?" He smiled.

"I'm sorry."

"No need to be sorry." He glanced at the wooded area off to the left. "Last year, we built a small outdoor sanctuary just through the trees over there. I find a few moments there every morning helpful. Maybe you'd like to sit there with me for a little while?"

"Are you sure it wouldn't be too much trouble?"

"Not at all. But I do make it a habit never to sit with anyone whose name I don't know."

"I'm sorry, Rabbi." I held out my hand. "Dinah Rosenberg Galligan."

"Nice to meet you, Dinah." He shook my hand, then gently put his hand on my back and guided me through the trees into a small clearing, arranged with a few benches around a memorial stone.

He sat down beside me on a bench. It was a beautiful late summer day, and the sunlight radiating down through the tops of the trees encircled us in a dazzling cocoon of light. We sat in silence for a while.

"Are you Jewish, Dinah?" he asked.

"I used to joke that my family growing up was 'unformed Reform.'"

The rabbi smiled. "Well, we're formed Reform. You never thought of joining?"

"My husband is Catholic. That made it difficult. Not that Sam is so religious, either. He used to call himself 'Catholic by Chore,' in the days when we used to joke about our mixed marriage."

"Used to?"

I looked down at my haunted hands. "Nothing seems too funny anymore." I took a couple of breaths. "Can I tell you about the dream I had last night, Rabbi?"

He nodded.

I told him about the dream where the undertaker calls, oddly compassionate.

"I see," the rabbi said. "You lost a child."

"No, my son Elijah lived, after all. He's my sweet, extraordinary boy. He'll be six next month."

"I don't understand. Why do you have such dreams?"

I folded my hands on my lap, trying to still them. "That is a very complicated and painful story. Very painful."

Rabbi Jacob Leiberman looked intently into my face for a moment, then said, "Tell me what you came to tell me, Dinah. Maybe telling me will help."

"No one can help, Rabbi. I'm not even sure why I came."

"I could listen. Maybe that will be of some help.

I stood up, moved toward the perimeter of our illuminated cocoon, at the edge of the clearing. I needed to stand away from him to say what I had to say. "There is no help for the doomed," I said.

He raised an eyebrow.

I looked away. I expected to see the demon standing next to one of the surrounding trees. I saw only a tiny sparrow, poking in the grass.

"Do you believe in ghosts, Rabbi?" I asked him. "And demons?"

He startled, then nodded slowly. "Yes, there are ghosts and demons. According to the book of *Zohar,* demons are linked to the *Sitra Ahra,* which exists in perfect balance to the *Sefirot.* Do you know what that is?"

"I've read about some of this." I had, during my exorcism attempts.

He explained that the *Zohar* was the basic book of *Kabbalah,* the Jewish book of mystical revelation. The ten *Sefirot* are the ten emanations of God, who is called *Ein Sof,* That Which Is Without Limit. By good works, and by prayer and meditation on the ten holy *Sefirot,* we could bring about God's divine grace in the world. He gave me some examples of the ten: *Keter*, God's will to create; *Binah,* God's understanding; *Hesed,* or loving-kindness, God's limitless flow of goodness.

"Where do demons fit in?" I asked, still keeping my distance, standing by the trees.

"Well, if you think about it logically, demons would be linked with the opposite processes, would they not? If God creates, evil destroys. If God loves, evil hates. If God is kind, evil is unkind. Do you see?"

"What about the death of innocents? Natural death, I mean. Is that from God or evil?"

"Well. You do get right to the big ones, don't you?" He smiled. "A certain rabbi, Nahum of Gimzo, used to say, 'This too is for the best.' No matter what happened, he would say it. Meaning even the death of innocents comes from God."

"Meaning God must have a reason for taking that innocent life?"

"It could mean that. Meaning we may not understand God's reasoning. Divine providence is just that. We call it *bashert.*"

I nodded. "Can you tell me more about demons?"

"There are different types. A *dybbuk* supposedly enters a human being and—"

"Enters?"

"Possesses."

"Have you ever seen this happen?"

"I, myself? No." He seemed stunned.

"Why would it happen?"

"Some people say the spirits of evil men live on after death. They have different names. Some are called *mazzikim.*" He stood up now and came over to me, as I said this word through my lips. "*Mazzikim.*" I whispered it softly, letting the "z" sound slide off my tongue. I couldn't help it. I was tearing up again.

"Tell me." The rabbi offered me a handkerchief, put his hand on my shoulder. "I'd really like to hear."

"I've told a lot of it before. The outcome wasn't good."

"Perhaps you told it to the wrong person."

"How do you know if someone's the right person?"

"Well, I don't think you always do. Speaking of deep pain to another human being is surely an act of faith, that what you say will be received compassionately."

As a psychologist, of course I knew this.

"The average person doesn't want to hear of pain," he said. "Can't bear it, would do anything to avoid it. Until it happens to him, or her, and avoidance is impossible. And then we wonder why there are so few people willing to listen, now that what we need *most* is to have someone to receive our story and accept it, no matter how disquieting the story is. It's really quite simple. It's also part of the reason rabbis and priests are in business."

"And psychologists," I said. "I used to be a psychologist."

He nodded. "Come and sit down. I'd like to hear."

"I don't even know where to begin."

"Begin in the most important place."

His face was kind. I knew he had sat at many bedsides, and held many hands, and said many *Mi Shebeirakh,* prayers for healing, and heard many horrific tales of sorrow and loss. I also knew he had heard no tale like mine.

We sat down again on the bench. "My son Elijah, he was very ill. He was in a coma."

By the time I finished telling him the story, the rabbi and I had been sitting there for several hours. I was out of breath and energy, exhausted with the telling.

He was silent for a while, then spoke the first few words he had spoken. "Do you know that tale your ghost told you about the two ghosts being overheard in a cemetery talking about the rain and the crops? That's a *midrash,* you know."

"The ghost told me it was just a story."

"Well, that's kind of what a *midrash* is. A story. But your ghost didn't tell you the end. After the man who overhears the ghosts uses the inside information to save his own crops, the two ghosts decide to stop talking. Because they realize that what they've been saying to each other has become known among the living."

"And that's not a good thing?"

"I don't know. What do you think? Is it?"

I didn't know how to answer so I said, "You sound like a therapist."

He smiled. "When in doubt, always answer a question with a question. It's getting hot, maybe you should tell me the rest in my office."

"I've been in your office, you know." I had described his office earlier, the way I knew it in my visions.

He stood up now and stretched. "So you said. I admit you've described it accurately."

"Then you believe me."

"Does it matter to you if I believe?" he asked, looking down at me.

I tried to smile. "I don't know? What do you think? Should it?"

"Not really," he said, sitting down again. Then, "I'll answer the question this way, Dinah. My mother's parents had been religious people back in Poland, but my mother wanted to leave all that behind when the family immigrated, and by the time my brother and I came along the only traditions my mother was keeping were gastronomic. She used my grandmother's recipes. To her death, my mother was not a believer. She was absolutely convinced that God was a fairy tale. Especially after Hitler. But, you know, she was a great cook. I mean great! Do you know who convinced me that God exists, absolutely?"

I shook my head.

"My mother. I was in high school and I was working after school at a plant nursery one day a week. I wouldn't take the time to eat that evening, I had to get right to work because I had a history paper due the next day. It was three o'clock in the morning when I finally finished. I went downstairs, hungry enough to eat nails, and sitting right there on a shelf in the refrigerator, I found that my mother had made up a plate for me. On it was her stuffed cabbage, which I loved, and some of her wonderful roasted potatoes, and green beans. She'd wrapped the whole thing in waxed paper, and there was a little note taped to the top with instructions as to how I could heat it up—microwave ovens were still years away—and a little message from her. I still remember the way my mother's handwriting looked. 'Dear Jake, the history scholar: Thought you might get hungry later. Love, Mom.' "

He smiled. "And that was the moment when I first truly felt the presence of God. I felt it in my mother's absolute love for me. I found her love in that plate, in that cabbage and those beans and potatoes, and that plate represented traditions of our people, that plate was the link all the way back, generations and generations. Objectively speaking, nothing had happened. But I'm convinced that God was there regardless of whether you believe He was there or not. Do you see what I mean?"

"I see." I waited a moment. "I'm sorry. I've taken so much of your time, I must be keeping you from something."

He bowed his head and muttered something. A prayer, maybe. For making such a bargain, perhaps I needed a prayer.

"Do you love your husband, Dinah?" he asked, looking me in the eye.

"He is my life." I put my head in my hands.

We sat there without talking for another minute or two. Then he told me that the spirits of evil men do live on after death, as ghosts, as demons, wandering the earth with no place to go and no place to hide, never mourned, yet never to see the face of God.

"But if they're evil," I asked him, "why don't they just go to hell?"

"There could be many reasons, I suppose. Maybe they haven't had a proper burial. Maybe that soul is so wicked it's simply exiled, denied even the possibility of rest. Maybe the dead are doomed to a punishment appropriate to the life they lived. Maybe they're condemned to wander because no one remembers their name."

It occurred to me that the young man I had known had made up his name, thinking the name Seth Lucien sounded evil or sinister.

"Could you do some sort of an exorcism for me?"

The rabbi sighed. "There are some rabbis who claim to know how to work with such things. But even if I believed these conceptions were real and not just metaphorical, I'm not convinced that's what you need, Dinah."

He bowed his head for a moment again, then looked at me.

"The ways of the Lord are mysterious and painful and wonderful, are they not? You know, Dinah, it's interesting to me that you named your boy Elijah. Elijah is the prophet angel, who gives himself completely to humanity, who shows humans the way to reconciliation. With the help of God, Elijah restores and reveals, and ultimately, shows the way to redemption. 'Lo, I will send the Prophet Elijah to you before the coming of the awesome, fearful day of the Lord. He shall reconcile fathers with sons and sons with their fathers.' "

"And mothers, too?"

"And mothers, too. I'd like to meet this little boy of yours, Dinah. The little boy who says he sees your ghost. The five-year-old vegetarian. That's kind of interesting, too."

"How so?"

"When the Prophet Isaiah imagines the world at its end, he envisions a non-carnivorous world, I think. The leopard lies down with the kid, the cow and the bear shall graze, their young shall lie down together, and the lion, like the ox, shall eat straw. The laws of *kashrut* could have been intended to be an intermediate step on the way to the ideal of vegetarianism. Keeping kosher is a way of respecting life, killing the animal without torturing it, respecting the lifeblood of the living being."

"He's a funny kid," I said.

"I have a feeling funny doesn't come close to describing it."

"No. It doesn't."

"But there is one thing, Dinah."

"What?"

"I want to thank you."

"For what?"

"For your story."

I shrugged. "It's my story."

"Yes," he said, "but our stories are all we have. You needed to tell this one. And I feel privileged to have heard it. And, having heard it, I feel I can give you my opinion, right or wrong. I think you yourself have the power to exorcise this demon. I really do."

"How?"

"Spirits have very little power in *this* world. They have the power to tease the living, and deceive, and confuse. They can tell lies about the future and the past, and worse, they can intermix the truth with lies. And that's all they can do. They certainly don't have the power of life and death that you're ascribing to this one, regarding your son. Only God has that. And we humans do, too, in a way, if we are weak and confused and if we allow ourselves to give in to the *yetzer ha ra,* the temptation to do evil."

"You mean, if Elijah had been fated to die, he would have."

"If the Angel of Death had been looking for Elijah, I suspect it would have found him. At least it seems so to me. Do you think a mere ghost could fool God?"

I took a deep breath. "And if Elijah had ended up connected to machines? Would I have been taking matters of life and death into my own hands by removing them?"

The rabbi sighed. "Ah. If machines are serving only as an impediment to inevitable death, prolonging life only in the technical sense without hope of any kind of recovery?"

"Yes, that's right."

"Then I think we, as human beings, after careful consideration, after we have looked unflinchingly into our hearts, have the right to remove them. That doesn't mean you would have been able to do it. Or that I would. In that situation, the mother and the father would have to struggle to find the answer. And struggle to keep faith while they're looking. I believe Jewish law would support the removal of life support in the circumstances you feared. There are certainly others in my faith who would interpret the law differently, and in other faiths who would also disagree."

He smiled. "But, thank God you aren't in that situation. If you were, I would tell you then what I told you just now. But I wouldn't tell you what to do. Judaism teaches us that we are responsible for ourselves, Dinah."

"I know that, Rabbi." I stood up.

"Perhaps if you turn your back on this demon and refuse to listen anymore, it will go away from you."

"Perhaps." He had helped me, I felt it, although I still didn't have a clue how I would begin to do what he was suggesting. "Well, I really have taken enough of your time now."

We walked toward the parking lot in silence, and when we got to my car, the rabbi said, "I'm sure you know the saying that there are some things that we as human beings cannot change, and there are other things that we can. And sometimes the hardest thing for us is to know which are which." He smiled.

"Come see me again sometime, all right?"

twenty-nine

When I came back from the synagogue, my mother was in the backyard with Elijah. The sun was still bright and hot, and they were on the grass in their bathing suits, playing ring-around-a-rosy. For a woman of seventy, my mother looked pretty good in her bathing suit, even with her hair soaking wet.

"All fall down," Elijah said, then the two collapsed on the ground, laughing.

The thought crossed my mind that she'd never played that way with me. But of course I knew she had.

"Mommy!" Elijah ran toward me.

"Oh, Dinah, thank God you're back. I was thinking about calling the police."

"I'm sorry, I got held up." I hoisted Elijah into my arms, slipping my hand under his buttocks. I realized that his bathing suit was wet. His hair, too.

"Elijah, did you go in the pool?"

He nodded, smiled. "Gramma took me."

"You got him to go in the pool?"

My mother grabbed her sunglasses from the picnic table and put them on her face. "Nothing to it. Right, Elijah?"

"Right."

"Well now, that's wonderful. But why now, Elijah?"

He looked at me for a moment, then said, "Because it was time."

"Time?"

"Flowers can't bloom in the winter when the ground is all cold, and the worms are sleeping."

I stared. When I found my voice again, I said, "So show me how you swim, okay?"

"Not now, Tuddy's inside. I left him." He scrambled out of my arms and ran to the door.

My mother put her arm around my shoulders as we walked toward the house. "I was really beginning to worry."

"I'm sorry I missed the swimming triumph—it really is, you know." I stopped walking. "Why did you come, Mom?"

"At first I came because your father was angry with me. I wanted to prove to him that I *had* been helpful to you when Elijah was sick. But really I think I came just because I love you. I want you to be happy. It was time, just like Elijah said. How about our wonderful boy?"

I smiled. "Do you think your mother wanted you to be happy?"

She shrugged. "My mother didn't care two bits if I was happy, Dinah. Or any of us, your uncle Lee, even Marshall and Bernard. All she ever cared about was her *dead* child and her bottle."

This was my mother's demon, perhaps as alive for her as mine was for me.

She stopped walking, looked at me. "I know I was sometimes out of control when I was younger. It was just that I . . . I don't know, I was just so . . . *hungry.*"

Hungry. My mother had found the perfect word.

After my mother left that afternoon, I called Sam at work. He answered the phone himself. "Sam Galligan."

"Hi, it's me. I wanted to tell you, Elijah finally went into the pool."

He groaned. "Without me? Jesus, Dinah."

"My mom came yesterday, she was here overnight. Today, I don't know how, she convinced him to go into the pool. Well, she may not have had to do much convincing—when I asked him why he went in he said it's like you can't have flowers blooming in the winter because the worms are all sleeping."

"What in the world does that mean?"

"I think it's his way of saying it was time."

Sam made a whistling noise. "He sure is something, that kid of ours."

"Will you meet us at Dr. Selson's office tomorrow?" We had a regular monthly checkup with the doctor scheduled for the next day.

"Of course I will, Dinah. Elijah is my son."

"Please come home, Sam. The children miss you. I miss you. I need you. We all do."

"I miss you, too," he said.

I lay down on my bed, exhausted. And I slept.

Elijah and I are on a boat, in the middle of a vast sea. The noonday sun is hot overhead, drenching us with warmth. We have been swimming with the fish, but now our skin has dried in the hot sun, and we hear the music, a progression of chords in a minor key, a chorus of arpeggios, a tenor voice.

"Do you hear that singing, Mommy?"

"Yes, I hear it. That's the demon's song."

I look over the side of the boat at the rippling water. Just beneath the surface I see brain corals, stag corals, honeycomb corals, tall and fat, tiny and towering, structure upon structure, in blues, reds, whites, greens. And crevasses between the coral for fish, resting places, free from predators. We all need resting places, do we not?

Elijah scoots over beside me and winds his arms around my neck. "No, Mommy," he says, "that's never been the demon's song."

"Everything seems fine," Dr. Selson said the next day, after he'd finished examining Elijah. Elijah and the doctor had developed a friendly rapport in the months since we started bringing Elijah to see him. Now Elijah was sitting contentedly on the doctor's lap, playing with Dr. Selson's purple dinosaur pencil puppet.

"I want to still keep him on the same medication," the doctor told us, "but next month, I think we'll do another EEG. At the next appointment, no hurry."

We booked the appointment with the receptionist, then Sam and I left his office, each of us holding one of Elijah's hands.

We waited for the elevator, not saying anything, trying not to catch each other's eye. When we came out onto the street, I pointed to the lot across the street. "We're over there."

Sam nodded. "Do you want me to walk you?"

"We can manage, but thanks." I wanted him home so much I could taste it.

"When are you coming home, Daddy?" Elijah asked.

I bent down to look him in the eyes. "Daddy can't come home right now, honey."

"Wait a minute, Dinah." Sam bent down, so that Elijah was between us. We parted the crowds walking on the street. Sam whispered something to Elijah, who looked at me with a big, big smile.

"Do you want Daddy to come home?"

I looked at my husband. "Of course I want him to come home."

Elijah looked up at us, back and forth, from my face to Sam's. "*He* doesn't."

"Who doesn't, Elijah?" Sam asked.

"The ghost."

My husband made a noise in his throat, but suddenly he and Elijah were gone, and with them that busy New York street. Another scene materialized in front of my eyes, inch by dreadful inch, a panorama of grass, sky, fields covered with snow, a farmhouse in the distance. Each visual fragment stacking one on top of another until the collection of fragments became a whole picture. A place.

I am standing in an icy rain, on a snow covered cornfield, under a black roiling sky. It is cold, very cold, and a raw wind whips around me. I hear a low rumble from the catastrophic sky, and there is heavy black smoke everywhere, hanging in the air, the smell of burning fuel. I am able to move through the smoke easily, but I hear coughing all around me, human beings suffering, burning, dying.

"Please," I say. "I left Elijah on the street."

The black smoke lifts with a gust of wind, enough for me to make out a death sculpture: jagged metal strewn across a cornfield like so much garbage, part of a wing, a propeller, a piece of tail, a section of fuselage, gunmetal gray, resting in the snow.

"Survivors!" I race across the field in that icy wind, stepping over bodies and pieces of bodies, a bloody arm, a torso, a white thighbone stripped of skin, protruding from the ground like a headstone. Finally I am standing next to the fuselage. I know the metal is fiery hot, but I feel nothing of life in this vision, no heat. I peer into one of the airplane's small windows. A woman's body is strewn like a naked rag across the floor of the cabin, clothes and skin in tatters. I hear a high-pitched scream—not the woman's, the woman is dead.

The screams come from a dark-haired boy, about ten years old, trapped under the woman's body. By instinct I reach in through the window and try to pull him, but I cannot touch him, and he is wedged in, screaming earsplitting shrieks more animal than human.

I hear another sound now, a slurp, and then a sizzle. The demon materializes next to me, bright and blinding against the leaden sky. In this gray light, I can clearly see for the first time what it is made of. Tiny wasplike creatures moving so quickly they create a kind of formed light, a whirlpool of stinging, buzzing, itching, swirling, agonizing torture. *That* is what I felt inside me, the churning cold, the motion of the wasps.

I stagger backward.

On a street in New York City, I stood very still.

"Dinah?" Sam's eyes were riveted on me. "What just happened? Your eyes rolled back, and you looked like you were going to collapse."

"All the dead people were there, Daddy," Elijah said.

"What are you talking about, Elijah?" Sam said. "What dead people?"

"In the field. An airplane."

I looked at my son. I hadn't seen him, but I realized I didn't have to see him for him to be with me.

"Where?" Sam looked at him. "*What?*"

"The airplane fell. The people aren't dead now. They're in heaven. But the white wasp man isn't in heaven."

Sam looked at me for a long moment, then gently took hold of our son's shoulders.

"Wasp man?"

"He's not really a wasp man, Daddy. He's just a silly ghost."

"I *told* you they'd get back together," Kate said that night, holding the pink rose Sam had brought her to her cheek.

Alex looked at us and made a face. "You two are weird."

He had no idea how weird at least one of us was. Kate might have had some idea, but so far it didn't seem she'd said anything to anyone about the mirror.

"Why are we weird?" Sam asked.

Alex shrugged. "John Harman's parents broke up, Sally Kershaw's, Larry Selwin's—and all their parents *hate* each other. John's mother says she wouldn't get back together with his father if he was the last man on earth—"

"Well, some parents do get back together, obviously," Kate said.

"Your sister has a point, Alex." Sam glanced at me. "Here we are, back together, you can see for yourself."

"Yeah, but that doesn't count because you're weird." There was a hint of a smile.

"You just have no faith in the power of true love, Alex," Kate said.

"True love," said Elijah, smiling.

After dinner Kate gave us a flute concert, playing the Bach sonatina she'd been working on tenderly, flawlessly. Alex and Sam played some video games, then Sam and Elijah looked through *Creatures of the Deep* together. Elijah told him about going in the pool, showed off his latest drawings, and they checked up on the fish named Elvis. Finally we said goodnight to the children, then Sam put his arm around me and we walked into our bedroom in silence. I had hidden all evidence of my possession—the candles, the books, all of it.

I started to take off my clothes and found that I couldn't bring myself to get undressed in front of my husband. It wasn't only that another man had touched me, it was more that our lovemaking had always been about mutual pleasure, and I felt as if my body were no longer my own. I took my nightgown into the bathroom, thinking I wanted to come to bed after he was already settled in. Afraid he'd leave again?

I kept the light off while I washed my face; I couldn't bear to look at myself in the mirror. I tried not to think about what had gone on in this room while he was gone. Though the vision I'd had that afternoon had been markedly different than the others, I believed I was still a long way from resolution.

When I came back into the bedroom, Sam was sitting up on his side of the bed, the covers drawn up to his waist. He didn't have his pajama top on. My husband's body, lean and long and smooth, was nearly as familiar to me as my own, even after an absence of six weeks, four days, sixteen hours.

I sat down next to him, on his side of the bed. "I've always loved you, Sam."

Sam looked into my eyes. "Who is he? The man you were with."

"He's no one, Sam."

"You have sex with another man, and he's no one?"

I put my hand on his thigh. I had hurt him deeply. Perhaps I would never again be able to look into his eyes without seeing the hurt that I had caused.

"You really want the details, Sam? I'll tell you if you want me to."

He sighed. "I guess not."

"It was just that one time, Sam. It won't happen again. I've told him I made a terrible mistake."

He held out his arms, drew me close. We kissed, then he pulled back just a little.

"Do you remember what I said when I asked you to marry me? That we'd be together always, no matter what?"

"I remember."

He smiled. "What I meant to say was 'no matter what, *except* adultery.' " He sighed. "You and the kids are my life."

"That's exactly what I told Rabbi Leiberman the other day. That you're *my* life."

"Rabbi Leiberman?"

"He's the rabbi at Temple Beth Elohim. I told him about all this."

Sam looked wary. "What did he say?"

I got up and went over to my side of the bed, got in, pulled the quilt over me. "He said the spirits of evil men can live on after death. He said demons have the power to taunt and deceive, and confuse. They lie about everything, the future and the past, and they mix up the truth with lies."

"And you really think this—whatever it is—*saved* Elijah?"

"I don't know what I think. I know *it* thinks it did. But Rabbi Leiberman said no ghost could fool God. He said that if the Angel of Death had been coming for Elijah, it would have found him."

"That seems right," Sam said. "Exactly right."

"It seems like it should be right. And I never know when the ghost is lying or telling the truth."

"Well, I certainly don't." He rubbed his hand over his chin. "I don't think I know anything anymore. Why don't we go to sleep now? We'll talk about it again in the morning."

He held out his arms and wrapped me within them, and we fell asleep that way together, nestled under the quilt.

In the morning we did talk about it, we talked about it again and again for several days. Early Saturday morning before the children got up, Sam asked me again to describe for him the way the ghost looked.

"Different ways," I said, sipping my coffee. "In the PICU it mostly looked sort of like Seth Lucien."

"What was he like?"

I sighed. "Not a nice guy. Let's just put it that way."

Sam sipped his coffee. "Come on, you can do better than that."

So I told him the whole story, all of it. I even told him about Seth's film. He made a joke about his wife, the porn star.

"Ha, ha, ha," I said. "Could we please go back to the matter at hand?"

"Oh, okay." A dimpled smile. "But I sure would have liked to have seen that movie."

"I dumped his whole lovely film collection in the garbage. Now. Enough. I was describing the demon. Since Elijah woke up, it's been less substantial, I guess you could say. The other day on the street in New York, I think I saw its true form. It's made of tiny wasplike things, always diving, moving, flying. In our bedroom, it was more like inert light."

"That thing has been in our bedroom," Sam said dully. "Boy, you are full of surprises. Has it been there when we were making love?"

"Yes."

"Oh Jesus, Dinah." He stood up and went over to pour himself another cup of coffee. "I'm sorry, I know it's not your fault. It's just so . . ." He shook his head, at a loss. "I mean, I may have had the odd *ménage à trois* fantasy, but this wasn't exactly what I had in mind."

I laughed, but he didn't join me. "What does it want from you, Dinah?"

"Possession. Or maybe love, though I guess to it, they're the same thing."

"Mother of God."

But I wasn't thinking about God, at least not directly. I was thinking about the visions. Sam and I had talked about them so much over the last few days, and I still didn't know which of the visions were truth and which were lies. Nor could I bring myself to ask Sam what he would have done if the worst of them had become reality, requiring a decision from us about the life support.

Now in the kitchen as the day dawned, Sam muttered, more to himself than to me, "It's like a war." He looked at me. "And I think we need to take the offensive."

I went over to him by the coffeemaker and gave him a hug. My husband was the rational sort, even in irrational circumstances

"You'll help me then?"

"Of course I'll help you."

"You believe me?"

Solemnly. "I'm not sure I believe, Dinah."

"But what about Elijah? He believes. He told you about the ghost. The wasp man, he called it. You heard him."

"Dinah, I want to believe you, but I can't help my nature. You *could* have described the ghost to Elijah, and he *could* be repeating what you told him."

"Why would I do that?"

"I have no idea. You know, Dinah, there are other explanations for all of this. It's hard for you to see them, I guess. For example, you tell me you never know whether this demon is lying or telling the truth. Let's just say, for argument's sake, that the whole thing is in your mind. Now, when the demon told you that Seth had poisoned your friend Jay, you automatically believed it was true. But if this whole mess comes out of you, is only in your mind, is made out of your imagination, and your guilt and your fear and whatever, it's reasonable that it would take credit for killing Jay. Because that's probably what you've always believed. You've probably always felt guilty about it, too, for not reporting what you knew to the police, for one thing, and now that guilt is haunting you, so to speak."

I was impressed with my husband's impenetrable logic, though it didn't persuade me.

"I do have one question though," he said. "Why in the world were you involved with a guy like that?"

"Because I was stupid and young and needy. Here's my question to you. Then you don't believe me?"

"I know I love you." He put his arms around me.

"I think that's good enough," I said.

When the Westport Library opened that morning, we were on the doorstep. It took a two-hour search on microfiche before we finally found a 1961 front-page story with the headline: AMERICAN AIRLINES PLANE CRASHES IN KANSAS CORNFIELD, 54 DEAD.

American Airlines flight 9960, we learned, had left Idlewild (now Kennedy) Airport at 7:30 A.M. that morning, bound for Los Angeles, with two stops scheduled. The plane developed unspecified mechanical difficulties after a stop in Chicago and crashed near Kansas City. On impact, the fuselage split into one small piece and one large one. Everyone not in the first few rows was killed in a conflagration, burned beyond recognition; eight passengers had survived. The story concluded with a list of the dead and the survivors, along with their ages and places of residence. Seth Lucien wasn't on either list, but among the survivors was one Andrew Cantrell, age ten, and Ronald Cantrell, age thirty-four. Wanda Cantrell, age thirty-two, was listed among the dead. Hometown, Greenwich, Connecticut.

Around noon we parked under the portico of a stately colonial house in the estate section of back-country Greenwich. The young woman who answered the door, holding it half open, was pretty and slim, elegantly but casually dressed in slacks and a sweater.

"We're sorry to bother you," Sam said. "I'm Sam Galligan, and this is my wife, Dinah. We're looking for someone named Andrew Cantrell."

The woman opened the door enough for me to see that she wasn't so young after all, in fact she was older than me, maybe in her late forties. Probably she owed the appearance of youth to health spas, constant exercise, and the ministrations of an excellent surgeon.

"My husband was his father. Ronald. He died last year, I'm afraid. I'm Mrs. Cantrell. Virginia."

"I'm sorry," Sam said. "Do you know where Andrew is?"

"Why?" She frowned. "Is he wanted by the police?"

"Why do you ask that?"

"If you have to ask, you've never met him."

"Do you have a picture of him?"

She gave a little snort. "Not in this house. I'm sorry I can't help."

She started to close the door; Sam put a warning hand on my arm. "Please, Mrs. Cantrell. Can't you tell us anything about him? You might prevent a tragedy."

She cast a dubious eye. "What kind of a tragedy?"

"We think Andrew Cantrell may be stalking my wife." Sam glanced at me, and I smiled, full of admiration for his quick thinking.

"Stalking? Why don't you go to the police?"

"It's very complicated," Sam said. "And if we're right, he's very dangerous."

She looked back and forth, from my face to Sam's, sighed. "All right, if you put it that way, I suppose I could tell you what I know about him. It isn't much."

She opened the door, led us into the house through a very large foyer and an even larger formal dining room, then into a small sunroom just beyond it. Open windows almost floor to ceiling on three sides gave it an expansive view of a formal English garden complete with manicured hedges, set around a small gray weathered statue of Pan.

"This is my favorite room in the house."

"I can understand why," I said. It was open and airy, full of greenery, wicker, and chintz. She sat down in a rocker and motioned for us to sit on the wicker sofa.

"Drew was gone before I arrived on the scene," she began. "That was more than twenty years ago. My husband hadn't ever said why he kicked him out, but eventually I learned that when Drew was seventeen he'd been accused of rape. The girl didn't press charges, and Drew insisted she'd wanted it, you know the old story, but his father believed Drew had forced her into it. He sent him to college, anyway, but then—"

"What college?" I asked.

She shrugged. "I don't really know, some small college, in Virginia, maybe. He dropped out before the end of his freshman year. Lived in Washington, D.C., for a while, I think." She crossed her legs and sat back, lit a cigarette from a pack of Virginia Slims on the glass-and-wicker coffee table next to the rocker.

"Forgive and forget, that's what I was always taught," she continued. "So after Ron and I got back from our honeymoon, I convinced my husband to give him another chance. Drew drove up on that big motorcycle of his, breezed in here that day like a cloud of bad air, hair down his back, bell-bottoms, black leather, boots, the whole hippie thing. I suppose some girls my age would have found him attractive."

"You didn't like hippies?" Sam asked.

She shrugged. "Hippies were rich people's kids. My friends when I was growing up were shipped out to Vietnam—I lost my high school sweetheart there, in some godforsaken place called Da Nang. Rich daddies kept their hippie kids out of 'Nam. There were a lot of us back then who couldn't afford to sneer at everything worthwhile, the way rich kids did."

"You didn't grow up this way, I take it," Sam said.

"Right. Lawrence City was just like Greenwich."

Not so very different. "Go on, Mrs. Cantrell," I said.

"Virginia, please. We had dinner together that night, just the three of us, right in that dining room." She took a long drag on her cigarette. "Well, you didn't have to be a psychiatrist to see that the young man was seriously disturbed. I was only twenty-three myself, and I knew some bad kids, growing up. But my husband's son? I've never met anyone like him, before or since." She looked out the windows for a moment, then back at us. "My husband's son was evil. Truly."

"Evil?" Sam glanced at me.

"I don't like to use that word, but I can't think of another way to describe it. My husband's son was evil just because that's what he wanted to be, no other reason. Being corrupt, depraved, nasty, hurtful, hateful, whatever—it turned him on."

She took another deep drag and blew the smoke away. "The evening didn't start out too badly, with Drew telling us about his interest in the arts. He said he had a new girlfriend, was in a theater group, doing a little filmmaking. Now, my husband, who was the CEO of a huge company, church deacon, pillar of the community, would have had higher aspirations than artsy college dropout for a son of his, but he listened without saying a word. Then Drew told us he played lead guitar in a rock band called Death Rap—no, it was Death Trip. That was one too many for my husband. He said, 'Why don't you go back to school, Drew? You're a smart kid, you could finish up in a year or two.' So Drew says, 'Go back to school, so I can end up like *you?*' Nasty and sneering, the way he said it. Still, my husband kept his cool. 'I just want what's best for you, son. That's all.'

"'You wouldn't know what's best for me if it bit you in the fucking head,' Drew said, excuse my language. 'I told you this was a bad idea,' my husband says to me. Then Drew starts imitating him, 'I *told* you this was a bad idea,' and then he starts calling names. Called his father an asshole, and me? Well, he called me a little gold-digging whore." She looked down at her lap.

"You realize I'm a good deal younger than my late husband."

We both nodded. She was just a little older than me, which meant she'd been married to a man thirty years her senior. What was it Seth had said in the theater that day, that his father liked young women?

"Well, my husband just lost it. He stood up and backhanded his son across the mouth. Twice, he did it. And the weirdest thing was Drew just sat there and took it, hair hanging in his face."

Maybe because it had happened before, maybe so many times, he was numb to it.

"What would *you* do with a kid like that?" Virginia Cantrell had caught Sam and me exchanging looks. "My husband ordered his son out of the house. Drew says, 'Fine. I'll leave, this is a fucking bore, anyway. Maybe we could liven up the party, have the' . . . well, I can't use the word he called me . . . 'service us both, maybe at the same time.' Well. I could see the smoke coming out of my husband's ears, but all he did was tell Drew, 'We don't use those kinds of words in this house, for Christ's sake.'

"Suddenly, Drew stands up and looks his father in the eyes and says, 'You know what I think about your Christ, Dad? I think he's shit. I think he's nothing.' And then he started to say some words, it was sort of a prayer, something like, 'He who stands on the most skulls sees the furthest.' And 'I lift up my eyes to stand before the Dark Gods.' My husband told him to get out and never, ever come back.

"Drew says, 'Fine. Here's a little something to remember me by.' And he hauls out this disgusting pornographic photograph, and lays the thing on the dinner table. Says, 'One for your collection, Dad. My girlfriend. She just loves to pose.' "

My whole body blistered with shame. Sam glanced at me.

"Your husband collected pornography?" Sam asked.

"Of course not. Drew just did it for effect."

"So then he left?" Sam asked.

Virginia Cantrell stubbed out her cigarette in the ashtray. "But not before he took his father's Rolex, his dead mother's diamond pin, and almost four thousand dollars from the safe. And that was the only time I ever met the adorable Andrew Cantrell."

"Thank you, Virginia," I said, standing up. "Before we go, I'd like to ask one more question. I was wondering if you know if Drew Cantrell is alive or dead."

She looked puzzled. "I thought you said he was stalking you."

"He may be." Sam stood. "We're not sure."

"And you can eliminate him as a suspect if he's dead. That's why you're here. Right?"

The woman had watched one too many cop shows. "Something like that," I said.

"Wouldn't they have notified my late husband if his son had died?"

Maybe not, if he wasn't using his real name. The police said they found no identification, none at all. Maybe he was buried somewhere in an unmarked grave. Or a grave marked with the name he'd made up instead of his father's name. Seth Lucien. Because he thought it sounded demonic.

After she closed the door behind us, Sam and I stood together on the portico. "I didn't pose willingly for that photograph, Sam."

He held me; I was feeling weak in the knees. "I know."

"Oh, Sam."

"I know."

"And we're no better off than when we started."

"It's all right, Di. We'll figure out what to do." He held me tighter.

"Well now, isn't this cozy?"

The demon materialized on the portico, dazzling in the noonday sun. I could no longer see the demon as Seth—that was a selling disguise, the best it could do, the best, the top, the max. Neither could I see it as inert light, another maneuver. Now it was what it was.

"If you hated your father, haunt him, haunt him!" I said.

"Dinah?" Sam said.

"He's dead," the demon screamed.

Of course. "Then if your father was cruel to you," I said, "he's suffering his reward. Just as you are suffering yours."

I took a step backward, suddenly remembering the sculpture of death. "Why did you show me that airplane crash?" I asked. "You wanted my pity with that, didn't you?" God. Even that had been just another tactic.

It said nothing.

"I can't help that child," I said. "He's been dead for years. Please. None of it has anything to do with my son. It isn't fair."

"Isn't fair?" the buzzing demon whistled, smacking itself, slapping at the tiny buzzing insects darting and zooming inside it, and out. "There's only One who isn't fair."

"You made your choice," I said. "You had a choice, everybody does."

The wasps buzzed and dived, and it slapped at itself with claws made of the same shifting torment.

A question formed in my mind. "Who saved Seth's life in that crash?" I asked.

The demon fixed me with cold, cold eyes.

"Satan," it whispered. I could see blackness in its mouth, wasps emerge from that blackness, swift as photons, and just as invisible.

"No," I said. "That was where Seth went wrong. Right there. Only God has the power of life and death. And he lived his life without God."

"Ungrateful woman," it screeched, rising.

I fell backward into my husband's arms. I knew now that whatever guise it fabricated to scare me, whatever accusations it hurled, whatever its threats and lies, this demon was constituted of its own torment, and not of mine. What a clever demon it was, too, exploiting my doubts, my regrets, and my guilt for its own ends. Yet I had swallowed it all. Seth had kept saying, "I'm only for you, I'm only for you," but this demon wasn't for me. It was for itself. And that was its biggest lie.

thirty

Dr. Selson had spread the pages of printout across his desk. It was shortly after Labor Day and Elijah was going to begin in a regular kindergarten class the next day. Now he was playing out by Dr. Selson's receptionist's desk.

"See?" The doctor pointed to the tiny blips in the long, continuous line. "Here. And here. And here. I'm very sorry. This is the seizure activity. Do you see?"

Sam nodded. There were tears in his eyes. "But we don't see anything in Elijah," he said.

"You wouldn't," Dr. Selson said. "These seizures are very slight."

After a few moments, I found my voice. "What does it mean?"

Dr. Selson clasped his hands together. "It could mean nothing. He'll stay on his medication. I'm going to increase his dosage. The medication could control the seizures, he could be fine."

"Or?"

"Or the seizures could possibly get worse. More frequent. Stronger. Or there could be another big one. There's just no way to know."

I sat down on the chair. There was no way to know. But I knew.

In a dream that night I dream again of a vast blue sea, and I hear music that lifts me up like the wind, and sings to me from the depths. The music has a kind of perfume, the fragrance of salty sea air and camellias, of pancakes browning and sizzling in a pan, of human sweat. The music soars, laughs, smiles, cries, loves. The music even hates. The secrets of the universe are contained in every chord.

In my dream, Elijah leans over the side of the boat, resting his chin on a forearm. His other hand is submerged in the water, rippling its surface in concentric circles like the parting of air when a ghost emerges. He is listening to the music.

"God is singing to us from the heavens," he says.

I turn to him in my dream.

"Believe, Mommy," he says. "Be still. Have faith."

I awoke then, and I sat up in bed. Who but God could hold a note so long without taking a breath? Who could warm me and ease my suffering, in the season of absolute zero? Who indeed?

I bowed my head and whispered words from my own heart.

God, I only ask this.
Grant me
gratitude for my fleeting gift,
grief without bitterness
sorrow without anger
the imagination to be happy again
the desire, the courage, to go on

"Dinah?" Sam opened his eyes and laughed. "What in the world are you doing?"

"Praying."

"Now?"

"Now. And watching you."

"That'd make a guy pretty nervous, having you watch him while he's sleeping and pray over him when he wakes up."

"I love you," I said.

"Love you, too."

The kids started school again the next day. We had a new routine. Kate, ecstatic about getting her driver's license, would drop Sam off at the train station every day, then drive herself and Alex to school. I would take Elijah to his school myself.

Miss Lerman was his new teacher. A pretty twenty-two-year-old, she informed me right away that she was very excited because it was her very first job out of college, and she explained enthusiastically that they were going to do all kinds of fun and wonderful activities, a few of which she described. It was obvious from the way she told me Elijah would be "just fine" that she was aware of his history. I explained his new medical situation to her, and took his medical form to the nurse. I told them both that if anything happened out of the ordinary, they were to call me right away, no matter what it was. They said they would.

Mary Galligan pronounced the foliage that autumn brilliant. She was right. The leaves were extravagant and uninhibited multitudes of color, each one a celebration. A bedazzled brush had painted those leaves. Every day, before the other children got home, Elijah and I would take a walk together through the neighborhood, just the two of us, collecting leaves in a little shopping bag we carted along. We took turns giving names to each color. The yellows were saffron, honey, and wheat and lemon and mustard and tawny, and there were tans like lion, sand, fawn. Some leaves were mottled yellow and green, spotted, like a certain fish pictured in *Creatures of the Deep.* The reds were ruby, apples and cherries, scarlet, watermelon, vermilion (that was mine). There were orange leaves the color of sienna, and fire, and Tuddy's orange bow tie, and mango (and oranges that reminded me of Julie's hair). There were flaming eggplant-purple leaves, and the Japanese maple in front of Mrs. Hurlock's house at the end of our block had leaves that turned the color of raspberries. When we got home each afternoon, we pasted our leaves into four scrapbooks, one book for each color category, yellow, orange, purple, and red.

Kate suggested that Elijah dress up as Elvis Presley for Halloween, and he thought that was a great idea. He looked pretty cute in his white spangled costume, knocking on doors, trekking through leaf piles now scattered all over the neighborhood, the four of us in tow.

The next day, we added the browns to his collection of leaves.

"Not as pretty as the other colors," I said.

"Just different," he said, pushing his glasses up on his nose. "Like me."

I looked out the window. In a gusty breeze, the leaves were falling from the trees like rain, whipping and dancing around the yard.

"Why do you think the leaves fall, Mommy?" Elijah asked me.

"Because in the fall they die, so new leaves can grow in the spring," I told him.

"Like the worms when they wake up?" he said, with a bit of a smile.

I kissed him. "Yes. Just like that," I said.

Every moment that Elijah wasn't in school, I spent with him. I kissed him as often as he would let me, smelled him, bathed him, dressed him, tried to commit the feel of his skin and his smell to memory.

If Sam thought I was hovering again, he didn't mention it.

October turned into November, and one night Sam and I were in Elijah's bedroom, Sam on the bed, Elijah in the rocking chair on my lap, Tuddy on his. Kate and Alex were both in their bedrooms; I could feel the pulse of Nine Inch Nails all through the house, even here. I was reading one of Elijah's favorite books to him, *Goodnight Moon,* and Sam was listening.

When I finished, Elijah spread his arms out and shouted, "Goodnight noises everywhere!"

We laughed. I was about to suggest that we look through the very battered *Creatures of the Deep,* but I was cut off.

"*EVERYWHERE.*" Sibilant, a whisper.

The demon materialized on top of Elijah's hand-painted chest of drawers, bubble-gum-pink skin and muddy boots. Back to its selling disguise. It'd been a long time since I'd seen that. I realized, in fact, that it had been two months since I'd seen the demon at all, in any form.

"Dinah?" Sam was searching the room with his eyes.

I nodded, put my finger to my lips. "*Shhh.*"

Elijah slipped off my lap and marched over to the bureau.

"Come away, Elijah!" Sam said.

"Wait, Sam," I said. "He's all right." I knew he was.

Elijah didn't come away. He stood right in front of the bureau, looking up at the demon. "You don't scare me. I see you."

"No one sees me unless I say they do."

"I do," Elijah said, then glanced back at me. "Don't I, Mommy?"

The air rippled backward, inward. Then the demon inhaled what seemed to be breath and shielded its face with a hand. The air quivered and I saw a claw.

Elijah turned his back on it and looked at me. "We know how to make it to go away, Mommy."

"Dinah, what is going on?"

"Wait, Sam. How, Elijah?"

"You know."

And I realized I did.

Elijah started to hum the tune, then to sing it:

So shut your eyes while mother sings
Of wonderful sights that be,
And you shall see the beautiful things
As you rock in the misty sea

I sang along with him, and the song filled me with strength and courage.

We sang another verse, and the ghost's black leather jacket rotted and dropped away, and the pink skin stretched and bloated out like a balloon, then fell off, until there was nothing but bone, and then even that crumbled like dust.

The demon appeared again as a woman with white, pointy sunglasses, then a woman with a stained dress and eyes so clear they seemed transparent. We sang and each of those rotted away. The demon came back again, as white and luminous as the moon. We sang and sang, and only then did I begin to see through that inert moonlike light, into the stinging, buzzing vortex of insects, the wasps.

We sang another verse together and there was a whizzing sound in the room, and then another, and another. They were too tiny to see, these micro-missiles escaping from a maelstrom; you could only sense the great speed of them, as each wasp bolted from the whole, one by one by one. With each wasp that fled, the demon shrank and paled and dissolved more and more, part by part. First the claws, then the arms, then the torso and neck, then the head, bit by bit like sugar in water, until the demon was nothing but air, until it was nothing. And the wasps had scattered to the four winds.

"Boo!" said Elijah.

The following Monday morning, the school nurse telephoned.

"Mrs. Galligan? You asked me to call you if we saw anything unusual. Nora Lerman just came to get me. She says they were having their snack a few minutes ago and suddenly Elijah just kind of froze. He's all right now, but—"

"Froze?"

"That's what she said. He sat there at the table with the other kids, staring ahead, not moving but his jaw was clenched, and his fists. She kept saying his name, but he didn't seem to hear. Then he just kind of came back to himself and started eating his peanut butter crackers as if nothing had happened."

I closed my eyes and realized they were wet. "How long did it last?"

"Maybe three minutes."

"Did she ask him if he remembered anything about it?"

"*I* did—she brought him to me, of course, right after it happened. He didn't seem to know what I was talking about. He's right as rain now, Mrs. Galligan, but it might have been a small seizure so I knew you'd want to know."

I thanked her and put the phone back in its cradle, slowly, softly. I sat for a long time before I picked up the phone again, to call my husband, and to call the doctor. Oh, and I also first said a prayer.

The next day we brought him to Dr. Selson, who made an adjustment in his medication, which didn't help. He had several more visible convulsions in the next few days. The doctor put him in the hospital, changed his medication again, poked, prodded, tested, and observed him. A neurosurgeon came to consult. His name was Dr. Manheim, he was reputed to be the best. A proper Brit, he somehow managed to be very formal without being aloof, but he told us that surgery wasn't an option, that it wasn't a lesion or something he could go in and go after, he was very sorry.

Sam and I met with Dr. Selson in his office. The purple dinosaur puppet sat idly on his desk. The doctor ran his fingers through his hair. "It's some sort of metabolic disorder. Unusual. He's having several different types of seizures. I'm truly sorry."

"Maybe another surgeon," Sam said, tears filling his eyes.

The doctor sighed. "We can certainly call in someone else. I think if he were my child, I would." He clasped his hands in front of him. "I wish I could assure you that he's going to be okay, that I have some magic potion, or some knowledge or skill to make this go away. I don't. Sam. Dinah. We know quite a bit about the brain. But there's far more about the brain that we don't understand. We're going to do everything we can, of course, I've seen some of these new anticonvulsant drug combinations work wonders. But I'm not going to lie to you, or mislead you. That I can't do."

I thanked the doctor for his honesty, and Elijah came home with us the next day. His convulsions were increasing in frequency and intensity all the time, he'd developed a weakness in his left side, and he was groggy from all the medication, but he carried on, bravely.

Near the end of that momentous year, Julie came. My mother had written to her, it seemed. And there she was, standing in my doorway. I hate the way people tell friends they haven't seen for years that they look exactly the same, but in this case it was true. Julie was still a beanpole, freckles still littered every square inch of her pale skin, and her hair was still a bright orange fuzzball, though she'd pulled the top half of it back in a barrette.

She was grinning. "*Charlotte* as peacemaker? Now there's something I never thought I'd live to see."

"You live long enough," I said, "and you see everything." I held my arms out, and we stood hugging in the doorway for a long time.

She whispered into my ear, "I thought you might need me, Di."

I told her that I did. My son's seizures were nearly constant now. He was beginning to lose the power of speech.

Elijah had a pretty good afternoon, nevertheless. And Julie and I were able to begin the slow process of catching up on all the lost years. When Sam got home, he managed to turn around an initial moment of awkwardness between him and Julie with a joke, then the three of us talked for hours. Kate got Elijah ready for bed, reading him his stories, and Sam and I went to tuck him in, then brought his monitor into the den with us. After Sam went to bed, Julie and I talked for a while more. Around midnight, during a check, I found Elijah lying awake in the dark. He seemed to want to be with me, so I carried him out to the den and sat him on my lap. I stroked him, tried to reassure him. Julie gave me the gift of being able to watch our suffering without turning away.

The next day, my mother and father came, insisting that I take a few hours off. Becky, Julie, and I met at a new restaurant on Main Street for lunch. A lovely place on the second floor, Mexican decor, overlooking the Saugatuck River. The waiter, lurking nearby, kept coming over to see if we were ready to order. Each time he asked we laughed as we realized we hadn't even looked at the menus.

For a few hours, I enjoyed the company of my friends, and even managed to accept their compassion and sympathy. Twice I called my parents to check on Elijah.

"Try to have a good time, and relax for a little while, honey," my mother said. "Elijah is doing fine."

Well, he wasn't doing fine, of course, but I took a deep breath, and went back to the table, where Becky and Julie were still covering the basics: our children (Julie had three, one starting college that year); our husbands (Julie's was "the best," a middle-school principal, a computer whiz, a lover of classical music); our jobs (Julie was a social worker for a Jewish family service clinic). The waiter was moving toward us again, and we finally ordered in self-defense.

Julie asked how Becky and I had met. I told her how Sam and I had been living in D.C., and Sam's about-to-be boss suggested Westport as a place we might want to live. The town may well have the distinction of being home to more advertising executives than any town in the nation. We fell in love with the place.

It was Becky's alliterative ad that found us our house: "*One acre, updated 1890s clapboard cream puff near Compo Beach: columns, character, charm and 4 bedrooms. Call!*" I showed up at her office on the Post Road not far from where I eventually opened my psychology office, hugely pregnant with my first child, holding the ad.

"I don't know how to resist at least *looking* at a something called clapboard cream puff," I told her.

She glanced at my swollen belly and said, "Honey, one more cream puff for you, and we're through!"

Becky had finished the story for me by quoting herself. Julie was laughing. "A woman with a sense of humor. All right!"

"How did *you* two meet?" Becky asked her.

I was finishing the last bite of my salad.

"Believe it or not," Julie said, "we were brought together by a frog."

Halfway through dessert, well after three o'clock, I went outside to the street, to feed the meter. And ran into Ellen Shoenfeld—again.

"Do you live near here?"

"What's that?"

"DO YOU LIVE NEAR HERE?" I said.

"I live right over there." She pointed to one of the side streets off Main, then turned her right ear toward me so that she could hear better.

"Ellen," I said, "maybe an aid would help your hearing."

"It wouldn't help."

"Why not? There are new kinds of hearing aids nowadays, fit right in the ear."

She made a little sound between her teeth. "I tell you, a hearing aid won't help." She pointed to her left ear. "They did this."

Of course.

"They did it with a club," she said. "A long wooden club." She demonstrated the length of it with her hands. Then she shrugged. "So you see, I do not want to hear better. I want to keep it this way all the time. The same with my hair." She touched her chignon of white. "They shaved my hair, and it was white when it came back in. They did these things to me, and this is how it will be forever."

I touched her shoulder. "I'm sorry, Ellen," I said. "I don't know what to say."

Another shrug. Then, "Even my children don't really want to hear. They want me to get over it. As if you could get over something like what happened to me, can you imagine? And I haven't even told them the worst of it. But they think, 'Enough already, Mother.' "

Maybe so. Maybe Ellen had buried her pain so deep within her that she really had never spoken of what happened to her. Yet if this were true, it was likely that she had played out her pain in so many ways that her children didn't even have to hear her story to know it.

And maybe Ellen has told her story over and over, so often that her children can no longer bear to hear it. Still. Isn't that what we have to do with our stories, tell them in different ways and at different times throughout our lives, changing our perspective and perhaps even our interpretation as we continue to learn and grow? If we don't tell our stories to each other, how can we find our common humanity, how can we move on?

I would not presume to speak for Ellen Shoenfeld, I can only speak for me. It's not a matter of getting over it. It's more a matter of going forward, holding it.

"No one wants to hear," Ellen Shoenfeld said.

"I do," I said.

epilogue

The seizures have left him this way now. Kept alive by machinery. No hope he will ever recover, the new doctor says. Never dance. Never walk. Never eat. Never see you, hear your voice, even know you're here. Never smile. Could he smile? With damage like this? Never seen it.

I'm sorry. Miracles are not my business.

His eyes are doing the rotating thing again. I never stop hearing the sound of the *whoosh*-pumping machine. The parallel lines on the monitors are inching their way across the screen, phantom-bright lines under my eyelids even when my eyes are closed.

He has been coming to me at night in a dream. In the dream, he is swimming in clear blue water that shimmers with a brilliant light. He is swimming as if he has sprouted fins and gills, and breathing underwater, as if water were air, or music.

"Look, Mommy, I can swim good now!"

He does an expert breast stroke, maneuvering easily and gracefully beside a tall stag horn coral, above a swimming turtle. He is buoyant in the water, weightless and free and unafraid.

"No, Elijah! Don't go! Stay with me!"

He stops swimming, and turns to look at me. He stays very still, floating upright, kicking his strong little legs, treading water. Keeping his distance.

"I won't drown, Mommy. Look!"

He flips himself over in the water, and does a little dance. Such agility, he is dazzling. I watch, amazed, as he swims away, and disappears into the light. He never looks back.

I open my eyes now in the hospital room, and I see him the way he is. I begin to weep, and I repeat the words of a psalm:

I will lift up mine eyes unto the mountains.
From whence shall my help come?
My help cometh from the Lord,
Who made heaven and earth . . .

I weep and I wail, and I thank God for the miracle of Elijah's life. A miracle very brief is still a miracle. God comes into me and fills me with the sights and sounds of another place, a future I could not before have conceived; to light a candle year after year, and have this simple ritual help me go on.

A room filled with flickering light, the brilliance of fire, the warmth. Alex comes down from his room for the candlelighting. He's left his music blasting upstairs, but he's come.

"Do you want to say something, Kate?" Sam asks.

Kate lowers her eyes, and her pale lashes rest as lightly as moth wings on her cheeks. "We love you, Elijah," she says softly. "Always."

"Alex?"

Our son looks back and forth from Sam to me, his tear-bright eyes flickering in the candlelight. He shrugs.

Sam touches Alex's cheek. "Yes, we love you, Elijah," he says.

I am thinking: This is all I can give you now, Elijah. A lit candle. Just a symbol, and it isn't much. It isn't anything like life. But it's all I have to give. And it is the best I can do.

Then I read the words of an ancient prayer, one that wisely celebrates life even in the face of death.

My family stands in silence for a few moments, then Alex says, "I gotta go. I have homework, I have to get up early in the morning."

"Go on, honey," Sam says.

Both of our children give each of us a hug and a kiss, then Alex and Kate go upstairs to their rooms.

"Sleep well, my children," I whisper. "See you in the morning."

How do you go on thinking this, whispering this in the night, when you know that it's entirely possible it might not be true? You do. You make the choice to find the way.

Now, in the hospital room where I believe Death is waiting patiently, I hold my husband's hand, and I stand over my son's bed. I close my eyes again, and I am filled with an awesome presence, with light and faith and love.

I do not need to understand to accept, just as I don't need proof to believe. Time has passed, and the demon has never returned to haunt me. Sometimes I ask myself if it was real: Did I bring it into existence, a being composed wholly of the darkest part of my soul, and then make it disappear forever? Or does it always exist as a formless spirit that chose me, used me once, took form through me, and may at some point choose another? These are questions for which I have no answers.

I tell myself that since Elijah saw it, too, it must have been real, but as Sam has pointed out, perhaps he only said what he thought I, his mommy, wanted to hear. It wasn't like that, I've told Sam, which of course he already knows. Whatever its origin, the experience has healed some things in me that badly needed healing, and helped me know that my son's illness has nothing to do with anything I've done or not done.

And this, too, I know: I have looked into my soul, and I will do now what I believe is right. I cannot be certain that my experience has been given to me as a kind of gift from a loving, caring God, and that my hand continues to be so guided. But I can surely hope. I do hope.

I open my eyes, and together Sam and I reach out to an electrical switch. We will let our son Elijah go.

acknowledgments

I am humbly grateful to Laura Mathews and Joni Evans, for believing, and for patience and guidance. Thanks to Rabbi David Wolfman, Rabbi Sharon Sobel, and Betsy Stone, Ph.D. Renni Browne, Nathalie Dorf, Jaci Fricks, Judith Kelman, and Sally Rothkopf have been incredible friends. Anne Ziff has been my absent mother. Nancy Sinacori has a natural empathy that is truly a wonder. And I am full of admiration for Christine Hart, M.D., who knows the soul and not just the art of medicine.

Finally, I wish to thank my husband and best friend, Bob Dorf, and my daughter, Rachel, the light of my life.